MURDER AFTER CHRISTMAS

MURDER AFTER CHRISTMAS

RUPERT LATIMER

With an Introduction by
Martin Edwards

Poisoned Pen
PRESS

Introduction © 2021, 2022 by Martin Edwards
Murder After Christmas © 1944 by The Estate of Algernon Victor Mills
Cover and internal design © 2022 by Sourcebooks
Cover image © Mary Evans Picture Library

Published by Poisoned Pen Press, an imprint of Sourcebooks,
in association with the British Library
P.O. Box 4410, Naperville, Illinois 60567-4410
(630) 961-3900
sourcebooks.com

Murder After Christmas was originally published in
1944 by Macdonald and Co., London, UK.

Library of Congress Cataloging-in-Publication Data

Names: Latimer, Rupert, author. | Edwards, Martin, writer
   of introduction.
Title: Murder after Christmas / Rupert Latimer ; with an introduction by
   Martin Edwards.
Description: Naperville, Illinois : Poisoned Pen Press, [2022] | Series:
   British Library crime classics
Identifiers: LCCN 2022006657 (print) | LCCN 2022006658
   (ebook) | (trade paperback) | (epub)
Subjects: LCGFT: Detective and mystery fiction. | Novels.
Classification: LCC PR6023.A755 M87 2022 (print) | LCC PR6023.A755
   (ebook) | DDC 823/.912--dc23/eng/20220211
LC record available at https://lccn.loc.gov/2022006657
LC ebook record available at https://lccn.loc.gov/2022006658

Printed and bound in the United States of America.
VP 10 9 8 7 6 5 4 3 2 1

Contents

Introduction

Murder After Christmas is an unusual and amusing Christmas mystery novel that has been out of print for three-quarters of a century. First published in 1944, this is a little-known book by a little-known author whose life was tragically cut short before he could continue his career in crime fiction.

The story is a Yuletide mystery in the fine old English tradition, but there are frequent reminders of the hostilities taking place elsewhere. The story opens at the home of Frank and Rhoda Redpath in the run-up to the festive season, and the couple reflect on the inability of Rhoda's stepfather, rich old "Uncle Willie," to take his usual trip to Italy. Rhoda reckons that "Mussolini had finally decided to take sides in the current European unpleasantness in order to make it finally impossible for Sir Willoughby Keene-Cotton to occupy his villa in San Remo."

The couple decide to invite the old man to stay with them, but their motives are by no means entirely altruistic. Rhoda points out: "It may be his last Christmas, and if we give him a really happy one and make him feel we all love him very much, even though there's no apparent reason why we should—." Frank brightens: "Rather a joke if, in the excitement of his happy Christmas, he revoked his will and left everything to us!"

So the invitation is sent, and Uncle Willie accepts. He duly suffers the customary fate of rich, elderly relatives in vintage detective stories, and is found dead. The body is discovered shortly after he has dressed up as Father Christmas and found a cache of chocolates in a snowman on the lawn. When Superintendent Culley and the Chief Constable, Major Smythe, try to discover what exactly has happened, they encounter all manner of complications.

There are some fascinating period touches. Early in the book, for instance, people try to master the rules of a game known as "Invasion": "One landed by parachute and made one's way to an important aerodrome, harassed incessantly by the most hair-raising perils and armed only with one's dice, which one rattled, however, bravely and hopefully." This is reference to a board game of strategy devised in 1938 by the thriller writer Dennis Wheatley, and anticipating the outbreak of war in Europe; these days, copies change hands on the second-hand market for high prices.

As the plot continues to thicken, the storyline pursues an increasingly eccentric course, but the light-hearted tone is maintained throughout. After the truth is revealed, Smythe observes that it is "almost a relief to realise there's still a war on after listening to all that stuff."

Rupert Latimer was the pen-name adopted by Algernon Vernon Mills (1905–1953). Information about his life and career proved hard to come by, and establishing the facts required extensive detective work. I'm indebted to the British Library's publications team for their research efforts, and in particular to a member of the author's family, Mrs. Sarah Balcon, for filling in some of the gaps in what is known about him.

Latimer (I'll call him that for convenience) was born at the wonderfully named Wildernesse Park, Sevenoaks, Kent. Today Wildernesse House is divided into apartments, but at that time Wildernesse was the home of his grandmother, the Dowager Lady Hillingdon. The earliest records of Wildernesse Estate date back to the fourteenth century. A deer park was established towards the end of the seventeenth century, and there was a grand house which changed hands a number of times over the years. The Duke of Wellington was one notable guest, shortly before the Battle of Waterloo, and a great avenue of limes was planted to commemorate his visit.

Charles Henry Mills, a director of the East India Company, acquired the property in 1884, and was raised to the peerage as Baron Hillingdon two years later. He was a philanthropist who built his own gasworks, a laundry, and an orphanage, all of which became a major source of livelihood and provided employment for people within the local communities of Seal and Sevenoaks. Latimer was Charles's grandson and the son of Charles's youngest son, the Hon. Geoffrey Mills and his wife, Grace. He could trace his ancestry back to William the Conqueror.

On the face of things, Latimer was undoubtedly born with a silver spoon in his mouth. But tragedy struck him during infancy. On a trip to France, he ate strawberries that had grown in the wild. They were contaminated and he contracted typhoid fever; although he survived, his elder sister and their nurse both died. For the rest of his life, he was lame and suffered from epilepsy.

He never married and had no children, but grew into a tall, handsome young man. For some time he pursued a career on the stage. Among those he worked with in repertory was Arnold Ridley, also a playwright whose plays included the popular mystery *The Ghost Train*, but who is today best remembered as Private Godfrey from the television sitcom *Dad's Army*.

Latimer was interested in writing and published a humorous novel, *Jam Today*, in 1933. He is also credited with publishing *The Unenchanted Circle* in the same year; whether they are alternative titles for the same book, I have yet to establish. In due course, he graduated to detective fiction, publishing *Death in Real Life*, which one critic described as "an all-time curiosity in thrillers which you must not miss," while another spoke of it being in a class by itself and striking a new note.

Duly encouraged, Latimer produced *Murder After Christmas*. Unfortunately his health, never robust, began to decline. His mental health worsened and ultimately a brain tumour was diagnosed. He died in 1953. A member of his family said, "I remember him as a sweet man, but different." Despite his privileged background, it is evident that he experienced serious difficulties in his life, but the gusto with which this novel is written shows an admirable sense of humour. Almost seventy years after his death, it is a pleasure to bring his entertaining, unorthodox Christmas mystery back to life.

—Martin Edwards
www.martinedwardsbooks.com

A Note From the Publisher

The original novels and short stories reprinted in the British Library Crime Classics series were written and published in a period ranging, for the most part, from the 1890s to the 1960s. There are many elements of these stories that continue to entertain modern readers; however, in some cases there are also uses of language, instances of stereotyping, and some attitudes expressed by narrators or characters, which may not be endorsed by the publishing standards of today. We acknowledge, therefore, that some elements in the works selected for reprinting may continue to make uncomfortable reading for some of our audience. With this series, British Library Publishing and Poisoned Pen Press aim to offer a new readership a chance to read some of the rare books of the British Library's collections in an affordable paperback format, to enjoy their merits, and to look back into the world of the twentieth century as portrayed by its writers. It is not possible to separate these stories from the history of their writing and, as such, the following novel is presented as it was originally published with minor edits only, made for consistency of style and sense. We welcome feedback from our readers, which can be sent to: Poisoned Pen Press, an imprint of Sourcebooks, 1935 Brookdale Road, Ste. 139, Naperville, IL 60563.

I
Bread Upon the Waters

I

"Uncle Willie?" echoed Frank Redpath in mild surprise, making passes over the electric heater on the sideboard to warm his hands. "What about him?"

Rhoda dropped the letter she had been reading in order to sit on her fingers and thaw them.

Just as she had managed to stop her teeth chattering and was about to reply, her husband broke in: "Don't tell me he's dead at last?"

"No; he doesn't say anything about being dead." Rhoda went through the mechanical procedure of reading her stepfather's letter again to make quite sure.

Frank nodded in absent approval of his wife's performance.

"He says they've commandeered his hotel," Rhoda continued. "They've all got to turn out. Before Christmas, he says." She clicked her tongue sympathetically.

And so did Frank.

Aunt Paulina, however, whose attention had been distracted from the *Daily Telegraph*, seemed to think Rhoda's piece of news called for a warmer, more colourful reception than either her nephew or his wife were disposed to give it. "Oh, poor Sir Willoughby!" she cried. "At *his* age! In *this* weather! Where *will* he go?"

"Well, he always goes to Italy about this time of year, in any case," murmured Frank, filling up his plate; then, pulling himself together: "Oh, no."

Rhoda reminded him superfluously that the present war was declared to make it as difficult as possible for poor Uncle Willie to cross the Channel and that Mussolini had finally decided to take sides in the current European unpleasantness in order to make it finally impossible for Sir Willoughby Keene-Cotton to occupy his villa in San Remo.

"Of course, of course!" Frank stemmed hastily, to her relief. "Keep forgetting about this beastly war. And then there was a revolution before that, wasn't there, so as to blow up his castle in Spain? Altogether, the old man seems to have caused a lot of trouble in the world, one way and another, doesn't he? And now the British Government have found out that he's still alive and pushed him out into the snow. Well, well!" He sat down and poured himself out some coffee. "He can't live very much longer," he consoled himself, "and then perhaps we shall have a little peace."

Aunt Paulina was obligingly shocked. But she surrendered to him the *Daily Telegraph* relentlessly; then, having finished her own breakfast, such as it was, opened the french windows of the dining-room and sailed out into an incipient snowstorm.

Husband and wife surveyed her through the frosted panes with reverence.

"Old people never seem to feel the cold," commented Frank.

"They wear a lot underneath," explained Rhoda.

"The whole armour of God?" suggested Frank.

"Possibly," Rhoda replied.

The commanding figure of Paulina Redpath remained standing outside the dining-room while some birds hurriedly ate the toothsome delicacies she had put out for them. Paulina smiled at the birds approvingly, deprecated their twittering gratitude, and passed out of sight.

"As an evacuated relation," Frank had to agree, "she's been a decided success."

"I knew she would be," said Rhoda, but without indecent triumph.

"I had my apprehensions," said Frank.

"Oh, but *why*?"

"Dunno. Always felt there must be a snag about her, though I've never found it. Chink in her armour. Having her permanently in the house, we'd be sure to find it sooner or later."

"No." Rhoda dismissed all this. "She's quite invulnerable. Look how she takes everything in her stride: the war, the weather—even the Wortleys. Nothing shocks her, nothing irritates her, and nothing is too much trouble." She looked quite distressed about it.

"We'll soon find something," Frank reassured her cheeringly.

He picked up Uncle Willie's letter idly. "Poor old turnip," he said. "He'll have to go and live with his wife in Chester

Square! Bad luck, I agree; but what's the use of having a wife if you don't live with her? And where's the sense in retaining an enormous house in London and keeping it shut up eleven months in the year?"

"I don't think at Uncle Willie's age he ought to be in London just now, do you?" ventured Rhoda.

"His ancestral home in the Highlands would perhaps be safer. Any port in a storm. Farther away, too…"

"No petrol," put in Rhoda.

"What do you mean—'No petrol'?"

"Read his letter. Besides, his chauffeur's been called up, and the one he's got now is nearly as old as he is and having a holiday for Christmas—"

Frank, who had been reading the letter, dropped it suddenly and glared at his wife in horror.

Rhoda hastily put on the whole armour of God, but Frank managed to swallow his wrath. "Dearest," he said, in tones of pity. "We can't have Uncle Willie here. It's quite out of the question."

"You did say I was to ask him," pointed out Rhoda.

"Didn't see that there could be any harm in *asking*. As an empty gesture of goodwill at Christmas. But there was one chance in a million that he would accept."

"Well, he *has* accepted. I thought he might. I really don't see how we can back out now, Frank dear—"

"You mean we've got to have him for the duration of the war?"

"Perhaps it'll only be for the duration of his life, dear."

Frank grumbled: "Wars do come to an end at some time or another, whereas Uncle Willie seems to be immortal."

"But he's well over eighty now."

"He's nearer ninety. But one of his aunts lived to be a

hundred and two—do you realise that? Looking on the brightest side, he'll probably die on us, which will be *very* nice."

Rhoda said calmly: "We'll ask him just for Christmas, then, shall we? After all, Christmas is a time to spend with one's flesh and blood, and he has been very kind to us, remember."

Which, of course, gave Frank the opportunity of retorting that a stepfather wasn't flesh and blood, adding: "And I don't call not pinching all the money your mother left him by mistake being kind, do you?"

Yes, Rhoda did. "He could easily have kept it," she said. "He's been very generous," she insisted.

"He hadn't any alternative," retorted Frank darkly. "Self-defence. Probably someone told him how we'd been planning to murder him all those years. Now we've no motive, so he's robbed us even of that little excitement in our middle age." He took a piece of toast and complained: "Don't enjoy reading the morning paper so much as I did now, either, not without the thrill of spotting Uncle Willie among the deaths. Wouldn't matter if he *was* dead now, would it? Not to us."

"There's the war for you to read about now."

"Wars are so crude and vulgar."

"So are murders, I expect—in real life."

Frank sighed nostalgically. "Uncle Willie," he insisted, "could have been murdered in the best of taste. Really artistically and with a hint of poetry." He sniffed morosely. "Don't you agree? Or aren't you listening?"

"Yes, dear," Rhoda stopped shivering to say, "but I was getting rather tired of murdering Uncle Willie."

"*I* wasn't. And now, just because he's given you your

own money, and you and Paulina feel you must wallow in insincerity at Christmas-time, we've got to have him snoring about the house and treating us like a couple of children. Why can't his wife look after him? Eh? She only married him so as to be Lady Keene-Cotton and inherit all his ill-gotten wealth; she might do something for her bread and butter."

Rhoda reminded him that the current Lady Keene-Cotton was not very strong and usually preferred to spend Christmas with some of her own family, probably in the tiny Rectory at Borrowfield, where they would be sleeping six abreast, in any case, during the Christmas holidays, and wouldn't like having Uncle Willie at all, "and Uncle Willie himself would simply hate it, dear, you know he would."

At which Frank could only repeat grumblingly: "What's the use of having a wife if you never see her?"

"Uncle Willie likes it," came from Rhoda in swift reply to this; "especially when they've got ready-made families. And this time, having all the money, he can write to them and order them about without the bother of loving them or even knowing them by sight mostly. I'm sure," she returned to her muttons, "he'd be far happier with us."

Frank snorted: "I don't doubt it!"

"And safer," he added, not referring to air raids either. But after due reflection he had to admit grudgingly: "Not that any of those Horshams would have the imagination or the guts to murder him. A more dreary lot would be difficult to conceive. Not that I blame the mother for hooking a rich husband with that helpless lot dependent on her, but she's only made them more helpless than ever. Angelina's the only one I've any respect for. She did at least have the decency not to hang around her mother but sell herself while the going was good. Who's her latest, by the way?"

"I think she's married now. Who to, I don't know. I don't think Uncle Willie does, either. She's lived abroad for some years, and I don't suppose he's ever seen her."

"Then he'll probably leave her all his money," said Frank.

"No, he's made a will leaving everything to his wife. I do know that. He told me so. She's had a hard life, he said, with lots of responsibilities, but a good head for business, and she'll be able to make good use of the money."

"By leaving it to her far-flung progeny! Actually, I don't see they've any more claim to it than we have."

No reaction from Rhoda.

"Eh? Do you?" from Frank.

Forced to answer this question. Rhoda said gently: "No, of course not. That's partly why I thought it would be nice to have Uncle Willie here with us. It may be his last Christmas, and if we give him a really very happy one and make him feel we all love him very much, even though there's no apparent reason why we should—"

"Ah, I see!" Frank brightened. "Bread Upon the Waters!" He chuckled. "Rather a joke if, in the excitement of his happy Christmas, he revoked his will and left everything to us!"

"It would be funny, wouldn't it?" agreed Rhoda.

"One in the eye for the Rev. Cyril Horsham & Co., eh?" Frank hugged himself. "Imagine their baffled fury!"

Rhoda obediently imagined it. "But of course we wouldn't allow him to leave us *everything*," she put in soberingly. "Just a codicil, I thought; so that we could give John a larger allowance, then he'll be able to marry that Margery person; she's far the best so far, and it would be such a relief to have it all settled."

"They're both coming for Christmas, I suppose?" said Frank, slightly sobered.

"I told John I'd write and ask her formally if Mrs. Dore is that kind of mother, and I rather think she is."

"Good. I like Margery. She's so real. Funny she should want to be an actress."

"There's nothing frivolous and artificial about actresses nowadays. Why, Gwendoline Lucas, who played Rosalind at the Old Vic last year, is a funny little plain thing, quite old, and wears pince-nez."

"How do you know?"

"She's staying with the Crosbies."

"Oh! I'd love to see her. Can't we ask them to our Christmas Tree?"

"I wouldn't dare."

"Never mind." Frank concealed his disappointment. "Who else have we got staying in the house for Christmas?"

"There won't be room for anyone else."

"Heaven be praised!"

"Not if Uncle Willie has the bridal suite."

"You mean we'll have to turn out?"

"He'll like somewhere he can *sit*; and write all his letters and fall asleep. He probably snores, dear. We'll be quite happy in the other two spare rooms just for Christmas. And if Uncle Willie does want to stay on—"

"Eh?"

"Well, as we've got the Coultards in the stables, I don't

suppose the billeting officer will worry us any more. Not with Uncle Willie *and* Paulina."

Frank was beginning to feel quite warm. He contemplated his wife admiringly. "You seem to have thought of everything," he said.

"It all fits in rather well," Rhoda assured him.

"There must be a snag somewhere," Frank decided in a moment. "Paulina and Willie," he said reflectively. "Uncle Willie isn't a vegetarian by any chance?"

"Oh, no! He has no fads. He eats anything and everything."

"Pity."

"Why?"

"I have so enjoyed Aunt Paulina's bacon."

Rhoda's face clouded a little at this. "Uncle Willie has always prided himself on being a *bon viveur*, but of course he's getting on now."

"He hasn't got diabetes or cirrhosis of the liver?"

"No, his health's wonderful."

Slightly oppressive silence until Rhoda remembered: "I believe his wife's got something like that the matter with her. Everything has to be boiled. She may send him some of her butter and perhaps a pound or two of sugar; so we won't do too badly with our rations. Besides, Uncle Willie's sure to be able to get us some illicit food for Christmas, if I know him. I should think he's got reserves of tea and marmalade hoarded away in his various houses. We'll make him send for them. And onions—" Rhoda was in danger of becoming reckless.

But Frank was quite happy now. "Uncle Willie's rather a dear old man," he said, picking up the paper with a contented sigh. "Like a beautiful antique. Just what one needs in one's house for Christmas. A link with the past. Damn." He put the paper down and frowned. "Paulina and Uncle Willie. I knew there was something wrong. Will they mix?"

"Because of her having been my governess? But surely being your aunt cancels that out?"

"No, I meant him being such a link with the past. A chink in her armour. Wasn't there some unpleasantness soon after he married your mother, and didn't Paulina have something to do with it?"

"Paulina would never have been mixed up in anything shady—"

"But she's dug herself in so happily here. Supposing Willie gets hold of the wrong end of the stick and starts to wave it about?"

"I'm sure Uncle Willie's entirely forgotten all about Paulina's early girlish predicaments. I don't expect he'll even remember who she is. Anyway, Christmas is a time for forgetting the past and burying hatchets, isn't it?"

"What about after Christmas?" said Frank.

"Now you're *making* difficulties," said Rhoda.

II

A few minutes later Rhoda Redpath was sitting at her not very tidy writing table in the drawing-room. Catching sight of her face in a small mirror, she rubbed her cheeks till they matched her nose. Satisfied with the reflected result of doing this, she ran her fingers through her short grey hair till it stood even more on end than ever. Then she placed on the blotting-pad before her a neat piece of pale-grey note-paper which was headed, simply and tastefully, FOUR CORNERS, ST. AUBYN,

MEWDLEY. She proceeded to write to her recently discussed stepfather, Sir Willoughby Keene-Cotton, Bart., while the mood was still upon her.

"...My husband and I are delighted to hear that you will be with us for Christmas," she scribbled quickly while this was still true, and, smiling with goodwill and affection, covered nearly five pages without pausing to think...

In any case, there was nothing to think about. People who paused to think made just as many mistakes. If Rhoda had paused to think in nineteen fourteen she might never have married Frank Redpath. Uncle Willie had certainly been against it at the time; but it made Paulina very happy, Frank being practically her only relation, and Rhoda being almost a daughter to her; and the marriage had certainly been a success, with Frank settling down to a job after the last war and retiring just before this one at the age of fifty-seven.

Uncle Willie had thought it necessary to object to Frank as a husband for his stepdaughter firstly on social grounds. Paulina's brother (Frank's father) had been an antique dealer in Liverpool whom Uncle Willie always insisted was a pawnbroker, and the fact that Gregory Redpath and his wife both died practically simultaneously and of the same disease in nineteen twelve, bequeathing Frank a fairly comfortable income, only made matters worse. Frank was an idler, a waster, and a dilettante of the worst description. Having no need to earn his own living and no one to thwart his ambitions, he went to an Academy of Dramatic Art, but soon learnt, however, that being good at charades, and once getting as far as Holloway Gaol in the guise of a fashionably dressed suffragette, was not at all the same thing as being able to act.

The next year found him at an Art School, where he designed a ballet which no one thought much of, but composed some incidental music for a production of *Romeo and Juliet* by their Dramatic Society, which everyone raved about; so he went to the Royal College of Music, where he wrote a novel which was sufficiently promising to be accepted by a reputable publisher. Which, of course, decided him to be a novelist for the rest of his life. But the war broke out and he found himself too busy being a conscientious objector to write silly books; also he was really working very hard in the Red Cross Hospital where his Aunt Paulina was Quartermaster (in a terrifying uniform), and in this hospital he met Rhoda Hepworth, a young and perspiring V.A.D., and became objected to by no less a personage than Sir Willoughby Keene-Cotton, which immediately raised his whole life into higher planes of conjecture.

The end of the war found him married, with a son aged four, called John, a steady, respectable job, and a solid, reliable wife. Indeed, he was presently earning such a comfortable income that when Rhoda's mother died in nineteen thirty-three, and Uncle Willie, owing to an unfortunate error, swept up the entire Hepworth fortune, which was considerable, it did not seem to matter very much. It was only when John went to Cambridge and became rather expensive that his harassed parents grew uneasy and brought their imaginations to bear on murdering Uncle Willie, for with his death the Hepworth fortune would revert to Rhoda automatically.

Murder was not necessary, however. Owing to the mellowing influence of Rhoda, Uncle Willie became their fairy godfather, no longer disapproving of Frank and taking quite an interest in John. He eventually handed over to them all the

Hepworth money, rightly considering himself quite rich enough without it, what with all the other fortunes he had managed to swallow up in the course of his long life. He must have enjoyed being a fairy godfather very much, thought Rhoda, and wanted to be one again, which seemed the only possible explanation for his marrying Mrs. Sinclair Horsham, with all her dependents, in nineteen thirty-three. He could not have found that worthy lady amusing or companionable. She didn't care for the Riviera, wouldn't live in London, and hated Scotland; so that, after walking up the aisle with her, he was not known to have met her since, though he corresponded with her a lot and someone introduced her to him at the Coronation of King George VI.

But Rhoda continued to love him and keep in touch with him and remember his birthday, even when he was no longer being fairy godfather to *them*, because being kind to people always paid, even if you didn't see how it could. (Aunt Paulina's bacon was perhaps a case in point?) And it was never a waste of time to keep on good terms with people. It was good practice, if nothing else. A lifetime's experience of keeping on good terms with Uncle Willie (who could at times be extremely *difficile*) had left Rhoda, in her maturity, with the habit of being kind to quite unattractive people entirely as a matter of course. Why not, after all? It was easier to be kind than not; it made one's daily life far happier, and always paid in the long run—were these, as Frank sometimes suggested, really valid reasons for *not* doing it? Morally speaking, for instance, should one be *un*kind to the Howard Wortleys, continually snubbing and avoiding them, simply because they made themselves a little too easy to love, being very rich and rather snobbish; and just because Howard owned a number of important newspapers and was in a position to pull a great many strings, and Ross & Weekes, the firm John worked for, might be closing down at any moment, and, although John had been medically exempted some time ago, he might be called up again at any moment, and it would be nice to find him a reserved occupation of National importance (as Frank didn't want a son of his to go off murdering people)?—well, Rhoda decided, if one always had to pause and think of such problematic ulterior motives, one would never be kind to anyone.

One certainly wouldn't be inviting Uncle Willie to stay and sitting there and writing him such a long and interesting letter, particularly knowing perfectly well that he would never bother to read it.

"But—Bread Upon the Waters—you never know…" murmured Rhoda as she read it through.

"…that you will be with us for Christmas," she read. "And we both hope you will stay with us for as long as you can after that, if you won't be too bored here. John will be here for Christmas, of course, and Margery Dore, whom I don't think you've met. Her father was M.P. for Middleswick and died a few years ago. Mrs. Dore has been managing canteens since the beginning of the war, and Margery, who was going on to the stage when the war broke out, has been helping her most nobly. Paulina has been with us for some time. At last we managed to persuade her to leave her little flat in London, and she's really bearing up remarkably well considering that, like you, she's used to spending most of the year abroad. It's nice for *us*, as we never used to see enough of her. She still paints, and has found an art club in the village. We never knew there was one—I'm sure there wasn't until she came! She goes to

Lady Bayham's First-Aid Point twice a week to sew bandages—
nothing seems to daunt her! The Howard Wortleys are still
next door—I forget if they were there when you were here
before? Rather impossible, but very kind. We don't see so
much of them now since the Crosbies have taken the house
up the hill—'High Winds,' I think it is called. Crosbie is an
American, but she *was* a Gibberd. They originally took the
house for week-end parties, but have lived there permanently
since the war. We've called on them, of course; but they're
having a large house-party for Christmas and haven't yet had
time to return it. The Bayhams, too, are having an elaborate
Christmas Tree for all their evacuees. Our schoolmaster and
his wife, Mr. and Mrs. Coultard, who live over our garage, are
taking their children. They're our only evacuees—except for
Paulina, of course. We're having our own Christmas Tree on
Boxing Day as usual. Last year quite a lot of people came, but
this time there seem to be so many counter-attractions that
we shall probably have to dance round it by ourselves.

"I don't think there's any other news. Except that you won't
know your old friend Major Smythe! He's now Chief Constable
of the county! Very grand, though we both feel he would have
made a far more effective secretary for the golf club. But I expect
he feels he ought to be doing what he can just now—so wonderful of him at his age—and I suppose the police must be extra
busy and short-handed in war-time. One never noticed them
here before. Now they whirl about in cars with megaphones,
and it doesn't seem to have gone to their heads; it's only some
of the specials who suffer from delusions of grandeur and think
they are a sort of Gestapo—but perhaps it's panic, poor dears!

"Talking of the police, we rather wish now we had sent

John to the Police College, although they might have rejected him because of his sight; but he really has the makings of a marvellous detective. There was a case of robbery at his office (Ross & Weekes still), and he solved the mystery entirely on his own. It was an inside job! Of course it was really rather interfering of him, because if he had left things alone probably no one would have guessed that there had been a robbery at all; but he's a very noticing sort of person and always wants to get to the bottom of everything, and once he starts a thing you can't stop him—so like Frank! However, it was all hushed up, so no harm was done in the end.

"I hope the weather won't delay you from coming here. It has been rather bleak lately; and you must begin taking care of yourself, Uncle Willie dear, now that you're an old gentleman of eighty, which is what we all keep forgetting, it seems so incredible.

"This morning it has begun to snow, which does make things *look* more cheerful, and perhaps we're going to have a Dickensy sort of Christmas like we did last year. I wish you had been with us then; Frank made me toboggan down the road into the village with him, which seems rather frivolous at our age, but actually it was the only really dignified way of *getting* to the village. How we got back I can't remember!

"Please come as soon as possible in case we're snowed up again and you can't come at all.

"Affectionately, Rhoda."

"I think it'll do," decided Rhoda as she licked it up. "It's fairly enticing," she thought, "and bristling with information for the reader. If any," she added.

II
Snow at Christmas

I

AUNT PAULINA DISPLAYED NO TERROR, NOR THE FAINT-est embarrassment, on learning from Rhoda that Sir Willoughby Keene-Cotton was to be with them for Christmas. All she said was, "Oh! Are we going to *like* that, dear?"

On being assured that we were going to like it very much, she meekly prepared herself to do so without further comment.

So her early girlish predicaments could no longer be used by Frank and Rhoda as a reason for wishing they hadn't asked Uncle Willie to stay. Vague forebodings and apprehensions had to be rationalised in other ways. The extra bill for lighting and heating which would result from Uncle Willie occupying the bridal suite. The extra work for the servants, and just at Christmas-time too, when Sills was having a holiday and a temporary parlourmaid would be adding to their confusion in any case.

"But he doesn't require much looking after," Rhoda

reminded Frank cheerfully. "In fact, he hates being fussed over. I'm sure he won't be any trouble."

"He's a wonderful old man for his age, I agree," replied Frank. "But what about our Christmas Tree? Even if he sleeps through it, won't he rather damp our high spirits? We're bound to make a certain amount of noise with tin trumpets and crackers. Hadn't we better put him off until after Christmas?"

Rhoda swept this aside. "Nonsense! Uncle Willie will enjoy the party as much as anyone."

But her own forebodings persisted.

Perhaps it was the weather. It had stopped snowing and become merely dark, slithery, and unpleasant. One would not, perhaps, have been feeling very cheerful in any case.

Then, a week before Uncle Willie's threatened arrival, it tried snowing again, which *looked* more cheerful; and, after it had snowed unremittingly for three days, there came a furtive hope that perhaps Uncle Willie would not wish to come after all but find another hotel across the road until the spring. "Oh, no," Paulina said, cheering them all up, "Sir Willoughby loves the snow; you needn't be afraid of *that*."

After it had snowed for the fourth day, Rhoda said: "Perhaps we oughtn't to *let* him come. I'll write and say that he'd better not attempt such a long journey at his age, in this weather..."

"If you like, dear," replied Paulina; "but it'll make him more determined to come than ever."

"So it will," said Rhoda.

There was nothing to be done.

During the next few days it stopped snowing and thawed

overnight, froze again, and snowed again. The village streets became impassable. Deplenished of traffic, St. Aubyn became more full of life than usual, the village pond being black with skaters and the surrounding hills squirming with tobogganing children. The proud young possessor of a pair of skis paraded the roads, ubiquitously aloof from his less fortunate elders who crept gingerly round familiar corners which had now become death-traps for the unwary. It was soon no unusual sight to find middle-aged ladies lying prone in gutters and sober, normally upright characters moving slowly uphill, virtually on their hands and knees. Frank observed that it was like crossing the Channel when one could die in public, and in the most frightful agony, and nobody would notice anything out of the ordinary.

Paulina had a theory that, owing to the mines in the sea, something had gone wrong with the Gulf Stream.

Frank upheld that the air battles in the sky had jolted the earth out of its course, so that we were rolling farther and farther away from the sun into another Ice Age and ought to have been making ourselves igloos instead of air-raid shelters.

Both Frank and his aunt were always unanimously anxious to end the war, but it was a pity they could never do so without ending the world with it, thought Rhoda; but it didn't really matter so long as they enjoyed themselves. Frank loved arguing, and Paulina was a really wonderful sparring partner for him; they agreed with each other more and more hotly; Frank never became rude, and Paulina was never offended, so that Rhoda never had to intervene and arbitrate, which made a nice change for her.

Why weren't there more people in the world like Paulina, and what was her secret?

She made friends with everybody. How did she do it?

One morning she came in out of the snow and announced: "Mrs. Howard Wortley has asked us all round after dinner to-night."

"Oh Lord!" groaned Frank, "and I thought they had dropped us."

"They've got a new party game for Christmas and they want to practise it," explained Paulina.

"Why on us?" demanded Frank.

"We're their next-door neighbours, after all," said Rhoda.

"I won't go," said Frank.

But he did. "They must be after something," he grumbled, as they set out in the snow with their torches. But Paulina had managed to allay his suspicions and at the same time arouse his curiosity. "I wonder what they want me to be now," Frank was then heard to say; "arty; highbrow; an escapist; a defeatist; a Peter Pan; or an irreverent jackanapes?" Because it had been very worrying for the poor Wortleys not to be able to tie labels on Frank. If it made things easier for them, why not let them do it, Rhoda had always told him vainly.

"Anyway, their house is always beautifully warm," she said.

And so were the Wortleys when they got there.

Mrs. Wortley was always vivacious and friendly, but rather spiky, as a rule. She had apparently abandoned her edges for the evening; one could hardly believe it at first.

And Howard, who had never had any edges to abandon, was looking very mellow and quite elderly in a smoking jacket.

He said something about Christmas only coming once a year and life being too short to remember petty squabbles.

Frank, who did not know he had been having a petty squabble with the male Wortley, but thought they merely shared a mutual antipathy, agreed quickly and surprisingly that Christmas was a time for peace and goodwill.

At which Howard laughed jovially and said that was Good; and his wife was heard to remark that there was always a comical side to everything, was there not, as she sailed round the warm drawing-room in search of the new party game. She was wearing something very Tudor in design, with long hanging sleeves and trimmed with ermine; and what *had* she done to her hair?

"She's letting it go grey," thought Rhoda. "It's a great improvement. In fact, they both look ten years older and really quite nice." Even Rhoda couldn't help wondering what it was all about.

A possible explanation came into the room next moment with a card table which was planted in an appropriate position under the still sailing direction of Mrs. Wortley.

"This is our niece, Esther," claimed the Wortleys proudly and simultaneously, disclosing a muscular but elegantly attired young woman of about twenty who defied the world behind unbreakable spectacles. "Esther Hobbs," elaborated Mrs. Wortley with formality; then, after a sufficient number of people had shaken hands: "My brother's only child, and such a time she's been having—all through the blitzes, weren't you, dear?—but she doesn't like us to talk about it." A few maternal pats from Mrs. Wortley on the one hand and proud smirkings from Howard on the other. "Anyway," Mrs. Wortley resumed, "we've persuaded her to spend a nice quiet Christmas here with us, right away from everything."

"After that," chimed in Howard, "we thought of getting her a few rags and showing her about a bit. All work and no play—"

"—and we're only young once," corroborated Mrs. Wortley. "Esther's a trained secretary, you know; and when the war came she gave up her career to help the poor bombed-out people in London."

"Plenty of stuffing, eh?" murmured Howard.

"Young people are showing such a wonderful spirit just now, are they not? Take off your glasses, dear."

Everyone sat round the card table and tried to master the rules of a game called "Invasion." One landed by parachute and made one's way to an important aerodrome, harassed incessantly by the most hair-raising perils and armed only with one's dice, which one rattled, however, bravely and hopefully.

Esther Hobbs, once she was sitting down and actively employed, warmed up and proved to be a sensible, capable young woman, not so much overawed by her aunt and uncle as one had at first supposed. She did not mind being classified with Mrs. Wortley as Howard's "womenkind," though both Rhoda and Paulina came to her rescue, swelling the ranks of what Howard called "The Ladies" or (worse) "Woman"; and even Frank soon began to find it quite interesting to peer at his wife through the wire netting of Howard's mental hen-run, where Rhoda was found to be lying, slandering, and even fornicating wholeheartedly with the best of them.

The party ended high-spiritedly, with Frank and Howard positively clinging to each other in the outnumbered inadequacy of being mere males of their species, and Mrs. Wortley soaring, sailing, and melting more than ever, and everybody—Frank, too—promising to call her Ida until further notice.

"*Wasn't* she looking nice?" remarked Rhoda on the way home.

"Exactly like a King's Mistress," Frank acknowledged.

"It *is* rather funny," said Rhoda, "that we've been included in the sudden thaw."

"Reaction to the snow, perhaps," suggested Frank. "No one else would bother to turn out in this weather."

"All the same," insisted Rhoda in dissatisfied tones, "it doesn't quite explain everything. That gown, for instance. Why, it was a positive creation!"

"Ah, well," Paulina said tolerantly. "It's natural she should be making more of an effort now, with a grown-up niece to take out. I expect they'll be wanting to marry her off."

Shrieks and slithers of dismay in the snow. "But not on *us*," the oysters cried (the oysters being Frank and Rhoda). And Rhoda ventured: "Perhaps we ought to have hinted tactfully that John is engaged?"

"We don't know that he is," pointed out Frank; "and a hint like that might cause a lot of trouble. But I shouldn't worry. I don't think it's John the Wortleys are so excited about. He isn't much of a catch, after all. If you ask me my opinion—it's Uncle Willie."

"Uncle Willie?" echoed Rhoda in a surprised voice.

"Someone must have told them he's coming to us for Christmas."

"But they don't know Uncle Willie. I don't think they ever met him last time he was here."

"Exactly," said Frank; "and they want to. They've probably looked him up in *Who's Who*. He *is* a bart., after all."

"So he is," exclaimed Rhoda. "I never thought of that!"

"Well, well," remarked Paulina.

II

A simple explanation! You only had to think of it and it surely accounted for the Crosbies suddenly returning Rhoda's call, outwardly covered with snowflakes but as warm as the Wortleys underneath. They were full of apologies for not having come before, but just before Christmas was such a bad time for calling, wasn't it? One really didn't want to be bothered with strangers at Christmas-time, did one?

But the Crosbies did not feel a bit like strangers to the Redpaths, seeing that Mrs. Crosbie's father, the late Humphrey Gibberd, had been such an ardent admirer of Kate Cameron, the erstwhile Virgin Queen of the Victorian stage, who had surprised everyone in eighteen eighty-six by marrying at the age of fifty-three, leaving the stage to become the mistress of a Scottish castle and dying in the same year as Queen Victoria, bequeathing a vast fortune to her husband, who was many years her junior and had survived to this day, and who was now coming to stay with the Redpaths for Christmas!

Furthermore, Rhoda's Uncle Willie (now that Rhoda came to think of it) claimed to have punched the head of his rival, Humphrey Gibberd, at a Royal Garden Party in eighteen eighty-five, which may or may not have been true, but sent the Crosbies away promising to come to the Redpaths' Christmas Tree on Boxing Day in order to meet this historical link between their two houses.

"Just fancy that wicked old man being still alive!" said

Evelyn Crosbie (*née* Gibberd) to her husband as they drove back to High Winds with chains on their wheels. "According to Papa, Sir Willoughby Keene-Cotton made an absolute *fool* of poor Kate Cameron. Took her away from the stage and buried her in Scotland. Yes, literally! Because I wouldn't be a *bit* surprised to hear he murdered her."

"Come now, Evie," protested Wilfred Crosbie tolerantly, and pointed out extenuatingly: "Anyway, he prevented the old dame from marrying your father. In which case," he added, scoring a point, "it's highly problematic you would ever have been born, honey."

"I suppose that's true," granted Evie broadmindedly. "But I wish he'd hurry up and die."

"Why, dear?" Crosbie raised his eyebrows.

"It's just occurred to me that Kate Cameron's biography would sell like hot cakes. What a character! Why have I never thought of writing it before? Truth is so much more market-able than fiction just now."

"There's such a thing as libel," ventured Crosbie.

"Well, that's what I mean, fathead," his wife replied. "I couldn't bring it out until after his death, naturally."

"I should stick to crime and romance, dear. You'll have to wait for all those Redpaths to be dead too."

"Oh, it doesn't matter about *them*. Do you think if I told the old man I was writing his wife's life he'd leave me her letters and things in his will? I must have a long talk with him. Do you think he's gaga by now?"

"Why not have a talk with the old lady, Miss Redpath? I figure she'll be able to tell you all you want to know."

"I have. As soon as I heard Sir Willoughby Keene-Cotton

was coming. She knew them both intimately. I imagine she played an important part in that Victorian drama; behind the scenes, you know. I always suspect those beatific old virgins. Either their own lives have been pretty giddy or else they've had all the fun they want arranging other people's. I think I'd make her the pivot of the story. A sort of Heavenly Procureuse."

"Why not write a play, dear?" suggested Crosbie soothingly. "Gwen could play the lead. Just the part for her, now she's getting on a bit."

"The character wouldn't be so interesting if it wasn't true," objected Mrs. Crosbie.

"Then you'll have to wait a few years," Mr. Crosbie told her. "Unless you start killing off a few of the characters," he said; "so as not to hurt their feelings," he added.

"What a lovely idea!" breathed Mrs. Crosbie (*née* Gibberd).

"There," Rhoda was saying meanwhile to Frank. "The Crosbies wouldn't have come to the Christmas Tree just to please *us*!"

"And John's friend will be most interested to meet Miss Lucas, won't she?" put in Paulina.

"Another motive for not murdering Uncle Willie, dear," Rhoda pointed out.

"Not until after Christmas, anyway," Frank had to agree.

III

A pity; because as soon as Uncle Willie arrived he really did seem to be the easiest person in the world to murder.

In fact, he almost succeeded in murdering himself twice

at the station: firstly by nearly falling on to the line while alighting from the train, then by nearly strangling himself at the ticket barrier in searching for his ticket beneath his many layers of clothing.

Quite a small, inconspicuous man he would turn out to be when disentangled, but easily recognisable even now by having one of those white moustaches with whiskers combined that seemed to have come out of a cracker.

He himself found Frank and Rhoda not so immediately recognisable. In the end, however, he took their identity on trust, but with a bad grace.

"How-de-do, how-de-do," he snapped ungraciously. "Needn't have come to meet me," he protested. "Shouldn't have brought the car," he presently objected; "not safe in this snow," he told them. "However, you know best. Get in, get in. Very good of you, I'm sure," he added more leniently in a moment. "Very kind of you both to ask me, of course," he remembered his manners in the back of the car, but wouldn't be wrapped in a rug by Rhoda ("Don't want a rug in a closed car," he said). "It's going to be a nuisance for you, having an old man like me just at Christmas-time," he prophesied depressingly. Then, since there was always a silver lining to every cloud: "Don't suppose it'll be for long, though. Can't put back the clock, can we, my dear?"

"Have you been feeling your age, Uncle Willie, dear?" asked Rhoda artlessly.

"Eh? Nonsense! Fit as ever."

In proof of which Uncle Willie at length alighted from the car and scurried up the front doorsteps of Four Corners with a heavy suitcase in each hand, and would have thus killed himself, had he been an ordinary mortal, for the third time.

Frank and Sills relieved him of his luggage in the hall, and Rhoda said, "I'll show you your room," and committed the tactical error of trying to assist him up the stairs.

"No, no, no, no!" cried Uncle Willie, throwing her off.

Frank and Sills were waiting at the foot of the stairs and luckily able to avert this fourth tragedy, in which it was Rhoda Redpath who would have been the corpse this time.

"Dear Uncle Willie!" she gasped as Frank caught her and tenderly removed her to a safe distance. "So chivalrous! He always was. Sills, see that Sir Willoughby has everything he wants."

"Yes, ma'am." The butler took the situation in hand, ascending cautiously in the wake of Uncle Willie.

"Easy to murder!" Rhoda echoed presently, feeling her bruises in the drawing-room. She and Frank watched a piece of plaster fall like a snowflake from the ceiling, which was also the floor of the bridal suite, where much scuffling was heard to be taking place. "It would need a strong man to do it; even then I'd put my money on Uncle Willie when it came to a hand-to-hand struggle for survival."

"You were too crude," Frank criticised. "Women have no patience," he went on in the idiom of Howard Wortley. "Give me a day or two," he told his wife, "and I could murder Uncle Willie with no physical effort at all."

"How?" Rhoda wondered, but she was still too out of breath to be really interested.

"Psychologically," said Frank.

"They didn't have any psychology in Uncle Willie's day," retorted Rhoda, "and he certainly hasn't got any now."

"I don't agree," replied Frank. "Only got to say 'Bet you can't jump out of the attic window at your age'—and that would be that."

"No one would believe it."

"Think not? We could get old Smythe to believe it all right, and he's the Minister for Murder in these parts."

"Major Smythe would believe anything."

"I've a good mind to try." Frank looked up at the ceiling, then out of the window calculatingly. "As an abstract experiment in Behaviourism. Eh? What do you think? After all, he couldn't hurt himself much—not with all this snow about. From the attic he'd slither off the projection over Sills's window, bounce off the porch there, miss the path, slither down the bank, and end up neatly and snugly in the nice deep snow we've shovelled on to the lawn. The perfect crime, eh? No motive, no clues, no bloodshed, and he'd still be alive for the party! What could be better?"

Rhoda might have been about to throw water on this attractive scheme, but Paulina came in briskly at this moment, followed almost immediately by Sills with the tea, and, later, Uncle Willie himself.

The next few hours were occupied happily enough by Uncle Willie trying to remember who Paulina was. It made rather a noise, because he shouted down anyone who tried to jog his memory. It wasn't that he had forgotten, it was only that he couldn't remember.

At last, by a process of elimination, he boiled her down to being a friend or relation of one of his earlier wives.

That in arriving at this conclusion he had got all his wives in the wrong order worried no one except Paulina, who found it worth the trouble of clearing the matter up. Without in any way teaching her grandmother to suck eggs, she impressed upon him that Kate Cameron had been his *first* wife, and it was not until after her death that he had married Rhoda's mother, when Rhoda was a gawky little girl of fifteen. Clear-headedly, she refused to allow him to marry any of his wives more than once; or to be married to more than one of them at a time, which would have been bigamy, she insisted obstinately.

After dinner, over his port, Uncle Willie confided in Frank that Paulina was, and always had been, a muddle-headed but devoted "gairl" who always got hold of the wrong end of the stick. "Bigamy indeed!" he snorted. Frank wasn't to pay any attention to such silliness. "But I think I managed to put her right," said Uncle Willie proudly.

He sat up till about twelve o'clock that night, talking to Rhoda about her mother, saying he that had a lot of her letters which he would show her some time, and that it was a shame no one had ever written her biography, as she was the greatest actress of her day, besides being, above all, a great lady, and there was no one alive who remembered her now, except as a name...

Needless to say, Paulina had, by this time, called it a day and gone to bed.

IV

What with the woolliness of Uncle Willie and the woolliness of the countryside, it was rather like living in a padded cell at first.

It also usually appeared to be snowing indoors as well as

out, for Uncle Willie not only wrote his normal quantity of letters but claimed to be writing his autobiography, amongst other things.

The letters which he wrote he insisted on posting himself—not that he didn't trust anyone else, but he didn't want to be a nuisance—and no, it was quite unnecessary for anyone to come with him, he'd posted letters all his life and was surely old enough to take care of himself by now. True, he had fallen over once or twice in the snow, but what of it?

Luckily, Paulina always arranged to have letters of her own up her sleeve. With these she was nearly always able to anticipate Uncle Willie in the hall, saying that a little stroll to the pillar box would blow away her cobwebs, but she hardly liked to venture out alone in such weather—oh, no, Sir Willoughby, why should you trouble?—no, really, Sir Willoughby—well, we'll go together, shall we?

She seldom failed to get away with this, and Uncle Willie never saw through her machinations.

What's more, she clung to him on the way back, pushing him up the hill, entirely giving him the impression that *he* was supporting *her*; no one but Paulina could have managed this so cleverly. "But isn't it rather too *much* for her at her age?" the Redpaths asked each other; and they wondered whether Uncle Willie, who naturally scorned the notion of having a trained nurse or male attendant, would perhaps take kindly to the idea of a strong young woman if it was put to him very tactfully? He could call her his secretary? What did Paulina think? She must put out her feelers, said Rhoda. "And perhaps you know of someone who would do, dear?"

"Someone pretty," added Frank.

"Paulina must find out the sort of thing that Uncle Willie likes," said Rhoda.

Accordingly, Aunt Paulina's feelers were put out; but drawn in again hurriedly. No, no, no, quite unnecessary, *quite*! Uncle Willie wasn't going to cause any extra trouble to *anybody*.

The house thereafter bristled with people to whom Uncle Willie was not causing any extra trouble.

Someone was always on hand to find his stick for him (not that he needed a stick, but thank you, thank you); and someone had to be standing by to switch on the wireless for him (not that he couldn't do it himself, but he was afraid of breaking it); to turn on the lights for him (the switches were in such a funny place), and turn them out again when he wasn't using them; to look through keyholes to see if he was still alive, and, if so, oughtn't he to have come out by now?

Frank had to drive him to Mewdley to do his Christmas shopping, about which he was very secretive, seeking neither advice nor human escort once he had left the car, so that it was only his white whiskers and distinctive colouring that prevented him from becoming lost in jostling crowds, and, although he did seem to know what he wanted, he never managed to get it and usually had to be driven home again at top speed to write to Harrods for it.

Rhoda seized the opportunity, while he was out, of picking up his scattered papers and trying to remember where she had put them in case he asked for them. Added to which, she was snowed over on her own account with correspondence. Not only were there her usual Christmas letters to write and answer, but the party on Boxing Day showed promise of being well attended this year, there being more and more people who apparently for some strange reason wanted to meet Uncle Willie; local powers who wondered if her stepfather would be interested in their current patriotic and entirely admirable, if sometimes somewhat vainglorious, schemes; people who claimed what could only be pre-natal intimacy with Uncle Willie's brother Roger in South Africa, and wished to renew youthful memories; someone very old called Professor Larkin, to whom Uncle Willie had evidently given his new address, who lived a mere dozen miles away and seemed undaunted by petrol-rationing and snowdrifts, threatening to pop over one day. To nearly all these people Rhoda sent invitations to the Christmas Tree, because it was Bread Upon the Waters, and you never knew what might transpire from such contacts. The more people the better, even if they did all seem rather old to dance round a Christmas Tree. At any rate, they would all have the pleasure of *seeing* Uncle Willie, even if they did not have a chance of cornering him, and it wouldn't matter how rude he was to them at his age, nor could people really expect him to know them from Adam in the circumstances. If nothing else more valuable came from the party, John would meet a mellowed Howard Wortley and Margery the Lucas woman, and Frank would have to be polite to a few of the neighbours for a change; so no actual harm could be done, at the worst.

Then there was taking Uncle Willie out to luncheon with Lord and Lady Bayham. This went off all right; but Uncle Willie refused to go to tea with the Crosbies; and when the Wortleys dropped in for cocktails Uncle Willie hid in his room and refused to emerge (he was too old for cocktails and didn't want to spoil the party; no one was to worry about *him*!)

The enterprising Crosbies cleverly kidnapped him in the village one day, offering him a lift, and he subsequently accepted their invitation to lunch on the spur of the moment, which was delightfully impulsive; only it happened that this was the day on which Professor Larkin popped over. Having driven twelve miles, he waited vainly for his old friend to appear, and Rhoda wasn't really any more interested in marine biology than Uncle Willie would have been had he turned up, which he never did; so Professor Larkin departed sadly, but optimistically hoping to get home before the black-out, and slightly cheered by being asked to the Christmas Tree, when Uncle Willie's presence would be a dead certainty, he was told.

Uncle Willie came in to tea, was informed of Professor Larkin's visit, said you don't want an old bore like that at a Christmas party, said he would write and ask young Smythe; also a jolly, high-spirited young feller who lived in these parts called Dingwall. Frederick Dingwall. Fickle Freddie, we used to call him, but had the most amazing luck on the turf. Follow Freddie and you can't lose. Quite a slogan, it was. On being told that Frederick Dingwall was the Bishop of Mewdley, Uncle Willie replied, "Yes, yes, I heard he'd gone into the Church—most extraordinary!—but he'll liven up your party for you. You can take my word for it." A long story followed which had a depressed reception.

The day ended with Uncle Willie wishing them the best of luck for their party, and they weren't to worry about him; he'd arranged to go up to London, anyway, that day. Not at all. No, no. He was too old to dance round a Christmas Tree, and wouldn't have come if he had thought he was going to be a nuisance.

Somewhat hysterical coaxing took place. The Christmas Tree would be nothing without Uncle Willie. He was to be the point of the party...

The ultimate capitulation of Uncle Willie was at last effected.

He agreed to do what he could to make the party a success. He'd order some extra presents and decorations; he'd think of something to amuse the kiddies, what?

Yes, yes! Everyone rallied hopefully.

"Ha!" cried Uncle Willie and left the room hurriedly.

No, it was all right, he hadn't been taken ill; he'd just thought of something, that was all, and it meant writing some more letters, apparently.

"I hope he isn't going to invite the Archbishop of Canterbury," said Frank.

No, it was all right, it was all right.

Mysterious and sly chucklings from Uncle Willie which continued for several days...

It was now evident that Uncle Willie had decided to enjoy his Christmas, even if no one else did.

V

One asked oneself, however, during the ensuing days of chuckling inspirations and sphynx-like facial expressions, whether this new and happy Willie wasn't perhaps even more of a strain on one's nerves than the erstwhile, disagreeable, and cantankerous one.

It was a personal triumph to have made him so happy, yes; but it had been far easier to sympathise with his concrete grumblings and (with practice) calculable reactions to daily life than it now was to share in his gleeful anticipation of one knew not what.

For no one could be sure *what* he would spring on them all at the Christmas Tree, nor whether his ideas for amusing the kiddies would necessarily correspond with the ideas of the kiddies on the same subject. There was, too, the awful possibility that he would die of happiness at any moment, and the party would, therefore, not take place at all, which, after all their trouble, would be simply maddening, to put it mildly. "Maddening, I agree," said Frank to his wife. "But it would serve you and Paulina right. Bread Upon the Waters is all very well. One of these days it'll return unto you again and choke you both."

And, ridiculous as it seemed, this is what Rhoda had begun to fear.

Particularly when Uncle Willie, after patting Rhoda's shoulder with his face wreathed in smiles and complimenting her on the cheerful, well-bred, home-like atmosphere of her establishment, announced that he had written and asked his poor wife Josephine to come to Four Corners for Christmas.

"Golly!" said Frank.

Uncle Willie had posted the letter, Paulina gave evidence.

But she won't come, Rhoda gave reassurance.

Supposing she did?

"In that case, darling, we'll just have to try and be nice to her, that's all."

"I absolutely refuse," shouted Frank, "to be nice to any more people!"

"Only till after Christmas—"

"No, no, I can't—"

"*Somebody'll* have to be nice to her," pointed out Rhoda desperately, "because I'm sure Uncle Willie won't be, even if he remembers that he's asked her…"

"Write and tell her we haven't room."

"I *might* do that," murmured Rhoda doubtfully.

But there was no need. It was a false alarm.

With the dawn came a reprieve in the form of a letter from Mrs. Cyril Horsham, who wrote to Rhoda direct.

Mother wasn't strong enough to make the journey…she had to rest as much as possible… We're having a very quiet Christmas this year…the weather just now is so treacherous for old people…

Rhoda looked out of the window. The dining-room had grown darker, but the outlook was brighter, for snow had begun to fall again thickly and with most merciful treachery.

She passed the letter covertly to her husband, who presently laid before Uncle Willie the reassuring if splutterily written information that Dr. Clark was not worried about Mother's condition so long as the poor darling avoided all rich food and excitement.

Uncle Willie put on his eyeglass and said, "Eh? Nonsense!" Then, after reading the letter, admitted that it all might quite possibly be true. "Over seventy, of course," he said, going on with his porridge. "Never had a chance to look after herself properly till now. Remarkably unselfish and capable woman, but never taken any ordinary natural precautions to safeguard her own health. Tremendous vitality and most astute business brain. Husband left her very badly off and she's had to think of every penny till now. Now she can relax and rest. Well, well! It's only to be expected, isn't it? We all come to it."

"I hope Lady Keene-Cotton isn't seriously ill?" Paulina felt someone in the room ought to have asked by now.

"No, no, no no!" Uncle Willie scouted, throwing Mrs. Horsham's letter into some marmalade. "But she'll be better off where she is. They'll look after her. Not that her son isn't a bit of an ass—like all clergymen—and Verna's not a lady, of course; but they're both very conscientious, and they'll see that everything possible is done. No excitement, eh? No mince-pies…no turkey…all the rest of it…we all come to it…" He had now finished his porridge and was piling up his plate at the sideboard. "Of course, I'm lucky," he admitted modestly, returning to his seat. "Fifteen years older than Josephine, yet I eat what I like. Always have. Eat as much now as I did when I was a boy. Eh?"

Murmurs of polite applause.

"Ha!" said Uncle Willie. "There's no need to be ill, you know, if you take ordinary, natural precautions and keep away from doctors with their serums, bacteria, and diets. Daresay there's something in it all. Suits some people." (No one was to think Uncle Willie narrow-minded and prejudiced.) "But the fact remains that your own inside is the best doctor in the world if you give it a chance and take ordinary, natural precautions…"

Uncle Willie's ordinary, natural precautions normally consisted of sprinkling his porridge recklessly with what appeared to be white arsenic; to-day he furthermore slipped a minute tablet into his coffee and stirred it vigorously with a gnarled and shaky hand. Later he was seen to swallow a vast capsule. Consequently he was enabled to eat more than ever that day of what he liked, only complaining that there wasn't enough of it. "Ought to be having mince-pies, oughtn't we?" he suggested. "And there should always be a few chocolates about; even in war-time, eh?"

"Soon there will be plenty of chocolates about, Uncle Willie dear," Rhoda assured him in comfort.

And Paulina reminded him that mince-pies were supposed to be unlucky *before* Christmas.

Paulina really was wonderful. Although it continued to snow more than ever that day, the weather becoming more and more treacherous for old people, she stood for nearly three hours on the lawn with Uncle Willie that afternoon while he watched the Coultard children make a snowman.

"It's too *much* for her," said Rhoda.

III
Mince-Pies
Before Christmas

I

The train moved slowly and stopped repeatedly.

"It seems rather silly," observed Margery Dore, clearing for herself a peephole in the misty window through which to survey the snow-clad countryside; "after spending so much of our lives pretending to be married when we're not, now we're going to pretend to be not when we are!"

"Yes, it does, doesn't it?" agreed John from his corner, but without much interest.

"Is it really necessary?"

"Only till after Christmas."

"You still haven't told me why," Margery complained.

"I thought I had."

"You said something about it being a better stage effect. Well, I think it would be far more dramatic if you rushed me in on them all and said 'Mother, we're married!' immediately. Why not?"

"Curtain," explained John patiently.

"Not necessarily," objected Margery Dore. "A lot of plays begin like that nowadays."

"Uncle Willie's old-fashioned."

"Well, so's my mother old-fashioned. That's why I always do what I like first and then spring it on her before she's had time to think."

"Very inconsiderate of you," said John.

"Not at all," retorted Margery. "It relieves her of all maternal doubts, apprehensions, and responsibilities—"

"So that the poor dear has to look elsewhere for her amusements. I call it a shame. My way's far more amusing for all concerned."

"Is it worth the trouble?"

"I thought you liked acting."

"I'm rather tired of lying and pretending. It isn't quite the same thing, you know."

"Yes, it is. So long as you know what the truth is—that's all that matters. What does it matter which side of the footlights you are if your heart is pure, dear?"

"I suppose that's true," admitted Margery, taking his word for it.

"We want to create an atmosphere of suspense over Christmas," explained John indulgently. "What a nice girl Margery Dore is! Is John coming up to scratch? Perhaps Margery hasn't been working it properly; perhaps she doesn't really love him; such a pity if she went out with the tide—"

"How lovely!" broke in Margery with appreciation. "The tide being—?" she prompted.

"The war, chiefly. Your estimable but ambitious mamma, perhaps. People are making such suitable marriages nowadays.

My poor old parents live right out of the world and only see life in the papers. And, of course, people in the papers always appear to be marrying complete strangers out of sheer affectation—"

"Yes, *don't* they?" Margery had to agree. "Or for purposes of propaganda…"

"Or *esprit de corps*. Well, the sober truth is I have no news value of any kind. Admit your mother has been hoping to hitch you on to someone in the R.A.F. with a father in the Middle East and a mother in the West End. And look at *me*! My father was a pacifist in the last war and has given nobody any reason to suppose he isn't one now. In fact, he's made himself quite unpopular in his bucolic retreat; and Mother just sits doing cross-stitch without caring a damn one way or another. They were both only too pleased that I was rejected for the army and don't even bother to go about saying how disappointed the poor boy was. Mother's only anxiety is to find me a nice soft reserved occupation in case I'm called up again. In fact, the less said about us the better." John lit his pipe.

"I don't see why you need be blamed for all that," Margery interposed. "You've been putting nails in Hitler's coffin as much as anybody."

"But it doesn't show. Where was I? Oh, yes. I mean No: our only hope is Uncle Willie."

"I didn't know your Uncle Willie had any National significance."

"Nevertheless Uncle Willie, to some extent—and even in war-time—is News. In his day he was a personage of some distinction. True, his glory is mostly reflected and his wealth entirely inherited; nevertheless the fact remains that his brother Roger fell down a gold mine or something during the Boer War and old Sir Willoughby Keene-Cotton is known to have been married to nearly everyone of any importance since attaining puberty, including my grandmother, and has accomplished the supreme triumph of remaining alive to the present day. Well, I mean, it does all give me at least a shadowy kind of background."

"Very shadowy," Margery commented.

"That's why we've got to push Uncle Willie in front of the curtain while we can," explained John. "He's an old man and can't live very much longer. At his death all his money will go to a lot of scattered, dreary people in whom he can't possibly take more than a dry, academic interest. A romance under his nose might kindle his enthusiasm—particularly if he can feel he's brought it about. I expect Mother's been saying how relieved she would be if I married you, but what can a mother do? Age cannot influence youth, etc. Your mother expects you to make a showy match, but as things are at present—"

"So I'm to vamp Uncle Willie into supplying a few Christmas decorations?"

"Darling, you will be careful, won't you?"

"You can trust me. He'll be my fairy godfather and bring me to my senses, show me the way to happiness, and so forth, and incidentally relieve your mother's feelings."

"Then he'll die happy."

"Yes."

Enchanted with the idea of being the cause of Uncle Willie's happy demise, they contemplated it in a rapturous silence which Margery broke at last, saying—"Darling, I'm only wondering—"

"What are you only wondering, dearest?" asked John tolerantly.

"Have we got to wait till Uncle Willie's dead before announcing that we've been married all the time?"

Pause, while John frowned. Then—"No," he said; "only till after Christmas."

II

A slight, alert figure was on the platform to meet them. This was Frank Redpath; and if fathers served as warnings to young girls of what sons could grow into, this particular father did so in the kindliest possible manner; because really, thought Margery, they were ridiculously alike, Frank being, if possible, the less sober and owlish of the two and far easier to live up to. But Margery's acquaintance with Frank was superficial as yet; she was not related to him and certainly not married to him, so she could afford to be appreciative. Being appreciative meant listening to a long dissertation on the character and habits of Uncle Willie, which began immediately after the perfunctory greetings had taken place.

"He was most excited when I told him you were coming," said Frank to Margery. "He's got an idea into his head that he's met you before."

"What?" said Margery. "No, I'm sure I've never met anyone called Sir Willoughby Keene-Cotton."

"He says you probably wouldn't have known it was him," pursued Frank.

"What does he look like?" asked Margery.

"He looks like somebody who had started to make up as Father Christmas but hadn't enough cotton-wool," was John's description, which Frank not only endorsed but applauded.

"No, I'm sure I've never met anyone who looks like that," said Margery. "Where does he think it was we met?"

"Oh, he hasn't the faintest idea," replied Frank gaily, arranging Margery by his side in the car and pressing the self-starter. "Some hotel or other, I gathered."

Minor commotion in the back of the car.

Margery caught John's eye in the driving-mirror. She smiled reassuringly. "No, I'm sure it wasn't me," she said to Frank. "*Ought* it to have been?"

"No, no, no!" Frank swept the car happily round the station yard. "Only you mustn't mind if he keeps insisting you're someone you've never heard of. He's rather anxious about his memory. Not that he can't remember, but he keeps forgetting."

"I don't mind *who* I am," said Margery. "I can always be anyone at a moment's notice."

"Good."

"Did you say he was ill?" asked John from behind.

"Nothing much. Wanted some mince-pies. Paulina said they were unlucky before Christmas, so of course he ate five or six. Then swore he had swallowed the threepenny-bit. Turned blue."

"Blue!" echoed Margery, being appreciative.

"That was partly through fury with Paulina. Said she'd put it there on purpose to justify her superstitions. Silly sort of joke. Might have killed him."

"And did it?" from John.

"Unfortunately not. Owing to having taken ordinary, natural precautions and having an iron constitution, he could have swallowed half a crown without noticing it. Determined to have his cake and eat it, however. Wouldn't sit still and sleep it off, walked up and down rattling, then went out into the garden to choke to death, refusing to let anyone come with him."

"What happened?"

"Coughed up tuppence three farthings and digested the change."

"Father, do be serious."

"As a matter of fact," complied Frank, "he had rather a nasty fall and twisted both his legs, so he's tied to his room at the moment. Thank heavens! We're fattening him up for Christmas. Got him a secretary to help him with his 'work'—really to keep an eye on him (nothing like being tactful)—so the house is now comparatively peaceful. Almost gloomily so. He's still huffy with poor old Paulina, who really has been wonderful with him, and snaps my head off every time I go and see him. Poor Rhoda is the only person who can do anything with him now. And Esther Hobbs."

"Who's she?" asked John.

"She's the secretary. Niece of the Wortleys, staying with them. Strong, capable young woman who is only too pleased to tootle over daily from next door. She's one of those girls who ought to be married as soon as possible, being absolutely lost with nothing to do and no one to look after. The Wortleys were going to try and push her into high society if they could find any; but we've saved her from that—for the moment, anyway."

"Isn't Uncle Willie high society?"

"But she can't marry *him*. And as his secretary she isn't expected to be a lady."

"Is she pretty?" asked Margery.

"She has a slight squint," replied Frank.

"Sounds perfect," remarked John.

"Yes, it's most convenient," said Frank. After a pause he went on (since talking appeared to keep him warm): "I don't know what we shall do if he *does* fall down dead suddenly. Won't have a doctor near him, so there's bound to be an inquest. Supposing they open him up? I should think the contents of his stomach—"

"Do shut up, Father—"

"—would make the most sensational reading in the local paper," finished Frank. "He's probably been an arsenic-eater over a number of years. Could swallow a whole sack now without noticing it. Ordinary, natural precautions."

"You mean it's no use ordering in an extra supply to put in the mince-pies?"

"Not enough shipping space."

"Anyway—I forgot—we don't want to murder him now, do we?"

"Not for his money," acknowledged Frank wistfully. "His wife gets it all."

"Do you think he began eating arsenic as soon as he married her—as a natural precaution, I mean—" John broke off from this idle prattle as they turned in at the gates of Four Corners. "Shades of Father Christmas!" he said. "What's that?"

Four Corners was not a large house, but it was an oldish one and stood back from the road with a presentable carriage sweep, at one point in which the terraced lawn at the back of the house could be plainly seen.

"That was a snowman," explained Frank needlessly.

"What a good one!" admired Margery. "Who made it?"

"Uncle Willie said he did; but it was those horrid little boys in the garage."

"Why was there a fence round it?"

"Because of that inquisitive black dog of the Coultards."

"Come on, Margery, let's knock it down and see what's inside it—"

"NO!" commanded Frank fiercely.

"Why not?"

"I want it to last over Boxing Day."

John groaned. "I'd forgotten about the Christmas Tree. Are there crowds of children coming?"

"On the contrary," replied Frank, "nearly everybody who's coming is over seventy, so I've had to provide some ponderous and intellectual amusements this year."

"What's the snowman got to do with it? Oh, yes, I see."

"No, you don't see," John's father reproved him. "Margery, dear," he said, "kindly restrain your young man from solving any mysteries until after Christmas, there's a good girl."

III

They were welcomed by the temporary parlourmaid, who was a muted and efficient elderly woman with a mechanical smile; she subsequently served them with an enormous luncheon.

"You seem to have done yourselves pretty well," John observed.

"We have indeed," agreed Frank and Rhoda, showing enthusiasm. "Uncle Willie insisted on giving us *three* turkeys," Rhoda told them, "several jars of mince-meat, two enormous Christmas puddings, and as for the Christmas cake he ordered at Buntings—"

"You wouldn't believe it was real," put in Paulina enthusiastically.

"We've been trying to persuade Paulina to be a carnivore," said Frank; "just over Christmas; to help us out; but she won't."

Paulina shook her head smilingly and planted her hoofs firmly.

"But doesn't Uncle Willie help you out?" asked John.

"Oh, yes," said Rhoda quickly.

"Oh, yes, he does," said Frank.

His parents seemed depressed, so John said cheerfully: "Well, now you've got us. Come on, Margery; let's get down to it. *Esprit de corps.*" But even they made very little impression on the turkey.

Frank and Rhoda hardly managed to finish what they had on their plates, which was curious, as they were usually such hearty eaters. John hoped they were not ill. Oh no, they said, they were only reserving their appetites for Christmas.

Esther Hobbs put in an appearance for lunch, but she was not a very helpful eater; she came in late and withdrew early to a small room where she was heard typewriting assiduously. She had a slight cast in her eye, it was true, and not much small-talk, but was evidently a young woman who believed wholeheartedly in whatever she was doing at the time, which, according to Frank, was at present typing out Uncle Willie's autobiography. "She laps it all up and takes it all down, whether it makes sense or not. If it's coherent enough to be published it'll create the most frightful uproar, I should think; but I don't think we need worry."

At which Paulina said, "I don't see why it shouldn't be

publishable with a little editing. It's only the events of the last few years that are a little hazy in his mind."

"Come now, Paulina," said Rhoda, "he gets his generations terribly mixed up."

"That could easily be smoothed out," upheld Paulina optimistically.

"And now, if you'll excuse me," said Frank, "I'll just go and see if he's had everything he wants for lunch; then I really must take some exercise. We'll take the Coultards' dog for a long walk, eh, John?"

"O.K.," said John.

"Darling, don't *excite* Uncle Willie," came anxiously from Rhoda, following him to the door. "And if you're going to the Coultards…" A strictly domestic conversation took them from the dining-room.

In the drawing-room, lulled by gentle conversation from Paulina, John and Margery fell into bloated slumber, waking up in turns to raise their eyebrows at her attentively.

The subject of Aunt Paulina's discourse was, inevitably, the wonderfulness of Uncle Willie; his bravery in coming all the way here, quite alone and by train; how he was looking forward to the Christmas Tree; how a large number of people were coming to the party entirely because they had heard about him and wanted to see him, and that was why dear Rhoda and Frank were taking such care of him, for it would be dreadful for him to be laid up on Boxing Day and miss all the fun; for the last few days he'd been chuckling over a little surprise for us all and we were all trying not to guess what it was, which was another hint to John not to try and solve any mysteries before Christmas.

And John woke up to hear that the Wortleys were coming

to the party, that Howard's newspapers had suffered from the War like everything else, but he was bringing out a new War Magazine, and he hoped that perhaps Sir Willoughby Keene-Cotton would be interested enough to write an article for their first issue even if he didn't care to invest any money in it; and Margery woke up to hear about the Crosbies and Gwendoline Lucas, and how they had suddenly thought of having a Kate Cameron All Star Matinée in aid of the Red Cross and wondered if Sir Willoughby Keene-Cotton would favour the idea; and how anxious Miss Lucas was to act in one of Mrs. Crosbie's books if only she could find a young playwright with time to dramatise it and a young actress for the girl who wouldn't want too big a salary...

Then, just as Aunt Paulina's subject-matter was becoming really interesting, though her delivery remained as soporific as ever, Rhoda appeared with the information that Uncle Willie wanted to see Margery.

"You will be careful, darling, won't you?" whispered John in her ear.

"And don't let him talk too long," implored Rhoda. "If he can be made to go to sleep for a few hours in the afternoon he's so much more manageable for the rest of the day. I'll come and turn you out at half-past three."

Margery was ushered upstairs. Rhoda opened a door through which a reverberating voice was heard to say: "Ha! Come in, come in. How-de-do, how-de-do..."

John was lulled to sleep again by a muffled drone coming through the drawing-room ceiling, also by a catalogue of his mother's charms and virtues coming from Paulina, who would never have pulled through a severe illness the winter before last if it hadn't been for dear Rhoda's visits. "She's always been like a daughter to me," said Paulina. "She's always had me *with* her, you see, ever since she was born. After her father died and her mother married Sir Willoughby, I stayed on looking after her *right* up to the day she married your father! And now you've grown up too, dear, and it seems only the other day that the nurse came down the stairs with you in her arms. Frank and I were sitting in the drawing-room…"

It was a sort of earthquake that woke John up finally. This was caused by the entrance of a fat black retriever which snuffled hilariously round the room, rolled on its back, then settled down to eating balls of ice off its feet.

"Just time for a mile or two before tea," said Frank.

IV

Esther Hobbs rejoined the family circle at tea. But Rhoda had tea with Uncle Willie overhead. Esther Hobbs disappeared with a large pile of manuscript and shorthand jottings and an even larger slice of Christmas cake. Aunt Paulina recatalogued, for Margery's sake, the charms and virtues of the absent Rhoda, who presently came in and said Where was Frank? Damn; and went out again. Paulina, observing mildly that Rhoda was very naughty, went to lie down before dressing for dinner.

John and Margery were left alone.

"Well?" said John.

"Isn't he lovely!" said Margery. "I'm sure I should have remembered if I'd met him before. Of course he's got me mixed up with Mother, whom he seems to have known quite well, although he seems to have got *her* mixed up with someone called Cornelia Hastings; and poor Cornelia Hastings, if there ever was such a person, can't possibly, on the circumstantial evidence, be less than a hundred and twelve by now, and that only on the assumption that he's mixing her up with her daughter. Just fancy his writing his autobiography! I'd love to read it!"

"But how did you get on with him?"

"Oh, very well. He asked if we were engaged, and I said we were too young to tie ourselves up."

"What did he say?"

"He said 'Nonsense! Get engaged as young as you can.' It was a good education, he said; always break it off if you like, and no harm done."

"And what did you say?"

"I sighed and said Love wasn't Everything."

John applauded. "Yes?"

"He said: 'No—no—no—no—no—no—no—no—no—no—.'"

"Goodness!"

"I thought he was never going to stop. Then he said Love or Money—didn't make any difference when I got to his age. Said if there was plenty of money about, Love would look after itself."

"What if there was plenty of Love about?"

"That's what I asked, of course. He said God took care of lovers."

John *was* disappointed. "Oh," he said. "Never mind, darling. You've made a good beginning."

IV
Parcels at Christmas

I

PARCELS ARRIVED BY EVERY POST. A GREAT MANY OF them were for Uncle Willie; nearly all of them were labelled— "Not to be opened till Christmas Day."

"You wouldn't believe the difficulty I've had trying to hide Uncle Willie's parcels," said Frank to Margery. "I suppose at his age you grab your pleasures while you can in case you die to-morrow."

"Why not let him be happy in his own way?" Margery asked.

"Because," answered Frank, "if we let him have all his fun now he quite possibly *will* die to-morrow; and we want him alive on Boxing Day."

"After which it won't matter," put in John.

"Quite right," agreed his father.

On Christmas Eve Frank had arranged to go up to London on some essential but highly secretive errand. Poor Rhoda was in a fluster that morning because Angelina was coming over for the day with her husband to see Uncle Willie. "I think you ought to be here when they arrive," she kept murmuring in rather a futile manner, rubbing her cheeks and scratching her head. But no one else appeared to agree that the presence of Frank Redpath to greet these flying guests was really important. And Frank himself, while admitting a mild curiosity to meet Angelina and whoever she was now married to, upheld that, on the other hand, the success of their party depended entirely on his visit to London. Probable snowdrifts and possible air raids could not deter him, so why should his mild inquisitiveness and even milder sense of social duty keep him at home? Rhoda gave way and broke the news to Uncle Willie. She found him with Esther Hobbs, dictating a letter to Professor Larkin, in which he thanked the Professor for his Christmas good wishes, etc., but refused to be blackmailed into showing the slightest interest, financial or otherwise, in the university where he lectured. "But you'll be seeing Professor Larkin at the party," pointed out Rhoda; "you can tell him all that then." "Want to enjoy myself at the party," retorted Uncle William.

"He was much cheered up, though, at the prospect of meeting the notorious Angelina," reported Rhoda at luncheon.

"Then he'll probably be out when she arrives," said John. "Hadn't you better lock him in?"

"He can't manage the stairs," replied Rhoda. "Anyway, Esther's keeping an eye on him."

"Is Angelina *very* notorious?" asked Margery artlessly.

John, indicating the presence of virginal innocence in the person of Paulina, frowned at his ingenuous beloved.

It was Paulina, however, who answered her question. "Oh,

no, dear. Poor Angelina was in love with a married man, you see; she lived with him for quite a time, I believe; then he left her in the lurch. Luckily there were no children, so it didn't matter, dear."

"Oh," said Margery rather blankly. Emboldened, she asked: "Is she married to the one she's got now?"

"Presumably," Paulina answered with an air of logic, "or she would not have brought him to stay in a country rectory."

Margery accepted this seal of respectability and went on with the book she was reading.

Presently a large car clanked up the drive and Keevil set Angelina's seal of respectability even more firmly by announcing in her temporary voice: "Mr. and Mrs. Freer."

Angelina was dark, exquisitely turned out and almost unbelievably slim. Her features were clear-cut but robbed of their severity by a generous and somewhat foolish mouth which was beautifully painted and incessantly revealed her flashing white teeth. "How do you do?" she said, shaking hands with everybody in her abstracted manner. "Dreadful of us to come butting in on you just before Christmas; but Puffy thought we'd better get it over before there was another snowstorm or an invasion or—or anything; didn't you, Puffy?"

Puffy was about forty-five, with completely colourless hair and eyebrows, but a very red face.

"Rather," he said, and stood about nervously, leaving everything to his wife but watching her anxiously. If *she* was at all nervous it showed only in an increased vagueness of manner, which was evidently her chief defence and charm. Rhoda, after introducing and explaining everyone, and apologising for the absence of her husband at far greater length than anyone else present thought the circumstances demanded, confided how Frank and Uncle Willie had both been very busy preparing surprises for the Christmas Tree on Boxing Day, about which they were both so serious and secretive that they were hardly on speaking terms with each other or anyone else; which was a pity, because Christmas was a time for goodwill, not petty squabbles about nothing in particular, wasn't it?

The Freers agreed that it was, and, having gathered round the fire, warmed up and simmered down, and jokingly confessed their surprised relief that Sir Willoughby Keene-Cotton was still alive.

"Very much so," Rhoda informed them. "His enforced rest has done him the world of good. Really, I think he's better now than he's been for some time."

"I *am* glad to hear that," murmured Angelina.

"That *is* good news," agreed Puffy.

Pause; while everyone wondered, perhaps, if they had been over-acting.

It was Paulina, of course, who asked the formal but leading question: "How is Lady Keene-Cotton?"

Which brought the Freers to the reason for their visit.

"To be quite frank, Mrs. Redpath," said Angelina, frowning at her own dainty feet, "we're rather worried about her."

"Not too good, I'm afraid," put in Puffy.

"In fact, that's why we're here," Angelina was distressed at having to confess.

"Thought it best to come along as soon as possible," mumbled Puffy.

General alarm. "Oh dear," thought John, who was sitting

in a corner of the drawing-room, "they think their mother's going to die before the old man! What then?"

"I quite understand," said Rhoda sympathetically, "and I *am* sorry."

("Perhaps it's a good thing Father *isn't* here," thought John; "Mother does this sort of thing far better when left to herself…")

"Not that we're really worried," deprecated Angelina.

"Doesn't do to put things into words," her husband shook his head wisely.

"Dr. Clark, of course, is an old man, and he advised us to have a second opinion. I'm afraid that may have made poor Mother imagine she's worse than she really is. It's made her worry about all of *us*, you know; about being a burden to us, you see, then dying and leaving us in the soup. It's made her a little light-headed. She's insisted on carrying on as usual over Christmas. I think she's an idea that if she once takes to her bed she'll never get up again. However, we've imported a trained nurse at last; otherwise I couldn't have come away, of course; Cyril and Verna have never been able to manage Mother at all—you see, she's always been the one to manage *them*."

"And she was much better this morning, wasn't she?" said Puffy, with an attempt to disperse the gloom. "Come now, Angy—this morning you told me she actually *recognised* you?"

Angelina admitted this, explaining: "When I first came, she didn't know who I was. I hadn't seen her for a very long time, of course. Not since her wedding to Sir Willoughby. And this morning she sent for me. She was sitting up in bed and knew my name and everything. She said she wanted to ask my advice. Sir Willoughby Keene-Cotton, she said, had asked her to marry him, which would be rather a solution to everything, she said; even if she hadn't always loved him dearly," added Angelina quickly. "Then she began making plans for the future, having forgotten all about the war and everything. I promised to try and get over for the wedding, then I rang you up and we came straight along."

"And *did* you get over for the wedding?" asked Rhoda foolishly. "I mean," she amended, "*were* you at the wedding? I don't remember seeing you."

"No. I couldn't make it," said Angelina.

Then Keevil came in and announced that Sir Willoughby would see Mrs. Freer.

It was decided that Mr. Freer was to remain in the drawing-room, leaving the interview in the capable hands of his wife. He was only too pleased with this arrangement, being obviously embarrassed by the present situation. Rhoda tried to cheer him up with some whisky, but he told her he was practically on the water wagon these days. He succumbed to temptation, however, on finding a decanter and syphon placed under his very nose by John, and made a few feeble jokes about not giving him away to his wife and cynical observations about married life in general which could hardly be taken seriously, seeing how difficult he found it to live through even a few minutes' separation from Angelina.

Paulina did her best to make the time pass by catechising him on his family and connections. Was he, by any chance, related to some Freers she once met in Rome? Or there were some Freers with whom Paulina Redpath was very nearly shipwrecked in the Caspian Sea? No? No, Puffy disclaimed all geographical and genealogical associations with the name of Freer until Aunt Paulina, having sailed with serene obstinacy round the world, came to port in Durban, where it seemed he was actually born; which implied that he was an off-shoot of Freer's Bathing Beach, if not actually born in a bathing machine.

"How very interesting," rallied Paulina, but it served her right, thought Rhoda.

Angelina returned at last with the news that Sir Willoughby had been most amiable to her and promised to provide for the contingency of outliving his wife, which he had triumphantly assured her he was going to do. The idea of making a new will, in fact, once it had penetrated, appealed to him enormously—so much so that he was going to make an orgy of it, sending for his solicitor and giving his whole mind to the matter. He would get down to drawing up the will at once, he had said, though he didn't suppose he'd be able to get hold of old Merivale until after Christmas.

"We'll see that he doesn't forget," promised Rhoda, wrapping the Freers up in the hall for departure.

It was very good of Mrs. Redpath, the Freers replied, to bother about *their* troubles. They departed full of good wishes for Christmas and looking ten years younger.

Their entire reliance on Rhoda's easily made promise was not, perhaps, so naively trusting as it seemed. It possibly occurred to both of them—as it certainly did to John—that once old Willie started on making new wills and redistributing his great wealth, it might not be altogether to the disadvantage of the Redpath family.

After they had gone there were three more parcels on the hall table labelled "Not to be opened till Christmas Day."

II

"Who *does* get his money if he outlives his wife?" wondered Frank, after being supplied with a character sketch of the Freers, and when the motive for their visit had been explained.

"He'll have to make an entirely new will, of course," said Rhoda.

"Not having any heirs of the body or next of kin," appended John.

"No, he wouldn't bother to have any of those," agreed Frank.

"They do sound rather scratchy," admitted John.

"Yes, *don't* they?" chimed Margery.

"Of course it's none of my business," said Paulina, "but I'm glad he's going to make a new will."

Everyone asked why.

"I've been trying to persuade him to for a long time," she said. "Oh, very tactfully. During his life he's been very generous to a number of people who have come to depend on him. It has always seemed to me a pity they should actually *lose* by his death, even if they don't gain very much. Mr. Merivale, I know, thinks his present will a little—well, quixotic. An altogether more satisfactory document can, I am sure, be devised."

"You mean he might leave something to *us*?" John asked without shame.

But Paulina refused to be drawn. "No, dear; I meant that a new will, made now that he's had time to think things over and remember that there are other people in the world than his wife, will simplify matters."

"Not for the Horshams," pointed out John. "It would be simpler for them if he died before his wife. In fact, why Angelina didn't stick him in the gizzard while she had the chance, I really don't know. And, personally, I can't share your happy optimism about more satisfactory documents. He's reached a dangerous and irresponsible age. He's quite likely to leave everything to somebody he's met for the first time at the party."

"There's an idea in that, John, my boy," murmured Frank appreciatively. "What can we lose, after all? We'll curtain him off in a corner of the room at the party, with a placard outside: 'WILLIE FOR WILLS! Legacies while you wait!' Margery and Esther can sit on either side of him witnessing away like mad, Eh? What do you think?"

Nobody paid any attention to this except John, who affected to consider the idea. "Mightn't be a bad idea to curtain him off," he granted. "People are only coming to our party to have a look at him. Most of them can afford to pay for the privilege. It could go to the Spitfire Fund. Can't see much point in the wills—they'd revoke each other as they went along, wouldn't they, and be just a lot of waste paper after Christmas."

"Well, what could be more valuable than waste paper these days?" said Frank, cleverly ending this futile discussion.

III

Next day being Christmas, John felt justified in complaining that he had hung up his stocking and nothing—absolutely nothing—had happened! This would not have mattered in itself, but at breakfast there were only the most nominal and peremptory gifts for everyone.

"Darling, how lovely! It's just what I wanted. How did you guess?" said Rhoda, undoing a trashily decorated matchbox.

"But, Mother," expostulated John in horror, "*that* isn't what I was giving you for Christmas!" He ran out into the hall. Dimly he had noticed there was something wrong. The hall table, which had become piled even higher on Frank's return the night before, was now completely bare.

V

Secrets at Christmas

I

Secrets and whisperings were allowed at Christmas, Aunt Paulina pointed out. Moreover, Uncle Jeff and Aunt Meg motored over for luncheon, encouraged rather than otherwise by the snow, which they considered most cheerfully seasonable; so John had to suppress his irritation.

Uncle Jeff and Aunt Meg pretended to be disappointed that Sir Willoughby Keene-Cotton did not descend from his room to meet them. He was a wonderful old man, they upheld; but if he was suffering from a slight cold, it was wise of him to remain in an even temperature; and if he was resting to-day so as to reserve his strength for the party to-morrow, perhaps they had better not disturb him.

"But I'm sure he'd *like* to see you," said Rhoda warmly. She ran upstairs, but came down again quickly. "I don't know, I'm sure," she murmured doubtfully. "He wouldn't answer me properly. He seems to have turned his whole room upside down. He's got a surprise for us all to-morrow and I don't like to force my way in… Perhaps, if you could both stay for tea…"

But no…Uncle Jeff and Aunt Meg quite understood, wanted to get back while it was light, left their very best wishes for the success of the Christmas Tree, a box of chocolates for everybody…and departed, their kind thoughts remaining behind, but their boxes of chocolates disappearing from the hall table just like everything else.

II

When Frank and Rhoda returned to the drawing-room from wrapping up Uncle Jeff and Aunt Meg, John was standing with his back to the fireplace, having apparently been airing his grievances on Aunt Paulina. Margery, disclaiming all responsibility, was trying to read a book.

Not that Paulina wasn't a most suitable person to air one's grievances on, and not that she couldn't agree with everything he said and turn away his wrath far better without assistance from her nephew and his wife; but John's father and mother didn't see why he should turn them out of their own drawing-room; besides, Rhoda wanted to write a few letters, and Frank, who had been on his feet all day, wanted to relax in front of a cheerful wood-fire.

"It's all very well for Father to say I'm not to try and solve any mysteries before Christmas," John was telling Paulina while she did her knitting, "but I didn't know he meant me to go about with my eyes shut. Anyway, to-day *is* Christmas."

"I meant Boxing Day," put in Frank.

John ignored him. "This morning," he said, "Uncle Willie

sent for me. *I* didn't particularly want to see him, but I very kindly go upstairs and knock on his door; he says 'Come in'—'*Come in*', mark you!—so in I go, to find him standing in front of a mirror in a red dressing-gown; he's absolutely furious, kicks me out of the room, and the rest you know."

Rhoda didn't have to stop writing to suggest: "He can't have said 'Come in.' It must have been 'Just a moment, my boy.'"

"He said 'Come in,'" stated John flatly. "And as for Father," he went on in a moment, "I think he's going off his head, I really do. I don't *deny* that secrets are allowed at Christmas, but a joke's a joke, and one should try to keep one's sense of proportion, however old one is. How can I *help* guessing what's going to happen on Boxing Day when I can't *move* without finding parcels at every turning, inside every piece of furniture that has an inside. Even the piano won't play. If I take a book from a shelf something is immediately exposed to view that I'm not supposed to know about. If I sit down something cracks and nobody's allowed to wonder why. If I walk across the room something creaks or crinkles and I'm not allowed to wonder what. It's all your fault, Mother; you've fed his megalomania for years; and, since you've both been living buried down here, he's come unstuck entirely and thinks he can get away with anything, however crude. Form of escapism, I suppose, poor old turnip; but I warn you, soon he'll have to be locked up. He'll begin murdering people left and right, in broad daylight, and go off in a huff if anyone dares to notice."

Rhoda's pen scratched, Paulina's needles clicked, and Margery was heard to chuckle appreciatively. John shot a grateful glance at her, but found she was only laughing at something in her book; and what could be more annoying than that? The jewelled aphorism that fell presently from Paulina's lips at least denoted that she had been listening to what he had been saying.

"If you let people keep their secrets, John," Paulina generalised, "they may let you keep yours."

"I don't know what you mean by that," grumbled John and defied her: "I have no secrets."

Frank looked at his son suspiciously, and Rhoda cleared her throat in all innocence.

Paulina affected to voice everybody's disappointment. "We quite thought that you and Margery had prepared a little surprise for us—after Christmas…"

"You make me sick," John told her bluntly.

"I'm sorry," said Paulina. "Perhaps it's Margery who's preparing a little surprise for *you*?"

"What?" said Margery, looking up from her book, keeping a finger on her place.

"All right, dear," Paulina reassured her; "I won't give you away."

Margery, not wishing to play, went on with her book.

"Either of you," added Paulina, still wishing to play and going on with her knitting.

"You won't give *us* away!" echoed John, furiously playing, whether he wished to or not. "I like that! *Us!* What were *you* doing, may I ask, snooping into Uncle Willie's room this morning?"

"When, dear?" Paulina enquired, looking only a little pained.

"When he was in his bath. Putting poisoned pennies in his porridge?"

"Something like that, dear. As a matter of fact," she explained fragrantly, "I was putting a few flowers in his room."

"As a peace offering?"

"Yes, dear."

"Hasn't he forgiven you for poisoning his mince-pies yet?"

"I don't know, dear; I haven't asked."

"You and Willie used to be rather thick. Almost a romance, from what I gather."

"He's got Esther Hobbs, you see, now, dear."

"That's another funny thing!" John pounced, allowing her no retreat. "He refused to have anyone in to look after him until after he had nearly been choked to death by those mince-pies; now he's only too glad of a smoke-screen. Looks as if he doesn't trust you any more, doesn't it?"

Rhoda put down her pen. "Oh, John, stop being so silly. We're getting tired of it."

"All right." John sat down. "But it seems to me that living under the Nazi regime will be a picnic after spending Christmas in this house. I can't think what I'm saying, let alone say what I'm thinking. And, like the poor Germans, you must all be very frightened or guilty about something or you wouldn't be so touchy."

"Touchy is the last thing we are," said Rhoda, licking a stamp.

"Then you ought to be," retorted John. "Here have I just accused my great-aunt Paulina of twice attempted murder… and she merely goes on with her knitting. It's—it's not *normal*."

Rhoda sighed and said, "Darling, why can't you read detective stories, like Margery?"

"I want to *do* something," said John.

"Then take these letters to the post, dear. When you come

back tea will be ready. After that Margery can take you to the pictures and not bring you back till you're satiated with thrills."

Margery said, "What a good idea!" but without any enthusiasm at all.

John said, "I'd rather go with Aunt Paulina. She's an older and far more interesting woman."

To which Margery replied, "And I'd rather stay here and be polite to your father. It's warmer."

"I shall be busy up till dinner-time, writing out the labels for the Christmas Tree," said Frank.

"Then I won't disturb you," said Margery. "What could be politer than that?"

She returned gratefully to her book.

III

Paulina took John at his word and appeared after tea, looking older and more interesting than ever, swathed about with everything in the house, including her gas mask. "You'd better put it on," advised John, bearing her off; "and I'll get Father's tin hat—in case we feel sick on the way."

"Paulina is *such* a stand-by," murmured Rhoda as the car drove off. "*Nothing* seems to daunt her."

"I suppose I ought to have gone," said Margery, with a twinge of conscience.

"Of course not, dear, if you didn't want to," soothed Rhoda. "Paulina always enjoys everything."

Although it was Christmas Day and Esther Hobbs was nominally off duty, she kindly looked in after tea to tidy Uncle

Willie up. She was the only person he had let into his secret and no one else had been allowed into his room that day. His cold, however, had not entirely been a polite fiction invented by Rhoda to explain his aloofness to Uncle Jeff and Aunt Meg. In the drawing-room, at irregular intervals throughout the day, there had been circumstantial evidence of a really rather nasty cough. But Frank had been too preoccupied with his own mysterious plottings to wonder if Uncle Willie was seriously ill, though Rhoda had just found time to wonder if it would be any use sending for Dr. Gosling.

"No use at all," Frank had opined. "Better let the old fool dope himself and have his fun; then, after Christmas, we can send him to a nursing-home and have him thoroughly decarbonised."

Which all sounded rather callous to a comparative stranger to the family like Margery. Rhoda, it is true, had made an occasional show of feeling worried about the cough overhead. But—"We don't want to have him collapsing in the middle of our party," was as far as her tact allowed her to express any concern to her husband. Frank, it seemed, was even prepared to take that risk. They both had complete faith in Esther Hobbs, and Uncle Willie himself evidently preferred her company to anyone else's; so why was Margery worrying? Nobody else was.

Rhoda confided in Margery what appeared to be her only real apprehension: "If only Frank and Willie could *collaborate*," she said, "instead of having separate secrets and running away from each other all the time. Surely it's a great mistake for *two* people to try and be stars in the same play?"

"Of course it is," agreed Margery, speaking professionally. "They'll kill each other stone dead."

"That *would* be such a pity," sighed Rhoda.

Even she was really interested in nothing but the party. It certainly wasn't normal, thought Margery.

IV

Perhaps it was a good thing John and Miss Redpath were out, she found herself thinking a little later, because Uncle Willie, after making quite sure that Frank was busy in his study and Paulina not in the drawing-room, came limping down the stairs, supported by Esther, to enquire why it was that as soon as he came down everyone went out.

Scouting the idea that it was the other way round, he insisted that Frank, Paulina, and John had been trying to avoid him. "Yes, and you too, my dear," he accused Margery. "Don't want to be bothered with an old man like me at Christmas-time." Not allowing her to interrupt: "All right, all right: I understand. No offence. But Paulina!" He was lowered gently into an armchair. "Don't know what's come over that woman. What's the use of being touchy about things dead and for-gotten years ago? Don't know what I've said, I'm sure—don't remember saying anything—but I seem to have offended her all right. Why else should she be avoiding me like this?"

"She hasn't been avoiding you, Uncle Willie," said Rhoda. "You've been rather busy, that's all, and she hasn't liked to disturb you."

"Pshshs!" objected Uncle Willie strongly to all contradic-tion, then admitted magnanimously: "Of course I've been busy—what with this Christmas Tree to-morrow coming on top of everything else—but I've been wanting to have a talk with her about old times. She would remember things, wouldn't she?"

"What sort of things?" asked Rhoda.

"That's just it," said Uncle Willie. "There's something she doesn't *want* me to remember. All buried and forgotten. But how," he enquired loudly, "can I tell her I've forgotten if I can't remember what it is? Eh?"

No answer but the telephone ringing. Rhoda left to answer it.

Margery and Esther Hobbs advised Uncle Willie not to worry trying to remember things.

"No-no-no-no-no-no!" denied Uncle Willie furiously; he wasn't worrying; and he wasn't trying to remember anything; "but Paulina married a man who we got sent to prison; or something. Must have taken it very badly. No idea. Didn't mean to bring it all up now. All over and forgotten. Never mind. It'll come back. Things always do in the end. Really only came down to put a little strength into my legs, so as to be fit to-morrow. Haven't taken enough exercise lately. Beryl and I used to be great walkers. I mean Paulina. Yes, Paulina. She and Beryl were great friends, you know. In it together. But we got her off. There was never any suspicion against Paulina. Nobody had any idea. Stupid to worry about it all now. She wouldn't have been happy married to a crook, now would she? Wish to the devil I could remember the whole story. But it'll come back to me. Things are coming back to me every day, aren't they, Miss Hobbs?"

"I think it's wonderful all the things you remember," replied Esther to this clue.

Uncle Willie pinched her and said she was using the best butter, but it was true, all the same, that he had a long memory, he remembered things that nobody else did, and that they came back to him at all sorts of inconvenient times when he couldn't write them down, and he wished he could do shorthand like Esther, then he could write things down and nobody would be able to read them if he left them about.

Then Rhoda came in and said that Uncle Willie was wanted on the telephone, if he felt equal to it.

Certainly he felt quite equal to it and dragged Esther Hobbs from the room. He eluded her in the hall and pranced, unaided, into Frank's study.

Frank was heard to make polite enquiring noises from within.

Uncle Willie said something about the telephone and Rhoda hoiked him hastily out of the study, leading him to the small cloakroom where the communal telephone lived.

Uncle Willie was most apologetic. "Sorry, sorry! Didn't know. Poor old Frank! Caught him at it! Treasure-hunt, eh? So *that's* what he's got up his sleeve..."

"Sssshhhh!" said Rhoda, steering him out of earshot.

V

Yes, decidedly it was a good thing, Margery thought, that John had taken his aunt to the pictures. Wisely she decided not to tell him anything about this little episode; he would never give poor Miss Redpath any peace. Not that she appeared to mind what he or anyone else said—but this in itself was a little unnatural, and must surely be a sort of armour? Even if it was all smoke and no fire, smoke could be almost as lethal, armed as she was, gas mask or no?

Margery, at any rate, would keep the secret until the Redpaths' precious party was safely over. And Miss Hobbs must be advised to do the same.

Was Esther Hobbs to be trusted with a secret, Margery wondered (not for the first time). She certainly appeared to be keeping Uncle Willie's secret quite competently...

And after Christmas John and she would announce that they were married and have no more secrets from each other (how lovely!)? After Christmas Uncle Willie was going to make a new will; there would be no need to pretend any more after that; it wouldn't make any difference one way or another...

What fun, thought Margery, cheering herself up, that Gwendoline Lucas was coming to the party! Miss Lucas had, for a few terms, been a producer at the R.A.D.A. and Margery one of her most promising pupils. And now she was hand in glove with some people called Crosbie who were gently angling old Willie, which was obviously their sole purpose in coming to the party. Well, even if they had no success with old Willie they would meet someone who was known to be a promising young actress and whose name was Margery Dore. Another secret. Because one didn't like to count one's chickens before they were hatched; and one hadn't liked to write to Miss Lucas and pester her—she probably had quite enough of that sort of thing—anyway, one was sort of semi under contract with Mother to stay put with the canteens for the duration. But if a job was actually *offered* to her!...even Mother would not expect her to refuse it, especially after she had already accepted it!

Good-bye, canteens and being picked up by officers...and Mother thinking she oughtn't to mind because there was a war on, really green with nostalgic jealousy, poor old darling, secretly hoping for an engagement, or at least some emotional predicament on the part of her daughter that a mother could talk about, instead of just somebody in spectacles dimly called John and practically unmentionable.

Perhaps all mothers were like that. And Mrs. Redpath, too, wanted to talk about John outwardly as well as think about him inwardly; and she was in a panic that he and her husband were going to undo all the good work she had put in with the Howard Wortleys...

Well, they wouldn't be able to do much harm at the party to-morrow, thought Margery...

VI

Some of the guests began arriving immediately after lunch and the whole house was blacked out by three o'clock. Collations were spread out in Frank's study and the dining-room; one fell to on arrival, overflowing into the drawing-room. The Christmas Tree was in the music-room. Uncle Willie's room, the servants' quarters, and most of the bedrooms were clearly marked out of bounds.

The Coultards arrived first of all, with their two horrid little boys; then came the Howard Wortleys, with Esther Hobbs and three well-washed, adolescent evacuees. Rhoda tried to stir up these preliminary guests to be going on with, but they weren't immediately mixable. The Coultards accepted the Wortleys as equals, but the Wortleys weren't able to place the Coultards at all, having merely been told that he was a schoolmaster, which gave him no social status at all. Mrs.

Coultard, well-dressed, stout, and cheery, bustled about help-ing Rhoda and calling her my dear (but in Scotch, which told one nothing), while Mr. Coultard referred to Frank and Howard as Sir (but in a cherubic and public-school sort of way, which told one even less).

A party of very young children arrived under the wing of the Bayhams' reliable secretary, Miss Hunt, but without Lord and Lady; then came two *nice* little girls with pigtails and a govern-ess; after that one lost count. Esther Hobbs cleverly removed a great many juveniles for the first heat of Musical Chairs, in which Marathon there were consolation prizes for all, but two extra special prizes for the champion and runner-up. This served the double purpose of making more room for others round the tea-table in the dining-room and more room in the shaken-down insides of the competitors for another tea in the study. And so, in Heaven, it might have gone on eternally, but luckily one wasn't in Heaven. Aunt Paulina had seated herself firmly at the piano, some of the notes of which did seem to play after all, and remained there, refusing all relief and refreshment.

A surplus scum of adults was carefully and selectively adjourned by Frank into the billiard-room, where an old-fashioned amusement known as a Bullet Pudding took place. Major Smythe, the Bishop of Mewdley, Mr. Crosbie, a friend of somebody's called old Bertie, and an elderly woman in a wig who was a complete stranger to everybody, but unabashed, were among the competitors in this tournament, which was finally won (or lost?) by Frank, who had to bury his head in some flour to eat a prune, then go away and wash his face. "No one's to touch the Christmas Tree until I come back," he left urgent instructions.

General conversation. Everyone wandering from room to room, secretly rather tired of Pop Goes the Weasel, ingeniously though Paulina varied the theme. More and more people asking Rhoda awkward questions about the whereabouts of Sir Willoughby Keene-Cotton, and Rhoda not knowing and not daring to guess, and presently only able to wonder why her husband was such a long time, but at last confiding in everybody with disarming candour that her stepfather was busy preparing a surprise for us all, and nobody knew what it was except Miss Hobbs (everyone looked at Mr. and Mrs. Wortley, who respectively smirked proudly and bowed graciously), but we must all try and like it when it came, she concluded—whatever it should turn out to be, she postscribed.

She felt much reassured by the way everyone supported this vote of confidence and there was a resulting burble of happy surmise.

Mrs. Crosbie suddenly said, "Oh!" during a silence; then, putting her hands to her mouth, she implored everyone to go on talking. "It's all right," she said to Margery during the renewed burble; "but I've just thought what it is Sir Willoughby is going to do. What a situation! What irony! We've all come here hoping to meet him and talk to him, perhaps corner him and bother him to death, poor old man; and I bet you not *one* of us manages to get a word with him! He's done it on purpose—the wicked old wretch!"

"Do you mean he's gone out?" asked Margery. "Is that his secret?"

"No, no. We'll see him all right. But you wait!" She chuckled admiringly. "Trust *him* to know how to protect himself! He always did. Never mind, Gwen, dear, I'm sure Mrs. Redpath will ask us again. After Christmas. *I'm* not going to let him escape. Not alive." She nodded emphatically, then screwed up her pale-blue eyes at the symphony of life before her.

"Well, dear, it *is* naice to faind you stying sow near," said the crumpled little woman addressed as Gwen, speaking affably to Margery in a clear, tiny voice (which always reminded Margery of the gnat in *Through the Looking Glass*). "With your fice, dear, and your nime, you ought to do well on the stige—haven't ai always towld you sow?"

(She didn't talk like that on the stage, of course; and not *quite* like that in private life, but that was the impression one always had on meeting her, for a minute or two.)

Margery murmured something about having given up the stage unfortunately, or perhaps it was the other way round, to which Gwen said, "What a silly thing to dew, dear. You're such a useful tape."

At this point the Musical Chairs came to an abrupt end and Rhoda had reverted to wondering why Frank was so long. "Surely," she decided, "there can be no harm in us all *looking* at the Christmas Tree?" She clapped her hands. "Come along, everybody. We're going to light up the tree."

Everyone now had somehow to wedge themselves into the music-room, which took some time.

Unfortunately it was the elder Coultard horror who had won the first prize in the Musical Chairs and he was consequently rather above himself. "Coo! Come on! Buck up, everybody," he kept saying to his elders.

("No, *not* out of the top drawer," decided the Wortleys, becoming much happier.)

As soon as the lights were turned out and the Tree was

being politely admired in all its splendour, the front-door bell rang dramatically.

"See who it is, John," ordered Rhoda. "It might be the wardens—oh, no, it's only half-past four, so we can't be doing anything wrong."

"Mother, keep calm," soothed John, patting her. He was about to depart, but something detained him.

This was the voice of Esther Hobbs, which had become extremely artificial and reverberating. "I *wonder* who it is," she said.

"Ah," said John and sat down comprehendingly.

"Shall we go and see?" she said, having a bold impulse and gathering up children left and right; then, in a more chatty tone: "Do you know what I think? I think it might be Father Christmas!"

"Oh, Lord!" groaned John.

"No 'might be' about it," said Evelyn Crosbie quite audibly.

"Bet you it's a policeman," said the Coultard horror. "Bet you it is. Come for a drink," he explained for the benefit of those less sophisticated than himself.

Quite a number of children pointed out to Esther Hobbs, quite kindly, that there wasn't such a person as Father Christmas.

"Well, *I* think that's who it is," Esther repeated obstinately.

"And he'll die of exposure, at his age, if they don't hurry up and let him in," said Evie. "I can almost hear him wheezing from here."

"Santa Claus must be pretty old by now," put in Crosbie.

"Ninety," his wife told him in a nutshell.

"I don't think they ought to have allowed him to do it,"

Major Smythe was heard to mutter to His Grace the Bishop of Mewdley, who made odd gestures which seemed to imply that the Redpaths were doubtless in the hands of God in these matters.

There was a commotion off-stage as Esther Hobbs let some cold twilight into the darkened hall.

A terrifying voice rasped: "Is this house called Four Corners?"

"This way, Father Christmas," from Esther.

Shrieks from the children. "It's Father Christmas! It isn't really, silly, there isn't such a person. Yes, there is…"

"No-no-no-no-no-no!" from Father Christmas, refusing to be relieved of a simply enormous sack, under the weight of which he tottered purposefully towards the drawing-room door.

A tremendous groan, a final wheeze, a graveyard cough… and Father Christmas was in the room!

Screams from the children, mostly delighted, some derisive; a few short-lived whimpers of sheer terror…

"It's almost *too* real," Mrs. Crosbie complained. "Perhaps it's a good thing that Hobbs child can't act; or there'd be a panic…"

"What a good mike-up!" (from the gnat).

"But he isn't made-up at all" (*sotto voce* information from Margery) "—except for the extra beard. He really *does* look like that, you know."

"I can see he does," from Mrs. Crosbie, screwing up her eyes appreciatively; "he always did."

"I can hardly believe it!" from Crosbie, impressed.

"It isn't really Frank?" everyone heard their flustered hostess murmur, then yelp as her son pinched her, then gasp as she recognised the blue-veined, knobbly hands of her stepfather.

Father Christmas dumped his sack, opened it fumblingly, and began his performance in earnest.

"...perhaps, dear, you'd better go and tell your father to wait until Uncle Willie's finished before..."

"Mother, do try and keep calm," implored John.

Father Christmas, having deplenished his sack, now began pulling things off the tree and distributing them at random.

("Frank will be furious," moaned Rhoda bootlessly.)

All the grown-ups received the trifles Father Christmas bestowed upon them in a conspiracy of solemn gratitude, at first fearful of shattering the illusion of reality, but presently warming up, overcoming their diffidence, shaking hands with him, applauding and congratulating him, but always calling him Father Christmas carefully, some hoping his reindeer wouldn't be cold waiting: had they got something nice in their nose-bags? and had Father Christmas remembered to immobilise them? and didn't he find the modern system of entering by the front door a little cold and formal after so many centuries of coming down chimneys?

It had certainly been warmer coming down chimneys, Father Christmas replied, which was not a bad piece of repartee for an old man of his age, everyone thought.

Uncle Willie had now denuded the tree, leaving only the purely ornamental trinkets, the tinsel, the candles, and the fairy on the top. There were now, however, seen to be a number of labels, hitherto obscured, twining like ivy round the trunk and branches. Father Christmas, after a defiant and triumphant chuckle in the direction of Rhoda, put on his eyeglass and now began to tear off these labels one by one in a thorough and business-like way...

"I expect Father's twigged," John was heard trying to soothe Rhoda not very confidently, "and that's why he's keeping out of the way."

Uncle Willie had invited all the grown-ups to choose a label, each of which transpired to bear a cryptic message in doggerel verse. "Treasure-hunt," he explained; and, having found a label for himself, pondered over it for a short time, then made off with it gleefully.

"I think we ought to leave *one* label for Father," said John mildly.

"Nonsense!" Father Christmas snorted, disappearing from the room.

No one appeared to think it unreasonable that Father Christmas should join in the fun himself, and, after he had left the room, everyone murmured what a wonderful old man he was, and began to frown over their own labels in pleasantly baffled and entirely preoccupied corners, from which they gradually emerged one by one, tentatively searching the drawing-room, presently percolating into the hall, and finally scattering about the house.

In the depleted drawing-room children were busy undoing parcels, blowing trumpets, pulling crackers, letting off squibs, dropping small bombs in the grate, hatching out "Pharaoh's serpents," sending up fire-balloons to the ceiling, making varied animals squeak and growl, and winding up mechanical toys.

No one heard the taps at the window until they had been repeated several times.

By now it was well past black-out time, so all the lights had to be put out so that the french window could be opened.

John disclosed a figure with a sack, shaking snow off its boots. "Is this Four Corners?" the figure asked in a rasping voice.

"Yes, yes." John dragged the figure in without ceremony. He shut the windows, drew the curtains and turned on the lights again.

"Oh dear, he's going through it all over again," said Mrs. Crosbie, who hadn't bothered about the treasure-hunt.

Rhoda emerged from an anxious conference with Paulina, who had merely smiled uselessly. She approached Father Christmas. "I think, Uncle Willie, dear…" she began; and then—"Oh," she said, and sat down.

It took everyone else a little longer to realise that this wasn't the same Father Christmas. The children, to their pleasure and surprise, received a further supply of presents from Father Christmas's inexhaustible sack, not noticing that the old man was a shadow of his former self, that his eyebrows were now obviously false and his moustache insecurely fastened, that his hands were comparatively firm and white and his face heavily daubed with paint.

Nor did Frank immediately notice that the Christmas Tree was practically bare, the guests dispersed about the house, the treasure-hunt in progress, and indeed the party nearly over.

This was what poor Mrs. Redpath had been afraid of, thought Margery, catching Rhoda's eye.

Oh, poor Father, thought John…

Paradoxically enough, it was the deliberate tactlessness of the Coultard horror that entirely saved the situation from all embarrassment.

Still terribly above himself, he crept up behind Father Christmas and whipped off his fur cap, exposing the neatly parted hair of Frank Redpath.

After which there was general laughter and the sport of chasing the Coultard horror round the drawing-room, catching him, and slapping him soundly.

Then Frank became the dutiful host once more and proudly watched his older guests poring in mystification over the cryptograms he had so ingeniously devised. Some hours after all the children and some of the adults had departed a good many treasure-hunters were still at it. Frank, after hearing about Uncle Willie's *succès fou*, had pretended to be very indignant and gone off to "have his blood," but Uncle Willie had wisely made himself scarce, and the door of the bridal suite was locked. "Don't worry him," said Rhoda, "I should think he must be almost dead."

"Quite dead, I should hope," replied Frank. "I'm not really going to knock his head off," he told his wife, "but all these people want to see him and congratulate him, and we'll never get them to go until they have." He was about to knock again.

It was Keevil who prevented him. "Excuse me, sir, but Sir Willoughby told me he was going to bed and didn't want to be disturbed."

"Oh, he did, did he?" said Frank, remembering that one of Uncle Willie's natural precautions was a tin box containing wax ear-plugs, in the wearing of which he was proud of being able to sleep through anything. "All right," he decided, much to Rhoda's relief, "we'll let him off for to-night."

They had a cold supper, to which some of the lingering guests had to be asked.

The Wortleys dragged John off to dinner with them, John being made to go. The Crosbies went home eventually, but Gwendoline Lucas was allowed to remain behind. The strange woman in the wig turned out to be the Bishop of Mewdley's wife; they (*and* their chauffeur) stayed on until nearly midnight, the mortal remains of Fickle Freddie having a great deal to say about the mortal remains of Wilful Willie, the former having been the latter's fag at school.

The Redpaths at last went to bed burdened with promises to congratulate Uncle Willie on behalf of a large number of people—emptily made promises which they could not have been expected to keep, and, as a matter of fact, never did.

VI
Murder After Christmas

I

THE FIRST INTIMATION OF TRAGEDY CAME TO RHODA
on her way down to breakfast next morning.

Keevil was waiting for her in ambush. "I beg your pardon,
madam, but I thought it a bit funny." She moistened her lips.
"Been up with his breakfast three times and knocked on
his door, but not so much as a murmur, madam. From Sir
Willoughby, I mean."

"All right, Keevil," said Rhoda; "I'll have a try." No amount
of refined and respectful tapping would awaken an old man
wearing wax ear-plugs, she thought, so she banged on the
door resoundingly with her clenched fist.

Nothing happened, so she went round to the dressing-
room door and banged on that. Still nothing happened. She
peered through all the keyholes but could see nothing.

"All right, Keevil," she said again to that hovering lady;
"I'll fetch Mr. Redpath."

She and Frank found a key which fitted a door behind

a cupboard in Frank's bedroom which led them into Uncle Willie's private bathroom, from thence through a small dressing-room into the spacious bed-sitting-room where Uncle Willie had been living.

The room now showed no signs of human habitation except for a certain disorder, which, however, had not affected the bed.

The bed was conspicuously and incongruously tidy. It was neatly made and turned down. It had obviously not been slept in.

Nor were there any traces of Uncle Willie's Father Christmas get-up to be found anywhere.

II

This was more than even John had bargained for.

"Dead or alive," Frank said crossly, "where is he?"

"You've done him up in a parcel and sent him back to Gamages," John accused.

"Darling—really—please," Rhoda protested, "we're not in the mood for jokes."

"Well, *I* haven't been playing any jokes," denied John hotly. "I've never been less amused in my life. And Margery's feeling sick—"

("No, I'm all right," from Margery.)

Frank rang the bell in the bridal suite. They waited, shivering. It was bitterly cold, the curtains were drawn back and the window wide open.

Keevil appeared very quickly.

"When Sir Willoughby told you he was going to bed

last night," Frank asked her, "did you actually see him go upstairs?"

"Oh, yes, sir. He'd just come in. Covered with snow, he was."

"He'd been *out*?"

"Yes, sir. And he was carrying a box of chocolates. That would be it, sir." She indicated a box on the table.

John examined it. The box was opened and one chocolate gone.

Frank dismissed Keevil with injunctions not to say anything to anyone just yet.

"Looks as though he went out *again*," said John. "Perhaps to look for some more chocolates. Father, *you* were out in the garden last night. Didn't you—"

Frank broke in testily—"Didn't I murder him and hide his body in the snowman? No, I didn't. I hadn't time. Now shut up." Frank crossed the room irritably. "I suppose he must have got hold of the snowman clue in the treasure-hunt. Even so—And why should he go out *twice*? Did he have his sack with him when he went off with his label?"

"No, I don't think he did."

"No, there were two in the drawing-room last night," vouchsafed Margery, chattering her teeth.

"Then I suppose he couldn't carry more than one box at a time, so went out again to—oh, the poor silly, greedy old fool!"

"What are you talking about?" moaned Rhoda, blue with cold.

"Come and look."

Everyone gathered round Frank, who was standing before the open window which gave on to the lawn at the back of the house.

The snowman had disappeared; in its place stood Paulina, who had evidently just risen from its demolished remains. Mechanically she was dusting the snow from her person. The wintery morning sun came out and shone for a few fitful moments on the gleaming chunks of snow that lay scattered at her feet; and also on what looked like a vast pool of blood.

"It's his Father Christmas costume," observed Rhoda reassuringly. The remark fell flatly on her shivering listeners.

"I'm afraid—it's—Uncle Willie," Frank spoke at last, reluctantly.

"Oh...*no*!" Rhoda prayed as the sun went in and Paulina looked up at the window.

Paulina, seeing the startled collection of faces at the window, raised her gloved hands in an oddly theatrical gesture of horror mingled with a sort of hopeless benediction; then she shook them quickly, as though to erase any indications of approach from her overlookers, and came towards the house.

"Then he *was* inside the snowman!" muttered John incredulously as they all went down to meet her.

"Idiot!" His father covered him with concentrated scorn. "You know perfectly well what was inside that snowman."

"Chocolates?"

"Chocolates."

"Somebody must ring up Dr. Gosling," Paulina told them in the hall. "But I'm afraid he can't help us."

Rhoda disappeared obediently.

"He may have only fainted..." came from Frank without conviction.

"He's quite cold and stiff," said Paulina. "He must have been lying out there all night. Fancy none of us thinking—"

"How could we know?" Frank cut short her reproaches. "He'd said he was going to bed, and his door was locked..."

"No, we couldn't have done anything," admitted Paulina. "And he must have died quite suddenly and painlessly or I would have heard him cry out from my room."

"Well, we can't leave him out there," said Frank. "Come on, John; help me carry him in."

"We oughtn't to touch the body, ought we, Father? Sudden death, I mean..."

"Better leave him there," agreed Paulina. "There'll be formalities...an inquest..."

Frank groaned. The front-door bell rang. "That's Esther. Go and break the news to her, Margery dear. Then go and have breakfast." Margery obeyed with alacrity.

Rhoda emerged from her telephoning. "Gosling's coming straight away; and I thought I'd better ring up Major Smythe too. He's sending a sergeant along."

"Conscientious woman!" approved Frank. "Now we might as well *all* have breakfast, what? I mean, there's no sense in *not* having any, is there?"

Nobody appeared to disapprove of his reasoning except John.

"Mind if we go and have a look at the scene of the crime, Father—before the police arrive and clump about?"

"Who's we?"

"You and me."

"All right," complied Frank, resigned. "But I'm afraid there isn't going to be a dark mystery surrounding poor old Willie's death. It's quite obvious to me what's happened."

"Then you can tell me all about it," said John, leading his father away, "because it isn't at all obvious to me."

III

The body of Uncle Willie, still in his Father Christmas make-up, was lying a few feet away from the capsized snowman.

Carefully making as few footprints in the snow as possible, father and son approached and stood silently for a few minutes.

Then, without speaking, Frank dislodged a piece of cardboard from the dead man's rigid grasp.

Gingerly, with his handkerchief round his hand (because of fingerprints), he handed it to his son, who held it by the edges and read:

> *"He is the whitest man I know*
> *Who stands alone in ice and snow,*
> *From groping mortal greed apart,*
> *Rich treasures in his head and heart."*

"I see," said John. "Yes; that's a good clue. You'd better put it back, hadn't you?"

Frank did so. "There were so many boxes of chocolates, you see, that I thought I'd better pool them and hide them until after Christmas."

"All of them?"

"We let him have a few of his own private parcels on Christmas morning, reserving some for the Christmas Tree."

"How long had those boxes been in the snowman?"

"Oh, a long time. They were such big ones and we thought they would be safer out of the house."

"How did you know that Uncle Willie was going to pick that particular clue?"

"How *could* I know? I thought that whoever got it and had the brains to solve the riddle would have the intelligence to hand it over to one of the children. I hardly expected a grown-up person to go slinking out in the dark alone."

"I believe you," said John, after thinking this over. "All the same," he added in a moment or two, "it's just the sort of thing Uncle Willie would do."

"Perhaps," admitted Frank; "but the chances were a hundred to one against his getting that clue and being able to decipher it."

John said nothing.

"Eh?" prompted Frank, jumping about to keep warm. "Don't you think so?"

"Yes, yes," soothed John. "What you say is so true, Father, that it sounds quite fishy."

"What do you mean?"

"Brrrrr," shivered John evasively. "What did he die *of*, do you suppose?"

Frank stopped dancing and tried to shrug his shoulders. "Exposure? Shock? Must have been less tough than he thought. Than any of us thought…"

"Why was his door locked?"

"I suppose he didn't want people to go treasure-hunting into his room."

"Is the key in his pocket, do you suppose?"

"I hope so."

"If not, he might have put it in one of the other doors?"

"Yes, yes, so he might."

"Why should he?"

"Eh?"

"Now, look here, Father—when the police come— don't you and Mother invent a lot of lies about what you think *ought* to have happened; you'll only make everything worse."

Frank groaned and asked, in what seemed to be innocent bewilderment: "Why should we invent lies? The facts are obvious enough. Can't see anything fishy myself."

"What about those footprints?" asked John.

"Oh, come and have breakfast," implored Frank.

IV

Sergeant Dawes was reporting the matter to Major Smythe.

The Chief Constable was a corpulent, silver-haired man with protuberant eyes and a tarnished moustache. He seemed as much awed and astonished by the thoroughness and effi- ciency of the fellow confronting him as he was by the death of his old friend.

Sergeant Dawes, having laid the bare bones of the case before his chief, was waiting with respectful lack of interest for the Chief Constable to say something.

The Chief Constable told Sergeant Dawes that he had the case very nicely taped, and that was very satisfactory—very satisfactory indeed, eh?

Sergeant Dawes continued to wait in silence, so Smythe

cleared his throat and tried again. "I must get over to St. Aubyn some time to-day, but—tell you the truth—rather a shock to me—all this—knew the dead man—not very well, of course—his brother better—all the same—well, never mind that—" He shuffled some papers with an air of throwing personal feelings aside and getting down to business. "I—er—was at that party last night, you know..."

"Yes, sir." Dawes found corroboration of this statement in his notebook.

"So I'm in a happy position to confirm the truth of what you've been tellin' me—er—"

"Yes, sir," said Dawes again.

"Of course they oughn't to have *let* him dress up like that and go careering out into the cold—but he was a wilful old man—so that I don't think any blame can attach to Mr. and Mrs. Redpath—"

"No, sir," Dawes actually interrupted this time.

"No. But we want to get everything absolutely clear, don't we, and make quite sure that everything's as it should be. Trevor's examined the body, eh, and had a talk with Gosling? They'll go into everything thoroughly—cause of death and all that—inquest and everything—"

"That's right, sir," said Dawes, becoming quite sympathetic. "Normal routine. Everything's got to be gone into. Sudden death, you see, sir, and he wasn't attended by a regular doctor."

"Quite. Quite," said Smythe. "No suspicion of foul play, of course."

"No, sir."

"No, no, no," said Smythe hastily, and then again: "No; I

must admit that everything seems to be explained very satisfactorily. No suspicious circumstances at all, eh?"

"No, sir. Unless—"

"Eh?"

Dawes met the slightly bulging eyes of the Chief Constable and confessed diffidently: "There's just a little matter of the footprints round the snowman, sir."

"Footprints, eh?"

"I don't know if it's worth following up. According to Mr. Redpath—Mr. *John* Redpath—there ought to have been another lot of footprints if the deceased had gone out a second time. Seems a very noticing young fellow. Worked it all out. There were the footprints of his aunt, who discovered the body, the footprints of himself and his father, and those of the dead man himself going up to the snowman—*and* back again. But it snowed again last night, so the dead man's prints weren't very clear. And it's snowing again now, so we've only Mr. Redpath's word for it, and it may be just an idea he's got, like."

"Very possibly," agreed the Chief Constable fair-mindedly. "No, I don't quite see the point about the footprints." He shook his head. "Do *you* see any significance in young Redpath's evidence, Dawes?"

To which Dawes replied: "If he's right, sir, it would mean the dead man *didn't* go out for a second time."

"What? Oh, come now! Then how did he get on to the lawn?"

"We'd have to check that up, sir," admitted Dawes. "It might be he had a fall and rolled down the bank on to the lawn the second time. There are some marks on the body that might account for that theory. Wouldn't bruise himself much with the snow being as deep as what it has been. Then, again, he might not have come out at all but fell from his window accidental."

"Eh? Eh? What's that?"

"*Could* account for them footprints that way," Dawes gently upheld. "Check it up if you like, sir." It was for the Chief Constable to say, of course.

"Yes, yes. Check it up, check it up!" The Chief Constable was saying it; and now he was grumbling: "Pity Trevor can't put the time of death a little nearer..."

Dawes thought it was a pity too, but one could never be very precise in these matters at the best of times, and, what with it freezing like it had, and the body lying all that time in the snow, the rigor mortis wasn't anything to go by, and the old man might have died any time that night between when he was last seen alive by the maid and an hour or two before he was found dead by Miss Redpath. All froze up, he was.

And there, in so far as the facts could speak for themselves, the matter lay beyond the realms of science and the scope of Sergeant Dawes's immediate business.

"Rigor mortis...frozen stiff," Smythe echoed, in no way flinching from these circumstantial technicalities. "But surely," he couldn't help feeling, "there are *other* ways of calculating the time of death? Without relying on circumstantial evidence, I mean—"

"We've made a list of all the people at the party," Dawes respectfully interrupted. "Maybe we can find one of them as saw the deceased after the parlourmaid."

"But that's all so circumstantial, Dawes," the Chief Constable objected. "Can't believe what people say; nor what they think they've seen. Even if they're speaking the truth it doesn't take us far enough. No, no, no! We must find out what he had to eat at the party—its position in—er—his intestines—all that—"

"You wish an autopsy, sir?"

"Yes. I—certainly feel an autopsy is called for. You said yourself he might have died at any time between the party and the following morning. Odd collection of people at that party, wandering about the house—there myself—ought to know; and a lot of people trying to buttonhole him—know that for a fact; and then again, as you say, he might have rolled down the bank or been pushed—fallen, I should say—out of his window. Frankly, Dawes, I don't feel happy about this business. Not at *all* happy," he insisted, cheering up enormously; "and I want a thorough investigation, please. Get busy, there's a good chap."

Dawes rose.

"And I'd like another talk with Trevor, if he's anywhere about."

"You wish to see the police-surgeon again, sir?"

"Yes, yes! And tell Inspector Brooke I can't wait about all the morning."

"Will that be all, sir?"

"Yes—er—thank you, Dawes. You've done a good morning's work. I'm very pleased with the way you've grasped the essentials of this case."

Dawes moved to the door but turned on hearing a throttled murmur from the Chief Constable. "Anything else, sir?"

"No, no!" Smythe picked up a pen hastily, then spoke very casually: "It was only—if you happen to see Culley—tell him I want to see him for a minute."

"Superintendent Culley, sir?" echoed the sergeant in awe.

"That *was* what I said," replied Smythe in an injured voice.

V

Sergeant Dawes found Superintendent Culley and gave him the Chief Constable's message, displaying neither surprise nor curiosity. Neither did Culley display any surprise or curiosity. His morning had been spent training a batch of war reserve constables, so he was too tired to have any private feelings, and was not in the habit of showing them even when he had some.

Major Smythe, on the other hand, could evidently have been knocked down by the feather with which he was cleaning his pipe when the Superintendent made his noiseless appearance.

"You sent for me, sir?"

"Why, yes, so I did! Indeed, yes. Sit down. That's better. Smoke?"

Culley waited patiently while everything came back to Major Smythe. "It's about the death of Sir Willoughby Keene-Cotton, Culley."

"Yes, sir," said Culley, comprehendingly.

"Yes; well, he's an important person, you know—and we don't want to make any mistakes—er—do we?"

"No, sir."

"No." Reassured on this point, the Chief Constable rustled some notes he had been making. "I won't keep you long—I know it's war-time and all that—but—yes…there are one or two curious points…"

Culley was heard to say, "Indeed, sir?" reverently.

"Yes," insisted Smythe, suddenly abandoning his notes and speaking from the heart. "You see—I *knew* the dead man."

"Ah," said Culley.

"Never very intimately, I admit; still, I've heard a thing or two about him. Quite apart from the fact that I was at that party last night and that there are several suspicious circumstances attending his death"—he flicked the notes away from him across the polished desk—"it's always struck me, Culley, that if ever a man was born to be murdered, that man was Sir Willoughby Keene-Cotton."

VII
Motives for Murder

Superintendent Culley's reaction to this was respectful and uncritical but by no means uninterested, a soothing negativity of manner being his chief professional asset; it worked wonders.

"You think it's murder, sir?" he said.

"Mind you, I haven't said so," Smythe replied sharply; "but—well—we don't want to make any mistakes. Just because there's a war on, the public mustn't think the police are no longer concerned with the prevention and detection of crime, *which must always come first*, extra work, depleted staffs or not."

"Naturally, sir," Culley ventured mildly.

"I agree," went on Smythe quickly, "that if anyone had wanted to murder the old man they could (and possibly would) have done so before, ten times over. And we've all got to die some time or another, and it can't always be in our beds. And at Sir Willoughby's age—he wasn't far off ninety, you know—it's not really surprising that he should fall down dead suddenly like that. All the excitement of the Christmas Tree yesterday might have killed a younger man. Well, there you are! Except for some nonsense about footprints, which Dawes is checking up for me, it's all perfectly natural and possible—quite open and above-board—nothing suspicious about it."

"You think it's a bit *too* natural and unsuspicious, perhaps," Culley suggested in a moment.

"Got to have an inquest in any case," Smythe explained, "so thought I'd have you along and ask your advice. Perhaps you'd like to nose about a bit and let me know how it strikes you."

"From what particular angle, sir?"

"All possible angles, beginning with the obvious one."

"Money?"

"That, of course. Sir Willoughby's death is going to make a difference to a number of people. Scandalously wealthy man. No one quite knows how rich he was. But a villa in Italy, a castle in Spain, another in Scotland, house in London—all for one old man! Could have been murdered from anti-capitalistic motives alone. Can't have lived on more than an eighth of his income; the rest was accumulating, eating its head off, no good to anyone. Don't suppose even the war and the surtax, and so forth, have affected it noticeably."

"How did he make it all?"

The Chief Constable snorted. "My dear Culley, he never earned a penny in his life. It simply fell into his lap! Married it mostly. His first wife was Kate Cameron, a very wealthy Victorian actress…"

"The Virgin Queen of the Stage… I can just remember her."

"I remember her well. And you can take it from me that

'virgin' was an understatement. More like a puritan maid; or a nun. Lived austerely and simply, piling up the pennies, until she lost her head in middle-age and married a man half her age."

"Sometimes happens," from Culley.

"Much sought after, you know—passion for her myself in my teens—trampled on hearts left and right. Then old Willoughby stepped in and conquered! Don't know how he did it, as he was a bit of a shrimp to look at even then. Lost her head and her heart and left the stage for good. There was a rumour going round at the time that what she's really lost was her voice, or her memory (some even said it was her reputation), and her marriage was by virtue of a necessity; anyway, from the day of her marriage she changed her character and personality—lived like a rich woman. And died like one, too—leaving everything to Sir Willoughby Keene-Cotton—"

"Who, to all accounts, was pretty rich already," put in Culley.

"Rich! His younger brother, Roger, made a fortune in South Africa—gold, I think—and then divorced his wife, also disinherited his son; so that Willie got it all. Most unfair, but there it was. And, if he wasn't rich enough already, what does he do within a year of Kate Cameron's death but marry the Jacob Hepworth widow!"

"He was a millionaire, wasn't he?" Culley seemed to remember. "Buttons, wasn't it?"

"May have been," Smythe admitted without interest, but added significantly: "He was also Mrs. Redpath's father. Another scandal. Owing to a criminally vague and trusting will, Mrs. Redpath never saw a penny of the money, her step-father swiping the lot for life."

"Mrs. Redpath being—?"

"Sorry—forgot you didn't know. It was Mr. and Mrs. Redpath who gave that party last night. Sir Willoughby had been staying with them." Smythe went on hastily: "She's a very nice woman and they're both quite comfortably off; but I happen to know that they've been waiting for the old man to die for some years now. Only natural, after all. I expect he knew it too; and that, if *I* know *him*, has helped to keep him alive so long…" He chuckled broodingly.

"And you think they might have at last grown tired of waiting…?"

Smythe gleamed; then frowned and said: "Nonsense!" But reluctantly he had to point out: "They had the best opportunity of anybody—if the idea wasn't so laughable." (He laughed, to show how laughable it was.) "You must have a talk with them, Culley; but I think you'll find that Rhoda Redpath is quite above suspicion. Her husband, I agree, is a more likely customer. Impulsive. Incalculable. Can't pin him down. Not a consistent type at all—that, I'm sure, is the main reason why people don't like him much—afraid of anything they can't stick a label on—am myself. Accomplished liar and talks a lot of disarming nonsense—well, you'll notice it, Culley, but there's always a feeling he may believe what he says and take his jokes seriously. However—" Smythe broke off and shook his head.

"But you don't think he'd go so far as to murder an old man?" Culley supplied helpfully.

"'Course not. Wouldn't have the guts, for one thing. Conchie in the last war. Won't hunt, won't shoot. Bit silly altogether. A dabbler. Artistic temperament, but no particular artistic talent. Intelligent enough to marry a sensible woman and earn an honest living. I shouldn't think *she's* had too easy a time."

"Oh?"

"Sobering him down, I mean. I think it was Frank Redpath who came along with a pick-axe early one morning and started to pull up Shaftesbury Avenue. Stopped all the traffic and quite a long time before the police interfered. Know for a fact he was once arrested as a suffragette."

"Suffragette!"

"Had quite a run for his money. Didn't find out he was a man till they got him in prison!"

"That must have needed plenty of guts," Culley pointed out.

Smythe objected: "But you'd hardly murder an old man just for a lark."

"Not for a lark, no," Culley agreed.

"Nor would a man like that commit a crime for money," Smythe insisted.

"Hardly the type," granted Culley amenably. "So let's get on, sir." He summed up: "That's three fortunes Sir Willoughby has been sitting on?"

"Four," corrected Smythe, explaining in apology: "Didn't I mention his own money which he came into on the death of his father?"

"No, sir, you didn't mention that he had any money of his *own*." Culley's voice held a note of faint reproach. He said, "For a moment I thought there was another widow he had married," and laughed.

Smythe gleamed and said, "Now we're coming to it! There was!"

"Indeed, sir?"

"In fact there *is*."

"She's outlived him?"

"And what's more, she hasn't a bean!"

"Ah! Married the third time for pleasure."

"Force of habit, more likely. Reaction, perhaps. Or pure chivalry. No use asking *me* why he did it. She'd been a widow for some years. A Mrs. Sinclair Horsham. Husband a clergyman who laid up for himself a lot of treasure in Heaven but nowhere else, apparently; died leaving her nothing but a large family. She borrowed some capital and opened a restaurant in Chelsea somewhere. Made it pay too. Clever woman, I believe. Married Sir Willoughby in nineteen thirty-three; he was well over seventy and they must have all counted on his popping off long before this."

Culley asked, "The present Lady Keene-Cotton benefits substantially by Sir Willoughby's death?"

"She gets every blessed penny!" Smythe replied.

There was a reverential silence...

"That is," Smythe amended, having made his effect, "so far as I know. Can't say if the Hepworth money was left to him absolutely; but, if so, it seems that the Redpaths won't get a look in."

"Bad luck," acknowledged Culley. "Still, if Lady Keene-Cotton gets *all* the money, it lets Mr. and Mrs. Redpath out of your murder, sir, doesn't it?"

"That will be a great consolation to them," Smythe said sarcastically. "And—what do you mean—*my* murder?"

"Well, sir," replied Culley easily, "we've been assuming it is murder for the sake of argument; in that case, it's the dead man's wife who's got the strongest motive—particularly if, as you suggest, she married him for his money."

"I had no business to suggest that," mumbled Smythe in protest. "Never met the lady, either; so how can I judge whether she'd be capable of murdering an old man in cold blood? Can hardly believe it."

"It's an easier thing to believe of somebody one hasn't met than somebody one *has*," Culley pointed out, and continued: "And if you've never met her, you can't say definitely that she wasn't at that party yesterday?"

"Eh?"

"Assuming her to be the murderer, we mustn't mind being a bit melodramatic," Culley apologised. "A party like that now would offer a most satisfactory opportunity to an enterprising murderer."

"I deserve it, Culley," said Major Smythe. "And it's a fascinating theory; but it won't work."

"No?"

"No. I happen to know that Lady Keene-Cotton was invited to Four Corners for Christmas; but, as a matter of fact, the poor lady's more or less bedridden. So I'm afraid that lets her out."

"It certainly gives her a very good alibi," admitted Culley.

"Couldn't have a better," Smythe agreed regretfully.

Culley sat back reminiscently. "Reminds me of the Hillman case... Husband pretended to be paralysed for two years so as to have an alibi for murdering his wife's lover... functional neurosis, bamboozled all the doctors, nothing was ever proved against him..."

"Good God, you think it's possible that—?"

"It has been done."

"What an idea! And that would explain why—"

The telephone rang. Smythe picked up the receiver. "Yes? Ah, Brooke…good man! You've broken the news to her?… Oh, to Mrs. Horsham! In a what? A taking, yes…naturally…" His face changed colour as he listened to the croakings of Inspector Brooke. With a muttered ejaculation he replaced the receiver.

He said to Culley: "Inspector Brooke has been on the telephone to the Rectory at Borrowfield where Lady Keene-Cotton has been staying. He broke the news of Sir Willoughby's death to Mrs. Cyril Horsham, who was very upset about her mother-in-law—"

"Her mother-in-law?" Culley raised his eyebrows.

"Yes, Culley. Lady Keene-Cotton died on Christmas Day."

VIII
Motives After Christmas

I

"Ah, that clears the air a bit," said Culley. "She can't have done it if she's dead. I'd better be getting along to Four Corners, hadn't I, sir?—take a look at the scene of the crime and have a talk with Mr. and Mrs. Redpath."

"Wait!" The Chief Constable put his head in his hands.

Culley waited.

"No hurry, Superintendent. Dawes and his lot will be there, checking up on clues and reconstructing the crime…" He sat back and grimaced at the ceiling. "Lady Keene-Cotton died on Christmas Day, Sir Willoughby Keene-Cotton dies on Boxing Day." He faced Culley. "Who the dickens gets the money now?"

"That," agreed Culley, "is the question, isn't it, sir?"

"The will lapses," decided Smythe. "And that lets out all the Horsham family. No motive for murder now."

"Not after Christmas Day. It would be shutting the stable door…"

"You express it very neatly. None of them get a penny. Don't you think that in itself is significant?"

"That Sir Willoughby should wait to die a few hours after his wife?"

"Too much of a coincidence..."

"But the sort of thing that happens."

"He died intestate," Smythe pursued his train of thought, muttering: "I wonder who his next of kin is..."

"We'll soon find out," Culley reassured him confidently.

"You always were a patient man, Culley..." He picked up the telephone directory. "We'll find out now. His solicitor used to be old Merivale. Think he still is. No harm in ringing him up..."

"No harm at all, sir..."

"Best to have some data in hand before you begin interviewing people...give you more confidence..."

"Thank you, sir."

"Ah!" Smythe had found the number. He applied himself to the long-suffering instrument; while waiting for the number he said: "For all we know, poor Willy was murdered solely to *prevent* his wife inheriting..."

"In that case they'd have to murder the old lady first."

"Murder out of Malice? Perhaps they did. Hullo? Merivale and Jorkins? Major Smythe here—Chief Constable of Blandshire. I should like a few words with Mr. Merivale. *Old* Mr. Merivale. What? But it's rather urgent...oh! Thank you... yes, I see... 'Out of Town,'" quoted Smythe for Culley's benefit ("But still alive," Culley murmured with inward relief). "Could you tell me when he will be back? Not till to-morrow? He's gone to see a client in the country and won't be back till to-morrow," Smythe told Culley and was about to replace the receiver.

"Ask them the name of the client," prompted Culley quickly—and just in time.

Smythe whisked the receiver back. "Just a moment! Hullo? Could you tell me the name of the client, please?" Smythe listened with unnatural calm.

Having finished his call, he gleamed admiringly at the Superintendent and said: "Smart of you, Culley. The client is Sir Willoughby Keene-Cotton; and old Merivale *took a clerk with him...*"

"Interesting," acknowledged Culley.

II

"Why must everything happen at once?" Frank asked nervily and rhetorically in the drawing-room of Four Corners.

"It never rains but it pours," replied Paulina from her store of ready-made answers to rhetorical questions.

"House full of policemen," Frank told everyone in case they hadn't noticed. "Mr. Merivale for luncheon," he reminded everyone in case they had forgotten. "And now Superintendent Culley," he announced to everyone in case they didn't know (for, if they did, they certainly didn't seem to care). "Who's he? And why?" Frank asked, wishing that somebody would take some interest.

"Major Smythe must have ordered a thorough investigation into Uncle Willie's death," explained Rhoda tolerantly and apologetically.

"At his age he ought to have something better to do— Golly, what's that?"

The house shook and some plaster fell from the drawing-room ceiling.

"It must be Sergeant Dawes and his merry men," said Rhoda, ready with her joke.

"They're reconstructing the crime," added John, pleasurably interested in the noises overhead.

"Why on earth can't they have us each in the dining-room and put us quietly through the third degree?" Frank enquired.

"Superintendent Culley's going to do that," prophesied John.

"Can't they respect our feelings?" said Frank. "It's bad enough having to have an inquest; I can see absolutely no necessity for playing leap-frog in Uncle Willie's room—"

He winced and everybody shut their eyes in agony while a heavy piece of furniture was rolled across the floor of the bridal suite.

"It *is* rather trying," even Paulina came at last to admit.

Keevil appeared, pinched and disapproving, to ask what she was to do with Superintendent Culley when he arrived. The etiquette defeated her.

"Show him in here," Frank ordered recklessly. "There's safety in numbers. A policeman in the drawing-room is worth three in the—" Another rumble followed by a crash. "What *are* they doing, Keevil?"

"Pardon, sir? I couldn't say," Keevil answered him retentively, but she told Rhoda in passing confidence: "They took all the sand-bags from outside the front door, madam, and Edith has given them some bolsters—"

"Bolsters!" Rhoda went so far as to raise her eyebrows.

"Then why don't they have a quiet pillow-fight instead of throwing furniture at each other?" wondered Frank.

"I really couldn't say, sir," Keevil answered him retentively and went out.

"She doesn't like you, Father," diagnosed John.

"Poor Keevil," sympathised Rhoda. "Being only temporary, she hasn't even the satisfaction of giving notice—"

The overhead rumble that interrupted her this time finished in an inevitable and familiar sound which rendered everybody speechless; except, of course, John, who nudged Margery: "Wake up, darling! Chamber music—"

Margery ignored him fiercely and went on with some knitting she had been reduced to beginning that morning.

Paulina looked out of the window and observed: "Why, I do believe it's stopped snowing!"

Which gave Rhoda the idea of suggesting: "John, why don't you take Margery to see the Spelmans' crater? Children have been tobogganing down it," she told Margery, not without bomb-snobbishness. "It was an unexploded landmine, you see, and *sank*—"

"I don't think any of us ought to leave this room," John said.

"Eh? Why not?" sharply from Frank.

"Who said so, dear?" enquiringly from Rhoda.

"Nobody's told us to sit cooped up in a stuffy drawing-room all the morning," reassuringly from Aunt Paulina.

"Then why are we?" asked John.

"*I'm* certainly not going to." Paulina began firmly rolling up her knitting. "I shall just look at the weather," she said; "then perhaps I shall take a little stroll down to the village and back. And if you ask me"—she rose and spoke to John as she went towards the french windows—"a breath of fresh air would do you and Margery the world of good."

"The murderer might still be about," Margery ventured lethargically. "They always strike again and again. Don't they, John?"

"She's only joking," explained John carefully to Paulina, who replied, "I can take care of myself," and opened the french windows.

She left them open while she sailed out intrepidly; everyone watched her, shivering patiently.

Suddenly there was a terrific shout and a crash.

"Jee—hoshephat!" exclaimed Frank as Paulina, white and shaken, came tottering back into the room.

She collapsed limply into a chair and Rhoda went to fetch some brandy.

"What was it?" Frank and John callously disregarded her and ran to the window.

What looked like a heap of clothes lay on the path which ran along the edge of the bank leading to the lawn.

"Only another body," observed John.

"Whose?" asked Frank.

"Dawes has fallen out of the window in excess of Zeal."

"Is he dead?"

"Yes."

"Good!"

Frank shut the french windows and returned to his seat just as Rhoda came in with some brandy, followed by Sergeant Dawes.

Sergeant Dawes, far from being dead, was most unnaturally alive. "Beg pardon, sir," he said, perspiring offensively, "but you'd best keep right away from the house or else stay indoors. We've had our orders to check up on all possible hypotheses…"

"Can't you do it somewhere else?" asked Frank.

"Check up on *what*?" asked John.

But the french windows were now wide open again and the sergeant was gone. He was seen and heard to be shouting frenzied instructions in the midst of a kind of funeral oration over the improvised body on the path.

Presently he backed expectantly and another body fell on the path, but a few yards nearer the bank.

"This is worse than an air raid," said Frank. "How long is it going on, do you think?"

"I expect they'll try all the windows on that side of the house," John replied comfortably.

"Thank you, dear; I'm all right now," said Paulina, being revived by brandy. "I do think they ought to have warned us," was her only grievance.

"Warned us!" cried Frank. "They've absolutely no authority to be doing it at all. Police think they can do anything these days. This is my house, and I won't allow it."

"You can't stop them, Father—"

"Shut up! It's all your fault for trying to be clever about footprints. Kindly mind your own business another time."

"Another time! Are you going to commit a lot more murders, then, Father?"

"John!" intervened Rhoda reproachfully, "we must try not to say things like that."

"Bit nervy, aren't you, Mother?"

"Nervy!" screamed Rhoda in reply as, amid manly cries of delight, a third body fell from an upper window and rolled triumphantly down the bank.

"They're nearly there," commentated John from the

window. "A couple more and they'll do it. I put my money on Keevil's bedroom. What was Uncle Willie doing there, I wonder—?"

"Hold your tongue," snapped Frank.

"I find your annoyance unreasonable," John told him. "We *want* to find out what really happened to poor Uncle Willie, don't we?"

"No, we don't," said Frank flatly.

"But if we never know the truth," said John, "we'll be under a cloud for the rest of our lives. How can I marry Margery when I'm under a cloud, Father?"

"I don't care if you do," said Frank.

"And it's not only us—we're young and can face the future together—but what about all those poor old things at the party? How can the Archbishop of Mewdley retain the respect of his diocese when he might be a murderer? And where was Professor Larkin during the party? I never saw him after the first two minutes—"

Keevil came in.

"Even Keevil," went on John, "may find it hard to get another place after being mixed up in a murder—"

"Superintendent Culley," Keevil announced vindictively and withdrew, her distaste for being mixed up in a murder making her look quite capable of committing one.

III

Keevil's vindictive announcement must have referred to a tall but inconspicuous-looking man in a grey suit who had somehow edged his way into the room when her back was turned. ("Quite a cosy-looking man," thought Margery with relief. "Quite sensible-looking," decided Paulina with relief. "We needn't be afraid of *him*," Rhoda told herself with relief. "Here's someone quite intelligent," thought John, "what a relief!" "What a relief," thought Frank, "here's someone we can trust!"...)

Superintendent Culley had not expected a hostile reception; on the other hand, he could hardly have predicted the warm welcome which he actually got.

Frank pounced upon him, introduced him to everybody, pushed him into an armchair, surrounded him with cigarette-boxes and matches, and plunged forthwith into speech.

"Just the very man we want," he was saying. "There seems to be a little misunderstanding about what happened last night. Dunno whose fault it is, but it's all quite simple really. What happened was this. We had a sort of treasure-hunt at our party last night. My wife's stepfather, who was dressed as Father Christmas, found a cache of chocolates in the snow-man on our lawn. He was inordinately fond of chocolates, Superintendent, and slunk up to his room with a box without telling anyone; then he must have decided to come down again to see if there were any more. Unfortunately he never would admit that he was a very old man and oughtn't to carry heavy sacks about and keep coming out of the cold night air into a warm room, and then going out into the cold again and coming in and going out again. He told the parlourmaid he was going to bed and didn't want to be disturbed; but he must have slunk out again and then fallen down the bank on to the lawn and died. Naturally we all thought he was in bed, so we never found him until this morning—"

"We were rather late to bed last night," came corroboratingly from his wife, "and I ought to have looked in on him last thing to see if he was all right," she reproached herself penitently; "but he'd locked his door and there didn't seem much point in waking him up—"

"We had no *idea*," Paulina joined in, "—how could we possibly *guess*—I mean it wouldn't *occur* to us, would it?"

"No," said Rhoda, who had forgotten to say this, "it wouldn't, would it—how *could* it?"

She paused for breath and was unable to prevent John from having his say.

"But, I keep telling you, Father," John was found to be saying, "if he had simply fallen down the bank, he couldn't have rolled all that way. If, on the other hand, he had got a little wandery—old men *do*—and walked out of the window, it's just possible he *could* have been found exactly where we found him. Not likely, but possible; and even more possible if he had wandered up to the attic. From there he could have bounced—"

"What nonsense!" brushed Frank.

"Not nonsense at all," retorted John; "it's the simplest explanation of the mystery. The police think so too, but they've got to make sure; so that's what they've been doing— don't you see? They're on your side, Father."

"I haven't got a side," Frank snapped. "All right," he capitulated suddenly and sighed wearily; "he fell out of the attic window, Superintendent. *I* don't mind."

"You see, he couldn't have fallen down the bank," John went on, without giving Culley time to say anything; "nor could he have walked back to the snowman a second time, or there would have been an *odd* number of footprints—"

"Yes, yes, I see the point about the footprints, sir," Culley was able to nip in.

"If he had just walked up to the snowman and died, he couldn't have walked back again," John had to finish tidily.

"No, no," soothed Culley, apparently oblivious to further police activity on the lawn. "Then you think your stepfather-in-law fell out of the window, sir?" he said to Frank.

"No, I don't," replied Frank.

"Then can you give a better explanation for these footprints?"

"Parachutist," Frank said promptly. "No, I can't. Yes, I can. Candidly, I think my son is talking through his hat."

John broke in: "Why on earth should I *invent* missing footprints? I made a very careful plan, Superintendent, before the photographers and police came and walked all over everything."

"May I see it?"

"Certainly," said John and produced it proudly.

Culley put on his pince-nez. "That's very clear," he approved. "It's certainly worth looking into."

"You think it's important?" groaned Frank.

"It'll have to be explained," Culley replied; and there were noises in the hall significant of strong men carrying pseudo corpses up the stairs.

"Can't we really explain it in any *other* way?" sighed Frank forlornly.

Culley regarded John's plan, pursed his lips, and thought deeply. "How'd it be, sir, if he died the *first* time he went out, and the snow obliterated the prints, the other lot being made by someone in the same size shoes who went up to the body, found him dead and went away without saying anything?"

"Yes, that's a solution," admitted Frank. "Could *I* have done that, do you think?" (Triumphantly:) "Why, yes! *my* Father Christmas boots were *exactly* the same size!"

John broke in once more: "It's absurd. He told the parlourmaid he was going to bed."

"So he did." Culley had to think again. "But she might have been mistaken. Or he might have been going out, not coming in."

"Rot!" scoffed John. "You must do better than that, Superintendent Culley."

("Darling," protested Rhoda.)

"Oh, we *can* do better than that," said Culley reassuringly, "if we've got to," he added.

"You can think of an alternative explanation?" asked Frank anxiously.

"Maybe he died somewhere else," Culley answered unemotionally, "and was carried on to the lawn and—planted there."

There was a pause while this sank in. In the silence you could have heard a body drop, and did.

"Oh—*no*," murmured Rhoda at last. "That would mean—"

Paulina stared at Superintendent Culley severely, but told him, in the gentlest of voices, and after a short, forgiving laugh: "Why, Mr. Culley, you're almost suggesting—"

"That he was murdered, madam? Oh, it doesn't necessarily follow; though, of course, we can't afford to overlook that possibility."

"But you can't seriously think—" began Rhoda; then picked up some mending to show her hands weren't trembling, but they were. "But of course," she found excuses for him, "you didn't know my stepfather; he was the kindest of men. No one could wish to murder him. Why," she beamed radiantly, "the Chief Constable, Major Smythe, was a great friend of his. *He* can tell you how absurd the idea is."

In reply to which Superintendent Culley was only able to make murmuring noises.

It was John who spoke. The stark unemotionalism of the Superintendent must have sobered him; or something had. "Look here," he said, "this won't do. Of course he wasn't really murdered—not seriously. I admit I may have been talking through my hat about those footprints and he probably fell down the bank—as Father said. There! No need for all this excitement, and I'm sorry to have caused all this bother—"

"Oh, for Heaven's sake let him be murdered and have done with it!" burst suddenly from Frank. He got up and walked to the window and back. "What the hell does it matter? I murdered him, Superintendent."

"No, you didn't, Father—"

"Don't contradict!"

"Now don't get excited, Frank dear." Rhoda went to him. "Nobody thinks you murdered Uncle Willie. Why, you've got an alibi, darling—"

"No, I haven't. There was quite a long time when he and I were out of the room at the same time. After I'd finished dressing up as Father Christmas I met him in the hall, killed him, carried his body on to the lawn and dumped it by the snowman. Faked the treasure-hunt clue afterwards. It was I who told the parlourmaid he was going to bed. One Father Christmas is very like another and the hall was practically dark. Faked the chocolates in his room and came back to the party. Worked it all out most carefully but forgot about those damn footprints. There you are."

"How did you kill him, sir?" asked Culley.

"What? I—hit him over the—no, I gave him a poisoned chocolate. Serve him right, the greedy old man."

Even Margery had woken up now. "But—I don't understand—why—"

"*Why* did I kill him?" shouted Frank, drowning the zealous shouting on the lawn. "Because he was a thundering nuisance," he threw out at random. "Because he was a meddling old fool—a blithering old bore—anything. *Anything*," he repeated loudly to Superintendent Culley, as another body fell, "if you'll only tell your men to stop throwing the poor old b—out of the window!"

IV

Superintendent Culley left the room softly. The results were quelling. He came back and settled down more comfortably. "I must apologise to you all," he said. "I didn't quite get on to what they were up to. We've an active lot of fellows in the police force just now. Now, sir…" He brought out a large notebook. "We'll just have all that again."

"Oh, no! I can't do it *again*!" said Frank weakly.

"You mustn't take my husband seriously," put in Rhoda, explaining, "we're all rather upset this morning."

"Yes, naturally, madam."

"We used to make jokes about murdering my stepfather, you see, and now we're all feeling—well, a little foolish."

"Quite so," murmured Culley.

"It had become quite a habit," said Frank, cheering up. "Why, on the first day he arrived I pointed out to my wife how easy he would be to murder; didn't I, Rhoda?"

Rhoda corroborated, "He was so obstinate, you see, Mr. Culley—"

Frank confessed: "I believe I actually said that if we told him he couldn't jump out of the attic window at his age he *would*!"

"So if he *has*," Rhoda felt sure the Superintendent would understand, "it makes everything seem rather gruesome, doesn't it?"

"And ironical too," chimed Frank.

"Ironical, sir?"

"Yes," said Rhoda, edging a little nearer in her eagerness. "Because we didn't want to murder him any more…"

"Not any more, madam?"

"Oh, *no*!" Rhoda sternly disclaimed; then, climbing down a little in the interests of absolute truth: "Well, we haven't for the last seven years…"

"Since his marriage, you see," explained Frank, "we haven't had any motive—"

"No motive at all, Mr. Culley: all his money goes to his wife. Of course," she admitted, "as my husband said, he *has* been rather a difficult guest—"

"Thundering nuisance…"

"Naturally we've *felt* like murdering him *frequently*…"

("Well, I'm damned," murmured John.)

"—but on the whole," went on Rhoda, "the advantages of having him to stay have greatly outweighed the disadvantages. Not so much for us, perhaps; but the people round here have been so interested to meet him; he was such a link with the past; he had glamour, Superintendent—if I may use an overworked word...?"

"Glamour, yes," appreciated Culley. "In fact, from all accounts, he was the life and soul of your party yesterday?"

"People came from miles around especially to meet him! People who wouldn't have turned out in the ordinary way. Not nowadays, in the black-out and with petrol being so precious. Altogether, our Christmas has been much more cheerful than it was last year. Having Uncle Willie here made it more worth while making an effort, and he himself was really wonderful, *nothing* was too much trouble or expense!"

"So it looks as if you had every motive for *not* murdering your stepfather?" Culley summed up pleasantly.

"Not until after Christmas," agreed Frank happily.

Rhoda frowned.

"Ah," savoured Culley; "*after* Christmas..." He seemed about to say something, but changed his mind and said something else. "About that money, madam, which should have come to you from your father..."—he made a slight pause to see what would happen, but nothing much did, except that the old lady in the corner stopped knitting—"... or so the Chief Constable was telling me—that would all go to the present Lady Keene-Cotton, now, wouldn't it—?"

The old lady went on knitting.

"It *would* have," admitted Rhoda. Culley sat back and looked at her intently. "But—that's just what I've been telling you," she went on, unabashed under scrutiny. "My stepfather was the kindest and most generous of men, when you knew him and how to manage him." Quickly without waiting for

Frank's mechanical snort: "He had made over *all* my father's money to me before his last marriage."

"Oh!" said Superintendent Culley. He looked round at everybody, but nobody did anything. "That's very nice," he observed presently. "I'm glad you've told me that."

"No mouse in that hole," said John kindly; "we don't gain a penny by the old man's death."

"In fact——" began Frank, but met John's eye and stopped.

"Yes, sir?"

"Say it, say it!" urged John. "All right then, *I* will. Your last hope of a case against us has fallen through," he told Culley. "We were hoping that our aged connection would make a new will and include us in it—if we were very nice to him. That's why Mother asked him here, of course. He was going to make a new will to-day. But he's dead. So the only person with any material motive for murder is the widow—and she's bedridden."

"How true that is!" murmured Frank, pleasantly surprised, regarding his son quite affectionately. "I'd forgotten all about that. It lets us out entirely, doesn't it?"

The old lady with faded yellow hair was still knitting; though the young one with the thick mouse-coloured bob had stopped, but only to pick up the pattern book which she had just dropped; she pushed back her bob, and her exertions had left her face rather flushed, which was only natural.

"So he was actually going to make a new will to-day?" Culley prompted hopefully. "Why was that?"

"It was after the visit of Captain and Mrs. Freer on Christmas Eve," Rhoda told him; and everyone, taking it in turns, obligingly described the entire circumstances in detail. "Lady Keene-Cotton has been ill for some time," Miss Redpath capably finished the narrative, "and Sir Willoughby had to provide for the possibility of her pre-deceasing him."

"I see," said Culley, and decided that the card had been up his sleeve long enough. "So you don't know that Lady Keene-Cotton died on Christmas Day?"

"What?" said Frank.

Rhoda was equally amazed, and also distressed. "Oh dear!" she said.

"Gosh, what rotten luck!" pronounced John.

"So they haven't any motive either," pointed out Frank; "the Horsham family, I mean. Not after Christmas. Things are looking brighter all round. *Nobody* has a motive now! Hurray!"

"Father, this isn't a game."

"Sorry."

"It's going to be very difficult to know what to do about the money," said Paulina, "but I'm sure Mr. Merivale will arrange things to everyone's satisfaction."

"It seems funny," Culley reverted, "that none of you knew about Lady Keene-Cotton's death. I should have thought they would have sent Sir Willoughby a telegram immediately."

"No," said Rhoda; "he never knew anything about it."

"He *died* without knowing," Miss Redpath informed him. "It was far better. He couldn't have done anything about it until after Christmas. He was in such good spirits and so looking forward to the Christmas Tree; it really could do no harm to keep the news from him until the party was over;

so I never said anything about it." She looked up from her knitting to find herself the focus of all eyes.

"You never said anything about *what*, madam?" asked Culley in his official voice.

"About Lady Keene-Cotton's death, of course."

"You knew?"

"What's that?... Paulina, what do you mean?... How could you know?..."

"Let me see," said Paulina, trying amiably to answer everybody's questions, "it was yesterday morning. I met the telegraph boy in the drive. I was surprised, because I didn't know they delivered on Boxing Day. It's all right"—she had sudden compassion on Culley, who was looking so stern and bewildered, poor man—"I put it somewhere *very* safe. Would you like me to go and fetch it?" she beamed as this happy, considerate notion occurred to her.

"If you please, madam."

"Paulina, *really!*" Rhoda reproached her when she came back flaunting the telegram as though it were a piece of barley sugar to console a child for having bumped his head. "Really," Rhoda repeated as Culley accepted the consolation prize ungraciously: "you might have told *me!*"

"Oh, no, dear," Paulina replied, "we all know how conscientious you are; and the harmless little deception didn't worry me at all. There, Inspector! I hope I haven't done wrong?"

She certainly didn't seem to think so herself. He decided to let the matter pass. He folded up the telegram neatly and stowed it away in his bursting wallet. Then he got up and said affably to Rhoda, "I think that will be all for this morning, madam. I can only apologise for intruding upon you at such a painful moment."

"No, no," cried Rhoda happily, "not at all!"

"Any time you happen to be passing..." murmured Frank hospitably, moving to the door.

Culley observed: "It looks as though the poor old gentleman couldn't have died at a more awkward moment, doesn't it?"

"Rather...indeed, yes!..." came a clamour of agreement.

"And I expect we'll soon find an explanation for those footprints," Culley reassured his host as he followed him out.

"I'm always at your disposal, Superintendent," Frank accommodatingly answered as the front-door bell rang.

"That will be Mr. Merivale!" exclaimed Rhoda. "Why not stay and meet him, Mr. Culley?"

Culley said he'd be having a talk with Mr. Merivale later on; at the moment he wanted to get back to the station to hear the result of the autopsy.

"Well, now you've found your way here..." Frank was saying as he helped Culley into his overcoat; then suddenly: "*What?*"

He backed onto the hall table, upsetting a lacquer bowl containing cards.

Culley remained half dressed and tottering in the ensuing petrified silence, which was broken by a wild whoop from John, who seized an unwilling Margery round the middle and waltzed with her round the hall, at last collapsing with her, completely winded, on to an ottoman. "Father's face!" he could only gibber helplessly. "Oh! D-d-darling, d-d-did you s-s-see Father's f-f-f-f-f-f—!'"

Keevil had silently appeared and obstinately opened the front door.

Culley, evading the muffled figures on the doorstep, escaped deftly into his own car.

V

"Are they *all* on the border-line?" he asked himself, driving cautiously back to Mewdley. "Or is it me that's going balmy? They can't think we're going to find arsenic in the organs of the deceased. What's the joke, I wonder? Something funny there." He shook his head as though funny was the last thing a joke ought to be.

When at last he heard the result of the autopsy he had another shock. There wasn't arsenic in the body, but there was a large quantity of laudanum, recently swallowed—and quite enough to kill three old men (which was how the police-surgeon finally expressed it).

Also, according to Major Smythe, Sir Willoughby Keene-Cotton had been seen to eat a number of mince-pies at the party; and, owing to the position of these in the intestines, death must have taken place within an hour of eating them.

"Hm!" thought Culley. "Is *that* the joke?... Something to do with mince-pies...?"

IX
Mince-Pies
After Christmas

BUT CULLEY COULD HARDLY BELIEVE THAT THE MINCE-pies were poisoned. Dr. Trevor could hardly believe it either. He shook his head sadly and patiently—a habit he had.

The three of them were sitting in the Chief Constable's room. "Then how *do* you account for the findings of the autopsy?" asked Major Smythe firmly.

More shrugs and head-shakes and a few despairing titters. "Overdose of some medicine, mmm?" he said at last in his small, cooing voice.

Exhibit 3 was patiently produced—an empty bottle of cough-mixture found by Dawes in the dead man's room.

Some sniffing and tentative licking followed. "Yes; why, yes—a preparation of laudanum certainly. Hm. Mmm? Very curious. But quite harmless, unless he drank *five* of those bottles straight off? He wouldn't do that."

Exhibit 1—the chocolates—proved scarcely more satis-factory. "You'll have to wait for the qualitative analysis," he reprimanded Culley and Smythe gently for their impatience.

"Don't see how that'll help us," grumbled Smythe irritably. "All the poison might have been in the one missing chocolate, which he ate."

"Phe-e-e-ew!" said Dr. Trevor.

It couldn't have been done?

Yes, yes, it *could* have been done; he didn't say it couldn't have been *done*...

(Oh Lord!...) What it boiled down to was that it would need great skill and make the chocolate taste very funny—what kind of chocolate was it?

There was a classified catalogue in the box; the missing chocolate was thus deduced to have been an Almond Whirl; there was, furthermore, found to be *only one* Almond Whirl in that particular box.

"That clinches it," said Smythe. "Must have happened. Somebody knew he would pick it out first. The others will be harmless..."

But Trevor advised a thorough investigation into all the other medicines the deceased was in the habit of taking.

Culley assured him that these would be gone into, of course. Now that definite traces of poisoning had been found, everything the deceased had eaten that day would have to be checked up all round.

Trevor said death from laudanum poisoning would take place within a few hours; the fatal dose varied according to the age and health of the deceased; in Sir Willoughby's case quite a small dose would be fatal; being oxi-di-morphine, it would cause sleep, coma, and collapse, especially in conjunction with over-eating.

"That narrows things down, eh?" Smythe commented to

Culley. "Little doubt that he'd overeaten himself. All those mince-pies!…possibly on top of a heavy lunch. But I can vouch for the fact that he wasn't at all sleepy when he came in as Father Christmas. Never seen anything like it! Couldn't have done it myself, and I'm more than ten years his junior. Well, well! Where does that get us, Culley?" He answered his own question: "On second thoughts I put my money on the mince-pies. Damn things are worrying me. Kept on eating them, one after another. *I* didn't know he had any special liking for the things; *but supposing someone did*?"

"Someone at the party, you mean, sir?"

"Well, candidly, I don't see how the chocolates could have been poisoned, Culley, if they had been in the snowman all that time; unless you're going to believe that pretty story Frank Redpath told you."

"I'm keeping it at the back of my mind, sir, of course; but—I agree with you, sir—I can't seriously think of him as a murderer—nor any of them, for that matter—even if we find a reasonably strong motive, which we haven't so far."

"Then it *must* be someone at the party," said Smythe. "Well, I'm blessed! What a thing to happen! I can't believe it even now. Knew most of the people at the party by sight— have for years."

"Was there anybody whom the deceased seemed particularly afraid of that you noticed, sir?"

"Let's think. Now you mention it…there was that old professor tryin' to buttonhole him—never met *him* before… and yes! Now you mention it there *were* two other people he was rather anxious to…'avoid,' shall we say?" Smythe gleamed.

"Yes?" Culley queried patiently.

"One was me," said Smythe. "Couldn't get a word with him; certainly avoided me in rather a 'marked manner'!"

"And the other, sir?" Culley asked even more patiently, after acknowledging the Chief Constable's little joke.

"The other was the Bishop of Mewdley."

"Quite so, sir."

Smythe then checked his own levity. "'Course, being dressed as Father Christmas, it was natural he should feel a bit sheepish at meeting anyone who knew him."

"That's very true," admitted Culley. "Anyone else?"

Dr. Trevor cleared his throat. "Do you want me any more?" he cooed diffidently.

"Sorry, Trevor. No, I don't think so."

Trevor got up to go.

"*You* weren't at the party last night?" Smythe asked him suddenly.

"Mmmm? Oh! Hm! Ha, ha!" Exit a police-surgeon with the giggles.

"That's something, anyway," remarked Smythe as the door shut. "There was the Redpath aunt, of course," he resumed. "What did you make of her, by the way? I had a talk with her and she told me Sir Willoughby had been rather quarrelsome for the last week or so. '*Difficile*' was what she said. French. But it was only about the plans for the party, I gathered. Wouldn't take any of the family into his confidence, so they had to engage the Wortley niece from next door to look after him. I should have an interview with her, Culley; she saw more of him than anyone else, and he's quite likely, in his perverse mood, to have taken a stranger into his confidence about other things besides the party. As regards the arrangements for the Christmas Tree,

I got the impression that he and Frank Redpath had almost come to blows, refusing to speak to each other and making their own plans independently; and, of course, it turned out they both had the same idea! Bit galling for Redpath; old man got his fun in first—even got wind of the treasure-hunt and tried to take all the credit for that—did his best, in fact, to steal all the thunder. Redpath pretended to be very angry, but actually kept his temper very well, I thought."

"But he might have been really upset?"

"Naturally, he probably was. Not a motive for murder there; surely?"

"Hardly, sir. And he had a quarrel with Miss Redpath too, sir?"

"Impossible to have a quarrel with a woman like that. Wears a sort of chromium-plated armour; everything slithers off her. Can't see her as a murderess either...unless she'd been in love with him, say, and has killed off all his wives in turn and finally the old man himself just at a moment when nobody gains a penny by his death. Might be mad, I mean," he explained apologetically. "Murder out of Malice, eh? Good title, that; but don't think much of it as a theory myself. True, she's a spinster and used to be Rhoda Redpath's governess and so on, but she doesn't strike me as an embittered, thwarted woman; on the contrary, I should say that, quietly in her own way, she has arranged her new life—and probably everyone else's—exactly as she's wanted to. Eh? How did she strike you, Superintendent?"

"I think you've taped her very nicely, sir." He recounted the episode of the telegram.

"There you are. Typical!" Smythe was gratified to have his psychological insight so happily corroborated by facts.

"So we don't think it was she who poisoned the mince-pies, sir?" said Culley presently.

"Oh, damn those mince-pies," said Smythe plaintively. "Even if somebody *did* poison one or two, I can't for the life of me think how they could make sure it would be Sir Willoughby who ate them."

"Couldn't very well force them down his throat," admitted Culley; then: "What's the matter, sir?"

Smythe was staring at the Superintendent. Suddenly he became abashed and muttered: "Must be going off my head. When you said that, I remembered a bit of damn silly nonsense at the party."

"About mince-pies, sir?" murmured Culley enquiringly.

"Yes—to hell with the beastly things!—now this is unofficial, Culley, and I don't think it's significant myself—"

"Well, let's have it, sir," encouraged Culley patiently.

"I remember Miss Redpath handing him some mince-pies. John Redpath was standing near and asked her if she was turning the other cheek, and she replied perhaps she was heaping coals of fire on his head. That's all."

"Wonder what she meant," Culley commented laconically.

"Nothing! If he *was* poisoned by a mince-pie, it must have been sent to him personally in a parcel; then it needn't have been anybody at the party at all. How's that?"

"Mr. and Mrs. Freer left a number of parcels when they came on Christmas Eve," threw out Culley. "But, so I gathered, the parcels were all labelled 'Not to be opened before Christmas'; and," he added, "they had no motive for murdering him *after* Christmas."

"Anyway," agreed the Chief Constable with a faint gleam, "if anybody wanted him to die before Christmas, they wouldn't have poisoned *mince-pies*."

"How do you make that out, sir?"

"Nobody eats mince-pies before Christmas. Isn't it supposed to be unlucky?"

"A good point."

"Thank you. But aren't we rather wasting time? A war's on and a murder has been committed—and we sit here talking nonsense about Almond Whirls and mince-pies!"

"We're trying to find out how the poison was administered," Culley explained soothingly.

"Well," said Smythe, "he was an old man. He wouldn't be attended by a doctor; preferred dosing himself; might have done it once too often."

"Easy to murder, in fact, sir. As the Redpaths said."

"The devil they did! But they've no motive, Culley."

"Nobody's got any motive. That's the most significant point about this case."

Smythe shrugged. "Put it like that, Culley, if you like. All the same, the findings of the autopsy may have a perfectly natural explanation when you consider that he must have been taking quack medicines for the last fifty years or more."

"I'm glad you've brought that up, sir," Culley said; "it would possibly explain Frank Redpath's excitement when he heard we were opening up the body?"

"Certainly," agreed Smythe warmly. "We must go carefully, Culley."

"I agree with you, sir," said Culley. "I'm not denying that it *may* be just a coincidence that he has died a few hours after his wife and just before Mr. Merivale was coming to draw up a new will. Can't honestly see, sir, how it can be to anybody's advantage that he's died intest—"

One of the many telephones on Smythe's desk rang.

"Yes?" queried Smythe, choosing the right one first shot. "Ah! The very man we're waiting for. Show him up at once."

"Merivale?"

Smythe nodded and glanced at his watch. "Hope he won't be *too* long-winded… Must be almost as old as Sir Willoughby…"

Which didn't sound too promising to Culley.

But a tall, thin man, as though kicked from behind, had already hurtled into the room.

"Phew!" said Mr. Merivale, removing a black felt hat, revealing a narrow, domed head which was completely bald—indeed he was entirely hairless except for a very small, close-cropped moustache which was quite obviously dyed.

"What weather!" exclaimed Mr. Merivale, throwing off his overcoat with energy and blowing on his hands. "Poor old Sir Willoughby! Dead at last. Intestate, of course. I'm applying for a deed of administration myself; best person. Lot of money involved. Should all go to the Crown. Superintendent Culley, eh? Ah, yes, we met on the doorstep. Police want to hear all about it, that's why I'm here. No next of kin, but moral obligations which the law will view kindly. Horsham family. Redpaths. Nephew and niece of Kate Cameron; girl on tour; boy in the R.A.F.—wife and child evacuated to the States. Should all get something. Then his brother Roger's wife, dead now, but left a son; army pension, last war, feet, pity, nice lad, married." He blew again.

Smythe, both looking and feeling like a very old and partially deflated balloon, managed to nip in. "You mean to say—all these people—er—can claim—er—"

"No claim at all. But Willoughby practically supported 'em. Don't see why they should lose by his death—"

"It seems a little hard, certainly, that they should—er—actually—er—"

Mr. Merivale rifled the Chief Constable's cigar-box, assuming the invitation to do so. "Ask me my opinion?" he said, biting the end off a cigar. "Tell you. Best thing that could have happened."

"Indeed?"

"Greatest good to the greatest number. Iniquitous will. Always said so. Everything to the Horshams and that would have been an end of it—"

"But—er—he was making a new will—er—"

"Might have been worse still. So if you're hunting for a murder, tell you where to look."

"Yes?"

"Fairy," explained Mr. Merivale succinctly. "Came down the chimney just at the right moment. Ha, ha! Often thought of doing it myself. Want to check up my alibi? All right, we'll fake one up for you. Must be getting along now. Tricky business intestacy, no time to waste, may all be dead tomorrow. Hope the war's killed off a few of Sir Willoughby's dependants. Save me a lot of trouble, eh? Ha, ha! Don't mean that really. Hate this war, scared stiff, waste of money, waste of time, waste of lives and proves nothing..." He had now resumed his overcoat. He replaced his hat and picked up his case...

"Er—one moment—" came anxiously from Smythe.

"Anything else?" rapped Mr. Merivale in surprise, revolving and raising what would have been his eyebrows if he had happened to have any.

"It was only—" Smythe floundered and looked to Culley for assistance.

"It's about this nephew, sir." Culley put it in a nutshell helpfully.

Smythe nodded gratefully and shrugged apologetically. It was not that Superintendent Culley and himself didn't believe in fairies, his expression seemed to say, "But this son of *Roger* Keene-Cotton—er—should normally be the next of kin...?" he had to ask.

"Of course!" Merivale emphatically agreed. "Should have been a millionaire long ago. And now that Sir Willoughby has left no will he ought to be able to buy up Europe and stop the war. However, there it all is—expressly disinherited; all perfectly legal."

"Did—er—*does*—er—"

"Does he *know* he can't inherit?" Culley interpreted.

"Certainly. No use crying over spilt milk. Had his allowance, and pension; enough to live on as a bachelor—"

"But you say he's married now—?"

"Think he did it? Surely not! Killing the goose. Lived abroad, anyway. May be in England now, can't say, soon find out, advertisement in the paper. Somebody's sure to spot it."

"Yes, yes," agreed Smythe. "Keene-Cotton is an uncommon name. Well, you must let me know when you find him."

"Not if you're going to string him up," said Merivale in flight. He staggered suddenly and whirled round, clutching at the door-knob for support. "Keene-Cotton? No. Took his mother's maiden name after the divorce. Can't remember why, but look it up for you—"

"Ah, yes, now let me see—" Smythe had the name on the tip of his tongue. "Roger Keene-Cotton married a Miss—"

"Freer," said Merivale. "Millicent Freer. Pretty girl, her father owned a row of bathing machines in Durban. Why not, after all?"

He was gone.

X
Family Party
After Christmas

I

Freer wasn't a very common name either.

Another coincidence, perhaps? But Culley decided it would be worth paying a personal visit to Borrowfield.

He made an early start the following morning by train—quicker than car with the roads in such a state.

Culley reflected that the Freers, in spite of the deep snow, had come over by car on Christmas Eve. They had been in a great state of anxiety, yet expressed relief on hearing that Sir Willoughby Keene-Cotton was in the best of health. Slightly over-acting, John Redpath had said, since they must have realised Lady Keene-Cotton couldn't last much longer. It was urgent, they had ostensibly pointed out, that Sir Willoughby should amend his will. And yet they had been quite content for him to do so after Christmas, and had departed—"Looking ten years younger," according to the observant Miss Redpath! And they had left Christmas presents, all of which were labelled "Not to be opened before Christmas" and placed them on the hall table with the others which (did they know?) were not going to be opened until Boxing Day!

And Sir Willoughby had died intestate; which *should* have made his nephew a millionaire ten times over. True, according to Mr. Merivale, the nephew knew he couldn't inherit; but Mr. Merivale was rather too sure of himself for an old man of over eighty; and, in any case, what about *Mrs.* Freer? Did *she* know?

Motives after Christmas, Not to be opened before Christmas, Mince-pies after Christmas, Murder after Christmas...

Rather a problematic motive; and they had chosen rather a haphazard way of committing a murder...

Yet they had departed from Four Corners looking ten years younger. As though they had averted some catastrophe. It didn't look as though they had taken a long chance; looked more as if they had planned something, or made some arrangement, that was a *mathematical certainty*.

Was that possible? How *could* they?

Well, it was no use Superintendent Culley asking himself foolish questions, though his speculations made a tedious train journey pass in no time.

He took a taxi from Ambledale to Borrowfield. He had purposely not warned the Horshams of his visit and wondered what his reception would be.

The ancient taxi was driven cautiously and incongruously by a very chic young lady in a peaked hat.

She decanted him on the doorstep of an unexpectedly ugly house covered with fish-scales and settled down to the

Literature, Philosophy and Politics of the World (pocket edition) until her professional services would be required again.

Many of the windows of the house were still blacked-out, presumably as an indication that the family were in mourning; and the front door was at last opened reluctantly by a flushed maid with chilblains.

Culley pulled out his most gentle and reassuring stops; also his professional card, which he handed her.

She showed no surprise. "I'll see who's in," she promised him briefly, and Culley waited on the doorstep.

Some chattering took place in the recesses of the house, then the maid reappeared, still alone, and hurried up the stairs.

Then the garden gate clicked and a flurried woman with a shopping bag joined him on the doorstep.

"Oh!" she said. "Good morning. I'm Mrs. Horsham. My husband—is there anything?—I don't know, I'm sure—won't you come in?"

"I'm a police-officer, madam," began Culley.

"Yes, of course," she broke in sympathetically. "I'm so sorry, but we're so worried just now. My husband, you know—his mother, I mean—as I told the Inspector last night—"

"The Inspector?"

"About the light in the boxroom—"

"I'm over from Mewdley, madam, and I'm making some routine enquiries into the death of Sir Willoughby Keene-Cotton."

"Yes?" Mrs. Horsham spoke suddenly in a hushed voice and closed the front door reverently. "In here," she said, and led the way on tiptoe.

Culley found himself in a small, nondescript room evidently

reserved for callers of doubtful social standing. Mrs. Horsham lit an imitation coke fire with a resounding pop and invited Culley to huddle round it. "Such treacherous weather for old people," she said, waving her fingers at it; "and just at Christmas-time, too; and the war and everything…and *everything*," she added quickly, in case she had left any points unexplained, and removed her woollen helmet, revealing herself a pretty woman who had lost all shape and colour in her determination to take life seriously.

She sat on the edge of a deep armchair and looked at Culley owlishly, pursing her lips expectantly.

"I'm sorry to intrude on you at such a time," said Culley with formality, "but Sir Willoughby Keene-Cotton died very suddenly, as you know—"

"Indeed, yes! You rang me up. I'm afraid I—it seemed so—three deaths within a few hours, I mean—it—"

"Three, madam?"

"Old Lady Turtle…she'll be *missed*…"

Culley clicked his tongue. "And your mother-in-law, Lady Keene-Cotton, died very suddenly?" he asked.

"Well, she was not strong. She kept herself alive by will-power, my husband says. That must have been truer than he thought. Why, when we told her the news she just fell asleep. She never woke again. Life's struggle was o'er."

"O'er…" Culley echoed feebly, then pulled himself together and asked: "What news was this?"

"I mean when we told her that her husband was dead," amended Mrs. Horsham, but without coming out of her trance.

No hint of the surprise and bewilderment that Superintendent Culley was feeling. "Lady Keene-Cotton died on Christmas Day," he merely said.

"Such a sad, *sad* Christmas," was all Mrs. Horsham replied.

"Sir Willoughby, you know, madam, did not die until Boxing Day—possibly later."

Mrs. Horsham shuddered. "It almost made us feel as though we had murdered him after all."

"After all?"

She came out of her trance at last. "You see," she explained ruefully, "we used to make jokes about murdering our rich stepfather. It's—it's not very nice to think of now, is it?" She went on: "Poor Josephine had been a little light-headed for some time; she really believed she *had* murdered her husband; and it worried her, you know…"

"Naturally," murmured Culley with great patience.

"Having letters from him, I mean, and realising that he was still alive."

Oh.

"Dr. Clark," she went on, "says it's quite a common delusion with old people. Such a thin line separates thoughts from deeds… There was his own wife, you see, only it was a baby with her—it's usually a baby, I believe. So dreadful to die with a sin on one's conscience, my husband says."

"That, however, was not the case with your mother-in-law, it seems. It was not her conscience that worried her?"

"We can't judge her by ordinary standards. She had to think about money all her life, so at the end, naturally, nothing else seemed very real to her. Only the horror of dying before her husband and leaving us all unprovided for. We'd all grown to count on our inheritance, you see…and now with everything costing twice as much and the two boys at school—the weekly *books*!—and then there's Archie and Dinah—I believe he's actually sold *his* share some time ago—so poor Josephine felt we had been depending on her and she was going to let us down—which was true in a way—that was why Angelina, my sister-in-law, decided to go down there in person—leave everything to *her*, she said, so we did; she and her mother always understood one another; so wonderful! She came back and told us that it was going to be quite all right about the money, but she would tell her mother that Sir Willoughby had died quite suddenly, it would be simpler; so she did. My husband didn't like it, but he had no idea that it was true, none of us had, and Josephine died peacefully without the tiniest suspicion that we—that Angelina had—"

She was interrupted by the sound of someone heltering down the stairs.

Next moment a dark woman of about thirty wandered abstractedly (but breathlessly) into the room.

"Oh!" she said, seeing the Superintendent. "I didn't realise you *had* anyone, Verna."

Since she was at that moment twirling Culley's card between her exquisitely manicured fingers, one had to take this as a somewhat figurative utterance.

"Ah, here *is* my sister-in-law!" proclaimed Mrs. Horsham, as though the interruption vindicated everything she had been saying. She got up and made gestures as though feeding invisible chickens which Culley assumed to be symbolic of a formal introduction.

"Mrs. Freer?" he asked. "That's very satisfactory. I should like a few words with you, madam. Alone, if convenient."

"It's about the death of poor Sir Willoughby," fluttered Verna impotently.

"I suppose they're having an inquest," Angelina Freer said coolly. "All right, Verna; go away. I'll look after Mr. Culley."

Verna departed with only a perfunctory show of reluctance, being evidently quite accustomed to taking orders from Angelina.

"Do sit down, Superintendent," invited Angelina with purring charm ("and you needn't be frightened of *me*," she implied). She wandered over to the gas fire, cleverly manoeuvring him into the deep, disreputable armchair, herself perching gracefully on a tattered club fender.

Having him thoroughly at a disadvantage, she offered him a cigarette which he refused. She took one herself. "Get anything useful out of my sister-in-law?" she asked as she lit it. No answer from Culley, so she added: "Verna's a terrible liar, you know."

"Is that so?" said Culley.

"Her conscience troubles her," Angelina Freer explained. "I don't know why it is, but the more conscientious people are, the more lies they tell. Cyril's far worse—or perhaps I should say better?—because he really believes all the lies he tells. Are you going to interview him?"

"Perhaps you can tell me all I want to know."

"Depends what it is."

"You and your husband motored over to visit your stepfather on Christmas Eve?"

"We did," answered Angelina, with nothing to hide.

"That was the first time you ever saw your stepfather?"

"First and last apparently."

"Would you mind telling me what passed between you?"

"What a lovely way of putting it! Nothing much 'passed between us.' As you know, I wanted to get him to do something about his will before it was too late. It wasn't easy to come to the point. He'd heard so much about me, and was so interested to meet me, that he kept making me sit in different chairs so that he could see me properly. I kept trying to impress upon him how ill poor Mother was, and how old *he* was, and he kept asking me how I was, where I lived, and who I was married to—"

"He didn't know you were married to his own nephew?"

"That's what was so funny! He must have known, but he seemed to have forgotten."

"Curious," Culley commented.

"Well, he was very old."

"You didn't try to remind him?"

"Yes, I did. But I don't know if he took it in. I asked him if he would like to see Puffy. And he seemed quite horrified at the mere thought! It was *me* he wanted to see. Then he asked me how I was, where I lived, and who I had married all over again."

"But in the end he promised to do something about his will?"

"Yes, at last he did understand that Mother was quite possibly going to predecease him."

"It was a shock to him?"

"Well, he was really rather excited at the idea of outliving her. I suppose very old people *get* like that. He was quite sure he was going to live for a great many years, but promised to send for his lawyer immediately after Christmas if it would make us any happier."

"Pity he didn't live a few hours longer," vouchsafed Culley.

"Quite damnable," admitted Angelina.

"Or die a few hours earlier..."

Angelina frowned and threw away her cigarette. "Yes, that would have come to the same thing, wouldn't it? But of course we don't know what sort of will he would have made, do we?"

"That's very true," concurred Culley. "Perhaps it's a good thing he died intestate. Mr. Merivale, the lawyer, seems to think so. I should write to him, if I were you, madam. It will save him advertising for your husband."

"What's that?" said Angelina sharply. "Puffy can't inherit, you know."

"Mr. Merivale thinks he may be able to do something," Culley told her placidly.

"That's absurd, surely?" Angelina snorted warily.

"No harm in trying," Culley pointed out. "I thought you might be glad to hear the news."

"Oh, I—I am, of course," said Angelina quickly; "but not"—and she smiled disarmingly—"if you're going to arrest us for murder."

"No question of arresting anyone for murder just yet," Culley reassured her.

"Oh, I thought there was," murmured Angelina in a crestfallen manner. "Why else have you come here?"

"We want to get everything nice and tidy for the inquest."

"I see. 'Foul play not at present suspected,'" she quoted, unable to disguise a note of relief in her voice. Her eyes, however, were still watchful. She took another cigarette and asked it idly: "How did he die, by the way? Er—actually, I mean?" The cigarette did not answer, so she put it in her mouth.

"He died from laudanum poisoning," Culley told her,

and the cigarette remained unlit. "We haven't yet found out how he came to take it. As he was in the habit of taking a number of patent medicines, it's a bit early to jump to conclusions."

"Of course," she agreed soberly, and, finding Culley looking at her, asked with interest: "What *is* laudanum?"

"Preparation of opium," replied Culley glibly. "Sometimes used in cough-mixtures, I've heard."

"He did have rather a cough, I remember," Angelina told him and lit her cigarette. "Didn't you find an empty bottle of cough-mixture in his room?"

"Quite right, madam, we did," said Culley.

He waited a few moments, then got up and said: "Well, well! I'll be off. Could I have a few words with your husband before I go?"

"You want to see Puffy? He's in the garden. I'll send him to you."

"Don't worry. You'd best stay here in the warm, Mrs. Freer. I'd like to have a look round the garden."

"Tell him he can stop shovelling snow and come in," commissioned Angelina; "and come in yourself and have a drink before you go."

"That would be very nice," accepted Culley amiably and wandered out into the garden.

II

Puffy was easily located. "Doing an odd spot of work," he told the Superintendent sheepishly. "Caught me in the act! Had a talk with my wife? Good! Well, if she hasn't managed to convince you that we didn't do it, I don't see how I can."

"Didn't do what, sir?" asked Culley innocently.

"The murder, of course."

"Which murder might that be, sir?"

"That's a nasty one! Might have done the old lady in as well! Never thought of that." He planted his spade in a heap of snow and led the Superintendent down the garden path.

"So you think Sir Willoughby Keene-Cotton was murdered then, sir?"

"No, not really," Puffy made concessions to the literal-mindedness of the police force. "Just a joke between Angy and me. Used to work out the most ingenious ways of murdering our one and only rich relation. Did you say anything?" he asked after a gusty guffaw.

"Did I, sir? No, I don't think so," answered Culley, who had merely sighed.

Freer went on: "So, you see, if we *had* done the odd spot of murder, we wouldn't have made such a mess of it. Got 'em in the wrong order, I mean. Bit careless, what?"

"I understand though, sir, that you are Sir Willoughby's next of kin?"

"What?" Puffy stood momentarily rooted. He recovered immediately and took the Superintendent by the arm, leading him away from the house from which such beguiling speculations must have emanated. "No, no, Inspector; that was just a bit of wishful thinking on the part of my wife. She thought we might go to law about it. Prove 'injustice' or something. But nothing doing, I'm afraid."

"Oh, why not?" said Culley sympathetically. "The law

doesn't view these exclusions any too kindly, you know, sir; especially when there's no other surviving kin."

"No good." Freer adjusted the battered clerical hat he was somewhat unbecomingly wearing. "Old Stick-in-the-mud will tell you—the lawyer chap—unless he's forgotten all about it. Fact is—my father always had the idea that I wasn't his son at all."

"Oh," said Culley as they came symbolically enough to a brick wall and turned back.

"That was what the rumpus was about," went on Puffy. "Daresay he was right. No one will ever know. It wasn't a suitable marriage at all. Mother had means of her own, so couldn't be bothered to kick up a fuss—her father was quite well to do and left her fairly comfortably off. Freer's Bathing Beach. Sold up the business long ago, of course."

"So that when your mother died—" prompted Culley.

"Quite right. I *should* have been a comparatively rich man. Oh, yes, I could have been still; I've only myself to blame… Lost a couple of toes in the last war, which gave me a pension for life. After the Armistice, mother dead, no wife, no home, no job. Nothing, in fact, but a lot of money. Well, I soon gambled all *that* away. What I didn't lose on the swings I lost on the roundabouts, and anything left over went on drink. Are you interested in all this, Inspector?"

Culley gave his assurances.

"Don't see why you should be. But I'd like you to know everything; it'll save you a lot of laborious research, won't it? So I'll be absolutely honest. Yes, I confess that at one period in my life I went to the bad—almost reduced to getting a job!"

"And what prevented you from doing that?"

"Sir Willoughby prevented me. After old Sir Roger de Covely's death he found me out and made me an allowance; so there I was again—saved from the final humiliation of work and back drinking again, like a gentleman!" Further guffaws. "Spent my life in hotel bars on the Continent, giving England a bad name. At the Towers Hotel in Nice I got a sort of half-baked job looking after tourists. That was where I met Angy. She'd been living with some bounder who had left her in the lurch, and she was picking up a few pennies in the same sort of way—arranging rubbers of bridge and so on. Never thought of marriage before, but found out who she was, and she found out who *I* was, and it sort of made a link, what? Angy's got a very forceful character, although she pretends to be silly. She told me something that I didn't know before which was beautifully sobering. When old Willie died my allowance would stop; so I would have to pull myself together and do something."

"So you married the lady," summed up Culley.

"Saved my life," Freer appended simply. "But here we are now, both without a bean, and I shall have to find work after all. Good thing, perhaps?"

After a few moments Culley noticed that the autobiographical sketch, to which he had been listening so patiently, had ended in a question. He decided to answer the question. He said: "I think Sir Willoughby's lawyer—Mr. Merivale—is considering your case amongst others. Doubtless you will hear from him in due course."

Puffy's surprise came very pat. "Really? Old Stick-in-the-mud? You think he can do something?"

"*He* seems to think so."

Puffy mustered a deep sigh and said: "Well, well! There seems to be a conspiracy against my earning an honest living, doesn't there? Have you told Angy this?"

"She doesn't know?"

"How could she?"

"She struck me as being intelligent."

"Yes, isn't she?" agreed Puffy with an enthusiasm entirely spontaneous and genuine; then the boyish expression left his face and he looked at Culley suspiciously. "I say," he protested reproachfully, "are you trying to catch us out?" Culley's face seemed *too* innocent, so he went on: "Trying to prove we've a motive for murder? Murder after Christmas, I mean. You can't do it. We've got an alibi."

Since the conversation *had* taken this direction Culley chose to point out: "In a poisoning case alibis don't mean much. If he'd been stabbed, now; or shot…"

"I get you." said Freer slowly. "Might have been poisoned in hundreds of ways, at any time, and by almost anyone. Might have swallowed it accidentally, I suppose? He was rather hot on tonics. My wife tells me there were a whole lot of bottles in his room. One of them might conceivably have contained laudanum—" He broke off as they approached the house.

"Yes, indeed," said Culley softly.

They entered the house in silence. Freer hung up his battered hat, exposing scanty, colourless hair which made his face look redder than ever. He said. "'That—er—*was* the drug you told me he died of, eh?"

"Why, yes, sir, it was," Culley replied.

"Ah," said Freer affably. "'Nothing like a little exercise to warm you up, eh?" He mopped his face and led the Superintendent to the drawing-room.

III

The drawing-room of the rectory was on the first floor; evidently a converted loft over the garage and approached by a long passage. Having three outside walls, it was made habitable by being heated with an anthracite stove, round which were found to be huddling, in addition to Verna and Angelina, the rector himself and a hospital nurse in full war-paint.

The Rev. Cyril Horsham was a sallow, lantern-jawed man; he had the big, foolish brown eyes of Angelina and the same very black hair. Brother and sister were startlingly alike. Culley could only marvel that, with the same features, Angelina could be so beautiful and Cyril Horsham so plain. A photograph of Lady Keene-Cotton told him where their features came from, and then he found himself marvelling that they could both manage to look so foolish.

He refused to stay to lunch but accepted a drink and listened sympathetically to the rector's description of his mother's last moments, which ended in an eloquent and lengthy tribute to the kindness and unsparing diligence of Nurse Hastings, who was remaining with them all until after the funeral; all of which passed over the nurse's impassive countenance without a ripple.

Presently, owing to some juvenile screechings from below, Verna left the room. Culley cocked an ear and asked if those were the two children coming in. The rector replied that they had been out toboganning—yes, two were his, the boy and the girl, one was a little orphan they had adopted, and the other two were evacuees.

At which Angelina murmured cryptically: "Poor Verna... after *all* her trouble...!" and Nurse Hastings fled suddenly to smooth over a domestic commotion on the stairs.

Culley managed to corner the hospital nurse before he went. From her he learnt that Lady Keene-Cotton had recovered from two strokes which had left her only with occasional fits of mental haziness. Death had come quite suddenly and painlessly from cerebral haemorrhage. Yes, she had been taking laudanum for a number of years, but not regularly until the last few weeks of her life, as she wasn't the sort of lady to give in to pain. Mostly she just liked to know it was *there*, if Superintendent Culley saw what Nurse Hastings meant.

Superintendent Culley thought he did.

He learnt nothing else of any importance. Unless it was that Lady Turtle died on Boxing Day, the Rev. Cyril consequently bicycling fourteen miles all told in order to despatch her into the next world and not returning home until late that night; which either gave him an alibi for being at the Redpaths' party, or not, as the case might be; and, anyway, could always be checked up if necessary.

XI
Inquest

I

"But, Great Scott, man—that absolutely clinches it!" exclaimed the Chief Constable, gleaming.

"Not necessarily, sir," replied Culley respectfully.

"How else do you account for the fellow knowing Sir Willoughby died of laudanum poisoning? Thought transference, eh?"

"That did strike me as a bit fishy," admitted Culley mildly.

"And his wife drawing your attention to that empty bottle of cough-mixture?"

"That's more understandable. She might have seen it there."

"More likely to have left it there herself."

"With a poisoned box of chocolates? But all the chocolates have been analysed and proved harmless, you say, sir?"

"All the ones he didn't eat, Culley. We know nothing about the ones he did."

"That brings us back again to the Almond Whirl," said

Culley thoughtfully, explaining: "If the doctor insists that he must have died within a few hours of swallowing the stuff."

"We've still got the mince-pies," reminded Smythe; "not to mention all his other patent medicines. The parcels on the hall table may have been left as a blind. Probably were. Easy for a clever woman like that to hit on a way of poisoning an old man like that—an old man who was easy to murder, remember—in such a way that he wouldn't swallow the laudanum for a day or two. Anyone who knew Sir Willoughby would be able to work it all out to a mathematical certainty."

"Funny you should say that," remarked Culley; "but she *didn't* know him, sir. She'd never met him before."

"Never actually *met* him, no, that's true…"

"And if only we could find the Freers a stronger motive, sir. After Christmas, I mean…"

Smythe was nothing if not obliging. He tried to think of one, frowning hideously. At last his face cleared; he gleamed again, and said: "Then how's this, Culley? They *meant* him to die *before* Christmas!"

"Ah-ha," said Culley; "that's better!"

"It fits!" pronounced Smythe, grateful for this encouragement. "As soon as she realised her mother was going to die, she decided to make sure that her rich stepfather died first!"

"So she murdered him, then, for the sake of her family, sir?"

"You said yourself she seemed to be the only one of 'em with her head screwed on the right way, and that they were obviously accustomed to relying on her to get 'em out of their scrapes."

"That's true enough," admitted Culley; "but she doesn't seem to have done so, does she, sir?"

"No, it didn't come off. But she couldn't know her mother was going to die on Christmas Day. It was a long chance, after all."

"Bit too chancy for a lady like that." Culley shook his head discouragingly.

"In this case we must take into consideration two important factors," said Smythe dictatorially. "First, that a lot of money was at stake; and second, that he was easy to murder. So we haven't got to look about for someone with a homicidal mentality. It isn't a question of finding out who killed him, Culley, so much as sifting the evidence until we discover who it was who let him kill himself. Now! We've got a lot of work before us and the inquest's to-morrow. I shall ask for an adjournment. You agree?"

"No, sir."

"Eh?"

"I think we've got quite enough evidence for a Coroner's jury, sir. In my opinion the sooner we get the inquest over the better. Even if we only get an inconclusive verdict, it'll clear the air a bit, and won't mean we've got to shelve the case."

"I suppose that's true," agreed Smythe reluctantly. He sighed. "An inquest can't make the case more obscure than you're trying to make it. Then you'd better run along, Culley, and have a talk with old Footring."

"Thank you, sir," said Culley, rising to do so. But, not wishing to leave the Chief Constable in such a gloomy condition, he said: "To my mind, sir, it'll be worth having the inquest if only to get a clear and satisfying explanation of those footprints."

Smythe started; then groaned: "Are we really still worrying about *them*?"

"They're still worrying me a bit, sir. Stands to reason, sir," he put it to Smythe lucidly, "the deceased can't have been murdered by Frank Redpath and planted on the lawn, and also fallen out of the attic window and bounced down the bank, and then been poisoned by Mr. and Mrs. Freer on top of everything else. Now, can he, sir?"

"Since you put it like that, no," agreed Smythe; "but then I don't see how he can—even if we do have the inquest to-morrow. Run along, man."

II

The inquest, accordingly, took place on the following day in a room at the Crown Hotel, Mewdley.

Mr. Herbert Footring, the Coroner, was a local solicitor and conducted the affair with tact and unflurried competence. He had mustered a shivering jury who were fiercely bored at the outset, the Coroner making no particular effort to interest them, nor exercise their brains to begin with. They listened patiently to the technical evidence of Dr. Trevor. They gathered that, from the findings of the autopsy, laudanum poisoning was the cause of death, and knew that it was their business to decide how, or by whom, the poison was administered. They were told by someone with a red nose, in a leather coat, about the various medicines her stepfather was in the habit of taking; these she described to the best of her ability, glucose, iodine, rhubarb, senna being the only names she was able to supply. The deceased had fallen down and twisted his legs some time before Christmas and had been allowed to straighten them out again and kill the pain in his own way. He had also had a bad cough, but he often had it and knew how to treat it. "Yes," she replied to a question from the Coroner, "he had brought a number of medicines with him. And I remember getting him some cough-mixture in Mewdley." No, she didn't recognise exhibit 2, when it was produced, but it had the label of a London chemist, so must have been one of the ones he had with him.

There followed the evidence of Edward Gover, the local chemist, who described the medicines he had supplied to Sir Willoughby Keene-Cotton at Four Corners. Among them had been a cough-mixture on December the nineteenth; the order had been repeated on December the twenty-first and again on the twenty-third as he wanted a supply over Christmas.

The next witness was Sergeant Dawes, who announced that no other empty bottles had been found except the one produced in court. The other medicines mentioned by Mr. Gover had also disappeared, empty bottles and all. His announcement caused a stir of interest among the jury, for surely here was a hint of mystery at last?

But they soon forgot to wonder where the empty bottles had gone to (where *did* empty bottles go to, anyway?), for Dawes was being even more interesting now and giving them an inkling of the efficiency and thoroughness of their own police force of which they had not hitherto dreamed.

"It comes to this, then," summed up Mr. Footring, turning to the jury; "the results of your investigations on the evidence of Mr. John Redpath were—er—negative?"

"Unsatisfactory, sir," corrected Dawes. "So far as we were able to tell, sir, from our practical experiments, it was not possible for the deceased to have fallen from any of the windows."

That was that.

John was called. He said he might have been wrong about the footprints, but he had certainly noticed them at the time and had felt they ought to be explained.

Frank Redpath was called. He had been with his son when the latter had noticed the footprints, but, personally, Frank Redpath had felt it was not at *all* necessary for them to be explained.

"Why not?" asked the Coroner after a short pause.

"Because, as I told the Superintendent next morning, it was I who carried the poor old man on to the lawn that night and left him by the snowman."

Mr. Footring's cool, unflurried manner momentarily deserted him. "You left him on the lawn—*all night!*"

"Yes, I did," said Frank.

Mr. Footring pulled himself together. "Perhaps, Mr. Redpath, you will explain to the jury why you did that?"

Frank turned obediently to the jury. "Because he was dead," he explained.

The jury gaped. "How did you know he was dead?" the Coroner asked helpfully.

"I've seen death too many times to make a mistake. I worked in a Red Cross Hospital during the last war. I was a stretcher-bearer in France for a year..." ("I never knew that before," murmured John.) "I'd just gone out into the garden in order to come in out of the snow as Father Christmas at the party. My stepfather-in-law was lying on the path. I had a torch with me and soon saw that he was dead. I hadn't time to think. He was clutching a large box of chocolates, also one of the treasure-hunt labels I had written. The snowman on the lawn had collapsed, so I put two and two together. Well, I couldn't leave him there. Somebody would have to help me carry him up to his room; then I was going to ring up Gosling. With luck, I thought, I could manage everything quietly without any of the guests at the party knowing what had happened. I found the parlourmaid lurking about in the dimly lit hall. 'Oh, Keevil,' I heard myself calling to her urgently. I was so upset that I hardly recognised my own voice. She didn't either. 'Yes, Sir Willoughby?' she said, and at that moment she put the whole damnable idea into my head. I found I was still clutching the box of chocolates. I told her I was going to bed and didn't want to be disturbed, didn't want any dinner, or anything. She quite understood and helped me up the stairs. I left the box of chocolates in his room, remembered that he always slept with his windows wide open, turned out all the lights, locked the door and came down again. Just in time. The guests were beginning to creep about all over the house, treasure-hunting. Then I carried the body back to the snowman, put the label in his hand and the key of his room in his pocket. It had been snowing steadily, so I suppose his own footprints must have become covered over. Then I came in through the french windows as Father Christmas out of the snow, according to my original plan. I thought that would be more realistic, you see," explained Frank anxiously, "than simply coming out of the lavatory."

"Quite so," murmured Mr. Footring, playing for time. "I am sure it was—er—most realistic…"

"Well, actually it wasn't," said Frank, "because Uncle Willie had just done the same thing far better. In fact, he had been a great success and the party was going with a swing. Everyone was talking about how wonderful Uncle Willie had been as

Father Christmas; obviously I couldn't announce that he was dead."

"No, no," the Coroner had to agree, "but as soon as the guests had gone…"

Frank groaned. "I thought they were *never* going…! I could hardly keep people from breaking into his room, everyone was so anxious to congratulate him! And after that the bishop and his wife and Miss Cameron stayed on to supper, all so pleased with Uncle Willie and so happily convinced that he was still alive and that they would see him again when he had recovered from his exertions. By the end of the day we were all very tired and slightly tipsy. My wife, my aunt, and Miss Dore hurried happily off to bed before I had time to stop acting. I waited for my son, who had been out to dinner, but he came in so pleased about something that I missed my cue again. That's all," said Frank, and waited.

"Thank you, Mr. Redpath," said the Coroner. "What you have told us is certainly enlightening"—he looked at the jury— "even if we cannot personally applaud your actions." (No; the jury certainly could not bring themselves to do *that*.) "We are not here, however, to criticise any lack of feeling or ordinary good taste you may have shown, but to examine the facts merely. You say that you told the Superintendent this on the following morning? I have no record of any such statement." He pretended to look through his papers. "No. But doubtless Superintendent Culley would now like to ask you a few questions himself?"

"Thank you, sir," said Culley, rising. "It would have saved the police a lot of trouble," he told the witness, "if you had been a little more straightforward, sir."

Rhoda got up suddenly. "I *do* apologise for my husband!"

she said in an anguished, rather gushing voice, "but he must have gone through such agonies at the party, and next morning we all had rather a trying time; it was difficult enough to hear ourselves speak, let alone think what we were saying—"

"I quite understand, madam," replied Culley soothingly. "Easier to confess to a murder than go into a lot of long-winded explanations…"

"And far quicker," added Rhoda, pleased.

"Just one or two further points, sir," said Culley. "The boots. The two Father Christmas fancy-dress costumes, yours and Sir Willoughby's, were practically identical."

"They came from the same shop—Furlong & Davenham. They only *had* two sizes."

"Then you knew your stepfather-in-law was going to dress up as Santa Claus at the party?"

"Oh, no! If so, he could have had my costume. I ordered it a long time ago. He ordered another one quite independently. I did have a slight suspicion after something my son said, but I wasn't going to alter my own plans. *Somebody* had to be Father Christmas, and it was no use counting on Uncle Willie—particularly after his accident. Frankly, I didn't think he'd feel up to it when it came to the point."

"And now, about those chocolates," went on Culley. "You had no reason to suppose they were poisoned?"

"The ones in the snowman? No, of course not."

"Were they the ones that Mr. and Mrs. Freer left?"

"No, he had those on Christmas Day. The ones in the snowman had been there a long time. I think they were some which he'd ordered himself."

"You're not sure?"

"I'm not absolutely sure, no. What does it matter, anyway? They've all been analysed, haven't they?" He knew only too well that every chocolate in the house had been confiscated by the police. ("If only one could feel that the police were *eating* them," Rhoda had lamented, "it wouldn't be quite so heartbreaking!")

But Culley continued: "I was thinking of that one chocolate that was missing when you entered his room the next morning. You see, sir, he would have eaten that one chocolate just before he died, and it's just possible he might have been poisoned that way."

Frank looked extremely uncomfortable suddenly. He blushed, and then turned pale. "But—but—I assure you— that's impossible—out of the question, Superintendent."

"Well, sir," returned Culley pleasantly, "that's what we don't know, you see."

"*I* know that chocolate wasn't poisoned," said Frank, shutting his eyes and speaking very positively.

"Then perhaps you'll tell the jury how you know, sir," suggested Culley kindly.

"Because"—Frank eyed the jury steadfastly—"when we broke into his room that morning and were standing about wondering what to do—I—er—as a matter of fact—well, you know how one *does*—I ate that chocolate myself."

III

Highly embarrassed, Frank sat down. There was a feeling that only a very courageous and conscientious man could have stood there and made such a fool of himself. Mr. Redpath seemed quite a nice gentleman to the jury, in spite of all they had heard, and especially if he had been a stretcher-bearer in the last war, which they had *not* heard. And they felt very sorry for his poor wife, having such a red nose particularly. Evidently this was not going to be a murder after all. The deceased must have taken too many of his cough-mixtures, because nobody would wish to poison such a harmless old man.

Even the diligent ingenuity of Mr. Merivale (who arrived late and blowing) in so generously apportioning his late client's money to divers and widespread characters, to whom (he said) Sir Willoughby's death, taking place when it did, was going to prove an unexpected windfall, failed to create an atmosphere of murderous suspicion at this inquest. Quite the contrary—whatever Mr. Merivale himself might have thought he was doing. He reeled off the tentative lists of suspects which he had concocted with such labour, then stated baldly (except for his moustache) that none of these people (who were all very nice) could possibly *know* that they gained a brass farthing, "but there you are, done my best, don't think money was the motive myself, want me any more, no, good," blew again, wrapped himself up again indistinguishably, walked excitedly into a cupboard, from which he was extracted laughing pleasantly at his own mistake and dispatched into the corridor of the Crown Hotel and the inquest resumed, and even endeavoured to recover some of its proper solemnity when Major Smythe rose to give the jury the benefit of his wide experience of the world and long (too long) associations with the dead man and presently to voice some of his (rather pop-eyed) suspicions, which were hardly taken seriously, so that he had to tone himself down and finally sum himself up, stating apologetically that, as Chief Constable of the County, he had felt bound to order a detailed investigation, but the facts doubtless spoke for themselves, eh, and he was the last person to wish to stir up any mud, and sat down to listen intently to old Footring, who naturally did this sort of thing far better.

Footring finished a brief but comprehensive speech in a sea of negatives. There was no reason to suppose that anybody gained—certainly no one *knew* they would gain—by the death. Nor was there now any evidence for supposing any of the chocolates, nor any of the food consumed during the time-limit prescribed by the police-surgeon, to be poisoned. It was by no means unlikely, and not at all uncharacteristic of temperament of the deceased, that he had absent-mindedly or inadvertently swallowed an overdose of laudanum in a cough-mixture. A single bottle of cough linctus would not ordinarily contain sufficient laudanum to cause death, certainly not sufficient to account for the results of the analysis of the organs of the deceased; but there were, according to Mr. Gover, five other bottles of medicine which, taken in the prescribed doses, should have lasted the deceased for several more weeks. Failing the production of these bottles, it was not unreasonable to assume that they had been thrown away, empty, by the dead man himself, who, one had to remember, was nearly ninety years of age, and of failing memory with regard to matters in the immediate present. Mr. Footring cited an instance of a woman who died of an overdose of sleeping draught, possibly owing to a new maid having washed out the medicine glass, the dead woman having been in the habit of accepting the state of the glass as evidence of having taken the dose instead of relying on her own memory. The evidence at her inquest had been pure conjecture; and so it was in this case. He would like to suggest, however, that if anyone had deliberately poisoned Sir Willoughby Keene-Cotton with laudanum, and wished to make it appear that he had taken an overdose of his own medicine, the murderer, probably, if not certainly, would have made sure that *more than one bottle was found after his death.*

Which seemed to the jury a very good point. And they retired to consider it.

"You have agreed upon your verdict?" the Coroner asked the foreman on their return.

The foreman, a little man wearing large spectacles made of *real* tortoise-shell, which were his most distinctive feature, cleared his throat importantly, then lowered his voice and told the Coroner impatiently and almost parenthetically that they had agreed upon a verdict of Accidental Death, since there was little or no indication as to how, or by whom, the laudanum was administered.

Mr. Footring nodded in acceptance of this verdict and was about to speak; but the foreman had cleared his throat again and told the Coroner, not at all parenthetically, that he wished to add a rider.

"Certainly, you are at liberty to do so."

"I should like to say, sir, that, in my opinion, the conduct of any man in—hrm—callously disregarding a dead body, merely for the sake of a Christmas party, calls for *the severest censure.*"

"Yes, yes," murmured Mr. Footring, much chastened. "I—quite agree, Mr. Dove—er—thank you."

IV

"Father! Was all that true?" asked John outside.

"Did it sound as though I'd made it up?" asked Frank in reply.

"No," John had to admit; "it sounded just the sort of thing you would do. Knowing you, I mean. But I'm surprised the jury swallowed it."

"Possibly," Frank suggested, "they had the sense to realise that there couldn't be any other explanation for your precious footprints. In real life, I mean. And, if you'd an ounce of real perception, instead of just a superficial nosiness, you'd have realised it too, and not made fools of us all—and yourself. Now come on."

John seized Margery and followed his muffled parents to where they had parked the car.

"Thank heavens that's all over!" said Margery.

"I don't see any reason to be so thankful," grumbled John; "and, as far as I can see, it isn't over by any means. We'll be under suspicion of murder for the rest of our lives. I daresay Father thinks he's solved the whole case brilliantly, but I don't think old Smythe was satisfied. And Superintendent Culley's no fool. And, speaking for myself, there are still several queer points about the case that are worrying me."

Margery pinched his arm—"Darling, don't," she implored.

"But we don't want to suddenly find ourselves accessories after the fact, do we, dearest?"

Frank wheeled round on him with a sarcastic laugh. "You can't be an accessory before or after a fact unless you know what the fact is. So don't worry. You're so abysmally innocent that you even split your infinitives." He walked on to the car, where Paulina was already encased; then came back and said, lowering his voice: "If you were such a good detective as you think you'd have realised by now what had happened and not keep talking about it."

"All right, Father," soothed John, "you needn't spit." He took off his spectacles and shook them. "Shan't wear spectacles any more if I'm not allowed to see anything. I thought I was going to be allowed to look after Christmas. Apparently not. Never mind, Margery. Let 'em all hang if they want to. Who cares?"

Paulina, making room for him in the car, pointed out refreshingly: "Just because people want to keep a few secrets, John, it doesn't mean they've committed murders."

"Poor idiots," said John, "what do their silly secrets matter?"

"They may matter *because* they're so silly, dear," came from Rhoda, catching sight of her nose in the driving mirror and looking in her bag for some powder.

"This is madness," said John, getting out of the car and dragging Margery with him. "You won't like being dead, Father, you know you won't. It's the worst thing that can happen to anybody. You've always said so."

"No doubt," replied Frank; "but being alive might prove far more embarrassing." He pressed the self-starter.

"Where are we going?" asked Margery, struggling feebly.

"Just seen someone I know," John offered no more reasonable explanation for leading her into the High Street, ducking suddenly into a doorway, then pouncing out with her at a tall, inconspicuous-looking passer-by.

"Superintendent Culley, or my name isn't John Redpath!"

"Why, so it is, sir!"

"You going back to the police station?"

"Why, yes, sir—I *was...*"

"Mind if we come with you?"

"Are we going to confess to the murder?" asked Margery, prepared for anything.

"Not necessarily," replied John.

"Inquest went off very nicely, sir," observed Culley.

"A very unsatisfactory verdict, I thought," said John.

"Did you, sir?"

"Didn't you?"

"I'm not complaining."

They turned into Worplesden Road, where conversation became a little easier. "Have the police washed their hands of the case now?" asked John.

"There are one or two loose ends here and there that have got to be tidied up," admitted Culley.

"I agree," said John. "Those medicine bottles, for one thing. They can't have evaporated. They must be in the dustbin, or returned empty, or something. Something fishy about those Freers, too. I suppose Smythe and the Coroner hushed all that up. Hushing things up is very stupid, I think." Culley looked at him and then at his companion. He wondered if the young lady thought so too. "We don't want to stir up unpleasantness needlessly," he said retentively.

"Hushing things up is the surest way of stirring up unpleasantness," John told him in case he didn't know, and added the gratuitous information: "Father and Mother have both been lying like hell for some fatuous and utterly trivial reason. Not that Mother cares a hoot, and Father hasn't any reputation to lose; so it must be something that affects someone else. It may even be me. If so, I want to know what it is. My—er—fiancée already thinks I murdered Uncle Willie, and I think *she* did—"

Margery broke in: "I'm sure we oughtn't to be wasting the Superintendent's time with nonsense, John."

"Not that we've either of us any motive, as far as I know," John went on, and Margery tugged his sleeve restrainingly, "but the fact remains that if my stepgrandfather had died before Christmas, the money would have gone to the Horshams, and if he had lived to make a new will, Lord knows what would have happened; he was an old man and a slave to sudden impulses. He might have decided to leave everything to Margery, or Miss Hobbs. He might even have decided, after a good dinner, to have his whole fortune glued on a shrine to contain his ashes. Something like the Taj Mahal—"

"Come along, John," urged Margery, looking at her watch, "your poor father's waiting in the car."

"He isn't. I don't care if he is. Where was I?"

"We'd got as far as the Taj Mahal," Culley reminded him as, in point of fact, they had got as far as Mewdley Police Station. "But you don't want to stand out here in the cold. Come inside, if you wish to talk things over."

"No, we can't wait now. I only wanted to tell you three things."

"Only three, sir? Well, I'd like to hear *them*."

"Firstly, you ought to realise that my father and mother have lived so long in their semi-rural retreat that they have lost all sense of proportion. Secondly, if my poor stepgrandfather *was* murdered, I don't think it ought to be hushed up."

"No, no!" Culley soothed him, equally shocked at the idea. "And the third thing, sir?"

"... Sorry, I was just looking for my fiancée—oh, there she is!" (Margery was gazing at a very dull shop window with great interest.) "Well, thirdly, Superintendent, I'm absolutely positive that he couldn't have been murdered by any of us."

"That's very nice, sir," said Culley affably, beginning to struggle with his getaway; but John hadn't finished.

"In fact," John said, "I'm so sure of our innocence that I've come to ask you if you'll stay at Four Corners for a day or two—at my invitation—and nose about a bit. Scene of the crime and all that. Two heads better than one. You and I together might be able to get at the truth."

"'Fraid I can't very well do that, sir," Culley broke in gently, with an explanatory movement of his head towards the Police Station, "got my routine work to attend to."

"Can't you shove all that on to a subordinate?"

"'Fraid not, sir."

"Oh."

"You'd best get on with a little detecting yourself, sir. Let me know what happens. I'll be most interested." He smiled kindly and disappeared into the station.

"That's that," said Margery, returning to the side of a gaping John.

"I believe he thinks one of us *did* murder Uncle Willie!" said John, this being the only excuse he could find for the Superintendent's gentle snub.

"He certainly thinks you're a little too sure that one of us didn't," Margery said; "and I think you are too," she added, leading him away.

V

Major Smythe, in his office, goggled his eyes more than usual on being told by Culley of this little encounter.

"Most irregular. Most—er—irregular," he thought he had better say, but was unable to help adding: "See his point of view, of course. I'd like to leave the case a little tidier myself—"

"Oh, we aren't stopping work on it, sir."

"No, no…but, as he says…scene of the crime…may be something in it. How'd it be if *I* went, eh?"

"Seriously, sir?"

"No…suppose not…but friend of the family, quite unofficial…might hit on something…"

"Might be a bit awkward?"

"Mmmmmm…" Smythe sobered. "Rather a dirty trick, too. And, personally, I don't share his sublime faith in the innocence of his family. Do you?"

"I'm not sure I don't," said Culley slowly.

"You *do*?" Smythe interpreted sharply, and became pensive. "I agree his story at the inquest had a realistic flavour, a ring of truth…"

"Yes, I noticed that too, sir."

"…in any case," Smythe came to the regretful conclusion, "you couldn't have accepted an invitation from John Redpath. Don't suppose his parents would be any too pleased if they knew what he was up to! And there's no doubt, as I told you, that Frank Redpath is a really first-class liar. The Coroner and the jury wouldn't have taken that into consideration. It's an old dodge, Culley, to confess to a small crime to cover up a large one—"

A constable came in. "A lady asking to see you, sir. In a hurry, sir. If you can spare the time, sir."

"Better have her in," instructed Smythe grumblingly. "Wonder who it is."

So did Culley.

"Don't suppose it's anything to do with this case," Smythe said; "gas mask...lost her identity card...nothing to do with me. However, courtesy pays."

But a picture had come into Culley's mind of a cold young lady gazing intently into a very uninteresting and heavily plastered shop window...

The door opened and the constable announced: "Mrs. Redpath."

In came Rhoda.

VI

She seemed very agitated and dropped her umbrella, then proceeded to rub off the layers of powder on her nose.

Major Smythe, recovering from his astonishment, put both her and himself quickly at ease. She'd met Superintendent Culley?... That was good. He apologised for dragging her through the painful business of a police enquiry and an inquest.

Rhoda waived all apologies and quickly came to the point, regaining her poise as soon as she had become a little warmer. "I understand," she said, accepting a cigarette and light from the now gallant Major, "that my son has just been here."

"He had a few words with Culley outside," Major Smythe modified.

Rhoda beamed at Culley. "I'm afraid you must have thought his behaviour very odd. I do apologise for him. He asked you to stay with us and continue investigating the death of my stepfather! I'm afraid he really is rather bossy sometimes."

Smythe made a boys-will-be-boys noise.

"Yes, he seemed very anxious for us to find out the truth," admitted Culley.

"Teaching you your business, in fact!" said Rhoda.

"Naturally," Smythe told her, "we've been investigating all possible angles. We're tracing the nephew and niece of Kate Cameron. Scotland Yard are making some discreet enquiries about the two other Horshams, and we've an inspector staying down at Borrowfield. We aren't calling off the investigation just yet, in spite of the inquest verdict. But you mustn't worry, Mrs. Redpath; you can trust Culley here not to tread on more toes than necessary—he has a genius for discretion."

"So I've heard," said Rhoda. "As a matter of fact, I'd no idea you were being so thorough."

"Got to be," Smythe said ruefully.

"So I suppose you told John you were far too busy to accept his invitation."

"Of course we didn't take the invitation seriously," Smythe reassured her. "I'm sure the young man had no authority to ask policemen to stay in your house. Wouldn't have accepted the invitation *myself*." He sighed wistfully.

"It was very naughty of him," agreed Rhoda warmly. "As I told him, it isn't at all the sort of thing one *does*, besides being rather irregular, I suppose?"

"Most irregular," concurred Smythe emphatically.

"That was why," Rhoda hurried on with her explaining, "I decided to come here myself—in the hope of finding you both here, I mean, and being able to account and apologise for what may have seemed to you rather *odd* behaviour on the part of my son…"

"Not at all," murmured Major Smythe politely.

"Of course, now that you've told me how busy you both are"—she rose, smiling at them—"I quite see how conceited it was of me to think I would be able to persuade Mr. Culley if I came here in person."

"Persuade me, madam?"

"To accept the invitation, I mean," said Rhoda, picking up her umbrella. "If only Major Smythe could have spared you, we would have been *so* grateful."

XII
Family Party
After Christmas

I

THIS PROVED ALTOGETHER TOO MUCH FOR MAJOR Smythe. Spare Culley indeed! We were none of us so important that we were indispensable. Needed a little reorganisation, but that was all. Run along, man, for heaven's sake, before they changed their minds.

Culley accordingly, after only a few faint and formal demurs, ran.

"You see," Rhoda was presently explaining in Frank's study, "we both can't help feeling that my stepfather was deliberately murdered, and we *do* want to be put out of our agony. Not that gossip can affect *us*, but there's my son's fiancée—her mother, I should say—and my husband's aunt—Miss Redpath—for *her* sake—she's made so many friends here—not that she can't look after herself, but…" Rhoda tailed off rather helplessly.

"But you know what people are," Frank finished for her tidily and went on: "Uncle Willie was far too fond of life to take an overdose of cough-mixture. And far too careful. If he had been as absent-minded as that, he would have killed himself a long time ago."

"But he wasn't getting any younger," observed Culley. "The verdict seemed to me quite a reasonable one on the evidence at the inquest."

"To anyone who didn't know my stepfather, yes," admitted Rhoda. "But he'd have been far more likely to throw himself out of the attic window from cantankerousness than poison himself by accident. You don't believe that, of course; but it's quite true."

"If *I* had wanted to murder him, for instance," illustrated Frank, "I would simply have told him he would die if he lay out all night on the lawn buried in snow; and he would."

Culley greeted this remark with due respect; then he asked: "So you want me to try and prove he *was* murdered, is that it?"

But, if he hoped to create a sensation by asking this, he was disappointed.

"No, no," Rhoda corrected him patiently.

"We want you to find out the truth," stated Frank simply. "If it was an accident we'd be most grateful to you if you could prove it. On the other hand, so many people could have poisoned him in so many different ways; and if, later on, one of them turns out to have a strong motive, it would be a relief to know who *did*—"

"If he *was*," put in Rhoda.

"—so that it couldn't be *them*, I mean," finished Frank.

"Ah!" said Culley when he had taken this in. "So that's what you think! Have you anyone in particular in mind?" After stemming their protests he tried again: "You don't know anyone, then, in whose associations with the dead man a motive may later transpire?"

Rhoda answered this with: "Practically everyone who came to our party claimed some kind of associations with my stepfather—most of them very remote and a few quite possibly fictitious. Some of them may have had motives for murdering him, but only, I am sure, in the sort of way one *does*."

"With so many detective stories written, murdering people has become a kind of intellectual sport nowadays," said Frank.

"That's the worst of this case," Culley sighed. "It started off being a detective story before it had begun, so to speak, what with Sir Willoughby dying like that so soon after his wife and just before he was going to make a new will…"

"One can hardly believe it!" Rhoda sympathised with him. "I've never heard of anything like that happening before, not in real life, have you?"

"Not in these parts, I haven't," Culley had to own.

"It isn't as if anyone *gained* by preventing him from making a new will," Rhoda reminded him.

"Nobody could *know* they were going to gain," agreed Culley in modification.

"Even if they did, I'm sure nobody would."

"And yet you both think he *was* murdered," said Culley.

"We both feel he *must* have been," amended Frank.

"But you don't see how he *could* have been," pursued Culley.

"We don't see how *anybody* could have been," was how Rhoda tried, expressing it.

Frank had been toying with a murderous-looking dagger on his desk, hoping, no doubt, for inspiration. "There's only one real motive for killing a human being," he said, "and that's fear; which I suppose covers pretty nearly everything, including courage. Vanity, too, is the result of fear. Think of it, Superintendent; we're all killing each other at this very moment out of sheer vanity! We're afraid somebody will tell us that we're ugly, mean, treacherous, stupid and of no importance whatsoever…"

"No, Frank, dear…" soothed Rhoda.

"We think we're the cat's whiskers," insisted Frank, "and, so long as we can go on thinking so, it doesn't matter who we kill. We *all* think we're the cat's whiskers—not only you and me and the Superintendent here, but the cruel, cruel Nazis in the sky and the poor downtrodden Poles and Whatnots…"

"Yes, of course, Frank dear," soothed Rhoda, "but Mr. Culley doesn't want to know that."

"I don't care if he does. I admit it. I'd murder anybody who dared to suggest I wasn't the cat's whiskers, so there!" He threw the knife on the table.

Culley hurried on before Mr. Redpath had time to think of confessing to the murder of his stepfather-in-law again.

"It comes to this, then," he said: "you feel Sir Willoughby must have been murdered, but you don't suspect anyone in particular, and—and you don't, in fact, see how he could have been murdered at all!"

"Only by someone driven mad with fear," said Frank.

II

They had put him in the late Sir Willoughby's room. It might inspire him, they said.

He had adjourned there, to unpack the few things he had

brought and tidy himself up a bit for dinner, when there came a tap at his door.

"Hullo?"

John came in.

"So you've changed your mind!"

"As you see, sir."

"Well, I'm damned! Can you give me an explanation, or have we got to wait until the last chapter?"

"Your mother persuaded me to come, sir."

"So *that's* what she was up to! Very extraordinary! Don't you think so?"

"Well, here I am, sir, so we won't worry."

"No wonder Father's been having a mood."

"Been having a mood, has he?"

"Yes, but he's all right now. Mother's calmed him down. She always does what she likes in the end. Have you noticed that?"

"No, sir."

"No," said John; "I don't think Father ever has either. By now he probably thinks it's all *his* idea having you here."

"When actually the idea originated with you, sir."

"To be honest," confessed John, watching Culley unpack, "I hadn't much hope you'd accept. I did it partly to annoy Margery—keep her in training, you know; she has far too many negative impulses—and partly to see what you'd say."

"Oh, yes, sir?" said Culley, taking off his coat, and John noticed that he didn't wear bicycling clips on his arms, which was *something*.

"Yes—you needn't bother to put on evening dress, you know—"

"I was only going to wash, sir."

"Don't let me stop you," said John, following him into Uncle Willie's bathroom, where Superintendent Culley washed in the thorough manner that was the hallmark of his calling. "There *was* another reason why I wanted you to stay in the house," said John strikingly (as Culley came up for the third time). "Would you like to hear it?"

"Yes, please, sir."

"Because Father said if I was such a good detective as I thought, I would have realised by now what had happened and not keep talking about it."

"Your father said that, sir?" said Culley with interest.

"Something like that," replied John, opening the door of a small cupboard, which was empty, so he shut it again. "And, damn it all, it rankled—wouldn't *you* be annoyed? If everybody in the house, I mean, knew something and were laughing up their sleeves at you. 'He hasn't seen the programme!' Naturally I want to find out what it is."

"Naturally, sir. And you thought I might be able to help you?"

"Serve 'em all right," said John, backing obsequiously before Culley as he emerged, dried, from the bathroom. He went on: "When I told them what I had done, I watched them like a lynx. At first they were highly indignant, and then I saw them look at each other. A few moments later Mother murmured something about Her Wool, so Father drove the car round in a circle and we all waited outside the Scotch House while Mother disappeared for more than an hour. And now you've turned up. The plot thickens, doesn't it?"

"Ah, maybe it does," said Culley, about to brush his hair and meeting John's eye in the mirror. "You say *everyone* knows something except you, sir?"

"Everyone," insisted John morbidly. "Aunt Paulina, of course, has known something all along. But she always does bristle with secrets. It's part of her charm and probably gives her that feeling of security in her old age. Even Margery—"

"Ah," said Culley.

"You needn't say 'Ah' like that. It's ridiculous!" John snorted impatiently. "Insulting! She's become a female oyster about something. I'm not even allowed 'to know what it is without being told'; I've just got to Keep Off the Grass. Nice thing, what, when a woman won't even trust her own hus—future husband? Quite frightening."

"Frightening," savoured Culley.

"It was bad enough before Christmas—enough to drive a chap crackers—and, now Uncle Willie's been murdered, *it's still going on*; and looks like going on for ever; unless we get to the bottom of the mystery, Superintendent." He flung himself into a deep, upholstered armchair which crackled protestingly.

III

The Redpath family gave Culley a really good dinner, and he didn't make peculiar smacking noises with his lips or clatter needlessly with his knife and fork, which Frank said he would and Rhoda said he wouldn't (which was perhaps what they had been quarrelling about in the study, thought John, but on the other hand perhaps it wasn't). Nor did he talk about his food, noticed Aunt Paulina, which was more than could be said for the Upper Classes nowadays; though he couldn't resist remarking that, considering the war and everything, they seemed to have done themselves pretty well over Christmas.

The Redpaths, guiltily, felt they ought to exonerate themselves, explaining about the generosity and unscrupulousness of Uncle Willie and his insistence on going "the whole hog" (!) at Christmas-time, war or not. "It was almost *too* much," complained Rhoda. "We felt quite ill, didn't we, Frank?"

"I don't see why you need have felt so guilty," said John. "If anybody could have been arrested for food-smuggling it would have been Uncle Willie—it wasn't *your* fault."

"Oh, no," said Rhoda, "but there was so *much*."

"There's just as much now," pointed out John, "and Father's just beginning on his third helping. With a policeman in the house too! *Ah!*" he said suddenly, finishing his own mouthful and turning to Culley. "A clue! Appetites at Christmas! Where had they gone to? And why…"—John swilled down some light wine ruminatively, then put down his glass and thumped the table—"*why have they suddenly returned?*"

"Since Willie's death," explained Frank, "we haven't had all his rations."

"Your stepfather didn't eat much, then?" Culley asked Rhoda politely.

"Yes, he did," John told him firmly.

"Yes, indeed," said Rhoda. "Uncle Willie was a *great* eater."

"Yes, he was," said Frank.

Followed a somewhat depressed silence during which Superintendent Culley certainly hadn't seen the programme. *Had* the appetites of Mr. and Mrs. Redpath really improved since the death?... Or was it, perhaps, since the inquest?

The old lady, Miss Redpath, whose vegetarianism removed her fluctuations of appetite to unfathomable planes of conjecture, slithering guiltlessly from the insinuations of this very tiresome young man, said: "Naturally at Christmas-time, with Sir Willoughby being laid up, and the party and everything, we were all too worried to eat much. Now that the inquest is over, as well as the party, we can all relax."

With which explanation Superintendent Culley tried to feel content.

He noticed, however, that Margery Dore, whether she had done her share of eating before Christmas, during the present meal had hardly opened her mouth—even to speak.

IV

It was too soon, he decided, to start cornering people and questioning them in turn. Better wait until he had found out what it was he wanted to know, because at present he didn't even know that.

The mystery of the Appetites before Christmas may have had no existence except in the imagination of John Redpath. The barriers of reticence surrounding Miss Dore might be a natural and inevitable defence against her fiancé's rude inquisitiveness and nothing more. "If you were such a good detective as you think you would have realised by now what had happened and not keep talking about it"... That might mean they knew who had committed the murder and wanted to have it definitely proved; it might mean they knew there was a very strong case against somebody in whose innocence they had complete faith but they wanted the case finally *dis*proved; it might even mean (yes, yes, it was possible) that they were trying to "frame" somebody and had asked him here to plant a lot of evidence on him... So Culley would have to proceed cautiously and keep an open mind. Well, well...he was quite good at doing that.

The ladies conventionally withdrew, leaving the three men to drink port. John Redpath relaxed a little: he and his father sat looking at Culley with wistful, melting eyes. Something like a couple of spaniels, they were. It was flattering but rather embarrassing.

They were only too pleased to answer questions, and their answers seemed honest enough. It couldn't be their fault that the more questions they answered the deeper the mystery grew; or *could* it?

Culley tried to probe to the foundations of the mutual antipathy that had grown up between his host and the dead man, but the foundations were shallow and of the most trivial nature and did not date back any farther than the week or so preceding the party. "He never *approved* of me, of course," Frank Redpath confessed disarmingly, "and consequently I have never bothered to love him as much as my wife did." And that seemed to Culley perfectly inevitable, and natural too.

The same with John. "Unless the old man was finding fault with me, he didn't really notice my existence; I was just another of Mother's liabilities—like Father—only slightly more expensive. Margery had been trying to put in some good work with him before Christmas."

"Oh, yes, sir?" encouraged Culley, since they *were* taking it in turns to be so candid.

"Yes. You see, we thought if she went in and vamped him a bit daily, and didn't seem too keen about marrying me, he'd perhaps begin to show an interest in our forthcoming nuptials out of contrariness. 'Yes, yes, when in doubt always get married,' he would say (*he* always had) 'doesn't matter who *to*,' and point to Mother and Father as final proof that it didn't."

Frank hugged himself with glee. "So that's what your young woman was up to in there! I wondered."

"I think she had been getting on rather well," John proceeded, reviewing the matter in retrospect. "Uncle Willie was beginning to feel quite kindly towards me—he might have left me all his money when he had used all the other ways of annoying Father he could think of—and then I went and upset the apple-cart by catching him rehearsing as Santa Claus in front of a mirror."

Frank subsided into paroxysms of silent laughter. "You certainly did!"

"He *sent* for me," pointed out John, aggrieved. "Silly old fool! His mind was so occupied with Christmas foolery there wasn't room for anything else."

"You don't think he had anything else on his mind," asked Culley, "—anything more important—that had nothing to do with Christmas?"

"Oh, no," said Frank positively.

But John qualified: "We didn't think so at the time; but, looking back, we're not so sure."

"Because it wasn't only *us*," explained Frank more thoughtfully; "he had a frost on with Paulina, too."

"He had a quarrel with Miss Redpath?"

"I don't see how anyone could quarrel with Aunt Paulina," put in John.

"Uncle Willie could," retorted Frank. "I don't suppose she knew she was having a quarrel with him."

"She did keep out of his way, though," remembered John.

"Yes. That's curious. Because usually when people want to quarrel with Paulina, she *lets* them quarrel with her, and there's an end of it. But she seemed to go out of her way to avoid contact with Uncle Willie. Most unlike her."

"You can't make a guess as to what the quarrel was about?"

"Well…Paulina is a sharp, clear-headed old lady. Old Willie was trying to write his autobiography and got his generations terribly muddled. On the first day he arrived here he got his wives in the wrong order, marrying some of them several times and committing bigamy with the rest; Paulina straightened them all out for him most tactfully, but after she had gone to bed he got them all muddled up again. And during the first part of his visit she was really wonderful: looking after him, seeing that he didn't kill himself more often than necessary… She used to help him up the hill, making him think that *he* was escorting *her*…all sorts of things…and then something went wrong…"

"They had a silly quarrel over mince-pies," volunteered John.

"Mince-pies?" Culley pricked his ears.

"Oh, never mind about *those*," implored Frank. "Come on," he said briskly; "we'll have a rubber of bridge. You don't want to begin sleuthing to-night."

"As you wish, sir," said Culley deferentially and followed his host into the drawing-room.

V

They entered in the middle of the News.

Margery had wound a large ball of wool and had begun some *more* knitting.

Towards the end of the Postscript, Rhoda began creeping about on tiptoe getting a card table. She quelled gallant motions of assistance.

Culley did not play bridge. He did the crossword puzzle in the *Telegraph* to tidy up his brain for the night.

Margery did not play, either, and soon lost patience with her knitting and began floating gingerly about the room. "Looking for a book," she explained, on adverse criticism from John.

"There are plenty about," John told her, in case she hadn't noticed.

"Not the one I'm looking for," she retorted.

"If it's the *Finer Points of English Law*, you've got it in your hand."

"No, it isn't." She put a heavy book back in a shelf, sat down, and resumed her knitting.

Later she disappeared and was heard playing the piano.

When bridge was over John disappeared too.

The piano continued for a few moments and then stopped.

"I hope they won't be cold," said Rhoda.

"I'm sure they won't," said Paulina.

"I'm not so sure," said Frank.

"Just a lovers' quarrel perhaps," admitted Paulina.

"Oh, dear!" said Rhoda. "I do hope she isn't beginning to get on his nerves already."

"Far more likely to be the other way about," opined Frank.

"Well, well!" said Culley, having finished the crossword puzzle (he was good at them). "I think I'll be turning in." He got up. "If you'll excuse me, ladies. Early to bed. We get the habit."

"I'm afraid we've got into the habit of sitting up to all hours," said Rhoda. "Otherwise one wakes up so early. So pointless in the black-out and before the paper has come or anything. Good night, Mr. Culley. Scream, if you want anything. Now promise." She smiled winsomely.

Culley promised he would scream, and on his way through the hall to the stairs he didn't intend to overhear a private conversation, but the door of the music-room was ajar; and, anyway, if these people didn't want to be spied on, what did they want?

And all he heard was John's voice saying: "Well, if you won't let me tell anyone else, let me tell Superintendent Culley. I don't think we ought to keep anything from him, and I'm sure we can trust him."

Margery's reply was inaudible, but evidently hostile.

"Why—*why*?" (John's voice again). "If you won't tell me why, darling, I shall begin to suspect—"

"Ssssshhhh!"—audibly from Margery, who presently emerged from the hall.

Culley put his hand on the drawing-room door to make it look as though he had only just come out.

She smiled at him. "Just off to bed," she told him and tripped airily up the stairs.

Culley was about to follow her example but was caught by John.

"Now!" said John, taking him by the arm and mounting the stairs with him. "I don't know what *you* think, Superintendent, but I'm absolutely certain there's a will hidden away somewhere in Uncle Willie's room."

"Indeed, sir?"

"Can you think of a better reason for anyone murdering him after Christmas?"

"Well, now, sir," replied Culley fairly, "since you ask—no, I can't."

"Good," said John.

VI

Culley saw at once that his hopes of an early bed had been over-optimistic. Indeed, he would be lucky if he did not spend the night tapping panels and searching for secret drawers.

He told his earnest collaborator (rather feebly): "Mr. Merivale has been through all Sir Willoughby's papers."

"Of course," John replied. "And the police have been over the ground with a fine toothcomb. I know all about that. Nevertheless—I'm absolutely convinced, Superintendent, that the old man was leading those two up the garden path."

"You're referring to Mr. and Mrs. Freer, sir?" gathered Culley intelligently.

"We don't know who they really were," pointed out John, who was assuming nothing; "for all we know, they were a couple of international crooks. Funny that Uncle Willie didn't know Angelina had married his own nephew until she told him."

"I noticed that too, sir; but his memory wasn't what it was."

"Convenient," said John. "And, even if she did tell him, she took jolly good care that Uncle Willie didn't *see* him."

"You think he was an impostor, sir?"

"I advise you to check him up very carefully, Superintendent, and not go on believing everything he says."

"Very good, sir," said Culley respectfully.

"And her too," went on John recklessly. "He'd never seen her before, remember. And, mark this, when she arrived home for Christmas *even her mother didn't know her.*"

"How about the brother, sir? I've been down to Borrowfield. Had a talk with the Rector. And the Freers. I noticed a marked family likeness between the brother and sister."

"How do you know you saw the same Freers that we did?" asked John swiftly, and before Culley had time to think of the answer: "Never mind; we'll let that pass. Assuming them to be the genuine article, don't you think it was fishy their going away happily satisfied with his vague promise to send for his lawyer some time after Christmas? With Lady Doings about to die at any minute—!"

"Yes, sir," said Culley, and asked the young man with interest: "Why do you think *that* was?"

"Either," replied John, finding explanations simple, "he made a new will then and there, and *they went away with it*—"

Culley had to protest: "Not as easy as all that, you know, sir. There's a question of witnesses—"

"Easy enough to get a couple of witnesses afterwards.

Impossible to prove they hadn't seen him sign. But I don't think that's very likely."

"No, sir—"

"If Uncle Willie did that, it would have been to save his own skin—"

"Yes, sir—"

"More likely that he sent them away with fleas in their ears—"

("That does sound more like the dead man to me," put in Culley.)

"—and, in so doing, signed his own death warrant."

(Oh.)

"You're surprised?" said John. "How funny, I wonder why? It seems to me such a reasonable solution. Old men don't like being asked for money. Don't like to think people are waiting for them to die. But the Freers didn't dare leave it to chance that he would die first. Even if their mother did live for another week or two, they weren't fools enough to trust an old man of ninety to keep his promises; so, when he fobbed off the bewitching Angelina, she left poison in his toothwater, not realising he didn't clean his teeth unless there was a party, or hadn't got any teeth to clean (the exact details don't matter), and departed telling Mother that Uncle Willie was sending for his lawyer after Christmas. *This gave them an alibi.* Mother, with an eye to the main chance perhaps, said she would see that he didn't forget (I heard her)—and mark this, Superintendent, it was *Mother* who actually rang up Mr. Merivale; so far as I know Uncle Willie never had anything to do with it at all!"

At this Culley could only subside reverently into the deep, upholstered armchair, which crackled protestingly.

"But Uncle Willie wasn't born yesterday," John was continuing happily. "After they had gone he does the dirty on them."

"He makes a new will," Culley took up the thread, "gets the parlourmaid, or Miss Dore, or Miss Hobbs to witness it, and hides it in a secret panel. Funny they haven't said anything about it."

"Have you asked them? No. In any case, they were probably bribed to keep quiet. Well, we can't very well put them through the third degree to-night, so—"

"So we're going to spend the night tapping walls, sir; is that it?" Culley began to muster sufficient energy.

"There may be no need to do that," John told him.

"Oh…" Culley seemed disappointed. "Don't let's be faint-hearted, sir…"

"No, we won't," said John, who was looking at the Superintendent expectantly.

"Go on, sir; don't mind me," said Culley, sitting back in his chair and regarding the young man with interest. "I can get my sleep at any time…"

"I wasn't worrying about you," said John, "I was only wondering what was making that funny crackling noise in your chair."

"What!" Culley sprang to his feet.

"You see," explained John, "I got sensitised to that kind of thing before Christmas. To the sound of crackling paper, I mean, whenever one sat down; and I noticed something funny about that chair before dinner. It may only be a hangover from the treasure-hunt. But why up here? Come on; we'll rip her open and have a look."

Without further ado he produced a large knife and proceeded to mutilate the upholstery without scruple.

There was certainly *something* beneath the chair cover. John worked slowly in order not to deface any interesting document that might transpire. Presently and gingerly he was wheedling and coaxing a mass of brown paper from its padded retreat. Next moment he was holding in his hands what seemed to be a flattened parcel. With trembling fingers he removed the outer covering. The contents proved to be a confused mess, at first entirely unrecognisable.

Then it dawned on them.

"Mince-pies!" breathed John in an awed voice after tasting a few mangled fragments and making sure.

"Mince-pies…" echoed Culley.

They stared at each other.

XIII
Mince-Pies
After Christmas

I

"Mince-pies!" repeated Culley.

"Quiet a moment," implored John. "Let me think. Mince-pies…mince-pies…(oh, God, this is awful!) mince-pies-before Christmas, they're supposed to be unlucky, Paulina said so; Uncle Willie wasn't superstitious, he ate five or six and swore he had swallowed the threepenny-bit; he went out into the garden to die, but he *didn't* die; but he *did* fall over and twist his legs. So Paulina was right, Superintendent, the mince-pies *were* unlucky! Aunt Paulina was right! Mince-pies before Christmas!… He got all his wives in the wrong order as soon as he arrived, and Paulina was a clear-headed old lady and straightened them out for him, but as soon as her back was turned he muddled them up again; it wasn't that he had forgotten, it was just that he couldn't remember; then Paulina said mince-pies were unlucky before Christmas, and he fell over and twisted his legs round the wrong way, but he wouldn't let Paulina twist them round the right way—where am I?"

"Couldn't say, sir."

"Well, don't stand there looking like a butler. Sit down, man, sit down; that's better; we're just getting on to something. Wish I knew what it was. Paulina. She slipped up over those mince-pies. Before that she'd looked after him so tactfully; afterwards he wouldn't let her look after him at all and agreed to have Esther Hobbs (I somehow feel that Esther has an important bearing on this story, but I can't see why. Never mind.) He didn't like Paulina being right about mince-pies being unlucky. Thought she would say I told you so, but she didn't. What happens next? She goes snooping into his room while he was in the bath. Putting poisoned pennies in his porridge, I suggest (in fun). She laughs. She was only putting a few flowers in his room. As a peace-offering? She says 'Yes, dear.' (*Were* there any flowers in his room? Has anybody checked that up? No, I suppose not.) 'Hasn't he forgiven you for poisoning the mince-pies?' I ask (in fun). She says she doesn't know, dear. Supposing the peace-offering wasn't flowers at all, but *mince-pies*? He hid them in the armchair because he *really did* think they were poisoned and didn't want to hurt her feelings. Bit fatuous? But a step in the right direction. Perhaps he thought they really were *unlucky* and was keeping them to eat after Christmas. No, that's even sillier. Haven't I really said *anything* at all helpful?" He paused wistfully.

"You've certainly plenty of ideas to spare, sir," acknowledged Culley.

"Good," said John. "I think I'll go to bed now, don't you?

I'm rather losing my grip. Good old subconscious mind. Enlightenment with the dawn; that's our best hope. But I tell you what," he said at the door.

"Yes?" queried Culley, feeling very kindly disposed towards the young man now that a good night's rest was in store, after all.

"I should have an interview with Esther Hobbs as soon as possible."

"First thing in the morning," Culley promised quite gaily.

"Sleep well," said John.

II

But Culley didn't sleep very well.

It wasn't only the mince-pies that kept him awake, though he did lie in bed thinking about them for nearly an hour. The Chief Constable had attached significance to the mince-pies at the party and mentioned that nobody ate mince-pies before Christmas; but Sir Willoughby had, apparently; and, even discounting young Mr. Redpath's vivid imagination, there still remained a faint mystery surrounding them; just a suspicion that they were poisoned, or that Sir Willoughby had *thought* they were poisoned; which may have put the idea into the murderer's head; a murderer who wanted him to die after Christmas and knew he'd been frightened off eating any more mince-pies before Christmas. Fatuous? But if this was a murder at all, it looked like being a pretty fatuous one. Was it conceivable that he did think Miss Redpath was trying to poison him and therefore sewed the mince-pies up in the armchair?

Superintendent Culley, lying in bed, tried hard to visualise an old man of nearly ninety on his hands and knees busy with a needle and cotton.

He failed. It was a *woman* who had sewn up that parcel in the chair; a man could not have made such a neat job of it.

A woman…but what was the point? If Miss Redpath had brought them to his room, whether as a peace-offering or for murdering purposes, where was the point in sewing them up in the chair? Another woman…who knew that they were poisoned, say, and didn't want him to eat them, but didn't want the murderer to know he hadn't…? Yet another woman who knew they were poisoned and wanted him to die, but not until after Christmas…?

Was Culley any hotter?

Mince-pies after Christmas…

Murder after Christmas…

Mince-pies and Murder. Mince-pies after Christ—

No, it wasn't only the mince-pies that were keeping Culley awake; rather were they lulling him to sleep in a soothing refrain; indeed, he *would* have fallen asleep—dreaming of murder, mince-pies and medicine bottles; with missing wills and Almond Whirls sorting themselves out in his subconscious mind, with his craziest thoughts fitting in with his most fatuous ideas like a crossword puzzle (he was good at them), pending enlightenment with the dawn—but something, which had nothing to do with his thoughts, had woken him up—suddenly and entirely.

It must have been a noise. A sort of creeping noise; or was it a slithering, flopping kind of noise? Ah, there it was again…more of a scratching kind of fumbling noise. Surely there could be no doubt about it—*someone was in his room!*

Scratch, scratch, pick, fumble.

Sounded as though someone were trying to open something. A drawer, like…or even a secret panel, maybe…

But surely if someone had wanted to search the dead man's room they wouldn't wait until Culley arrived…and was in bed…? Unless it was a silly joke of some kind; that they'd asked him here deliberately to make a fool of him. Culley was not blind to this possibility.

He switched on the lights.

The room was empty. He got out of bed and switched on the rest of the lights to make sure.

No one.

He stood still and listened. Nothing. He waited. Yes, there it was again…

Scratch…scratch…(slight crackle?)…click…flop!…Yet the room was empty!

Ah, but the scratching was coming from behind the door of a built-in cupboard.

Stealthily Culley advanced (wondering if he ought to have a revolver).

The cupboard was not locked. He flung open the door suddenly.

Out pranced an enormous black cat.

It arched its back and made indignant, inarticulate noises; then, deciding to accept the situation, purred ingratiatingly. It rubbed its head not only against the legs of Superintendent Culley but the legs of all the furniture too—in fact, against anything within reach—so anxious was it to create an atmosphere of goodwill.

Then it went back to the cupboard and began clawing at a corner of the floor.

"Mice," Culley could only diagnose patiently. "But I shall never get any sleep if this goes on."

He went into the cupboard and picked up the cat with the idea of transferring it to the kitchen quarters, where, normally, cats ought to spend the night, if anywhere. In doing so, however, he happened to walk on one of the floorboards in the cupboard, which was loose: beneath it came no protesting squeak from subterranean mice, but—yes, positively—a crackle!

"Oh, Lord!" groaned Culley. "If it's some more mince-pies I shall throw up the case. And if it really is a will this time I shall retire from the force. About time, perhaps."

After breaking the blade of his knife, and a nail file, he at last prised up the board with a poker (wish I'd noticed it before). The immediate result was a faint and not very pleasing smell.

He put in his hand and dragged out another brown-paper parcel, bigger this time and not so flat.

It was neatly done up and addressed to Sir Willoughby Keene-Cotton in clear if rather shaky writing.

He opened it irritably, impatient with his own idiotic curiosity.

It contained two turkey-wings, a drumstick, and a large slice of plum-pudding, all congealed in a mess of bread-sauce, breadcrumbs, mashed chestnut, and stuffing; and goodness knows how long most of *it* had been dead, from the circumstantial evidence…

He sat back and scratched his head. "I suppose if this were a tale the whole case would be clear to me now…"

Thoughtfully and carefully he preserved the brown-paper

wrapping and put it in a drawer. He put the rest of the mess where he had put the mince-pies—in the empty medicine cupboard in the bathroom. With the exception of one turkey-wing. This he took downstairs with the cat and flung them both out into the garden.

He didn't really think that the cat would be found dead in the morning from laudanum poisoning. Cats have nine lives and too much sense to poison themselves. "But if the cat *does* die," he consoled himself as he got back into bed, "it'll save the trouble of having all that stuff analysed. And it *asked* for it."

III

The cat didn't die. In point of fact, it returned with the dawn, having decided that kitchens, in these days of national economy, were barren territory compared with bridal suites, particularly those in which there had been a recent and suspicious demise.

"Out of it, you little vulture," said Culley ferociously, but without effect. "No more clues," he tried telling it painstakingly; "you've eaten them all."

But the cat knew better.

It stood in the middle of the floor gazing up at the ceiling in a soulful way, looking like the Infant Samuel.

The ceiling was lofty; and of course Culley, by now, was unable to feel really surprised to find a great many more parcels hanging from various parts of it.

Standing on a table, he removed two (which contained whitebait and a nice piece of grilled steak, respectively) from the imitation candelabra; with the addition of a chair on the table and his old friend the poker, he hoiked two or three more parcels from the ancient beam which crossed the ceiling (more plum-pudding and crystallised fruit); and, hot on the scent, he unearthed a further supply of mince-pies in a paper bag blocking up a small ventilator.

The conscientious Superintendent carefully undid all the parcels, preserved their wrappings, and classified their contents with the other exhibits in the bathroom.

"Waste," he muttered. "If it's a joke, they ought to know better. Wasting food's almost as serious as murder nowadays. If I can find out who planted all this stuff about, perhaps I can arrest them for waste, even if I don't ever prove the murder case."

But the thought of doing this did not console him very much.

His eyes returned to the desecrated armchair. Here, at least, was a definite line of approach. A woman! *Cherchez la femme!*

Mentally he made a list of all the women in the case and determined to interview each of them in turn, bringing mince-pies into the conversation. No enlightenment had come to him with the dawn—quite the contrary; but he now knew *one* of the things he didn't know, and that was A Step—whether forwards or backwards, it was hard to say, but anything was better than standing still.

It was too early to expect any of the family to be about, so he captured the cat and went down with it to the kitchen quarters (which was better than doing nothing).

The house was still blacked-out and silent, but there were sounds of domestic activity below, stoves being raked out and cups rattling.

Softly he entered a warm, brightly lit kitchen.

"My!" said a stout woman in astonishment; but on seeing the cat she thawed.

"Kept coming in through the window of my cupboard," Culley explained.

Having effected this friendly introduction, the cat washed its hands (or rather its stomach) of further social obligations, and Culley found himself quite a welcome visitor.

Indeed the cook was only too delighted at no longer having to disguise her curiosity concerning the death of poor Sir Willoughby. Hitherto it had evidently been her duty to damp a number of presumptuous but interesting theories proffered by Keevil, who, it transpired, was departing that day, so hadn't seen no reason to mind what she said like she should. Mr. Sills was coming back from his holiday and would be that grieved to hear of the death, having thought a lot of that old gent, he had, him being a chip of the old block, and a wonder the way he had kept young like he has, Sir Willoughby she meant.

"Hearty appetite the old gent had?" ventured Culley.

"That's a fact," replied the cook. "Enjoyed his victuals without false shame—not like some, with their prattle about proteins or such, and wanting things special."

Not that Miss Redpath wasn't a very nice lady and you couldn't somehow take her up, like if it was anyone else to come snooping into the kitchen. "Fancied to do a bit of cooking sometimes, you see," the cook explained leniently. "Liked to try her hand at things out of them books, and I'm not one as won't learn—it takes all sorts, doesn't it?"

Culley agreed that it did and admired the cook's magnanimity in allowing amateurs in her kitchen.

"I wouldn't allow no one else," came in swift reply.

Except the master or mistress, of course?

"Oh, *they* don't mind what they eat so long as they can have plenty of it! Quite a job, these days, to keep things like what they've been used to."

"Was Sir Willoughby particular about his food?"

"Not him! Ate everything sent up, and to spare! The amount that old gent put away you would hardly believe, to look at him! Not as if he was a big gentleman."

"Put away," savoured Culley thoughtfully; then asked: "He was fond of mince-pies, I know?"

"Quite right, Mr. Culley. And he wasn't superstitious, neither. Mrs. Redpath come in here and said to me there was to be a few mince-pies sent up with every meal; before *or* after Christmas, she said, as he didn't mind about bad luck; and I've always said myself that mince-pies after one Christmas is mince-pies before the next, so why worry? So up went the mince-pies regular, just like in my first place there was always eggs for breakfast whether they was ate or not. Seems wicked now, doesn't it, to think of the waste that went on in them big houses before the war? Before the last war it was worse, I've heard tell—the things people just used to nibble into and leave on their plates. I'll say that for Sir Willoughby, he was one of the old school and brought up rich without having to think, but he never left anything on his plate nor sent nothing down!"

Culley greeted this with the applause it deserved.

She went on: "As soon as we heard he was coming Mr. Sills said to me, 'You'll be at your wits' end to let him have what he's accustomed to.' Meaning the war, you see, sir. But, what with the extra things he got us, we managed quite nicely, after all."

"And nothing wasted," commented Culley with admiration.

"No waste goes on in this house," the cook assured him austerely. "What little we can't manage ourselves the pigs have, unless it's our own chickens; and Miss Redpath, she always saves up something of her own so that the birds can have a bit while the snow's lying so deep."

"Miss Redpath sounds a very economical guest," remarked Culley.

"Being a vegetarian, you mean? Well, yes, it makes more to go round, so to speak."

"That's very nice, I'm sure," said Culley affably, surveying his surroundings with approval. "And you keep every scrap of waste paper, I see"—as his eye alighted on an overflowing hamper. "When did they last collect?"

"Well, the boy from the grocer's, he usually has our lot. He's a scout and gets something for it. But while he's been on his holiday—and what with all the parcels at Christmas— looks like he'll be having a bit more than he bargained for when he comes again, doesn't it?"

"Ah!" said Culley, his eye lighting up. Here was another definite line of investigation. The waste paper! A soul-destroying job, but one which might repay a little extra patience—especially the wrappings of the parcels at Christmas, most of which had been "put by" for future domestic use; but Mr. Culley, being the police, was welcome to them, said the cook conspiratorially.

Busy at last, Culley removed every fragment of waste paper to his room, assisted by a gaping, slightly giggling woman called Edith Moxon, with whom, after satisfying her curiosity by telling her the truth so flatly and starkly that she thought he was "having her on," he contrived a short interview, introducing the topic of mince-pies chattily, and asking her if she didn't think it was funny that the seat of the armchair should have bust open suddenly like that, which she did; on the other hand, there had been lots of funny things like that happening at Christmas, and she had been told in particular not to move nothing until after the party was over. There'd been some parcels hanging from the ceiling too, she told him, but—oh, dear—they'd gone now, the police must have took them...

When Keevil came in to call him at half-past seven he asked her point-blank if she had sewn up a parcel of mince-pies in the upholstery of the armchair. She did not deign to take the question seriously. She looked at the chair, clicked her tongue, and said some people didn't deserve to have nice things. She then looked down on Culley, who was just discernible among piles of paper on the floor, and asked him expressionlessly if there was anything more he would be wanting. He reassured her that there was not...

When at last he looked at his watch, and found it was time to undo the black-out, he was in possession of an interesting fact.

For some minutes he sat by the window staring at two pieces of cardboard in the cold morning light. They were both seasonably edged with holly leaves. One of them was inscribed: "To dear Willie, wishing him many more happy Christmases, with love from Josephine," and the other—"A Merry Christmas and a Happy New Year, with love from Josephine"...

So far as he could judge, the handwriting on each was the same; and hadn't he seen writing something like that quite recently—*something* like it, but even shakier? He groaned. He would have to look through the parcel wrappings all over again. People wrote more shakily on brown paper parcels—no! He remembered; no need...

He went to a drawer; then returned to the cold morning light with a piece of folded brown paper. He flattened it out. It was that same piece of paper which had wrapped up the mince-pies which had been sewn up in the armchair. "Sir Willoughby Keene-Cotton, Four Corners, St. Aubyn, Mewdley, Blandshire." (Mince-pies after Christmas... Murder after Christmas...)

"This is the malt that lay in the house that Jack built," Culley heard himself humming softly to a tune of his own invention.

Was this the woman who sent the parcel which was sewn up in the chair...etc...? *Lady Keene-Cotton?*

But Culley was not a handwriting expert; he could not be sure.

Nor could he be sure about those two cards. One of them might, quite possibly and innocently, have been written by someone else, especially if the poor lady was too ill to see to her own Christmas presents. It was perfectly understandable that Mrs. Freer should have brought a present from her mother. She could not know that Lady Keene-Cotton had, in point of fact, sent her husband a present already. The parcel of mince-pies had come by post. Funny thing to send by post, and loosely wrapped up, too, not even in a box. And he couldn't have been poisoned by the mince-pies, because they had been sewn up in the armchair and he *hadn't eaten them*.

What on earth *had* he eaten?

IV

Idiot! They couldn't have come by post. Culley was making a fool of himself over those mince-pies; or someone was making a fool of him; but, never mind about how silly he looked; he *had* to get to the bottom of them.

He sprang them on the assembled house-party at breakfast. Rhoda giggled weakly and Frank roared with laughter. Paulina smiled sadly and said it was typical of Sir Willoughby's vanity, wasn't it? Margery said, "How lovely!"

No one was worried about them at all. The old man had hidden them because he wouldn't admit that his appetite was at last beginning to let him down, and he didn't want to hurt the feelings of his host and hostess.

There you were! A perfectly rational and innocent explanation! He had wrapped them up in a piece of brown paper from one of his Christmas presents and sewn them up in the armchair. Nobody—not even John—saw anything funny in an old man (who had been brought up rich in the old school or whatever the cook had said) being an expert needlewoman; and Culley decided to keep this point to himself for the present.

He pointed out to Miss Redpath and to Rhoda Redpath independently that as far as he could see there could be no sinister motive for sewing up the mince-pies, so if they had done so they might put him out of his misery and own up. But neither of them did, both of them latterly conveying that Superintendent Culley's little joke was wearing rather thin. Margery Dore thoroughly enjoyed being accused of doing something so silly and purposeless; so, whatever it was that had been worrying her, it had nothing to do with mince-pies.

Damn the mince-pies!

But this sewing business had simply *got* to be cleared up.

He had drawn a blank, it seemed, with all the women in the house; and that left only Miss Hobbs.

Culley had nearly forgotten all about Miss Hobbs.

V

The Wortleys welcomed him warmly. They now appeared to have known Sir Willoughby Keene-Cotton all their lives, and his death had bereaved them shockingly, particularly as Mr. and Mrs. Redpath were not only their nearest neighbours but their dearest friends. They were so thankful that the inquest had passed off so satisfactorily. Poor Esther had dreaded it so. She was only nineteen and terribly conscientious, poor child, and felt responsible for what had happened. But the Coroner had been so gentle with her, hardly worrying her at all. "And I won't be worrying her, either," Culley told them reassuringly. "I just came along hoping she'd be able to help me in one or two little matters I'm trying to clear up."

The Wortleys looked at each other. "I'm sure she'll be only too pleased to do what she can," said Ida, "I'll try and find her for you."

Culley allowed her to do this, and said chattily to Howard when they were left alone, "So Sir Willoughby was an old friend of yours?"

At which Howard rose gently on his toes, subsided, and rocked imperceptibly backwards and forwards while he thought out his answer. He sizzled slightly. He spoke as man to man with womenfolk out of earshot. "Hardly old friends, Superintendent. Neighbourly we were. Yes, neighbourly—that's more like it. In a small place like this, and with a war on, we can't afford not to be neighbourly, can we?"

"Then you didn't know Sir Willoughby before you came to live here?"

"We never actually met him, no," replied Howard reluctantly.

"You met him last time he stayed with the Redpaths?"

"We saw him once or twice, yes."

"You saw more of him this time perhaps."

Mr. Howard Wortley rocked. "Just in a neighbourly sort of way," he said. "War-time…Christmas-time, and all that…"

But by now Superintendent Culley was satisfied that the Wortleys had met Sir Willoughby for the first and last time at the Redpaths' Christmas party.

"You never had any business relations with the dead man?" he had to ask, if mainly for the pleasure of watching Howard rise on his toes again.

He did so. And answered, "As to that, Superintendent, a man in my position has to be careful. I still control a number of newspapers, you know. I heard that Sir Willoughby was interested in a new weekly I'm bringing out; and that may have been why he was so anxious to meet us."

"Oh," said Culley.

"Not that I would have minded having a little talk with him about it," Howard confessed generously, "and I daresay I might have been able to give him what he was after—especially him being who he was, if you get me. We are none of us so rich, nowadays, that we can turn up our noses at a good investment."

"In fact"—Culley was so impressed by the ambiguity of

Howard's speech that he found himself infected by it—"it was a pity he died."

"A tragedy," Howard agreed, blowing his nose with gusto and no longer toppling. "But tragedies, like wars, are sent to put stuffing into us, eh? Bring out the best in us and make us stick together."

Culley listened patiently to a few more philosophical generalisations born from Howard's long experience of the world and human nature, at the end of which he gathered that Sir Willoughby's death had forged a bond between the Wortleys and their next-door neighbours, the Redpaths. Howard expressed approval that Superintendent Culley was tidying up the case. We didn't want to leave a lot of loose ends about, as, sooner or later, people would start talking. Not that people could be stopped talking, anyway, human nature being what it was. It was bad enough for John Redpath, being rejected for military service on account of his eyesight, or whatever it was, and people hinting he was a shirker or a fifth columnist just because his father happened to be a pacifist in the last war, and, not having a son in the army, he didn't have to make a virtue of a necessity and be false to his own ideas, like some. "Not that I'm a pacifist myself, but I admire any man with the courage of his own convictions. That's why I'm not going back on my offer to young Redpath. Young men are scarce nowadays and the arrangement suits me very well, so I won't make a virtue of it either."

"That's very nice," murmured Culley, trying not to visualise Rhoda Redpath murdering her stepfather expressly in order to forge this bond with the Wortleys and get her son on the staff of Howard's new war-time weekly.

Nor had he time to applaud Howard Wortley for aiding and abetting pacifists and murderers (for the words seemed to have become curiously synonymous during the last few minutes), because Mrs. Wortley entered with Esther Hobbs and swept her now happily inflated husband from the rather chilly little morning-room where Superintendent Culley had been holding his court.

Esther Hobbs sat on the arm of a chair and peeped warily round the edge of her unbreakable spectacles at the Superintendent. She patiently heard Culley through his little speech about clearing up loose ends tidily.

He asked her about her family and the general trend of her life and ambitions, hoping to put her at her ease, but realised she would feel more at her ease when he came to the point and asked her questions which she could answer impersonally. So he did. And she did. For her age she was a very solemn, impersonal young woman. High time someone kissed her, or shocked her, or tried to make her laugh, or something; but no doubt there was plenty of time for that.

She said she'd been having a holiday, staying with her aunt and uncle (who had been so kind), but she hadn't liked to refuse taking on the job as Sir Willoughby's secretary to please Mr. and Mrs. Redpath (who were also very kind).

What was the job like? Sort of nurse attendant?

"Well, actually," said Esther, "I was just his secretary. And he kept me very busy, with his autobiography and everything. But I was really there to keep him occupied and—and make him feel important. He was more or less confined to his room and they found him rather difficult to manage just at

Christmas-time when he was being so secretive and wouldn't confide in any of the *family*, you see."

"Yes, yes, I see. What about this autobiography? How far had he got?"

This wasn't very easy to answer. "I'd *typed out* a lot, and he was always very pleased when I brought it to him, but quite honestly I don't think he actually ever read it through. His sight wasn't very good and he couldn't really concentrate on anything for very long. Not actually," she added (the word was a great comfort to her).

"You don't think it would ever have been published?"

"Oh, no!" Esther Hobbs laughed kindly at such a funny idea coming into Superintendent Culley's head.

"I'd like to see some of this typescript if you've got any."

She peered out of one side of her spectacles, then the other, but there seemed no escape either way, so she blinked and said: "What a pity! Actually I did have quite a lot, but I'm afraid I—" and she paused in conscientious doubt.

"You tore it up?" ventured Culley uncritically.

"Oh, no! But, it was after the death, and I was wondering what to do with it, so, as a matter of fact, I actually gave it to Miss Redpath."

"Oh?"

"She said she'd like to see it. She actually knew Sir Willoughby very well. She was sort of companion to his first wife."

"His *first* wife?"

"Perhaps it was his second wife. He got his generations terribly muddled, I'm afraid…"

(Yes, this always seems to be cropping up, thought Culley.)

"…Miss Redpath would be able to sort of sort it out and see if it was worth keeping; and, anyway, she would know what to do with it."

"What did she do with it, I wonder?"

"She said she would give it to Mr. Merivale when he came. With the other papers. I'm sure I don't know whether she did."

"There wasn't anything—scandalous in what you typed, Miss Hobbs?"

"About Miss Redpath?"

"About anybody?"

"No, I'm sure there wasn't."

"Quite sure?"

"Yes, of course I am. Because actually, as a matter of fact, I made most of it up myself. And it was all very dull."

"You made it up?"

"It wouldn't have made sense if I hadn't—and he didn't seem to notice; so I did."

"Then," said Culley thoughtfully, "Miss Redpath only saw the typescript O.K.-ed by you. What happened to all his notes?"

"Notes?" (Did Culley detect a faint blush?)

"Didn't he make a lot of notes?"

"Oh, yes; a great many." She had a smooth, tight forehead, but she managed a frown. "They were all over the place. He used to keep remembering things, you see, and jotting them down."

"Ah. Funny they've never turned up."

"Yes," agreed Esther, "it *is* rather funny; because actually he was rather the sort of old man who *kept* things, if you know what I mean. And when I went through his papers with Mr. Merivale there wasn't a single note in his own handwriting to be found!"

"And not amongst the waste paper either," Culley appended, "because I've been through it all."

"It *is* rather funny, isn't it?" repeated Esther, sticking to her guns.

"Curious," agreed Culley. "Do you think he hid them away somewhere?"

"I suppose he must have. But I can't think why."

"Perhaps he had a habit of hiding things away?"

"I don't remember his ever doing such a thing. Not letters and notes and things…"

"Mince-pies, perhaps," said Culley.

"What?"

"Mince-pies and things."

"Mince-pies?"

"That was what I said."

Esther Hobbs wondered whether Superintendent Culley had gone quite mad.

So did Superintendent Culley.

"*You* didn't sew up a parcel of mince-pies in that big arm-chair in his room, Miss Hobbs?"

"Sew up—Why on earth should I?"

"*Did* you?"

"Of course I didn't."

No, of course she didn't, that was obvious enough, and now Culley's last hope was gone!

"Did you *find* a parcel of mince-pies sewn up in the arm-chair in his room?" she enquired incredulously.

"That's right," said Culley.

"When was this?" asked Esther.

"Last night," Culley told her.

"How *funny*!" said Esther, who really wanted to help the poor Superintendent, who seemed so worried about the mince-pies, which must have *some* explanation if only she could think of it. She racked her brains obligingly.

But Culley had risen departingly. "I won't worry you any more this morning, Miss Hobbs..."

"Not at all," said Esther politely. "I wish I could have helped you more. Are the mince-pies an important clue?" Her eyes widened—with interest rather than apprehension, Culley diagnosed.

"Perhaps not," admitted Culley; "but I'd like to find out who put them there, all the same."

Esther Hobbs appreciated this point and would like to find out too; but—"What on earth," she simply had to ask, "made you think of looking for *mince-pies*?"

"We weren't looking for mince-pies," Culley found himself telling her in self-defence. "We were looking for a will." Which sounded even sillier, but Esther Hobbs's face cleared immediately.

"Yes, I see," she said comprehendingly; "and you thought he might have hidden it away somewhere."

"Something like that, miss," confessed Culley and was happy to find she was going to let him get away with this.

Indeed, he got away with it as far as the door, and then it wasn't any further words of hers that brought him back.

It was one single word which stood out from what she had last said. "*It*"...?

Not so much the word, either, so much as the way in which she had said that sentence: "And you thought he might have hidden it away somewhere."

Superintendent Culley not only came back but sat down again. "What makes you think Sir Willoughby made a new will before he died, Miss Hobbs?" he asked her quietly.

"It wasn't a will, it was only a—a codicil, or something." She answered him conscientiously.

"What makes you think he made a codicil, then?" Esther was a little thrown off her balance. "I know he did because I witnessed it."

"When was this?" (Culley was asking the questions now.) "It was on Christmas Eve." (Esther had *wanted* to help him, and now she was doing so, apparently.)

"Morning or afternoon?"

"Oh, morning."

"Before the visit of Mr. and Mrs. Freer?"

"Yes."

"Before he decided to send for his lawyer?"

"Yes, of course."

"And you haven't any idea what he did with it?"

"Yes, I—he—I suppose I ought to tell *you*…"

"Yes, please."

"I promised not to say anything, really."

"Oh? Why was that, I wonder?"

"Because—I typed it out for him, you see, and he signed it, then Miss Dore and I witnessed it and he gave it to her to keep; it was to be a sort of wedding-cum-Christmas present to her future husband—to John Redpath—and a secret until after Christmas—she wasn't to tell him, and I promised *I* wouldn't either—why, what's the matter, Mr. Culley?"

Superintendent Culley had turned pale.

XIV
Motives After Christmas

I

"So that's it!" he was saying to himself on his way back to Four Corners. "That's been it—all the time! A missing will! *The only possible motive for murder after Christmas!*"

But John Redpath had said that himself, so he couldn't have known about it. Leastways, he couldn't have known that Miss Dore had it, or he wouldn't have been looking for it.

Unless the pair of them were in it together and were pulling wool over his eyes. Unless they had *intended* him to overhear that conversation in the music-room and had planted the codicil somewhere for him to find. The mince-pies and stuff were just padding so as not to make his search too easy.

That was a nice simple solution, thought Culley, and explained everything. Half of him wished it were true and the other half hoped it wasn't; the whole of him was afraid that it was. It all fitted in so well. He told himself that it fitted in too well to be true, but this was wishful thinking.

The codicil was the Motive after Christmas which Mr. and Mrs. Redpath were afraid would turn up, incriminating somebody whose innocence it might later on be impossible to establish; somebody in whose innocence they themselves had complete faith. "It can't be any of *us!*"... Frank Redpath couldn't imagine a murder being committed for money. The only possible reason for killing a human being was fear.

But fear covered everything, *including* love of money. Money was the only safe armour for those who feared to face the future...

Yes, there was a motive all right. Frank and Rhoda Redpath knew the old man had been murdered, but didn't see how he could have been! That was perfectly natural, but wasn't it rather inconsistent? Hadn't they themselves pointed out how easy he would be to kill?

No one had to kill him at all; someone simply had to let him kill himself. And who, Culley had to ask himself, had seen most of the dead man during the last days of his life—apart from Esther Hobbs?

An easy murder! If it hadn't been for those footprints there would have been no suspicious circumstances at all.

But John Redpath had drawn attention to those footprints, so that let him out.

Idiot! No, it didn't: it let him *in!* Fool, not to see the point of those footprints before! They *had* to be noticed; just as the missing codicil *had* to turn up. The real murderer would have known that the footprints had nothing to do with the murder; *but they had to be explained.* If those two were in it— either together or independently—the whole thing would have been neatly planned out; it had been an easy murder and everything was foreseen—but nobody, not even his own son, could have foreseen that Frank Redpath would remove the corpse to a safe distance from the house because there was a Christmas party in progress!

Had John Redpath been trying to plant the crime on the Freers, against whom nothing would ever be proved?

But this again fitted in too suspiciously well, surely?

It jarred on Culley that this case should have all the ingredients of a detective story. Beginning with the snowman, where the body should have been hidden but wasn't. Going on to the long-lost heir, who wasn't one. The sinister and scandalous autobiography, which was neither sinister nor scandalous, but just drivelling and incoherent, apparently. The footprints that had nothing to do with the murder. And all the poisoned food, which not only wasn't poisoned but he hadn't even eaten any of it.

And now a missing will and a couple of murderers with motives after Christmas.

"Well, well; if they want to be consistent, they haven't, and aren't." Thus thought Culley. Wishfully?

II

He located Margery Dore easily enough by the sound of a piano. She was in the music-room. Miss Redpath was sitting by her side. Some of the time they were playing together—one hand apiece.

Bach...

Culley admired Bach. Sometimes he played it himself; it made a change from crossword puzzles and a difficult case seem quite clear sometimes. Bach didn't go putting in any-thing that had nothing to do with his theme: he made life itself feel tidy and well-ordered, with God in the middle. Take away God and put in a murder instead, then go to bed and let Bach do your thinking-out for you; the result was astonishing...

It was Miss Redpath who noticed him first. She pretended to be very frightened.

"Why, Superintendent Culley!" she cried.

"As you see."

"Have you been sitting there detecting us?"

"Something like that, Miss Redpath."

"What a good thing you caught us so innocently employed! Which of us do you suspect most?"

"I'm not particular," said Culley cheerfully. "I've just received some highly suspicious information about you both."

"Oh, damn," said Margery, "he's been to see Miss Hobbs." She played a conclusive major chord, then turned round, confronting him. "I can see it in his face."

"Well, I won't deny it," said Culley.

There was a pause. Paulina began tidying up some music.

Margery burst into conversation. "Now she is *the* most suspicious person in this case. Don't you think so? No one knows where she comes from. The Wortleys have never men-tioned having a niece before, and I don't see why she need be so carefully explained unless she's Ida's illegitimate daughter or Howard's mistress—"

Miss Redpath said, "Now, now!" severely and went on with what she was doing to the music.

"Or blackmailing them," Margery finished unabashed, adding, "Sir Willoughby might have known something about

Howard's past life." She cleared a slight frog out of her throat and began again in her clear, melting young voice. "Ida might be the illegitimate daughter of one of his wives. Where does all Howard's money come from, anyway? No one knows. I should look all three of them up very carefully if I were you, Superintendent."

Mechanically, Culley was about to promise to do so, but Margery shook out her brown bob and went on quickly before he had time to utter. "One of them might even be his next of kin. They heard his wife was dead and that he was making a new will next day. Or he might have been the only person alive who knew 'Who the Wortleys were'; he recognised them at the party and signed his own death warrant."

"Seems to have been a habit he had," murmured Culley interjectingly.

Paulina clicked her tongue tolerantly.

Margery summed up: "So, you see, the Wortleys may have motives for murder. Murder after Christmas, I mean."

"Motives after Christmas," said Culley; "so they might!"

"They *wormed* Esther Hobbs into his employ to remove any incriminating documents in the dead man's possession, of course. She had access to all his papers, remember."

"I haven't overlooked that fact," Culley reassured her, after admiring her performance (she'll do well on the stage, he thought, but if she wants to act in real life she'll have to learn how to believe what she's saying: John Redpath's performance was far more plausible); "and it has struck me as curious," he told her, "that everything written by the deceased within the last week or so should have disappeared."

"*Has* it?" cried Margery with incredulous excitement. Then rather feebly: "Well, there you are!"

"Is that really so?" came chattily from Miss Redpath.

"So it seems," Culley replied in a gossipy kind of way. "Someone been in his room and had a good tidy up!"

"Esther!" breathed Margery (without believing it).

"Miss Hobbs denies it, of course," Culley said.

"Of course," echoed Margery.

"I don't think she'd tell you lies, Superintendent Culley," Miss Redpath put in charitably; "she's only nineteen and very, very conscientious."

"That's how she struck me," Culley agreed with her entirely. "She also told me that he left a lot of scrawlings all over the place. And if *she* didn't destroy them, *who did*?"

Paulina agreed with *him* entirely. "It's very, *very* curious," she said. "I'm sure he wouldn't have destroyed them himself. He would never have thought of it."

Culley regarded her in perplexity. "Was it *you*, then, madam?"

"Oh, no!" she replied patiently. "If so, I would have told you. That's what has been puzzling me. I couldn't find anything to destroy."

She dumped a neat pile of music and dusted her hands.

"Then you *did* have a look?"

She grunted amiably. "Perhaps I did," she told him as a favour. "Dear me, it's Thursday, isn't it? I must fly." But she melted in the doorway and came back to the gaping Superintendent. "Poor Sir Willoughby," she explained, giving him the benefit of her personal knowledge of the dead man which he would not have been able to obtain elsewhere, "was so indiscreet about leaving rather compromising papers about—diaries, you know, and letters from people he had lent money to, or thought he had. It would have been very nice if all these things had fallen into the hands of the police—after his death. Besides making *so* much work for them, and all for nothing, probably; but I really must fly now, I'm so sorry. Don't let him bully you, Margery dear; but I'm sure he won't." And with that she was gone.

"Does she always fly every Thursday?" was the only thing Culley could think of asking for a moment or two.

"She runs an Art Class in the village. All sorts of people go. She thinks it's a pity Art should be neglected in war-time. I agree with her, don't you? She's rather a wonderful person, really. She seems so respectable and conventional on the surface, but she's not in the least touchy like most old people, and nothing shocks her. She doesn't care a damn what she does, either."

"So it appears," Culley was heard dimly to murmur.

"I hope you're not going to arrest her," said Margery, noticing his thoughtful expression.

"What for?" asked Culley innocently.

"Oh—suppressing clues, or whatever it is you think she's done—"

"No, I don't think I'd dare," Culley confided.

"It was all rather silly, really," Margery went on, returning his confidence; "the poor old man couldn't remember anything for two minutes consecutively—not in the immediate present. He was trying to have a huff with her about those mince-pies. But she's the most terribly difficult person to keep up a huff with. He sat up in his room reliving the past, and soon he couldn't remember what it was he was having a huff about! I suppose she would have reminded him if he'd ever allowed her in his room, but he didn't. So at last he concluded it must be about something which happened in the reign of Queen Victoria. He came tottering downstairs to ask her what it was, so that he could tell her he'd forgotten!"

"And *did* she tell him?"

"No, unfortunately she was out."

"Oh!"

"We didn't say anything to her about it, of course."

"Who's we?"

"All of us. Except John, who'd taken her to the pictures. I didn't tell *him* anything about it, as he was quite suspicious enough already."

"What about?"

"About all the secretiveness and whispering at Christmas. Oh, yes; and then Sir Willoughby was wanted on the telephone and went clumping into the study where Mr. Redpath was writing out labels for the Christmas Tree. It was then that he guessed about the treasure-hunt. He was very pleased with himself."

"When did all this happen?"

"It was on Christmas Day."

"Christmas Day," said Culley, thinking. "What else happened on Christmas Day?"

"Some people called Uncle Jeff and Aunt Meg motored over for lunch. He was too busy with his Christmas presents to see them. We said he had a nasty cough, which was true, and wondered if he'd be well enough to appear at the party."

"*You* saw him on Christmas Day?"

"Yes, I told you. And I sat with him for an hour or two in the morning. Esther Hobbs had the day off."

"Oh? So Miss Hobbs wasn't there when he came down?"

"Yes, she was. She came back after tea to tidy him up. He wouldn't allow anyone else in his room. Not while his presents were spread about."

"Ah. So Miss Hobbs heard about this mysterious occurrence in the reign of Queen Victoria?"

"Yes, she did. But it wasn't anything sensible. Only extremely muddled about having Miss Redpath's husband sent to prison. It was nothing to do with *her*, he said, and it was stupid of her to worry about it now. He wished he could remember the details. But things, he said, were coming back to him every day; and he wished he could do shorthand like Esther, then he could jot things down and nobody would be able to read them if he left them about. I suppose that was why she snooped. If we had known he was going to die we would have told her about it, of course, and she could have reminded him about it and he would have realised it was nothing at all. But how could we know he was going to die suddenly like that?"

"How, indeed? So Miss Redpath didn't know he was trying to remember why her husband went to prison."

"I certainly didn't tell her; because it couldn't have been her *husband*, could it? And it probably *wasn't* anything to do with her at all."

"Miss Hobbs might have told her."

"Yes, I—I suppose she might." A slight frog returned to be cleared.

"Miss Hobbs doesn't seem very good at keeping secrets," observed Culley tentatively.

"She kept old Willie's secret all right," pointed out Margery.

"Secrets at Christmas, yes. But not so good at keeping them after Christmas…"

After a pause Margery said: "I suppose all this means that she's given me away?"

"Bit dangerous to trust another woman with a secret, Miss Dore?" suggested Culley.

"Yes, I thought it might be," agreed Margery with a frown; then, after a shake: "But you mustn't blame her, you know. It's just that she hasn't enough imagination to invent lies, so she's usually reduced to telling the truth. I mean she can't think of anything else to say, that's all."

"Yes, I expect that's all," Culley said, but he waited a few moments in case it wasn't; then he prompted her: "And now, Miss Dore, supposing you tell me all about it?"

"I suppose I'll have to," admitted Margery reluctantly, "if that's what you're sitting there for. I can't go on sidetracking you for ever, can I?"

"I *would* rather you didn't," Culley told her with candour.

"You haven't said anything to John?" she asked him anxiously.

"He doesn't know?"

"He doesn't know what a fool I've been. A she-ass of the worst description! Poor John!"

"Would you mind being a bit more lucid?"

"I don't mind how lucid I am. In plain English, I've just about torn it!"

"Well, let's see what we can do about it," said Culley, sounding more hopeful than he felt. "It may not be as bad as you think."

"I don't see how it could be worse," Margery contradicted.

"So futile and unnecessary. So altogether typical of me. I suppose I *must* tell you?"

"You're under no compulsion; but I'd like to hear about it."

"Oh!" Margery got up exasperatedly and walked round the piano, then sat down again. "Then why don't you bully me—*browbeat* me, or something—instead of sitting there waiting for me to make a fool of myself. It's maddening."

Culley cleared his throat obligingly. "Sir Willoughby made a codicil before he died," he confronted her with severity. "He left John Redpath an income of five hundred a year. You and Miss Hobbs witnessed the signature. He gave it to you to keep. He asked you not to say anything about it until after Christmas, as it was to be a wedding-cum-Christmas present—or so Miss Hobbs said."

"Quite correct," approved Margery. "'You'll *have* to marry him now,' he said. Wasn't it lovely? I thought I was so clever, too, because that was what I had been fishing for—more or less. I suppose you think it was terribly sordid and crude, but it wasn't really so much the money. We thought if we got Sir Willoughby Keene-Cotton interested in our nuptials it would give John more of a social *status*. From my mother's point of view he wasn't much of a catch, you see, not nowadays. And we thought Uncle Willie might *like* being a fairy godfather. I wonder if you understand?"

"Very thoughtful of you," said Culley, understanding. "I'm sure it gave him great pleasure. The money was only incidental, wasn't it? You really wanted him more as a kind of decoy."

"Yes! A sort of lay figure. Fancy your seeing that!"

"Well," Culley owned up in all modesty, "I've heard part of

the story before; and it's struck me that you and your young man aren't the only people who were using Sir Willoughby in that role."

"Really?"

"Mr. and Mrs. Redpath, now, they'd been using him as a link. Indirectly through him they've landed Mr. John with a job, I hear."

"What? *Have* they?"

"That's right. Didn't you know Mr. Howard Wortley is having him on the staff of his new weekly?"

"No! So that's what John's been so secretive about! How do you know? Who told you? I want to hear *all* about it!"

"I got it from Mr. Wortley just now. Didn't hear any details, of course; but you can take it from me it's all right. Even Sir Willoughby's death seems to have clinched the bargain more than not."

"But how *funny*!" cried Margery gleefully. "Perhaps he thinks John comes into the title or something. Oh, I'm so glad! Dear old Uncle Willie! I suppose John didn't want to count his chickens before they were hatched."

"They seem to have hatched all right," put in Culley.

"Even if it all falls through," said Margery, brushing away all doubts and apprehensions, "it doesn't matter very much, because *I* landed a job too!"

"Indeed?"

"Through the Crosbies. They were at the party with their tongues hanging out hoping to meet Uncle Willie, but he was so busy being Father Christmas that they didn't; but they met *me*; and I met Gwendoline Lucas. It's only a small part, but in London, and may lead to something. Oh, whoops!" She got up and danced. "And likewise Alleluia! I can tear up that bloody codicil now, it doesn't matter any more!"

"Shouldn't do that, miss," Culley intercepted her restrainingly.

"Why not? Why not?" Margery was unrestrained.

"Because it's evidence," said Culley uncomfortably.

"Evidence?" Margery stopped dancing in order to be slightly puzzled. "Evidence what of? Oh, you mean it's a clue."

"That's right," replied Culley, "I'll have to take charge of it, if you don't mind."

"I don't mind at all," said Margery. "You can have it analysed, prove it a forgery or anything. It's completely valueless now."

"It will be if you destroy it, certainly," agreed Culley dryly. "But don't you see, Miss Dore, that codicil gives you and young Mr. Redpath a motive."

"A motive for the murder?" Margery was suddenly sobered, "Yes, I'm sorry about that. I suppose it does—in a way."

"Motives after Christmas," Culley laboriously explained. "There aren't so many that I can afford to neglect any," he found himself apologising. "I'm investigating a murder case," he went on, appealing to her, "and you see the fix I'm in? Sir Willoughby made that codicil on Christmas Eve. He was an old man and next moment may have forgotten all about it, like as not. What happens then? Mr. and Mrs. Freer come along and he promises to send for Mr. Merivale to make a new will. *A new will might have revoked that codicil.* Mr. John was in danger of losing that nice little income." Culley paused to mop his face.

"John?" said Margery in amazement. "You don't think that John—why, he didn't know anything about it—"

"That may be," agreed Culley, "but he's good at guessing…"

"That's true," Margery said slowly, "and he may have thought… But you can't think he would have murdered an old man…"

"I don't *want* to think that either of you did. And if you can prove you never showed the document to Mr. Redpath, of course, it weakens his motive—"

"I should think it does!" Margery snorted.

"But the fact remains," pursued Culley doggedly. "You are the only two people who benefited by the death taking place when it did. The only people with reasonable Motives after Christmas in the case. I can't shut my eyes to that fact, now, can I?"

There was a long pause and then Margery drew a deep breath and spoke with what sounded like relief. (Relief?)

"In that case I'd better *not* destroy it," was what she said. Then, looking at the Superintendent with dawning horror: "How awful! I very nearly did. Thank Heavens I was fool enough to go on hoping that there was just a chance we would be able to get away with it; but there isn't, of course—not the faintest. It doesn't matter now. Nothing matters. I'll go and fetch it."

She returned a few moments later with the precious document, which Culley examined minutely. She stood over him, breathing down his neck. When he came to the end she said: "There you are, you see—Esther Hobbs, The Larches, Kilburn; Margery Dore, The Grange, St. Anselms, Nr. Middleswick—that's me. It lets us out beautifully, doesn't it?"

"Eh?" said Culley, startled. "What does it let you out of?"

"The murder, of course. As I said, the document's completely worthless. Doesn't that prove our innocence?"

Culley frowned. "You mean you didn't see him sign—"

"Oh dear," sighed Margery in exasperation, "you *are* being stupid! And I thought that was why you were so anxious to have it. It's completely valueless because *I* witnessed it. And the husband or wife of a witness can't benefit under a will."

Culley did not speak, so Margery went on: "In fact, we lose. Because, if Sir Willoughby had lived, I would have shown the codicil to Mr. Merivale and he would have seen it was properly witnessed. That's why I wasn't worried at the time. I knew it wouldn't work as it stood, but would be all right when Mr. Merivale came. But Sir Willoughby died, so I'm afraid there's no hope now—I've looked it up in all the law-books I can find…"

But Culley was still shaking his head slowly and maddeningly. He had to point out to Miss Dore that what she said was all very nice, but there was nothing to prevent John Redpath from marrying either of the witnesses *after* the signing of the codicil. "He's perfectly free to marry either you *or* Miss Hobbs if he wishes."

"But—" Margery began to object.

"That law would only hold good," Culley told her firmly but kindly, "if you and Mr. Redpath were *already married.*" At which Margery appeared to lose all hope and patience. She returned to the piano stool and said crossly: "But—didn't you say John had told you? I tried to prevent him, but he said he was going to all the same. We *are* already married. That's the whole point. We've been married for over a month, but were keeping it a secret until after Christmas—What on earth's the matter? Have you got a pain?"

No, Culley was only laughing…

XV
Motives for Murder

"So you think that lets them out, eh?" said Major Smythe wearily.

The Chief Constable was not in the best of tempers and wanted to go to bed more than anything. His was a rotten sort of job: if it hadn't been for the war he would never have taken it on. He was too old. He had done quite enough for his country in the last war; it had only been his vanity that had made him feel he ought to be doing something important in this one. Just vanity, that's all it was...sheer self-indulgence! Why couldn't he just go sensibly and unimportantly to bed, instead of sitting up half the night waiting for Culley to come round and report progress, and now sitting and listening to all this twaddle about mince-pies and missing wills? It was too *late*; and he was too old. It wasn't as if there was anything for him to *do*; except worry and take the responsibility for everything. He oughtn't to have let Culley go off staying with those Redpaths, and then careering round the countryside interviewing all the nobs. It wasn't as if *he* was doing anything, either. Dammit, he wasn't an inch nearer solving the case! Hadn't cleared up a damn thing! Just listened to what everybody said, lapping it all up and believing every word of it! Not the way Major Smythe would have tackled a murder case, if anybody had ever allowed him to *do* anything—but no, he was too old, high time he was dead, and he wanted to go to bed...sensibly and unimportantly...more than anything...

He suppressed a yawn. "Eh?" he said, loudly, since Culley appeared to be deaf, amongst other things.

"Let them out? No, sir," replied Culley with maddening reasonableness. "I suppose she might not have found out about the witnessing business until after she had poisoned the old man."

"Murder for Nothing, eh? Good title and a pretty little story. Don't believe it myself, but it doesn't do to believe everything you're told, Culley."

"No, sir."

"And as regards to Motives after Christmas, I think, personally, these disappearing notes are your best line..."

"They've got to be explained, I agree," Culley was kind enough to admit.

"This Redpath aunt, now," Smythe went on. "Something fishy there. Snooping around. You certainly caught her out nicely. But why the devil didn't you question her more?"

"She said the notes and things had disappeared *already*."

"*Said*..." echoed Smythe, too tired to snort.

"And we don't want to stir up a past scandal until we can feel sure it has something to do with the murder. So I thought I'd look about a bit for someone else who might have done a bit of snooping for the same reasons."

Smythe murmured something about all of us being enti-tled to our feelings and to use our own methods of approach, however circuitous they might seem to the lay mind; then he asked patiently: "On to anything?"

Culley brought out his large notebook. "Plenty of motives, sir, but I don't fancy any of them much."

"Well, let's have 'em." Smythe lay back and closed his eyes. He opened them to say, "Something might strike me that you've missed," and shut them again. But his conscience smote him suddenly. Here he was sitting comfortably in front of his own fireside, having done absolutely nothing all day, while poor old Culley had been rushing about listening to other people's chatter about the deceased. What could be more exhausting? Poor chap looked absolutely done in. "Have a drink, man, for Heaven's sake," he ordered irritably, but meaning it kindly.

"Thanks," said Culley, impressed with the idea.

"Now," said Smythe amicably when the glasses were filled. "We'll hear a few of these motives, eh? And try and decide which is the strongest. Right! Fire away!"

"Well, sir," Culley kicked off without further ado, "prac-tically everyone in the house, or at the Christmas party, had some kind of motive for murdering Sir Willoughby Keene-Cotton."

Naturally that went without saying. "Such as—?"

"Mr. John Redpath and his wife had their motives, as we know: money. If you don't think it's plausible enough, how's this? When Miss Dore first arrived the old man was evidently under the impression that he had seen her before—in some hotel or other. Later it turned out, according to Miss Dore's own account, that he hadn't. But *supposing he had.*"

"Eh? Well?"

"Supposing he actually *had* come across her in some hotel, perhaps on the Riviera where he lived mostly, and perhaps *with* someone, but *not* John Redpath."

"Oh, I say—"

"Or—what is to my mind far more likely—she *was* with John Redpath. They may have been passing themselves off as a married couple before they were married—in fact, I'm nearly sure, from what I've heard, that they had—and they wouldn't want their parents to know."

"Parents always do know; and nobody seems to mind about that kind of thing nowadays…"

"Mrs. Dore doesn't seem to be quite that kind of mother; and Sir Willoughby used to know her quite well; he was fond of writing letters—what could be more natural, particularly at Christmas-time, than that he should write her a chatty note, sir, upsetting their little apple-cart?"

"Brilliant, Culley," commended Smythe; "but go on. I'm gettin' rather tired of those two…"

"Then Miss Redpath…"

"Ah!" said Smythe more happily. "But skip her. She'll keep."

"Then the Wortleys."

"Surely not!"

"Oh, yes, sir," Culley assured him. "The Wortleys have been hit by the war like everyone else. Bringing out a war-time weekly and hoping for financial help from Sir Willoughby, but didn't get it."

"So he *loses* by the death."

"Apparently. But was that the real reason why they wanted to meet Sir Willoughby? Mr. Wortley suggested it was the other way about. *Supposing it was?*"

"Oh, Lord!" groaned Smythe. "You mean...?"

"Supposing it was Sir Willoughby who wanted to meet *them*? Because he had seen Howard before and wanted to remember where it was and what it was all about. Same theme again, you see; but fitting in with the Wortleys. An old man with a long but precarious memory might be a great danger to someone with ambitions of becoming a press baron, say. No, I don't think it'll be wasting our time to have his past looked up and find out how he made his money and so forth."

"Credit Clubs," said Smythe after rumbling and grumbling for a minute or two.

"Pardon, sir?"

"Credit Clubs. You know. Midlands and Lancashire. Pernicious system, but not criminal. Don't see how Sir Willoughby could have known about it. Don't suppose he knew there was such a thing. Not his walk of life. Still," Smythe brightened, "old Willie might have had him put in prison. He might even be Miss Redpath's problematic husband. Thought of that, eh?" He mustered a faint gleam.

"Yes, sir. But he's the wrong age. Old lady's well over seventy. Still, it's an idea."

"Don't see how we can use it, though. Pity."

"Now we come to Miss Hobbs," proceeded Culley. "It was she who made me try and think up a case against the Wortleys. She's had the best *opportunity* of anybody, not only for committing the murder, but destroying incriminating papers. She might have been used quite innocently. If not by her uncle and aunt, by someone else."

"So she might. But who?"

"There are the Crosbies."

"You've interviewed *them*?"

"Just returned." Culley paused to drink, then chuckled. Smythe eyed him with disfavour. "I suppose they'd been making jokes about murdering the deceased."

"Quite right, sir. Mrs. Crosbie wanted to write his life, but not until after he was dead. Didn't know he was writing it himself, either. But she told me she would have to kill off Miss Redpath and Mrs. Redpath before the story could be published. She thinks she knows something, but wouldn't tell me what. Personally, I don't see how she can know very much."

"She might," admitted Smythe. "Her father was old Humphrey Gibberd, you know. I remember him well. Always running round after Kate Cameron. But, as I told you, Willie stepped in and conquered."

"That's right, sir. There would be their motive, in fact."

"Where? Don't see that they're serious motives for murder."

"Well, you might look at it like this, sir. The Crosbies have no children, but one strong mutual passion: The Stage. Kate Cameron is something of sacred legend now. From the way the Crosbies went on about her she might be the Virgin Mary, like." Culley coughed apologetically.

Smythe said: "That's true enough. She was a good actress— not a patch on Ellen Terry, of course—but it's not as an actress she's remembered now; it's her personality, her character— erhm, yes, there's no other word for it—her saintliness..."

"So, if anyone was capable of debunking the good lady," Culley boiled it down to, "it would be the man she lost her head and married, wouldn't it, sir?"

Smythe admitted this but could hardly take it seriously. "In that case," he pointed out to Culley (*taking* it seriously), "it gives the Cameron nephew and niece motives for murder, apart from the money. And they've got alibis thousands of miles long and twice as many feet high. Let's get nearer home. Who else?"

Culley searched his notebook, saying: "Now let's see… Besides the Redpaths—"

"We can't have them *again*," Smythe objected plaintively.

"I meant the mother and father."

"So did I—"

"We won't worry about them for the moment, sir; but it did just occur to me that, while *Mrs.* Redpath was very keen to have her stepfather as a glorified evacuee, her husband might not have felt the same about it. Not after Christmas. The extra food he might get them, the social contacts he might indirectly make for them, the fact that he might leave them some money, or buy their son a partnership in some nice safe business—these things wouldn't weigh so much with a nervy sort of chap like Frank Redpath who only saw Sir Willoughby as a permanent and inescapable source of irritation foisted on them for the rest of their lives. While the war was on the old man had nowhere else to go, and they couldn't very well have turned him out at his age—"

"Silly," came from Smythe.

"Possibly," Culley granted; "but both the war and Sir Willoughby looked like going on for ever; and I've often wondered why more murders aren't committed simply to *get rid* of people—"

"For Heaven's sake, man! Get on, get on!"

"Yes, sir," obliged Culley, returning to his notebook. "Lord and Lady Bayham," he found there, apparently to his mild surprise; also: "Mr. and Mrs. Coultard (they live over the Redpaths' garage); Professor Larkin, who lives East Maddle way. But I confess I haven't been able to cook up *their* motives."

"Not even Professor Larkin?"

"He *may* have heard the dead man was making a new will, and he may have believed his University benefited under the current one," conceded Culley; "otherwise he just loses by not being able to touch the deceased for a donation, like most of the others. Possibly he tried harder than most, so wasn't exactly the life and soul of the party in consequence. A dusty old man. Something like talking to a haystack."

"You've interviewed him?"

"I think I've interviewed pretty nearly everybody who was at that party, except—yes, I did jib at calling on His Grace."

"The Bishop! Great Scott!"

"Thought he might not have cared to have his admirable early virtues (as a turf expert and extremely dexterous lady-killer, apparently) published—not in book form, shall we say? Hardly a motive for murder there, though. If so—"

"It lets *me* in, you mean? Yes—well—I think we've enough motives to be going on with. And the fact is, Culley, we haven't really got very far, have we?"

"I'm not feeling discouraged, sir," said Culley.

"You don't think this is a bit of a mare's nest I've let you in for? If so, you'd better be frank about it. If you can't make out a case against the Freers, we'd better let the whole thing drop. Let it go at Accidental Death, eh?"

"As you wish, sir," said Culley politely.

Which appeared to irritate the Chief Constable. "It's nothing to do with what I wish! Pshshshs! But, after all, old Footring is an experienced lawyer and conducted the inquest quite impartially and conscientiously. Gave the jury a perfectly fair view of the case. Didn't gloss over any of the evidence…except, perhaps, those medicine bottles…without them, as he said, there was no real evidence to justify any other verdict." After grumbling for a few inaudible moments, he worked himself up into quite a rage. "And dammit, Culley, we still haven't a shred of real evidence that a murder has been committed at all!"

"I think we have, sir," said Culley soothingly.

"Have we? I haven't noticed it."

"Negative evidence perhaps."

"What's the good of that? We're no nearer finding out how the laudanum came to be administered. You seem to have neglected that line entirely. Until we discover what happened to those bottles we have no business to assume that Sir Willoughby was murdered or not—"

"Ah, but I do happen to know what became of those medicine bottles, sir."

"How can you possibly know?"

"Because I found them."

"What?" Smythe put down his glass. "Good God, why didn't you say so before?"

"I only found them last night."

"Where were they?"

"In the medicine cupboard in the dead man's bathroom."

The Chief Constable was not able to speak for a moment or two; and then he had to turn purple before he did. "You mean to say—they've been in his cupboard *all the time*?"

"Not all the time, sir. They weren't there when I arrived. I remember Mr. John Redpath looking in the cupboard and noticed it was empty. Later I used it myself. Looks as though the bottles were put back some time while I was out yesterday."

"You didn't lock your door?"

"Good thing I didn't, perhaps. Anyway, there are a good many doors in that house, *and* a good many keys to fit them."

"Then—they must have been put back by someone in the house! By the murderer! And it must have been someone who attended the inquest."

"How do you make that out, sir?"

"The point Footring made about the empty medicine bottle. If the murderer wanted to make it seem that Sir Willoughby had died of an overdose of cough-mixture, more than one bottle ought to have been found. They *had* to be found! Culley, that's the reason why you were asked to the house! To find the empty medicine bottles."

"Very likely, sir," admitted Culley placidly; "but, as a matter of fact, they weren't empty—none of them were."

"They were *full*?"

"Unopened. All four of them."

"Oh." Smythe didn't know what to say. This was an unexpected development and most, *most* confusing. If they were unopened it meant—no, it didn't—yes, it did—

"It doesn't prove he was murdered, of course," Culley was saying. (But it did; yes, it did, surely...?) "As I say, sir, it's only negative evidence. Just proves that he didn't die of an overdose of that particular cough-mixture…"

"Then how the devil *did* he swallow the stuff?" Smythe demanded testily.

"That's just what we do keep coming back to, isn't it, sir?" agreed Culley sympathetically.

"Bloody mince-pies…" Smythe got up impatiently and knocked his pipe out into the fender. He put a large piece of wood on the fire and sat down again. "That settles it," he said. "We can't back out of the case now. I don't understand about those bottles—why should the murderer put them back if they hadn't been opened?—however, I leave that to you. Whoever put them back must have *been* in the house, if not actually living in it. Seems to let out the Horsham family, doesn't it?"

"Unless," Culley suggested happily, "one of the Horshams was actually in the house."

"Then Sir Willoughby would have been murdered before Christmas. And I don't see how anybody in the house could be a Horsham… Except the parlourmaid, perhaps—she was only temporary, remember, and Sir Willoughby had never seen her before."

"We've checked her up. She seems perfectly genuine, sir; and, besides, she's too old to fit in with any of the Horsham family."

"And Esther Hobbs is too young, I suppose. But he'd never seen *her* before, either. What's the matter, man? Don't gape at me like that. I can't help bein' a fool, but I'm doing my best. Have another drink?"

"Thank you, sir." Culley blinked and pulled himself

together. He filled up his glass thoughtfully. "I don't know which of us is being the fool, sir; but you've just suggested to me a rather disconcerting idea."

"Good," said Smythe. "Let's hear it."

But Culley shook his head. "I'd rather stick to facts for the moment."

"So would I," said Smythe, but mused: "Keevil and Esther Hobbs...too old and too young... Am I hot?"

"And then there's Margery Dore again; and some people called Uncle Jeff and Aunt Meg, who knew Sir Willoughby quite well, and motored over to lunch on Christmas Day, leaving everybody their best wishes and a lot of parcels on the hall table. *On Christmas Day Sir Willoughby had a nasty cough...*"

"Sorry, Culley, but I'm too tired to be Dr. Watson any more to-night. I'm going to bed. I advise you to do the same. I'm afraid, I'm very much afraid, that now we've found those bottles this murder case isn't going to be so amusin' as we thought."

"You think not, sir?" Culley swilled off his drink and put down his glass.

Smythe rose to speed his parting guest. "Best of luck to your disconcerting ideas about Uncle Jeff and Aunt Meg, but personally I'm afraid we're going to find it was Miss Redpath who poisoned poor old Sir Willoughby."

"In the mince-pies? You think she fits in with all the evidence?"

"Not *all* of it, perhaps. There's so much; and it's all so circumstantial. Somebody's been leading you by the nose, Culley, trying to 'take your mind off the food,' as it were."

"Hardly an apt simile, sir."

"Ha, ha!" acknowledged Culley's now genial host, having piloted his guest as far as the hall. "Well, good night, Culley; and don't let them make a fool of you. Glad I'm not in your shoes. Wish the devil I hadn't let you into this case. She's a nice old lady, and if it hadn't been for you and me the whole thing would have blown over and nobody any the worse off. But there it is. We can't go back now... Why on earth she had to poison him in the middle of the party I can't imagine. She must have known her nephew well enough to realise his reactions. I suppose poor old Willie had begun to babble at the party about her guilty past. Wonder what she *did*? (Is this your torch?) Well, well, old Merivale's coming to-morrow—to see about the funeral—perhaps he'll—*Culley!*"

Superintendent Culley had to shut the front door and come back. "Anything else, sir?"

Smythe stood in the hall, gleaming his eyes. "Yes, Culley— *that's* it! That's *it*—don't you see? *That's* the significance of Mr. Merivale! Nothing to do with a will at all!"

"You mean—?"

"I mean Mr. Merivale would know all about her guilty past—and jog the old man's memory!"

"Why, so he would, sir," admitted Culley handsomely. "Very smart bit of deduction on your part, sir."

"Oh, *damn*," said Smythe. "I wish I hadn't thought of it. Good night."

"Good night, sir."

"Something to do, anyway," thought Culley. "I'll get busy first thing in the morning and clear Miss Redpath out of the story. She's the person the Redpaths have been suspecting, of course. They know she didn't do it, but want me to prove it. Well, I only hope I can. But it doesn't look as though I'm going to be able to prove a darn thing in this case. I shall have to go very carefully, one thing at a time, get things in the right order…the medicine bottles…the mince-pies… the fluctuating appetites of the Redpaths…the poisoned chocolates *not* being poisoned…the body *not* being hidden in the snowman…the Freers *not* being murderers…the missing notes…the temporary parlourmaid and the temporary secretary…Uncle Jeff and Aunt Meg…

"Funny, the old man not knowing his nephew had married his stepdaughter…"

He garaged his car and was presently making his way into the darkened house. Everyone had gone to bed.

He didn't turn on any lights but crept softly up the stairs with his torch.

On the landing he switched out his torch and crept even more softly; for a yellow, ghostly gleam percolated through one of the bedroom doors which was slightly ajar.

He then found, to his surprise, that it was the door of his own room!

He entered, turned on the light, shutting the door after him.

Miss Redpath was in his room, wearing a pink woollen dressing-gown and holding an electric torch.

"Oh! How you startled me!" she said, adding in explanation of her hypersensitiveness: "You came in so quietly."

Culley made due apology. (For catching her in his room!)

"Been looking for another will?" he then asked her affably.

"No, of course not," she replied after polite laughter. "I was just looking for a book."

"A book!"

"Yes. I was reading it a few days ago, but Miss Dore took it and says she can't find it. I'd finished the one I was reading, and I can't sleep unless I have *something*—just to *hold*—and it was such a nice trashy book. Sir Willoughby might have taken it, you see, so I thought you wouldn't mind my just nipping in—since you were out, I mean."

"I hope you've found it?" was all Culley could think of saying.

"No, I'm afraid I haven't. It's really too bad!"

"We'll make an investigation," said Culley amenably. "What was it called?"

"*Murder After Christmas*," said Miss Redpath.

XVI
Murder After Christmas

"Murder," said Culley very clearly into the telephone. "*Murder After Christmas*. No...*murder*... M for mincepies, U for—that's it! No, I don't know who the publishers are, nor who wrote it, but try and get hold of it if you can. Read it; or find someone who has... Daresay not, but I can't afford to neglect *any* clues... No, I can't get over this morning; got Mr. Merivale coming; in fact, he ought to be here now. Good-bye."

He emerged from the small room which contained the communal telephone.

Was this book a further attempt to take his mind off the food, as the Chief Constable put it? Funny, all the same, frowned Culley ferociously; meaning, of course, that it wasn't funny at all—Inspector Carter had no business to be laughing up his sleeve like that.

His enquiries had elicited that Miss Redpath had only read the first chapter before Miss Dore had pinched it and lost it. Miss Dore admitted she had been searching for it spasmodically, but only half-heartedly, as it was the usual drivel, she said. As soon as the piano-tuner turned out not to be the *real* piano-tuner, you knew that his dead body was going to turn up somewhere or other sooner or later, probably in the snowman and presumably after Christmas (why else was there a snowman in the story?), and that he would have been killed by the *artificial* piano-tuner, or the other way round—what did it matter? Meanwhile, whichever piano-tuner wasn't the body was disguised as someone *quite else*, and one of the guests at the party… (Why that young lady bothered to read books, Culley didn't know; she would be better employed writing them.)

Rhoda Redpath remembered the title among the library books imported for family reading over Christmas (it had seemed so appropriate at the time, she said); John had turned up his nose at it, while Frank disclaimed ever having seen it at all but suggested that Uncle Willie would have taken it—not that he ever *read* books, he only dropped them on the floor at regular intervals.

Anyway, where was it? Did it contain a clue to the murder? And had it been removed by one of the guests at the Christmas Tree? Last night Culley thought he had arrived at a fairly idiotic solution of the mystery; but supposing he was wrong and the real solution was even more idiotic than ever? Someone, for instance (Professor Larkin, say, or the Bishop of Mewdley), had *tried* to murder Sir Willoughby at the party, and had *meant* to hide his body in the snowman; but Sir W. was a tough old man and not so easy to murder as one had thought; he had turned the tables on his murderer, changed clothes with him and left him on the lawn dressed as Father Christmas, dead!

In that case the vague old man Culley had interviewed in East Maddle was not Professor Larkin at all but Sir Willoughby Keene-Cotton, still living, and having the laugh on everybody!

Or the Bish—

Well, well! Come, come! Keep your feet on the earth, man; one thing at a time; idiotic solutions would keep. Mr. Merivale was the next item on the programme; Mr. Merivale, who was going to help him settle up with this old aunt who was making the story not so amusin' as the Chief Constable had thought... Mr. Merivale, who would be here at any moment and scurrying about into corners...so Superintendent Culley had better sit down quietly somewhere and sort himself out a bit.

He was not allowed to do so, however.

Mr. Redpath had put his study at Culley's disposal for interviewing Mr. Merivale in, and Culley made up his mind to sit there, going over his notes in cold blood until the lawyer came; but Rhoda Redpath frustrated this intention.

"Is that you, Superintendent Culley? Come in here a moment, will you?"

Culley was obligingly about to join her in the drawing-room, but she frustrated him again. "No, we'd better go upstairs, hadn't we? It's more private."

"As you wish, madam." Culley followed her with some curiosity.

"In here," she said, welcoming him into a small room. "This is where I've been sleeping," she explained, "since my stepfather has been staying here. My husband is next door. All the bedrooms lead out of each other, which makes it rather difficult to arrange one's guests respectably; but this house *was* very old, you see, and they didn't think of that sort of thing in those days. There!"—she turned on a switch—"I must say these electric fires do warm one up quickly, and I always maintain that being warm is a joy you can appreciate however old you are. So sad for people of Paulina's generation, who were brought up to think electric fires in one's bedroom immoral; though of course they didn't have them in her day, did they?—" She paused, but only for breath.

"You wanted to speak to me about something?" Culley nipped in.

"Oh, yes, so I did. It's rather embarrassing; but we *did* ask you here to detect us, so we oughtn't to keep anything from you. It's about Paulina. Miss Redpath."

"Ah…"

"I hope you don't think that she had anything to do with my stepfather's death?"

Culley could only manage to clear his throat at this.

"Yes, I can see you do," said Rhoda commiseratingly. Then, being quite sure she was taking a great load off his mind: "You can take my word for it that she hadn't."

"Thank you," said Culley, displaying the expected relief, but not able to feel that the interview was satisfactorily at an end, any more than Rhoda really could after they had been sitting there immovably for more than a minute.

"Oh dear! I suppose you want me to tell you all about it?"

"As you wish, madam; but I shall be seeing Mr. Merivale in about a quarter of an hour—"

"Yes, naturally," said Rhoda, "that's why I wanted to see you *first*. Mr. Merivale wouldn't know anything about it—only what was thought at the time, which isn't ever quite the same thing, is it?"

"Perhaps not—"

"I can vouch for Paulina, Mr. Culley. I've known her literally all my life. She was my mother's best friend. When my mother married my father, Paulina stayed on as a sort of companion housekeeper and general stand-by. We should have all been lost without her! You mustn't think my father had an affair with her or anything like that. Quite the contrary, if anything—I mean if *anything* he was a little jealous of her affection for my mother, and vice versa; but even that was a relief in a *way*—if it hadn't been for Paulina he might have felt he was neglecting us."

"Yes?"

Rhoda swallowed and proceeded: "And then, when he died, my mother married again as soon as he was free."

"As soon as Sir Willoughby was free?"

"Of course. They had to wait for Kate Cameron to die first."

"Naturally, madam…"

Culley was gazing innocently into the electric fire, but he knew that Mrs. Redpath was watching him, and she knew that he knew.

"It's no use trying to deceive you," she said. "Yes, it's quite true, what you're thinking…" (Culley blinked.) "My mother had been seeing a great deal of Sir Willoughby *before* the death of my father Mr. Hepworth. And they had to be very discreet because of Kate Cameron's reputation. Paulina used to help them. I expect it was she who made up all the lies for them to tell. She always says, you know, that so long as you know what the truth *is*, lying doesn't matter; only the lies you tell to yourself. I think that's so true, don't you?"

But Culley was only able to make murmuring noises.

"Oh, I quite agree," went on Rhoda quickly, "one couldn't have *everybody* thinking like that. People are so self-seeking and unscrupulous. But Paulina was always devoted to us all. It was *us*—the people she loved—who meant more to her than her own conscience or anything; people like that are so rare; such a pity! She's really rather wonderful. She *likes* very nearly *everybody*, and that must be why nearly everybody likes her. So she never feels she's wasted her life, or ought to have got married or anything, and it would have been a waste if she had, really—for everyone else, I mean."

"She's never been engaged or anything?" prompted Culley gently.

"She *was* engaged to one of my father's secretaries. Cecil Hargrove his name was. Fortunately he was not at all a nice man and it never came to anything. That's what I was going to tell you about. He tried to blackmail her, you see."

"Pardon, madam?"

"He tried to blackmail her. Cecil Hargrove did. About my mother and Sir Willoughby, of course. Because of Kate Cameron the faintest hint of a scandal would have been *most undesirable*; and he knew that. Paulina was very young at the time and it must have been a great shock to her, and she doesn't like having to talk about it; although, oddly enough, the episode seems to have strengthened her faith in human nature more than otherwise, in spite of the way my mother and Uncle Willie behaved at the time. 'As you sow, so shall you reap,' she always says; and Cecil certainly doesn't deserve one's pity at all."

"Sir Willoughby got him put in prison?" Culley

asked—apologetically, in case she might think him over-preoccupied with the facts of the case.

"They got Cecil on the wrong side of the law. I can't tell you how they did it, I'm afraid. I was too young then to know anything about it, but my dear old mother was never at a loss for ideas, and Sir Willoughby was cunning—"

"And rich!"

"Money *does* give one power," Rhoda conceded him the relevance of this side of the matter; "we were *all* very rich in those days, so we were luckily able to get Paulina's young man under lock and key."

"I see. What happened then?"

"Oh, that's all. When he came out of prison Uncle Willie had him emigrated somewhere—I don't know where, but I should think he's dead by now; anyway, we've never had any further trouble from him."

A bell rang and she rose. "There's Mr. Merivale! How lucky! He does time his entrances so beautifully! Well, now that I've cleared Paulina's character, I don't mind what he tells you. And you mustn't forget, Mr. Culley, that he's over eighty now. He *must* be!"

Which seemed even harder to believe than ever this morning. He came plunging into the hall, with a snowdrift having fallen on him while he was waiting in the porch. He had also been shot at in the drive, he announced chattily. Bad shot, though; and he had given the young devil a good hiding. "Evacuees. Bored stiff. Can't blame 'em. Blame the war. Give 'em toy guns, tell 'em they're in the Home Guard, shoot at sight, what can you expect, what will they all grow up like, thank God I shall be dead then—well, I won't waste your time, Chief Constable sent me along, bad business, tragedy after all these years, can't we hush it up, suppose not."

He blew, disrobed and Culley hurried him into the study (in case he got shot at again—you can't be too careful).

"Well, Mr. Merivale, it's like this," Culley explained firmly, "I'm not exactly suspecting anyone of murder at the moment; I'm just trying to eliminate as much as possible first."

"Don't think you need eliminate any further," said Mr. Merivale, stumbling into an armchair by the fire and warming his hands with enjoyment. "Ha! Only question now is—can we get her off? I'm sanguine. Yes, I think so. Plenty of money. Brief Marshall Hall—oh, no, he's dead, damn, forgot."

Culley opened his notebook and ejaculated prefatorially: "Well, now that—since you—as it's—whether we" and other conjunctions and unattached pronouns in vain.

Mr. Merivale was continuing, professionally speaking: "Insanity's the *obvious* line. Know a private asylum. Happy there. Better than Broadmoor. Defeatism, perhaps. Think we can do better, if we put our heads together, eh? Murder after Christmas! So that's the solution. *Said* it had nothing to do with the money. Expect you're glad the case is over. Should be, in your place!" Hearty laughter.

In the midst of which Culley had time to interject: "The case isn't over by any means, sir." But he had to say it twice before he was heard.

"Trial, of course," said Mr. Merivale. "Wonder if she will live through it? Better if she didn't, perhaps. Oughtn't to say that to a policeman, I suppose. Want to get 'em strung up, eh? Rotten job yours, prefer my own—"

Culley wheedled hastily, averting another gust of laughter:

"Perhaps you can give me a few facts, Mr. Merivale. I've been working in the dark, you understand; and I've nothing to go on but surmise and deductions from my own observations."

"Of course not." Mr. Merivale scoffed at the idea of anyone knowing any facts except an experienced lawyer. "Clear case, though. Tell you all about it. That's why I'm here. Facts, not theories. It was all strictly within the law; shouldn't have known anything about it if it hadn't been. But the law's elastic. And between you and me, Culley, there's such a thing as graft, even in England, even in those days. Keep within the letter of the law, and you can get away with anything. Could have had her jugged, of course, but managed to prove the fellow put her up to it. Daresay he did, too," Mr. Merivale appended conscientiously, reviewing the episode and finding it mellowed with time; then hoiking his thoughts sternly back to present realities. "However, that won't help her now, will it?"

Culley asked, while Mr. Merivale was getting out his handkerchief to blow his nose sadly: "What was it exactly that this Mr. Hargrove put her up to?"

Mr. Merivale, handkerchief poised, raised the skin on his forehead, positively crinkling his bald head. "You don't know? Why, she stole a whole lot of the late Kate Cameron's gew-gaws from Mrs. Redpath's mother! In it together. *He* was jugged, but, as I say, we got *her* off scott free. Keene-Cottons kept her on ever since. Dunno why."

"Very possibly," ventured Culley, "they felt under an obligation to her?"

"For making off with the family plate? Surely not!"

"I've heard that Miss Redpath was being blackmailed."

"Eh?"

"About something which would have involved Sir Willoughby, and more particularly his late wife, in a scandal." Merivale shook his head. "Never heard a word about *that*."

Culley reminded him: "If they were in some fix, sir, they might not have wanted you to know. Even if it *was* within the letter of the law."

"Pity. Could have got 'em out of it. Must have been something worse than a fix. Yes—smart of you to twig—explains everything! Poor woman—what did I say?—misplaced loyalty, victim of circumstances, more sinned against than sinning, absolutely in his power, do anything he told her, no choice in the matter, no feelings of her own, bottled them up all these years, getting on now, well over seventy, must be, something snapped at last, a wonder it hasn't before, thought she was safe down here, sleepy little village, no one knows her, loved and respected, but old man finds her out, her one surviving source of danger, too bad, had to kill him, stick at nothing, murder the only way out, murder after Christmas, phew, yes, I see the whole thing so clearly, but we can't let her off, her first murder may not be her last, what a tragedy it all is, good God what's that?" He sat up with a gasp.

It was a knock at the door.

Culley, who had locked it to avoid interruptions, was now not ungrateful for one; so he got up and opened it.

Miss Redpath was standing outside.

"Oh," she remarked pleasantly, "have you and Mr. Merivale been having a private conversation? You mustn't let me interrupt you—" She elbowed her way past him into the room, all the same, giving him no choice in the matter. "Good morning, Mr. Merivale," she said to the aged lawyer, who rose politely but gibbering faintly to himself. "Now, now," she told him severely, seating herself in the chair behind Frank's desk where Culley had been officiating, "no more whispering!" She came upon Culley's notebook, virtuously refrained from looking through it and handed it to him politely. "Please sit down," she invited, reproving them gently: "Secrets are not allowed, you know—except at Christmas."

XVII
Secrets at Christmas

Superintendent Culley seated himself obediently. But Mr. Merivale was found to be sidling stealthily round the room towards the door. "Just off," he explained briskly on catching Miss Redpath's eye; "getting late, lot to do…"

"Oh, please stay, Mr. Merivale," Miss Redpath entreated; "we may need your advice."

Mr. Merivale pirouetted impotently. "Quite so, lawyer present, always at your disposal, put our heads together, something can be done, leave it to me, never despair…"

A faint movement of Culley's head brought him to a standstill. "Better stay and listen to anything the lady has to tell us," Culley suggested reasonably.

Mr. Merivale returned rather unhappily to his chair by the fire.

"By all means, by all means, if you say so. But if I may advise you, Miss Redpath, I should say nothing. You are under no legal obligation to volunteer any statement to the police. Anything you say will naturally be—"

"No question of that just yet," came from Culley brusquely without moving his lips. "But since you *are* here, madam, I'd like to get one or two points cleared up."

"But of course," said Paulina Redpath. "I was upstairs in my room when I saw Mr. Merivale's car drive up." She turned to him, explaining: "I was putting on my things to go out. I was going to ask you to come and see me first when all that snow fell on top of you! So startling. I felt quite guilty for not warning you in time. Then I heard the Superintendent come out of Rhoda's room. I worried and *worried*, Mr. Culley—my conscience wouldn't give me any peace! As a matter of fact, I've been *rather* worried for a long time, really—ever since Sir Willoughby was murdered, in fact, I've had to keep it all to myself, you see; there was absolutely no one I could tell, no one at all. Secrets like that are so much worse when you can't share them, aren't they? I knew, naturally, that I would have to speak in the end. For Rhoda's sake, and because of the Horsham family. Though I tried to delude myself that it might never be necessary, after all. What I did *had* to be done. According to the law"—she favoured Mr. Merivale with a roguish glance—"I am sure it was very wicked indeed, but there was no other way out at the time. Now it's different. The truth must come out in the end, so why not *now*? Why *not*, after all? It was a shame, I thought, not to put poor Mr. Culley out of his misery. He's been working *so* hard on the case, Mr. Merivale, and deserves a rest. So I took off *all* my things again and just popped in to see how you two men were getting on."

"That was very kind of you, madam," said Culley.

"You see, I know lawyers," explained Miss Redpath. "My Uncle Godwin, poor Father's brother, was such a busy country solicitor and doing *so* well; then he had to sell his practice and live on the coast. He was a martyr to nervous dyspepsia and died three years later—from a duodenal ulcer, they said. But it was worry that killed him. Even after he had retired he couldn't relax. Their minds are like that. Lawyers, I mean; and it grows on them. They won't come out into the open and face things, they simply scurry into dark, dusty corners and worry round in circles. Try and pull them out of one corner, and they're so frightened and defenceless that they hurry into another as quickly as possible! It shocks them dreadfully to find that life is so simple, really, and that human beings have loves and hates that may not necessarily be guided by strictly legal rights and wrongs." Satisfied by Mr. Merivale's facial expression that he agreed with her in this matter, she turned once more to Culley. "And you, too, have to write everything down and weigh the evidence. 'How did poor Sir Willoughby come to be poisoned?' It seems quite inexplicable, doesn't it? 'And who benefited by Sir Willoughby dying after Christmas?' Nobody! On the other hand, it was the best thing that could happen, wasn't it, Mr. Merivale? If the money had all gone to his wife, I mean, and through her to the Horsham family, the fortune would have disappeared and nobody else, with perhaps more moral right to it, would have seen a penny of it. 'Who else had motives for murder after Christmas?' I know for a fact, Mr. Merivale, that Superintendent Culley's been round in his car and interviewed every *single* person at our party. He hasn't *spared* himself! But I don't suppose he's found a single person with a real motive for murdering such a harmless old man." She gave one of her grunts and chuckled amiably. "Apart from his money," she went on, "one really can't visualise *anybody* wishing him dead." Her eyes alighted on the murderous knife which lay on Frank's desk. She picked it up and felt the point absently. Mr. Merivale stirred uneasily. "It's so hard to think of poor old Sir Willoughby as being a menace to anyone and having to be 'silenced,' as they say in detective stories. One wouldn't believe it possible in real life, would one?" With the knife grasped in her hand, she turned to Mr. Merivale, who screamed.

Then, turning his scream into a cough, he managed to reply courteously: "No, no, one wouldn't, certainly not"... and moistened his lips (Superintendent Culley appeared to have fallen asleep, dammit).

"No," Miss Redpath went on; "and to do him justice, I don't think he himself ever realised what a danger he was. His memory was going, you see. He was trying so hard to remember the truth, but I think he died without remembering. For that we must all try to feel thankful. Next day his lawyer was coming to draft a new will and he might have been *obliged* to remember."

She put down the knife, and Culley appeared to have woken up slightly; but to be on the safe side Mr. Merivale was edging towards the bell, murmuring "Quite so"...

"If he had lived until you came, Mr. Merivale, everything would have been quite all right."

"...yes, yes, quite so, quite so..."

"What's that, madam?" said Culley, waking up entirely. Mr. Merivale, in the act of ringing, withdrew his finger suddenly as though the bell-push had stung him—"Eh?"

"But of *course*," said Paulina to the lawyer; "you and I together could have told him the truth. We could have put our heads together. It would have come so much better from you. As a matter of fact, I thought I had managed to convince him of the situation; but after that fall he had he seemed to get so strange in his mind and I could never get a word with him at all—to find out what he was doing about it, I mean."

"You thought he might be taking some kind of action in the matter, madam?" Culley asked very patiently.

"Oh, I hoped so!"

"You—?" Mr. Merivale boggled and gave it up.

"It was all arranged so pleasantly, I thought. He was going to amend his will—oh, it was arranged *long* before the Freers came—making provision for Rhoda and John; if only, I said, to avoid an ugly scandal which it might be my duty to make known—"

"You threatened him," ejaculated Mr. Merivale, seeing the light, "you—good God—threatened to expose a scandal about *him* if he didn't leave some money to Mrs. Redpath!"

"I did put it something like that," admitted Paulina; "it seemed the only way of making him take the matter seriously. But you can't say I threatened him, that's not fair. I wouldn't have given him away. Indeed, it was most undesirable that the truth should ever been known. He saw that too. But you can't keep a secret unless you know what it is, can you?"

"If you know what the truth is, you know what lies to tell, in fact," murmured Culley.

"Exactly." Miss Redpath applauded this lucid way of expressing it. "Sir Willoughby was getting so old and hazy. He might have told the truth simply because he couldn't think of anything else to say."

"Like Miss Hobbs," thought Culley. Aloud he said: "Please go on, Miss Redpath; we're waiting to hear what the truth is."

"Of course," said Paulina. "You don't know. As soon as Sir Willoughby died intestate I realised that I would no longer be able to keep the secret. Dear Rhoda, you see, is his next of kin."

There was a bewildered silence which she broke by pointing out: "So, of course, all the money comes to her automatically."

Mr. Merivale began: "My dear Miss Redpath, I don't see how—" but Superintendent Culley quelled him impatiently. He smoothed out his notebook, sighed stoically and said: "Well, go on, Miss Redpath. Let's get it all down as quickly as possible. I take it that *Sir Willoughby* was actually Mrs. Redpath's father—*not* Mr. Hepworth. Is that right?"

"I'm so afraid you won't think it a very pretty story," murmured Miss Redpath doubtfully. "Dear Rhoda herself has never heard it, of course."

"She was never told?"

"It would hardly have been suitable for her to know. She was brought up to believe that Mr. Hepworth was her father."

"Did Mr. Hepworth believe that?"

"I hardly think so," said Paulina. "He was a self-made man, rather vain and sentimental. He married mainly for social reasons. His marriage was not a—hrm—reality, if you know what I mean; he was always far too busy; a man of affairs; and kept everything separate."

"When you say affairs, madam, you mean—"

"Yes, he had those too. But he'd always wanted to marry Beryl—*marry* her, I mean—as she would have made him such a suitable wife in every way; but it wasn't until the baby that she—she found he was only too pleased to make an honest woman of her! Hrm. Very naughty. But her people never knew about Sir Willoughby and had always wanted her to marry Mr. Hepworth-—he was such a catch—so she did. I couldn't blame her."

Culley hadn't time to go blaming anybody, either.

Being scandalised was left entirely to Mr. Merivale, who presently managed to say: "And Sir Willoughby went off and married Kate Cameron of all people!"

"Such a tempting thing to do," said Paulina; "so hard for a young man to resist. *She* got what she wanted; Mr. Hepworth got what he wanted. Everyone was happy. There seemed no reason for publishing the truth."

"Should think not!" Mr. Merivale gasped. "Truth, indeed!—Kate Cameron!—Heavens above!"

"Perhaps the truth would *not* have seemed relevant at the time." Culley saw her point of view cautiously. "Sir Willoughby and Beryl Hepworth, though, remained on friendly terms, I understand? That was a little unwise?"

"*Very* unwise," Miss Redpath agreed warmly. "But they were only human, after all, and had always been *so* devoted to each other."

"Hm! Funny sort of way of behaving. Can hardly believe it, even now."

"They were very, *very* discreet. If it hadn't been for Mr. Hargrove…"

"How did *he* find out about it, I wonder?"

"I'm afraid I was foolish enough to trust him with my confidence. He seemed so nice and such a trustworthy secretary. So very loyal, I thought—but he was paid to be, of course; I soon realised that."

"Paid by Mr. Hepworth; later on by Mrs. Hepworth; and after that by Sir Willoughby Keene-Cotton into the bargain! He must, in fact, have found loyalty a very lucrative profession!"

"Well, of all the—! What a—! Well I'm—!" Mr. Merivale was heard to be exploding (impotently).

"He's dead now," Paulina reminded him soothingly.

"Surely—surely—*surely*," cried Mr. Merivale, having murmured his way into comparative coherency, "he was making enough money out of—no bones about it—*blackmail*—"

"—to find it unnecessary to force you into collaborating with him in a series of robberies," Culley came to his assistance.

"He never did," said Miss Redpath gently but clearly.

"Certainly he did," Mr. Merivale contradicted her flatly. "Nasty mess, got you out of it, remember all about it distinctly, might be yesterday—"

"No." It was Miss Redpath's duty to clear up all misapprehensions now that the conversation had taken this turn. "That was all poor Beryl's idea. Such a very, *very* dirty trick, but so clever! Really, you know, as I quite saw at the time, there was nothing else to be done. The law provided no acceptable way of dealing with blackmailers in those days. Beryl just gave me the jewellery two or three times a week; I simply sold it and gave Cecil the money. Then she made Sir Willoughby put the police on my track; they followed me from one pawnbroker to another, I remember; and I took care to wear something very bright, so as to make it easy for them. Oh dear, and it was *such* hot weather just then! *So* exhausting! Beryl said it was so exciting and I ought to be grateful for the experience; but it was *I* who had to do all the really tiring part—I could never make her see *that*. When I was caught, I just burst into tears and gave the game away. That part was easy. I said Cecil had been blackmailing me and I was at my wits' end to get the money. Sir Willoughby went to Mr. Merivale, who was simply wonderful; Cecil went to prison and nothing ever came out!"

"Well!" Mr. Merivale was dumbfounded. "Put-up job, pack of lies, swallowed every word of it, more fool me—"

"What we told you was perfectly true," Paulina returned sweetly; "it was you who made up all the lies."

Culley thought perhaps it was time to intervene again. "All this happened after Sir Willoughby had married Beryl Hepworth; and they continued to pass off Mrs. Redpath—Rhoda Hepworth—as their stepdaughter—"

"Yes."

"When actually she was their own daughter."

"Naturally they couldn't suddenly tell everybody that."

"Not then, no. Perhaps not. But *now*…" After pursing his lips, tapping his teeth, and frowning at the ceiling he asked Mr. Merivale: "*Does* that make her the next of kin?"

Mr. Merivale jumped and began grumbling reluctantly something about being born out of wedlock and the Law of Legitimacy, and having to *prove* something or other…

These grumblings, overheard by Paulina, appeared to give her a rude shock. "Mr. Merivale," she said in great concern, "I hope I haven't suggested—no, no, there'll be no need to try and prove that dear Rhoda is *illegitimate*. Oh dear, I didn't mean to suggest *that*!"

"Can't have it both ways, miss," pointed out Culley mildly.

"Should you wish to withdraw your statement—" began Mr. Merivale, cheering up a little.

"But it isn't true!" Paulina became quite hot and bothered.

"I'm afraid I must have let you think we were all making a fuss about nothing. Of course, if Rhoda had been illegitimate it wouldn't have mattered at all. How silly! No wonder you're both laughing at me!"

Which was far from being the case, although both of their mouths were wide open.

"An illegitimate daughter," she explained to them, "could have been adopted legally and everything would have been quite all right. People might have talked," she admitted, "but so long as both the parents were respectably married in the end there could have been no real scandal. It would have been a most natural, indeed common, situation; and you, Mr. Merivale, would have known all about it. But dear me, no, I'm afraid it *wasn't* like that." She perspired with horror.

"No?" "Oh?" (The queries floated on the air without apparently being actually spoken by anybody.)

"I'm afraid, you see," Miss Redpath said, "that poor dear Rhoda was their *legitimate* daughter."

"Leg—" began Mr. Merivale and stuck.

"—itimate," finished Culley and wrote it down.

"That was the real scandal." Paulina paused, feeling it was superfluous to tell them any more, but very kindly did so in the end: "Kate Cameron's marriage to Sir Willoughby was bigamous, of course; and so was Beryl's marriage to Mr. Hepworth. It's dreadful to think of, even now. It was all because of their parents opposing the match. *Beryl and Sir Willoughby were secretly married for over a year* before Miss Cameron and Mr. Hepworth came into their lives at all."

"I see," said Culley; "and they married again afterwards." During a throttled "Good God" from Mr. Merivale, he wrote it all down. "Then it's like this, madam," he summed up, putting in a full-stop. "When Sir Willoughby first arrived here—and kept getting his wives in the wrong order—"

"He really got them in the *right* order," said Miss Redpath. "And it was *you* who kept muddling them up again."

"I *had* to," said Miss Redpath.

"We're getting on," said Culley.

XVIII
Parcels at Christmas

"Well?"

"Case turned upside down, sir. Wasn't the old man who knew the old lady's guilty secret, but the other way round."

"So she didn't do it," finished Smythe.

Silence in the Chief Constable's office.

Superintendent Culley cleared his throat diffidently.

Major Smythe waved his hand irritably. "All right, all right. You needn't apologise. You don't suppose I *like* sending maiden ladies to the gallows, do you?"

"No, no, sir." Culley fluttered the pages of his notebook and fiddled about with a large envelope.

"Only too pleased, of course," mumbled Smythe. "But all the same, Culley, if you come into this room again and tell me that anyone else didn't do the murder—well, I shall either shelve the case or call in Scotland Yard."

"That's quite all right, sir," said Culley, not taking offence.

"It's *not* all right. You've been messing about, then comin' here and tellin' me a lot of damn-fool theories, and you're no nearer solving the mystery than you were a week ago. Now are you?" he asked, imploring his subordinate to face the facts.

"Found out one thing now," his subordinate told him meekly.

"Wonderful!" Major Smythe applauded; but his sarcasm was short-lived.

"Found out where all Sir Willoughby's money goes now that he's died intestate."

"You've found out *that*? Then why on earth didn't you tell me?"

"I am telling you, sir."

"All right, all right. Go on; break it gently; next of kin, I suppose. What's that?"

"Marriage certificate."

Culley, who had extracted a faded document from his large envelope, now placed it under the Chief Constable's very nose. While Smythe was looking for his tortoise-shell spectacles, Culley attempted to summarise the situation: "Mrs. Redpath is his daughter, not his stepdaughter. Bigamy. Second wife really his third wife who was actually his first wife."

Major Smythe, having just found his tortoise-shell spectacles, immediately dropped them on the floor. "Oh, no, Culley, *please*," he entreated.

"It's quite simple, really, sir."

"Is it?"

"Married the same woman twice."

"I didn't know that was bigamy."

"Both of them committed bigamy in between like."

"How awful. Now do keep quiet a moment…" He came to the surface with his spectacles, put them on and perused the document with silent concentration. It was some time before he could trust himself to words. Then he said: "He married his second wife first, his first wife second, then his first—I mean his *first second* wife—third!"

"You've got it, sir!" cried Culley.

"*Have* I? Have I *really*? Yes, I believe I have. And that makes his third wife his fourth wife, doesn't it? Or doesn't it? No, of course it doesn't, how could it?"

"Why not, sir?"

"Because there were only three of them all told."

"Only three *wives*, sir, yes; but he actually got married four times."

"Yes, I see," said Major Smythe hastily. "So he did; yes, of course." He went on, taking things in gradually: "Rhoda Redpath…! You say she's his daughter? How do we make that out? Doesn't say anything about her in this thing. No… nothing…"

"Well, hardly, sir. She wasn't born till after her mother had bigamously married Mr. Hepworth, in any case."

"But old Willie was her father all the time! No wonder she was so fond of the old man and wanted him to stay for the last years of his life! Blood thicker than water, eh? And she's kept the marriage certificate all these years! How did she come to get hold of it, I wonder?"

"It wasn't Mrs. Redpath I got it from, sir; it was *Miss* Redpath." Culley gave Smythe a synopsis of Paulina's life story which the Chief Constable approved and annotated from his own personal memories of Sir Willoughby, ending: "Sounds absolutely typical of the Redpath woman, too. Explains *her* all right. I suppose that was why she went snooping into his room?"

"That's right. Half-truth in the wrong hands might have caused a lot of mischief. And it wasn't necessary for the whole truth to come out just then, either."

"But it's got to come out now, eh? Explains a lot, doesn't it? Pity she couldn't have told you all this before; it would have saved you a lot of careering about. It was Miss Redpath who destroyed those notes all the time, of course."

"No, sir, I think she was telling me the truth. They had been destroyed already."

"By someone else? Mrs. Redpath?"

Culley shook his head. "You'd be surprised if you knew *why* those notes were destroyed, sir." He chuckled.

"Would I?" Smythe looked at him with distaste. "Then you'd better not tell me; I'm quite surprised enough already. So all that money goes to Rhoda Redpath! I must say I'm glad about that. She's a very nice woman. She won't keep it all to herself like the Horshams; nor scatter it about at random like old thingummy. So that settles the money side of the mystery, eh?"

But Superintendent Culley appeared to say nothing rather noticeably.

"*Eh*?" repeated Smythe more loudly.

"Knocks everyone else's motive on the head from the money angle, sir?" Culley found his tongue. "Well, yes, in a way, I suppose it does."

"Everyone else..." echoed Smythe. "Culley! You can't think that *she*—! Did she *know* she was his next of kin?"

"Says not. Not until I told her. Says she didn't know of Lady Keene-Cotton's death, either, until Miss Redpath produced that telegram."

"There you are!" said Smythe.

"Yes, sir," said Culley.

"You think she was lying?" asked Smythe.

"No, I *thought* she was speaking the truth," replied Culley.

"That leaves her husband, of course," said Smythe dubiously and reluctantly. "He *might* have found out, I suppose. It was he who destroyed those notes, perhaps?"

"Ah, perhaps he did," agreed Culley promptly, looking stuffed.

Smythe regarded him suspiciously, but went on viewing things impartially. "He's clever, you know, and might have got the whole story out of his aunt. All the same, I still can't think of Frank Redpath as a cold-blooded murderer."

"Oh, no, sir. Mr. Redpath wouldn't deliberately and cold-bloodedly plan a murder, sir…"

"I'm glad you agree with me about that, Culley," said Smythe, but found himself wanting to be a little gladder.

"He was too busy, by the looks of it, planning that Christmas Tree and treasure-hunt to go worrying about murdering anybody, wasn't he, sir?"

"That's truer than you know. You can take it from me that if either of those two had conceivably planned to do in poor old Willie (which is *quite* unthinkable) they would *not* have done it in the middle of their party. I'm not saying that to defend them, but because I know it's true. From the social point of view that party meant as much to Rhoda Redpath as it did to her husband, who revels in that kind of thing almost to a point of madness. Look at the trouble he took planning out that treasure-hunt!"

"I am looking at it, sir. Took a bit of planning, I expect. Needed brains."

Smythe looked up sharply. "Eh? You don't think there was anything sinister behind that treasure-hunt, surely?"

Culley replied mildly: "The dead body of an old man was lying out on the lawn half the time and Frank Redpath, on his own admission, knew it! No one guessed anything was amiss from his manner at the party. That's a *little* sinister, you know, sir."

"It's absolutely consistent and typical," dismissed Smythe, "and proves what I've been saying."

"Yes, sir, of course it does," agreed Culley thoughtfully. "And he didn't know that Sir Willoughby had been murdered then, did he?"

"Even if he had known, I don't suppose he would have stopped the party."

"If he had known that a murder was *going* to be committed, say—do you think he would have *put off* the party, sir?"

"Here—what are you getting at, Culley?"

"I'm trying to get at his psychology, sir—that's all. You know better than I do how people like the Redpaths would behave."

Smythe plumed himself, slightly mollified. "Mmmm… Daresay I can help you there, yes. If Frank Redpath knew that his father-in-law was going to be murdered at the party, of course he would have put it off. But how could he possibly have known? Unless—" he broke off. Then he said: "You're not trying to tell me that the murder had anything to *do* with the party? That—no, really, Culley—Frank Redpath planned the treasure-hunt to account for Sir Willoughby's sudden death?"

"You said something like that yourself, sir. After the inquest."

"I said it was a well-known trick to confess to a small crime to cover up a large—"

"Plant a forest to hide a leaf," Culley continued for him, since he appeared stuck; "declare a war to explain one dead body…"

"Absolute tosh!" Smythe came unstuck. "Shades of Father Brown! Clever, Culley, but you can't make it fit—not with Frank Redpath."

"Can't I, sir?"

"No! Conceal a corpse for the sake of a party, perhaps. In fact, that's what he did. But the other way round—plan a party to conceal a corpse—! Absolutely out of the question! *Entirely* out of character!"

"Well, you should know, sir…"

"Certainly I know. And so do you. You said yourself that Frank Redpath wouldn't plan a murder in cold blood."

"I'm not suggesting that he did, sir; I suggested, if you remember, that he might have known that the murder was *already planned*—and carried on with the party just the same…"

"Already planned…?" echoed Smythe blankly.

"That's all I'm trying to get at, sir," Culley told him cheerfully. "The murder was planned; but it was meant to take effect *before* Christmas, like you said. Somebody left him some poisoned chocolates, say, like we thought at first. It struck me at the time that we were a bit stupid about those parcels. Nobody who knew Sir Willoughby would count on his not opening his Christmas presents till Christmas, particularly if they were chocolates, however clearly they were marked 'Not to be opened till Christmas Day'. Of course they counted on his opening them at once and gobbling off all the best ones—the Almond Whirls, perhaps. But they didn't know that Frank Redpath had arranged a treasure-hunt and was in point of fact hiding all the parcels, making it *impossible* for him to open them until Boxing Day. And, of course, they didn't know that Lady Keene-Cotton was going to die on Christmas Day…"

"The Freers!" ejaculated Smythe. "Did *they* know about the treasure-hunt?"

"I've been under the impression that they did."

"Oh!"

"But it didn't seem to me important at the time, so I may be wrong."

"Yes, yes. Go on, go on. Wait a moment! Frank Redpath was in London when the Freers came—"

"But when he came back, sir, all the parcels disappeared from the hall table. All of them! Now we come to the curious fact that no *poisoned* chocolates were found. According to Mr. Redpath's own vague account, the Freers' chocolates were eaten by the dead man on Christmas Day, so the ones he ate could *not* have been poisoned, or he would not have been alive at the party. The Almond Whirl from the snowman lot was eaten by Mr. Redpath himself. But so far, sir, we've been assuming that Mr. Redpath was speaking the truth. *Supposing he's been lying all along?* It makes everything much simpler, doesn't it? He could have arranged the chocolates however he liked, and if he knew one particular lot was poisoned he would have taken care to substitute an innocent box after the death."

"I don't really *quite* see all that," complained Smythe.

"Surely, while he was about it, he could have arranged for the death not to take place in the middle of the party?"

"Ah, but you can't have everything, sir. He couldn't force poisoned chocolates down the old man's throat."

"Really!" intervened Smythe, pained.

"All he could make sure of was that Sir Willoughby Keene-Cotton should not be murdered until *after the death of his wife.*"

"No, no!" pleaded Smythe. "Culley, really, please! Anyway, how on earth could Frank Redpath know *when* Lady Keene-Cotton was going to die?"

"He couldn't know that," conceded Culley. "But, on the evidence it must have been obvious that she couldn't last very long. If she hadn't died on Christmas Day, all he had to do was to hang on to the chocolates and put back the time of the murder till she did!"

"No, Culley, you mustn't. You mustn't really. All this is nonsense, and you know it. It's murder, Culley—you're accusing Frank Redpath of murder…"

"But not *his* murder, sir. That makes a difference, doesn't it? No possible blame could attach to him. It need not have troubled his conscience very much, either. Indeed, far from murdering his father-in-law, he was, in fact, *saving* him from being murdered. For a few hours; perhaps days; say a week at the most. As soon as that telegram came on Boxing Day—"

"Which was suppressed by the aunt," cried Smythe, clutching at this straw. "You're forgetting that, Culley."

"No, I'm not, sir. *You're* forgetting that wires are mostly phoned through these days. The one the aunt kept was what is known as the 'confirmation.'"

Losing his straw, Smythe allowed himself to drown for a few minutes.

Coming up for the third time, he pointed out reasonably, keeping his head well above the water, that it was all conjecture; why couldn't all that have simply *happened*; just as he had said: the murder had been meant to take place before Christmas, but had gone wrong.

"I only wanted to know if you thought it could have been *meant* to go wrong, sir," said Culley.

"No, I *don't* think it could," replied Smythe firmly.

Culley sighed. "Pity. It seemed to me the perfect crime."

"Too perfect for this world," diagnosed Smythe. "Most people aren't as clever as you are, Culley."

"You said Frank Redpath was clever. And he struck me as being an intelligent gentleman who hasn't had much scope for showing his brains off till now."

"That's quite true, I suppose. But he's too intelligent to commit a murder at all."

"Well, there you are, sir; he *didn't* commit it!"

Smythe groaned.

"The most perfect crimes," Culley diagnosed, "are those which aren't committed at all. You see, the stumbling-block of this case, all the time, has been to prove how and why Sir Willoughby was murdered *after* Christmas. Well, *you* say he couldn't have been; while *I've* had to try and find out how he *could* have been. For it can't have 'just happened' like you said unless the Redpaths had a hand in it."

"Still don't see why not," complained Smythe obstinately.

"No? And I thought I'd made that so clear!" Culley concealed his disappointment. "Think of it this way then, sir," he said kindly: "If the time of the murder was just chance, and not deliberately manoeuvred in some way like what I've said—what *have* the Redpath family been up to?"

"Oh, something damn silly, I expect!" Smythe spoke with harassed impatience. "Certainly not all that horrible drivel you've been tellin' me. Can't you really think of anything else?"

"Well, yes, sir. I can. In fact, I thought I'd hit upon a solution of the mystery that night I came round to your place—after what you said about Keevil—remember? I would have finished off the whole case then and there that very night—if only I could have been sure of one fact."

"And what was that one fact?" asked Smythe with a gleam of interest.

"The fact that I hadn't gone completely balmy," Culley told him.

"Oh," said Smythe; "and had you?"

Culley shook his head. "Don't think so. But I decided to sleep on it. My theory, you see, would have accounted for everything—if only it could have happened at all; and, now after what you've just told me to-day, sir, I think it could. But next morning this new money element came cropping it; and that sent me right off the mark again."

"Oh, is *that* what it was!" Smythe was grateful for the information. "Well, I hope you're satisfied now that the Redpaths would be incapable of planning a cold-blooded crime to get hold of an old man's money."

"Yes, I'm satisfied enough now, sir. But I'd like to prove it."

"Quite so," agreed Smythe soberly. "Yes, I'm with you there. Been a lot of talk going on. More than ever now that they look like cleaning up all the Keene-Cotton fortune. Only to be expected."

"Not only that," pointed out Culley, "but according to the law a criminal may not benefit from a crime; so we'd like to prove that they haven't committed a crime, wouldn't we, sir?"

"By all means. Yes, yes, I agree. Now you're talking, Culley—have a cigar?"

"No, I can't wait now, sir. Thank you for being so patient. Now that I've got the psychology of the Redpaths, I can get busy and tidy up all the circumstantial evidence. Solidify it like, sir, and fix it all together in its proper place and right order."

"*All* of it?"

"Yes, it all fits in now all right. Like a crossword puzzle—a good one; once all the words are down you know there can't be any other solution. The medicine bottles; the Christmas parcels; the snowman; the book called *Murder After Christmas*; the missing notes in the dead man's handwriting; Miss Redpath being a vegetarian and an economical guest, always saving up something of her own for the birds; Mr. and Mrs. Redpath not caring what they ate so long as there was plenty of it, but suddenly going off their food at Christmas, which should be a time for over-eating; Sir Willoughby never sending nothing down; no waste going on in that house, wasting food being a crime in war-time; Mr. Howard Wortley not being a pacifist—"

"Won't you *really* have a cigar, Culley..."

"The butler being on a holiday; Keevil being only temporary and not minding what she said, like she should; Esther Hobbs being busy and impersonal; Margery Dore; Uncle Jeff and Aunt Meg; Professor Larkin; the Bishop of Mewdley; the Crosbies living at High Winds up the Hill; the Coultards in the stables—"

"Did they *all* do it…?" wondered Smythe, unheeded.

"The cat in the cupboard; the turkey under the floor-boards; two pieces of cardboard seasonally edged with holly leaves; the parcels, more and more Christmas parcels, hanging from the ceiling; the mince-pies sewn up in the armchair; the mince-pies that were sent up in case he felt like it; the mince-pies in the ventilator; the mince-pies he so eagerly ate at the party; the mince-pies—"

"No, no," stemmed Smythe; "that's enough mince-pies."

"The mince-pies he ate *before* Christmas," Culley insisted on finishing with.

"I really don't see why you need bother about *those*…"

"The mince-pies before Christmas, sir? But they're the most important of the lot!"

"Oh?"

"Barring the ones he ate at the party."

"Ah!"

"And the ones he never ate at all. See you after the funeral, sir, if I'm back in time."

"Eh?"

But Culley was gone.

XIX
Mince-Pies
Before Christmas

I

JOHN AND MARGERY BURST INTO THE WARM DRAWING-room. John flung himself into a deep armchair, while Margery sat on the fender. "Now we can giggle in comfort," said John.

"I don't want to laugh any more," announced Margery with surprise. "What is there funny about a funeral, after all?"

"Nothing whatever," replied John. "Hysteria."

"It was mostly Esther's face that made me want to laugh. She *has* got a funny face, hasn't she? Sort of surprised and defiant. What was she doing at the funeral, anyway?"

"Representing the Wortleys, perhaps."

"And I suppose Major Smythe was representing the police."

"Superintendent Culley having the good taste to keep away."

"I wonder where he is?" said Margery.

"He's probably behind that screen," said John; "so be careful what you say, my loveliest."

"We've nothing to hide any more now," Margery reminded him.

"Speak for yourself," John retorted. "Now that Aunt Paulina has spilt the beans and Mother swipes the money we're all under suspicion; only question is who knew what, and which of us actually did the foul deed."

"The police aren't really still searching for a murderer?"

"How else do you account for Smythe's face?"

"I don't see how anyone *could* account for that," Margery answered.

"Now you've started me off again," said John, hooting in comfort, continuing, whenever he had the breath: "Angelina Freer thought she'd made a conquest. Kept showing him her favourite profile! Puffy looked puffier than ever. Query: Was it guilt, jealousy, or an assumed brow of woe for the occasion?"

"I wonder if they did it," said Margery.

"It seems pretty awful," said John, gratefully sobered; "but we've got to hope that they did."

"Is it really as bad as that?"

"Pretty much. Smythe won't be happy till he's avenged the death of his old friend; or at least jugged somebody for something. And of course he'd rather it was the Freers, too. Poor devils! But I don't think he feels too sure of them. He was popping out his eyes at *us* most of the time...hoping to catch us with triumphant, gloating expressions. It's so difficult *not* to look like a successful murderer at a funeral."

"Yes, *isn't* it?" said Margery.

"I had to keep telling Father to look *sad*, not fierce. Then I had to prevent him from whistling nonchalantly whenever Smythe looked at him. Poor Father! Such a responsibility!"

"And I thought Major Smythe just wasn't feeling very well!" said Margery as Sills came in with a tray.

"Baked meats!" cried John. "Come on, let's go to the pictures!"

"You will kindly remain in this room," ordered Major Smythe sternly, having entered in the wake of the butler.

"Why?" asked John.

"Mr. Merivale has particularly asked me to see that as many of the family are present as possible."

"What on earth for?" asked John.

"He's going to read the will."

"But there isn't any will."

"He's going to read it whether there is one or not," retorted Major Smythe cleverly. He sat down and began to fill his pipe, making himself quite at home.

Esther Hobbs, the vanguard of a large crowd, came in, looking not quite so funny and rather bewildered, so Margery took her into a quiet corner.

"Oh, hullo, everybody," said Angelina, elegantly attired in black, and peering about her through a boldly unfashionable cobweb hanging from her hat halfway over her face (which made her look more like a lady burglar than a murderess, John decided, as she advanced upon him); "I do know you, don't I? Is that your father over there? I knew he would be like that from your mother. Wives do give their husbands away, don't they? Is it true she gets all the money, or is it a rumour?"

"I'm afraid I—er—don't know, exactly," said John.

"I shouldn't have asked. But I've never been to a gathering of vultures before. The suspense is going to be terrible,

I should think; so, if there's nothing doing, it would be a kindness to put us out of our misery and we'll go away..."

"I believe Mr. Merivale wants as many of the family as possible to stay and—hear about something—or something," John told her, making the best of his hearsay knowledge.

"Oh," said Angelina, disembarrassing herself of her veil and taking in the details of her surroundings for the first time. "Are all these people members of the family? I'd no idea Uncle Willoughby had such a large one! But sit down, Puffy, some of them are sure to turn out to born on the wrong side of the blanket—"

"Ssshh! Dear!" said Puffy.

"—or go away as soon as they've had tea; or something. Is that the Duke of Windsor?"

"No," said John, "that's Father."

"But you said—then who's the other one? The one with the pipe?"

"Major Smythe. He's our Chief Constable."

"Ah, yes... What a good thing he isn't the Prime Minister, or he might *stay* like that. A bishop! What next! And here's something *quite* new...good gracious, whatever *can* it be?" Fascinated, her eyes followed the quavering form of Mr. Merivale as it pranced dramatically over to the fireplace to warm itself. "Surely, surely, surely..." she murmured incredulously, then, turning with enlightenment to her husband: "Surely that must be the deceased, Puffy, look!"

"Quiet, Angy," commanded Puffy, perspiring, "not so loud!"

She accepted a light for her cigarette from John. "Now I want to hear all about the murder," she told him in more confidential tones. "Or wasn't it one, after all? Such a nice

Superintendent came to see us. He seemed to think there was something fishy about the death, and that Puffy and me were the most suspicious characters, and, really you know, I *quite* saw that we were—"

"It was only because of having to have an inquest," John assured her hastily, feeling very uncomfortable.

"Then he wasn't poisoned at all?"

"Yes, but he took an overdose of cough-mixture, or something. The verdict was Accidental Death…"

"Yes, I know," said Angelina; "but we thought that was just to put us off our guard, and that, as soon as he'd got enough evidence, he was coming back to arrest us."

"Oh, no," said John scoffingly, "nothing like that!"

"Then why has he just come into the room?" asked Angelina, stiffening warily. "He can't be a vulture, surely? No! Puffy, he's looking for *us*; I can almost hear the handcuffs jingling!"

"Rotten business, a sudden death in the house," remarked Puffy sympathetically. "Lot of formalities and police enquiries—no respect for private feelings—er—I wonder what the fellow wants now?"

"He's staying with us," explained John.

"Oh, I see! Just a friend." Puffy gave a short laugh at his own stupidity. "So he hasn't really been investigating the case officially at all? Just a few discreet private enquiries among the family for the sake of the inquest."

"That's all," said John hastily as Culley bore down upon them.

"Very decent fellow, I thought," murmured Puffy. Angelina decided that the time had now come to powder her nose.

"How do you do, Mrs. Freer," said Superintendent Culley, now upon them. "Sorry I couldn't be at the funeral, but I've only just got back from Borrowfield."

Angelina's bag rolled from her grasp and fell to the floor, bursting open in all directions.

II

John helped her to replace the contents.

"Been to Borrowfield?" said Puffy feebly. "Good spot!"

"And you found us out and had to come all the way back!" commiserated Angelina with apology.

"Found us out!" laughed Puffy pleasantly. "That's good! Ha, ha!"

"Did you think we'd fled—flitted, I mean?" asked Angelina.

"No, no," began Culley.

"Now you've run us to earth, eh? Funeral and all that. All open and above-board what?"

"Yes, yes," soothed Culley. "I hoped to find you here. I only went to Borrowfield to have another talk with Nurse Hastings. Thought she might still be there."

"What a pity," said Angelina. "You ought to have rung up or something. She only stayed for the funeral."

"Never mind, madam. I found out what I wanted."

"Good."

Culley found himself a chair and sat down, stretching out his legs comfortably. He explained how tired he was, proving himself only human, and made his speech about staying with the Redpaths to clear up loose ends. "Given me a twisting, this case has," he confided, since people were always so anxious to feel sorry for him, and he didn't mind if they were. "We've found out, you see, that the late Sir Willoughby could not have died from an overdose of cough-mixture, even if he had swilled off the contents of that empty bottle at one go!"

"How *difficult* for you," Angelina felt for him. "So I suppose you've had to search the house for more empty bottles."

"That's just it, madam; but when we found them they weren't empty! Seems he must have swallowed the poison some other way. That's meant checking up all his Christmas presents in case someone thought to poison him that way."

"Good gracious! You'll never be able to do that," said Angelina, pale at the mere thought (of such a Herculean task, wondered John?).

"Don't envy you your job, Superintendent," stated Puffy, turning all the colours of the rainbow except green (which proved that he didn't, John thought).

"I've done it," said Culley, and rested on his laurels for a few moments. Then he went on: "You and your husband, madam, left him some parcels when you came over. One was from your mother—a box of chocolates. You didn't know that your mother had sent him some chocolates already?"

"No, I'm sure she didn't. She was far too ill to see about her Christmas presents," she reminded him reproachfully.

"But, according to your sister-in-law, Lady Keene-Cotton sent off a lot of parcels *before* she was taken funny, some time before Christmas. And we know one was a box of chocolates for Sir Willoughby because he wrote and thanked her for them. That was when he wrote asking her to Four Corners for Christmas."

"Oh, Verna!" dismissed Angelina. "I don't see how *she*

could know anything about it, and the letter doesn't prove anything; the old man was very muddle-headed—he probably *thought* they were from her, that's all."

"Exactly," said Culley with a slight pounce. "They *might* not have been from her at all."

"They certainly might not. And, in any case, they can't have been poisoned, so what does it matter?"

"Why can't they have been poisoned?"

"Why? Because—because—why, yes, of course! Because, if they had been, *he would have been already dead*."

Game and set, thought John.

So did Superintendent Culley; but he was a good loser. "That's very true, madam. If he ate them he would have been dead when you came down to see him. And he *must* have ate them or we would have found them by now. Well, thank you very much. I'm glad we've cleared up that point. I won't worry you any more now."

Angelina inclined her head graciously and Culley was about to retreat ingloriously when John spoke.

He pointed out encouragingly: "There are still some mince-pies, you know. You haven't forgotten them?"

"Which mince-pies?" asked Culley innocently.

"Ah, that's just it."

"That, as you say, sir, is just it." He was about to retreat again but thought of something and turned to Mr. Freer. "Oh, by the way, sir; did you know that Mr. Redpath was going to hide your parcels until Christmas?"

"Suspected something of the sort," Puffy replied easily. "Some sort of treasure-hunt or something. Mrs. Doings was talking about it while Angy was up with the old man."

"Funny, Sir Willoughby not remembering you had married his stepdaughter, sir; and not asking to see you?"

"Frankly, I was rather relieved…"

"But he must have known your name, particularly if he was giving you an allowance. But he hadn't met you personally, perhaps?"

"Not for donkey's years, anyway."

"He'd never met *you* before at all, madam?"

"No, but he seemed to have got hold of a very flattering photograph of me from somewhere. I did my best to live up to it."

"You weren't either of you at his—*last*—er—wedding?"

"Wasn't in England," said Puffy.

"And I couldn't make it," said Angelina.

"Thank you," said Culley, really departing now.

"I'd give a lot to know what all *that* was about," said Angelina. "He can't think we're impostors, surely?"

"No, of course not," said John.

III

The crowd in the drawing-room thinned. Culley had been ambling unobtrusively in and out of it, apparently without aim. Nobody knew who he was, except those whom he had already officially interviewed, and he steered clear of *them*. The Bishop of Mewdley accepted him as a mutual friend of the deceased, and Superintendent Culley, who, like Miss Margery Dore, could always be anyone at a moment's notice, or no one at all if no one was wanted, listened effectively to Fickle Freddie's epitaph on Wilful Willie; how death could have held no terrors for him; that old age itself was just a part to be played; "the aged pantaloon, yes…and so he died in the midst of make-believe, with the laughter of children in his ears and so life goes on," he finished impatiently, having made this speech five or six times already and his wife was waiting in the hall to wrap him up and take him home.

Superintendent Culley then removed himself from the doorway to facilitate the departure of two more aged guests in sombre mourning but pink and smiling. "My mother's youngest brother and his wife," Rhoda felt trapped into introducing them as. "Jeff, dear, this is Mr. Culley I was telling you about who's been such a help to us with everything."

"I'm afraid it's How-do-you-do and Good-bye," said the pink, smiling lady sadly and turning out to be Aunt Meg, logically speaking.

"Beastly weather, hey?" from Uncle Jeff.

Sir Willoughby Keene-Cotton had figured largely in their lives in the old days and it was so sad they hadn't seen him on Christmas Day, as he remembered things which no one else did; but he must have been a sicker man than we all thought and better dead, from his point of view—though, of course, we shall all miss him terribly. "He had a good innings," said Uncle Jeff. "Yes, a good innings," agreed Aunt Meg, which gave them both a good exit.

Culley had a few words with Margery and Esther in their corner and heard about someone called Cornelia Hastings whom the dead man had mixed the former up with, and how the latter had been kept so busy reading the paper to him, taking dictation, and typing out his autobiography that he hadn't had time to mix her up with anyone, she was glad to say…

During which prattle the drawing-room had become

depleted of all supernumerary characters, leaving the Freers, marooned in their corner with John, and Paulina, conversing high and dry with Major Smythe. Frank and Rhoda were still seeing people off in the hall; and Mr. Merivale, who had taken up a strong position in the middle of the room behind a small table, and had been blowing on his hands and clearing his throat and looking at his watch for some time, was asked by the Chief Constable to wait for the return of his host and hostess before doing whatever it was he was going to do.

The door opened and Mr. Merivale said "Ah!" excitedly… but it was only Sills coming in with some early-morning tea on a tray for Paulina (knowing as she didn't drink sherry nor anything. Oh, how very kind and thoughtful of you, Sills!)

Mr. Merivale was disgusted. Despairing of ever being able to read a will, he decided that the time had now come to make his own, so removed himself to a warmer and less noticeable corner of the room apparently to do so and die in peace.

Smythe, still quite at home, accepted some whisky from Sills and asked him affably how he had enjoyed his holiday.

Sills replied that, what with the war and everything, Christmas had passed off very adequately.

The company were given, at Major Smythe's instigation, character sketches of Sills's family, their ages, ambitions, and present war-time preoccupations. Smythe was insincerely astonished at each piece of information—particularly at the fact that Sills had a grown-up family. "Always thought of you as a young fellow who ought to have been called up long ago."

"Oh, no, sir," replied Sills, flattered (for he prided himself on his youthful figure and *mountains* of black, wavy hair). "I'm fifty-two, sir."

Smythe raised his eyebrows extremely high. Angelina was frankly bored. Mr. Merivale was now at death's door.

"Eh, Culley? What do you think of that?" said Major Smythe, under the impression that he was breaking down all social barriers and putting everyone at their ease. "How old are *you*?"

But Culley wasn't going to give himself away that much. He embarked, however, upon an animated conversation with Sills, continuing even after Frank and Rhoda had returned. (Mr. Merivale being now dead, there was no one to stop him.)

Imperceptibly he led Sills on to the topic of the late Sir Willoughby Keene-Cotton, unobtrusively bringing out his notebook.

"Let me see now," he was presently saying, "you went for your holiday—when?"

"It would be on the twenty-second of December, sir," Sills confided.

Culley squinted at his notebook. "So it was you who served dinner on the twenty-first—the day of the mince-pies? The mince-pies *before* Christmas?" He squinted at Major Smythe, but squinted back quickly.

"Yes, sir," said Sills woodenly.

"Did everybody at dinner have mince-pies? Or was it only Sir Willoughby?"

Sills didn't quite know how to reply. "Miss Redpath mentioned something about them being unlucky," he ventured at last; "so nobody had any except Sir Willoughby. He wasn't a gentleman to be put off his food so easy, being quite unsuspicious in these matters." Sills paused, wondering if he had said too much.

"Unsuspicious," savoured Culley. "It was only *after* dinner, then, that he became suspicious?"

"What *do* you mean, Mr. Culley?" asked Paulina quite anxiously.

"As to that, sir, I can't say." Sills could not have given his personal opinion, even if it had been his place to do so. "I didn't see Sir Willoughby again," he pointed out, "and next morning early I went off on my holiday."

"Exactly," said Culley. "*Next morning you went off on your holiday!*"

"I hope you don't think, sir, that I—"

But Culley ignored him and shut his notebook with a snap. He said to Major Smythe: "That dinner was the last meal Sir Willoughby ever had. Those mince-pies were the last things he ever ate. Almost immediately afterwards he began to feel queer. Swore he had swallowed the threepenny-bit. Went out into the garden to die—"

Frank Redpath had risen apprehensively, but Superintendent Culley confronted him mercilessly: "And he did die, didn't he, sir?"

XX
Snow at Christmas

FRANK SAT DOWN AGAIN, ABRUPTLY. "SO YOU'VE guessed it!" was all he said.

"Ha," said Culley good-humouredly, bringing out his notebook again, but only to caress it affectionately, apparently. "Thought that was it! Yes, I've got it all fitted in now, sir. *That* was when Sir Willoughby died," he told the gaping assembly, "*Before* Christmas! On the evening of the twenty-first of December. Immediately after eating those mince-pies. Mince-pies *before* Christmas. So you were quite right, Miss Redpath," he made magnanimous acknowledgements where they were due. "The mince-pies were unlucky. Fatally unlucky."

"I hope you don't think that I—" Paulina began, but Rhoda had hurried to her side, protecting her from all accusations, and, anyway, Sills had just said that.

And, besides, her gentle voice could not have been heard, for Major Smythe spluttered: "My dear Culley—" and sought assistance from Mr. Merivale, who merely rose from the dead to squeak: "What, what, what did he say, wasn't listening, missed it all, damn..." and John broke in with: "Gosh, what an idiot I've been!" and stared at his father, who said: "Quite so."

"But I don't understand," came Angelina's undrownable voice plaintively. "What's happened? Who's dead now? Who else *is* there?"

Her large brown eyes sought each baffled face in turn. Nobody, however, seemed able to enlighten her except Superintendent Culley, and he waited for the hubbub to subside, then repeated for her benefit: "Sir Willoughby Keene-Cotton, madam, died on December the twenty-first."

"But—how *could* he have?"

"Nonsense, of course," Major Smythe muttered in apology.

"Drunk," explained Mr. Merivale for her ears alone.

"But surely, sir," Culley insisted respectfully to the Chief Constable, "that's been the most obvious explanation all along? He'd never seen Mrs. Freer before and he didn't see Mr. Freer at all. Mr. John Redpath suggested the interesting theory that they might be a couple of impostors" (John perspired), "but I didn't see how that could be so at the time; any more than I saw how Keevil could be one of the Horsham family like *you* said, sir" (Major Smythe blushed). "It wasn't until you pointed out, sir, that Sir Willoughby *hadn't seen Miss Hobbs before, either,* that I began to get the sense of it. That made three of them—not counting Miss Margery Dore—" ("What?" said Margery.) "—three women he had never seen before! No wonder I felt I was going balmy. After that I just had to try and believe it."

"And did you?" asked Major Smythe politely.

"No, sir; I couldn't somehow believe it until I had got it all fitted in and the facts confirmed. And now I have. I got the last bit of confirmation just now. Early on the morning of the twenty-second of December the butler departed and a temporary parlourmaid arrived—Keevil! And that, to my own deductions leastways, must have been the beginning and end of the whole idea. It would be Keevil who brought up his meals; she would be always in and out of his room; and, if he had never seen her before, it was almost certain that *she* had never seen *him* before, either! So far, so good. She had unimpeachable references. And, being only temporary, she had nothing to gain by telling lies, and no more she did. But, to make it even better, next day Miss Hobbs was engaged, who had never seen him before, either, and was to act as chief witness to the fact that he was still alive."

It was Margery who broke the silence. "But he *was* still alive," she said. "*I* saw him."

"You saw him, yes," admitted Culley. "But, if you remember, as soon as you arrived you stated positively that you had never seen Sir Willoughby before, even if he thought he had met *you* somewhere. That being so, it simplified matters even more. You could see as much of him as you liked—because it wasn't him at all."

"Then who was it?"

"Me," said Frank demurely.

Margery stared at him, trying to take it in.

(Idiot, idiot, idiot, groaned John.)

Culley reverted to Angelina. "So you see, madam, it was Mr. Frank Redpath you saw that day. That was why he made you sit in the light, remaining himself in the shade. Mr. Redpath didn't know *who* you had married. He only knew that Sir Willoughby had always been curious to meet you and would have told him if he had. But, because he knew that you had both lived on the Riviera, and particularly after his wife found out that your husband was born in South Africa, they decided to keep Mr. Freer downstairs to be on the safe side."

Angelina was unable to cope.

Culley went on musingly: "So your stepfather couldn't have made a new will in your favour or anyone else's. But Mr. Merivale was sent for; and that's why the death had apparently to take place immediately after the party—"

"Great Scott! Utterly impossible! Don't believe a word of it!" burst from Mr. Merivale.

"No, I don't *quite* see how you worked it, Father, even if Mother was in it too..." John felt abashed by Culley's superior professional deductions. "Do you really think they could have got away with it?" he asked in wonder. "It's not as if Uncle Willie was in his room all the time—that would have been easy—yes, but it *might* have looked fishy—"

Culley pulled him out of his bog of doubt with: "He actually only came out of his room on two occasions, sir. On the first of these you and Miss Redpath were out. You were the only two people in the house who knew him by sight; except for the cook, who never saw him, and the housemaid, who always did his room when he was in the bath. Easy for Mr. or Mrs. Redpath to get into the bathroom for a few minutes and splash about, just as your father managed to nip up and cough a bit while your uncle and aunt were in the drawing-room."

"Yes, Father could have done all *that*," agreed John, waving it aside as unimportant. "If it's only a question of being *nippy*, no one could be nippier...but..."

Margery came to his assistance, joining in his objections: "But, when Sir Willoughby came down that day, he went prancing into the study *where Mr. Redpath was writing out clues for the treasure-hunt*—"

"Oh, that's an old trick," scoffed John. "*I* could do *that*! What a lovely witness you are, darling! But *I* saw him, Superintendent Culley—oh, no, I only saw Father dressed up as Santa Claus. That explains everything, of course. Explains why he and Father avoided each other too. Very clever. And at the party Uncle Willie could meet people who knew him quite well—if he was dressed as Father Christmas; particularly as he was exactly *like* Father Christmas, even on dry land! And I never guessed it! It all seems so painfully obvious now. I suppose I'm too intelligent to think of anything so silly," he finished, consoling himself.

"That's right, sir. We were both a bit too suspicious to suspect the truth. Even after I had found all that food scattered about I didn't get on to what had been happening."

"It was Mother who sewed up those mince-pies!"

"Yes, dear," said Rhoda. She swallowed and hurried into explanations: "You see, we had to eat all Uncle Willie's meals as well as our own. It was rather—*much*, although we did our best. He always had such a hearty appetite, remember, dear, and Paulina, being a vegetarian, didn't help us at *all*!"

"And we couldn't risk putting him on a sudden invalid diet," chimed Frank; "partly because it might have looked suspicious, but mostly because of the mince-pies he had for dinner before he died. He ate so many that I wasn't surprised that he choked him."

"I don't get this point about the mince-pies," complained John. "*Were* they poisoned?"

"It was in case of an autopsy, wasn't it, sir?" Culley said to Frank. "You didn't know he had been poisoned by anybody, but you were always afraid that, when he did die, it would be through dosing himself once too often, and that the divisional surgeon might think to have him opened up, him not being attended by a regular doctor and there having to be an inquest probably. So when you staged his death he had to have *just eaten as many mince-pies* as on the day he *really* died." He turned to John: "That's the point about the pies, sir." And to Smythe: "So the evidence of the organs, sir, was just as circumstantial as all the rest was!"

"Well I'm blessed!" said Smythe.

"Then they weren't poisoned at all?" said Angelina, sounding both annoyed and disappointed. "What a shame!" Her husband did his best to console her.

"Course not!" Culley told her cheerfully. "And the other ones, sir," he told Major Smythe, who showed signs of growing bored—"the ones he didn't eat at all—and which Mr. and Mrs. Redpath didn't somehow fancy—"

"Didn't somehow fancy!" came in groaning echo from Frank and Rhoda.

Culley broke off with momentary compassion, but hardened his heart and said: "Christmas being a time for over-eating, and Sir Willoughby ordering so many things in extra and not being in the habit of sending anything down" (they groaned again), "you had to put away even more than you bargained for, perhaps. And it wasn't only Christmas, either; it's *war-time*; and wasting food is a serious matter; you didn't dare send too much back to the kitchen, nor throw it away anywhere that it might be found."

"Yes, he does seem to have guessed everything," remarked Frank.

"And it was you who put back those medicine bottles, wasn't it, sir?"

"Well, naturally. You could hardly expect me to poison myself with all his drugs on top of everything else."

"Why didn't you empty them, sir?"

"Eh?" But the answer to this proved easier than he thought: "Because I didn't want you to arrest me for murder, of course."

"Perhaps we can let that pass for the moment," Culley said; and he had to, in any case, because Major Smythe suddenly flipped his fingers and slapped himself for a fool.

"Of course! That's why you were chuckling over those confounded notes. They had to be destroyed because they weren't in his handwriting."

"Quite right, sir," applauded Culley.

Smythe beamed, then pulled himself up sharply. "The whole thing's the most outrageous piece of—of—irreverent buffoonery I've ever come across. Never in my life—nobody— *nobody* in their senses could *think* of such a pointless, callous, puerile scheme—far less carry it out—no one but Frank Redpath," he finished rudely, goaded with indignation.

"Well, no one but Mr. Redpath and his wife *did* think of it, sir," pointed out Culley.

"I don't believe it!" shouted Smythe. "They've been pulling your legs, Culley. They asked you here to detect their nonsense, and you *have* detected it. I'm surprised at you, really I am! I shall never trust you with a murder case again. How you have had the cheek to sit there and talk all that drivel beats me. Good heavens, man, pull yourself together! Can't you see your whole theory falls down the moment you look into it? It's not even *physically* possible. I know what I'm talkin' about. To hide a body for a few hours so as not to spoil a party—well, that's quite another thing, and perfectly possible, I agree—"

"And that's just what we did," put in Frank mildly; "only instead of being for a few hours it was a few days—"

"Days!" snorted the Chief Constable. "Well, there you are. Just what I say. It couldn't have been done—for obvious reasons."

"No," confessed John unwillingly, "I don't quite see how you could have concealed a corpse for *days*, Father; not unless you put it in the refrig—"

His father interrupted him with the admission: "Concealing the body *was* the most difficult part. But then it always is, isn't it?" Without waiting for any sympathetic murmurs of agreement, without even really expecting any, he went on: "We didn't want it to turn up too soon, you see. That would have spoilt everything. However, so long as Uncle Willie appeared alive and well, who on earth would go hunting for his dead body? There would be no question of his being dead at all until after Christmas, and the snow was so deep it would be sure to last till then, even if a thaw set in at once."

"The snow," murmured John. "Yes, I see."

"We did think of the refrigerator first of all; but that was, of course, before we had decided to do it seriously. After the first shock of finding him lying dead and cold on the lawn that night, my immediate thoughts naturally were, 'Why couldn't he have waited until after Christmas?'"

"Naturally. They would be," agreed John.

"Such a fuss we'd had arranging our party. He'd asked a lot

of people, and we'd asked a great many more because they wanted to meet him and we wanted to meet some of *them*. And he himself had spent so much money, had so many bright ideas and was so looking forward to dressing up as Father Christmas, and we were so looking forward to being surprised when he did, it was such a tragedy to think that he never *would*, and that the party would never take place now… *He* would be more disappointed than anybody if we had to put it off—if that's any consolation to Major Smythe…" But he had hardly hoped it would be. He continued, however: "When actors die, the play goes on with an understudy and nobody is shocked at all. Hitler himself may be dead ten times over for all we know, but the war still goes on with his deputies and doubles, and nobody thinks it bad taste. Uncle Willie told us that at Queen Victoria's Diamond Jubilee the Queen herself very wisely stayed in bed that day and it was the one from Madame Tussaud's in her carriage sitting on a spring to make her bow. A Princess whom Uncle Willie knew for a fact had died on the morning of the Royal Garden Party (or it may have been the Trooping of the Colours) was quietly kept on ice that day to die with better discretion on the morning after. That sort of thing was often done, dear Uncle Willie assured us, so why shouldn't we do it to him? His wonderful spirit had departed from his aged body, so what did it matter about his mortal clay? He was only enamoured of his own flesh and blood as a vehicle for remaining in this silly world; but now that he had gone to a better one (for he can hardly have found a worse)—"

"Can't listen to all this twaddle," muttered Major Smythe; so Rhoda had a shot. "It was Uncle Willie who really gave us the idea," she said. "The dead bodies in the Russo-Finnish war—on the wireless, I mean—*last* time he was here—he wouldn't let Frank turn it off—and even when it was over he couldn't keep off the subject of bodies frozen stiff in the snow—Captain Scott, you know—and he told us he had nearly gone on an Arctic expedition, which went off without him in the end, and never came back. He said he wished he *had* gone now; because they had died in the flower of manhood, 'at the height of their ambitions and enthusiasms,' he said, and if anybody took the trouble to look for their bodies they would find well-preserved young men in the twenties although some of them were very nearly ninety by now. That's what he said," she ended apologetically, not really feeling she had been very helpful; but she must have been, for Culley turned to Smythe and said, "You see, sir? This exceptionally cold weather only had to last a bit, and the body could have been preserved like it was when it died."

Smythe grumbled that it was all right, he could believe anything now; and Frank hurried to the defence of Rhoda. "My wife," he said, "didn't *like* the idea, of course. In fact, I didn't take it seriously myself until I went into the house to look for Sills and realised he was going off early next day. That seemed such an extraordinarily happy coincidence that we began to plan the whole thing seriously. The people who were coming to the party were only going to see him dressed up as Father Christmas, and, as I have already pointed out, one Father Christmas is very like another. Hardly any of them had ever seen him before, and those who had only knew him as an old man with whiskers that looked as though they came out of a cracker in any case. So, instead of guarding an empty room, which *might* have looked suspicious, as John said, we decided to let him be seen by as many people as possible. The rest could be done with circumstantial evidence and mass-hypnotism. I've always had a talent for that sort of thing—for taking people in, I mean—although I have never been any use as an actor on the stage. If you make a study of professional actors you will find that, contrary to the conventions of fiction, these two talents are entirely separate. My wife, for instance, can't act at all in a *play*, but she's a really wonderful liar in real life, which few professional actresses are; they invariably act too well and give themselves away. The more natural you seem on the stage, the more artificial you have to be—eh, Margery?"

"How clever of you," appreciated Margery. "No one knows what agony it is!"

"*I* know," said Frank, "because I've tried. I never got over to an audience, I had to have *real people* to deceive. Being Uncle Willie would be easy, but it was no use my doing it if no one was looking. Keevil wasn't enough. Making noises in his room, swishing and rustling in the bathroom for the benefit of Edith wasn't enough, either; so we engaged Esther Hobbs, who couldn't have been more perfect for the purpose. She was a little short-sighted and wore spectacles out of doors and at the pictures, but *not* for secretarial work and playing cards. When I first met her I realised she was the sort of young woman who, given a job of work to do, concentrated her whole mind on it and was in consequence dead to her surroundings. Also she's very conscientious, honest, and quite incapable of deception: genuinely deceive *her*, I thought, and she'll genuinely deceive everybody else. As for young Margery, she was too busy deceiving me to wonder if I was deceiving her!" He chuckled.

"To think that it was you all the time," Margery lamented. "It seems such a waste!"

"Not at all," Frank consoled her. "I appreciated far more than poor old Uncle Willie would have."

"I can't imagine why I didn't *smell* something," Margery kicked herself—"grease-paint, I mean."

"Didn't risk grease-paint, my dear. Just took off my toupé, whitened my hair round the edges, and the rest was whiskers. If you had smelt spirit-gum—well, there was a large bottle on the dressing-table which Uncle Willie was going to use for his Father Christmas beard, and he left the cork out sometimes. Secrets are allowed at Christmas," he told the assembly, "which gave us a lot of latitude; so I needn't go into any more details. The whole thing needed very careful working out and timing, but it wasn't really difficult. We had to be careful that neither Keevil nor Esther nor Margery should see the body of the real Uncle Willie, of course, but that passed off all right. Paulina discovered the body. Paulina was really the most difficult part—even worse than having to eat all that food—"

"Surely not?" said John.

"It was easy enough having a huff with you," his father told him; "and not being on speaking terms with myself was child's play; but anyone who has ever tried to quarrel with Aunt Paulina will realise what uphill work it was."

"You really upset me very much," Paulina reprimanded him mildly. "I thought I really had upset poor Sir Willoughby about his will. Why couldn't you have told me all about it?"

"Because if we had, you wouldn't let us do it," replied Frank with candour.

"Well, *me* then," said John; "you might have taken me into your confidence, Father. I could have helped you a lot."

"Perhaps that's what we were afraid of…"

"Oh, no, darling, it wasn't so much that," intercepted Rhoda pacifically. "Your father and I decided—didn't we, Frank?—that if we had to deceive *you* it would prevent us from getting careless over details."

"All right," agreed Frank amiably, "so we did. We felt that if we could deceive you, dear boy, we could deceive anybody."

John was greatly consoled by all this.

"If you had only told *us* about those footprints," Rhoda went on, "instead of keeping them for the police, we would have come clean then, dear; but you made them so suspicious—Sergeant Dawes and everybody, I mean. And, on top of that, Paulina producing the telegram—it was really very naughty of her to keep it like that—and having had to make Uncle Willie die just before Mr. Merivale was coming—and trying to answer poor Mr. Culley's questions—we really hadn't had time to *turn round*, dear—and after that it became a murder and we were really rather frightened, weren't we, Frank?"

"When we heard the result of the autopsy, yes," corroborated Frank. "But we weren't really surprised, and hoped all that would blow over in a day or two if we behaved unsuspiciously. So when I found Margery reading a book called *Murder After Christmas* I thought I'd better hide it for a bit; then Aunt Paulina found it, so I—"

"So you burnt it," said John.

"No, I took it back to the library and changed it, that's all."

Superintendent Culley felt it was time *he* said something.

"The body *was* in the snowman," he told Margery, "but neither of the piano-tuners were real ones."

"Er—thank you," said Margery, "how do you know?"

"Routine," replied Culley.

"I don't mind *your* knowing," said Frank generously; "but you see that it wouldn't have done for Sergeant Dawes to get hold of it. He might have arrested somebody at the party for murdering Uncle Willie and trying to put him in the snowman but making a rotten job of it. Or something."

"Quite so," said Culley.

"So he was in the snowman all the time," said Major Smythe, unable to feel shocked any more.

"It was safe enough before Christmas," Frank reminded him. "He hadn't been murdered then, and wasn't even dead; besides, no one was allowed to touch the snowman because of the chocolates inside. It was better than a snowdrift or a bomb-crater, even if it *had* been done before in fiction. Snowmen, you see, sometimes remain standing for weeks after the rest of the snow has melted. And we decided, too, that the night of the party was the best time for him to die. We thought sending for Mr. Merivale would make it less suspicious still. Besides, I wanted witnesses for the mince-pies he ate, the more the better. He was nicely propped up in his Father Christmas get-up. All I had to do was to go out into the garden, tip him out of the snowman and throw away the supports. Then I hardly had to alter my make-up at all—just make it a little less real and wash the blue veins off my hands—to return to the party as myself and be a flop. This, you see, was necessary to explain the two Father Christmas gowns and boots."

"That's very nice and clear now, sir," said Culley. "I see how it had to be at the party. You had him dressed up in the snow-man, *with* the treasure-hunt label in his hand, from the first."

"Yes," said Frank. "Before he got stiff," he had to add.

"That's very nice," said Culley.

"*Is* it?" said Frank, rather astonished.

"I mean," explained Culley, "if it's true, it all helps to prove that the time of death had nothing to do with the death of Lady Keene-Cotton. You couldn't have known she was going to die on Christmas Day all that time back."

"I should think not!" exclaimed Frank.

"Father's shocked," announced John.

"You don't think we went through that business for the sake of the *money*, Culley?"

"But it did rather *look*—" began Rhoda, quite seeing all points of view.

"Well, you don't get it now," said John, not without malicious glee. "It all goes to the Horshams after all."

"Of course it does," said Rhoda warmly to Angelina; "and we can only apologise for all this fuss and delay."

"Oh, not at all—I mean—*does it*?" She was rather taken aback.

"Original will holds good after all," said Puffy, waking up Mr. Merivale.

"Eh? What's that? Dead before Christmas. Yes, yes! Prove the will as soon as possible! Save a lot of trouble! Where is it?"

"He's thrown it away!" gasped Angelina.

"No, no, here it is, lucky I didn't, ha, ha, ha!" He flourished it, entirely rejuvenated at the prospect of reading something at last. He licked his lips. He was already in the middle of reeling off a speech of condolence to the bereaved when Superintendent Culley interrupted him.

"Before you begin reading the will, sir," he said. "I'd just like to get the situation quite clear…"

"Couldn't be clearer," Mr. Merivale brushed him aside and drew in his breath.

"According to the law, sir, a criminal may not profit from a crime," Culley pursued dauntlessly.

"Of course not," snapped the lawyer impatiently. "Found out, confessed the whole thing, should have consulted me first, something might have been done, too late now—"

"Oh dear, have we committed a crime?" cried Rhoda.

"Failing to notify a death, you mean?" said Frank.

"Grave misdemeanour; heavy fine; police court; no defence possible, but keep you out of prison perhaps, can't do more."

"Well, that's something," Frank told him.

"Yes, indeed!" agreed Rhoda; then, with a rueful smile: "It's far better than we deserve. Of course we never expected to *profit* from our crime, Mr. Culley! It's sweet of you to think of it, but—"

"Well I'm—" John was heard to murmur, then Culley spoke again. "That was not the crime I meant, madam."

"No, I suppose not." Rhoda pulled herself together and picked up some knitting.

"*Murder* was more the sort of crime I had in mind," observed Superintendent Culley.

"Murder…" Angelina was heard to gasp.

"Murder…" Puffy was seen to perspire.

Mr. Merivale gaped and Major Smythe popped.

Every eye was turned to Superintendent Culley, who explained, unabashed: "Before or after Christmas, murder is murder..."

There followed a silence which Rhoda felt she had to save from becoming oppressive. "Yes, naturally," she agreed, with common sense, doing her knitting. "Poor Uncle Willie has still been murdered just as much as ever. Did you ever find out who did it, Mr. Culley?"

XXI
Bread Upon the Waters

I

"Good-bye," advanced Angelina loudly. "Thank you so much for the lovely party, Mrs. Redpath, but we really must be getting back."

"Oh, but"—Rhoda was distressed to hear it—"aren't you both going to stay the night?"

"I think we'll try and make it," said Puffy.

"Just stay and hear who did the murder then," pressed Rhoda entreatingly.

"What a pity, we'd have *loved* to," exclaimed Angelina hastily. "Some other time, perhaps."

"It shouldn't take me more than five minutes, madam," Culley assured her.

"But five minutes is five minutes," she objected smilingly.

Major Smythe cleared his throat officially. "I'm afraid, Mrs. Freer, I must—er—insist on your staying and—er—listening to what the Superintendent has to say."

Angelina murmured "If you *insist*—" graciously. She and her husband sat down again.

Mr. Merivale muttered something about flogging a dead horse, while Smythe implored Culley not to make any more mysteries if there weren't any.

"Oh, no, sir," Culley replied to the latter; "it's all plain sailing now. 'Murder after Christmas' was the only mystery that had to be explained, and I've done that."

"Indeed you have!" complimented Rhoda gratefully. "While it was still 'Murder after Christmas,' my husband and I were the most suspicious people, weren't we?"

"If you knew you were the next of kin, certainly," conceded Culley.

"But I always guarded the secret from her most carefully," Paulina broke in anxiously. "Except for Sir Willoughby himself, I was the only person alive who could have known."

"Quite so," Culley soothed her. He waited for her agitation to die down, then told her: "You were also apparently the only person who knew that Lady Keene-Cotton had died on Christmas Day, so you were really the most suspicious person of all." He looked in his notebook and went on: "You still are a highly suspicious person because you might have poisoned Sir Willoughby with the mince-pies before Christmas—if you had been afraid of his giving away something you didn't want known."

"But that's nonsense!" Rhoda cried quickly. "Paulina doesn't know what fear is."

"True enough," Culley acknowledged handsomely and turned to Smythe, who sighed. "Miss Redpath isn't the kind of lady to commit a murder from a selfish, personal motive like that. Nor did she seem to fit in with the psychology of the murderer, any more than Mr. and Mrs. Redpath did from the money angle. None of them did, in fact—"

"Get on, man," urged Smythe testily.

"—so I had to ask myself this, sir," Culley *got* on: "what *was* the psychology of the murderer? It was then that the truth came to me suddenly, sir—this was an *altruistic* murder."

"No such thing," scouted Smythe.

"Why, yes, sir," Culley insisted patiently. "Miss Redpath, now, wouldn't commit a murder so as to prevent something in her past coming out that wouldn't look well if it were known—she wasn't all that much preoccupied with what people thought of her—quite the contrary, if anything, being accustomed to taking the responsibility for doing what others might feel a bit squeamish about—"

Smythe yawned sarcastically. "Meaning she might have taken on the murder because no one else fancied the job?"

"Well, she had been persuading him to make a new will, remember, sir. Then Lady Keene-Cotton died on Christmas Day. Miss Redpath knew that if Sir Willoughby died intestate Mrs. Redpath would inherit everything as next of kin—"

"Oh, shut up, Culley," implored Smythe.

"But that was the psychology of our murderer, sir!" insisted Culley with some animation. "Someone whose own life was behind them, who wasn't afraid of pulling the chestnuts out of the fire for the sake of those she loved, whose lives were still ahead…"

"Fiddlesticks! My dear Miss Redpath, I need hardly say we none of us believe—"

"Oh, but I quite agree with Mr. Culley," Miss Redpath began.

"Nonsense, Paulina," Rhoda interrupted, "you *don't* agree—"

"But, my dear," Miss Redpath pursued serenely, "I *was* the only person who could have killed poor Sir Willoughby. That was what made it all so baffling. Knowing that I hadn't, I mean, dear," she explained to Rhoda.

"That's right," concurred Culley. "Baffled me a bit, too. Suspected you from the first, I did, and kept your name down to the last. As the fairy," he made acknowledgements to the aged lawyer, who came to life suddenly. "Down the chimney," Culley reminded him.

"Chimney!" Everything came back to him. "Ha, ha! Murder after Christmas, best thing that could happen, thought of doing it myself, remember saying so—" He caught Angelina's eye. "Hrrrm! Joke, of course. Murder before Christmas all the time!"

"Murder *before* Christmas, Culley," prompted the Chief Constable with supreme patience: "*not* after—you've just proved it."

"Yes, sir," agreed Culley. "But then that was why Mrs. Redpath asked me to stay in the house, wasn't it, madam?"

Frank rose indignantly to this, but Rhoda put down her knitting and laughed. "How clever of you to guess, Mr. Culley! Yes, that's perfectly true."

"Oh, good lord," groaned Major Smythe, "you're not going to tell me that all those mince-pies and the snowman were faked up to deceive old Culley into—and—and—" he choked.

"No, no," Rhoda rescued him. "You see, our little plot seemed quite harmless before the inquest because we knew how fair Mr. Merivale was going to be about the money; but afterwards—when we all thought the murder had blown over—Paulina told me about being Uncle Willie's daughter and she was going to take the marriage certificate to Mr. Merivale so that I could get all the money! That was *dreadful*! Our harmless little plot had become a *crime*! Almost worse than murder! We were obtaining money on false pretences. I wanted to go straight to Major Smythe and tell him the truth. Then John announced that he'd asked Mr. Culley to stay and detect us, which we decided was a *much* better idea. He would be able to prove it and explain it all to you far more convincingly than *we* could." She beamed at the Chief Constable.

"Do we *want* to hear all this?" asked Smythe plaintively.

"It was just a point I was trying to clear up," apologised Culley. "Then you didn't really think your father had been murdered, madam?"

It was Frank who answered. "Well, I knew *I* hadn't drunk five bottles of cough-mixture—that was why I put the bottles back just as they were, so as to be quite fair with you—and none of the chocolates *I* ate could have been poisoned; so we did *rather* wonder how the laudanum got into his organs."

"Yes," Rhoda agreed, "we did rather wonder about *that*. So if you can explain that too, Mr. Culley, everything will be *perfect*." She resumed her knitting hopefully.

"Well," Culley decided to tell them after a short pause. "The explanation's a very simple one. The chocolates *you* ate, sir, and the ones we had analysed, were all what you had been keeping until after Christmas. The poisoned ones were in a box he received by post only a few days after he arrived."

Puffy drew in his breath and Angelina kicked him.

Then Frank said, "Oh. But I ate those too."

Culley stared hard at him. "Not *all* of them, sir."

"Oh, well," Frank climbed down. "Uncle Willie had, of course, gobbled up all the peppermint creams—he always did—but the Almond Whirls were the ones I liked, and he'd left me plenty of those."

Culley turned to the Chief Constable. "There you are, sir. That's the explanation of the whole thing."

"But—" Angelina found remnants of a voice—"*those* chocolates can't have been poisoned, or—or—"

"—or he would have been already dead? Well, so he was already dead, madam."

"Damn!" said Angelina. "So he was."

Puffy took up the offensive. "What exactly are you hinting, Superintendent?"

"I'm not hinting anything, sir. I'm telling you what happened. There isn't any doubt about it now, though I'm sorry it's got to come out, knowing all the trouble and worry you've both been put to."

("Save us!" prayed John to heaven, and Margery made Esther hold her hand.)

Culley went on, speaking to Angelina: "I know, you see, that this isn't the first time you've come home and had to get your family out of a fix, and it wasn't your fault that you didn't succeed on this occasion. You removed the empty box that day you came over, didn't you, and left an empty bottle of your mother's medicine which you brought with you for that purpose?"

"I'm sure I did if you say so," replied Angelina courteously.

Culley turned to Smythe: "And that explains, sir, how Mr. Freer knew the drug was laudanum when he couldn't have."

"A pack of lies!" Puffy burst out.

Angelina restrained him. "Keep calm, Puffy. It's no use blustering. The game's up now."

"I don't agree," Puffy retorted with heat. "Fellow can't possibly know who poisoned those chocolates—can't prove that *anyone* did."

"Well, it stands to reason, sir," Culley said gently, "it can't have been either you or your wife, or you wouldn't have come tearing down in such weather to prevent him eating them."

"What's that?" Smythe sat up alertly.

Culley reminded him: "If Mrs. Freer had wanted to poison her stepfather, she wouldn't have done it through the post in a chancy way like that."

"I should think not!" said Angelina.

Smythe complained in bewilderment: "But it can't have been either Mr. or Mrs. Horsham, surely?"

"Cyril and Verna committing a murder!" Angelina was reduced to temporary hysteria.

"Well, except for Lady Keene-Cotton herself," grumbled Smythe sullenly, "and Nurse What's-her-name…"

"No need to make exceptions, sir," Culley told him. "Nurse Hastings can't have had anything to do with it, I agree, unless it was she who actually posted off the parcel. I found out from her, however, that Lady Keene-Cotton always had some laudanum by her of nights in case she was in pain. Easy for a bold lady like that to bear the pain and suppress the drug until she got a lethal dose—quite tasteless it would be in strong peppermint. And she was his wife, remember. Although she hadn't known him as long as some—as Miss Redpath, for instance—it was long enough to know what his favourite chocolates were and that he was a bit greedy over such things. And, even more so than Miss Redpath, was she used to managing other people's lives for them and pulling their chestnuts out of the fire. Her own life was over, sir—"

"That's enough psychology," Smythe implored.

Culley flowed on: "The family used to make jokes about murdering their rich stepfather, and I expect she made a few about having married a rich husband who would predecease her. But then, you see, sir, she realised that she was going to die first...and it wasn't a joke any more. She'd led her family into a false sense of security, only to leave them stranded at the last. Lying there in the shadow of the grave (Smythe shifted), she decided to make one last effort to save them all. But time was short, moreover she knew that a dead woman could not be hung; which was perhaps why she didn't plan things as carefully as she should, overlooking an important fact, which may have occurred to you and your husband, Mrs. Freer?"

"You mean that we'd all fall under suspicion of murder?"

"I mean that the law does not allow a criminal to benefit from a crime."

Rhoda rose and her knitting went flying. "Oh, but poor Mr. and Mrs. Freer haven't committed any crime at all!" She appealed to the lawyer: "*They* don't lose their share of the money, surely?"

Mr. Merivale having lost touch again, it was Culley who answered: "Lady Keene-Cotton is precluded from benefiting, so naturally she can't will the money away."

"Oh, dear!" said Angelina. "So *I've* let the family down now!" She seemed to find this funny in a heart-broken sort of way. "Quite right, Puffy: we *ought* to have bluffed it out."

Puffy shoved another feeble oar in: "I hope you don't

think, Superintendent, that we came here on Christmas Eve just to remove the incriminating evidence?"

"Well, naturally we wanted to do that too," admitted Angelina; "anyone would. But—believe it or not, Mr. Culley—the idea of poor old Mother going and murdering an old man was just so absolutely bloody that we couldn't think of anything else. I didn't believe it at first—I thought she was just babbling until she actually described the way she had poisoned the chocolates—it reminded her of blowing eggs, she said—and began to worry about not hearing that Sir Willoughby was dead. After that it was all a little too circumstantial to be dismissed as the delusions old Clark diagnosed. So we hurried down here, hardly hoping to find the old man still alive. The relief was painful, wasn't it, Puffy?"

(So they weren't over-acting at all, thought John.)

"Particularly as he had eaten all the chocolates," corroborated Puffy. "Must have been delusions after all."

"Or else," chimed Angelina, "he'd taken so much that he was immune—the action was delayed, or something; so I took away the box and left the bottle to be on the safe side. I suppose I ought to have left a larger one. What else ought I to have done?"

"You didn't find the wrapping of the parcel," Culley said. "And you did?"

"As it happens, yes. It had been used to wrap up the mince-pies which had been sewn up by Mrs. Redpath into the armchair. I also found those two cards amongst the waste paper—"

"One of which was written by me. We always imitated each other's writing when sending off each other's Christmas presents in any case, but very fishy, I agree. Is that all the evidence against us?"

A pause while Culley wondered if it was; then he told her: "There's a letter written by the dead man on December the eighteenth thanking his wife for some chocolates and inviting her to Four Corners for Christmas."

"Oh well, I suppose you can make out a case if you want to," capitulated Angelina. "And we did both rather plant our feet straight in it when you came to the Rectory. Naturally we were in a flap when we heard about the death: I thought I must have come away with the wrong box and Mother's ones had been kept for the Redpaths' Christmas Tree, or something."

"I very nearly thought that too," Culley confided to her pleasantly as she rose to depart.

"Good-bye, Mrs. Redpath. Now you're not to worry about doing us all out of the money."

Rhoda said *they* weren't to worry either and must both come again when the evenings were longer, *promise*.

"We'd love to," Angelina promised. "Say thank you to kind Mrs. Redpath, Puffy," she prompted, explaining: "He's always wanted to have to earn an honest living, and at last he's going to. As for Cyril," she added, "it'll do him good not to live with his head in clouds of expectations with Mother to fall back on in every emergency. He'll have to fall back on Verna instead. She'll like that. That's what she married him for. It's a dreadful thing to say," she shook hands with Frank, "but strong, capable women like Mother do have the most demoralising effect on their nearest and dearest. I was lucky to escape young, and I think the other two are still young enough to recover. Nothing"—she shook hands with Miss Redpath—"can be so mentally constipating as financial security, I always say. Good-bye, Mr. Culley. I think you've been absolutely wonderful. Now that we really can't afford it, Puffy and I are going to try and have a baby. I wonder if I still *work*?" She shook hands with Major Smythe.

II

"Phew!" The battered Chief Constable drew a deep breath of icy air as he drove away from Four Corners with Superintendent Culley in his car. "Do you good to get out of that house for a bit. Come along to my place for a drink, eh? We'll just be in time for the seven o'clock news."

"That will be most refreshing," acknowledged Culley gratefully.

"Almost a relief to realise there's still a war on after listening to all that stuff," Smythe prophesied.

"But we had to get it all in, didn't we, sir?" Culley pointed out.

"I admire your patience," approved Smythe.

"Bread Upon the Waters, sir. Now we know everything."

"You must be tired. How you've got all the way to Borrowfield and back since I saw you this morning beats me! Wouldn't have thought it possible!"

"Luckily that didn't occur to anyone but you, sir."

The car swerved. "You mean to say you *didn't* go to Borrowfield?"

"She'll find that out when she gets home. That letter was a guess. So was the bit about Lady Keene-Cotton's medicine. We haven't any direct evidence, really. It's been like a crossword puzzle. Started off with the first two lights wrong, so we had to get all the other words filled in first, before we saw those two jokes."

"'Murder after Christmas' you mean?"

"That's right, sir. It wasn't."

"And the other joke?"

"Why wasn't the body in the snowman?"

"And it was. Yes, I see…"

"After that it was just a question of waiting. We knew none of those people could be murderers, but we had to make sure. Let 'em talk it off! Once we'd got it all fitted in so that it *couldn't have happened in any other way* I judged that Mrs. Freer would be glad of the excuse to get it off her chest. And so she was. No positive proof, as I say, but plenty of witnesses— including a lawyer. So that's that."

"And Mrs. Redpath gets the money after all."

"Presumably. It's a nice little problem for Mr. Merivale."

Smythe had become pensive. "I wonder if that's why she asked you to stay, Culley? To prove that Lady Keene-Cotton had murdered her husband—so that the Horshams shouldn't get the money."

"Well, yes, sir; that was one of the things I tried to get out of her, if you remember. Not that it makes any difference."

"No," decided Smythe, driving cautiously round a slippery corner. "They certainly couldn't have known he was murdered when they found him dead: or they wouldn't have done that stunt."

"No, sir," said Culley. "Of course not." Something seemed to occur to him and he was about to speak; but Smythe, finding himself on a nice straight bit of road, broke in cheerfully: "To think of all the trouble we had lookin' for a murderer after Christmas! Lucky there wasn't one, eh?" He gleamed.

"Lucky, sir?" queried Culley, not quite there.

"Supposing, say, it had been murder before *and* after Christmas?"

"Before and after," supposed Culley obediently. "You mean—?"

"Why," gleamed Smythe. "Frank Redpath would be dead too!"

Culley threw back his head and laughed. "That *would* have served him right, sir, that would!"

Two distinguished members of the Mewdley Constabulary were vastly amused...

III

"Remember, dear," Rhoda was saying to Margery that evening, "John is very like his father, so if he wants to be clever, my advice to you is, let him, however silly it may seem to you at the time. Cast your Bread Upon the Waters always. I know you don't want advice from an old woman like me, but I've found out from experience that kindness *always pays*. Really, you know, it's sometimes *quite startling* the way it does! It must be a law of nature, dear—older than Christianity, or anything."

Margery gave up trying to read her book. "John says that kindness is the most effective defence in the world."

"Oh, it is, dear, it *is*!" pounced Rhoda. "Why, look at Paulina! She's so kind to everybody that nobody can help being kind to her. And no one ever thinks of her as a bore, however boring she is being."

"Yes, that's true," observed Margery. "One can go on listening to her for hours. I wonder why."

"It's because she's always so happy when she's talking; and when people are happy it's never a waste of time. I remember when she was ill I went and sat with her in her nursing-home every day. Most of the time she was unconscious, so didn't know I was there; but it was Bread Upon the Waters, darling, and one of the things I *mean*."

"Oh? Why?" (Margery gave her cues.)

"Because I knew Paulina would have done the same for me, however tiresome and pointless it seemed. And *look* what happened!"

"What?"

"While she was delirious, dear, I pieced together the whole story about me being Uncle Willie's daughter from her ramblings."

"Oh," said Margery blankly.

"After that," continued Rhoda, "I was always very, very kind to dear Uncle Willie—even after he had given me all my mother's money. Bread Upon the Waters again."

"Was it?"

"Of *course*! When I asked him to stay I had no *idea* his wife was going to murder him; but, now that she *did*, I get all his money!"

"Oh," said Margery blankly.

"Astonishing, wasn't it?" remarked Rhoda, holding up her knitting to review it in retrospect.

"Then did you know his wife had murdered him all the time?"

"Not all the time, dear—what a silly question!—I didn't real-ise that until *quite suddenly* in the middle of the inquest—that we would have got the money just the same, I mean—and that poor Frank needn't have gone through all that agony after all!"

"Needn't he?" said Margery giddily.

"Well," Rhoda thought back conscientiously, "we *did* want Uncle Willie to be alive for the party *too*."

"Too?" echoed Margery, bewildered.

"Oh, but, *darling*," Rhoda reproached her accusingly, "you don't think I would have let Frank put poor dead Uncle Willie in a snowman—just for the sake of our Christmas party? No, darling—that really would have been *too much*! Even Frank would never have considered doing anything *so* wicked if I hadn't realised—quite suddenly, dear—that it might be worth trying for the sake of the money, darling. I knew, you see, as soon as I got Mrs. Horsham's letter, that poor Lady Keene-Cotton was unlikely to live more than a day or two longer. And it did seem to me such a *waste*, dear, that they couldn't somehow be made to die *the other way round*. That's why I warned you, darling, not to get into the habit of throwing cold water on John's little amusements. You never know! If Uncle Willie hadn't been poisoned and John hadn't made Major Smythe so suspicious about those footprints, I really believe we would have got away with it! Lady Keene-Cotton *did* die before the party, just as I thought; and as we'd staged Uncle Willie's death for *after* the party, all the money would have come to me as next of kin! Just think, darling—darling, *think*—how *useful* Frank would have been for once!"

"What?" said Margery blankly.

"Bread Upon the Waters, dear," insisted Rhoda.

THE END

If you've enjoyed *Murder After Christmas*,
you won't want to miss

MURDER BY THE BOOK,
edited by Martin Edwards,

the most recent BRITISH LIBRARY CRIME CLASSIC
published by Poisoned Pen Press,
an imprint of Sourcebooks.

Praise for the
British Library Crime Classics

"Carr is at the top of his game in this taut whodunit... The British Library Crime Classics series has unearthed another worthy golden age puzzle."

—*Publishers Weekly*, STARRED Review, for *The Lost Gallows*

"A wonderful rediscovery."
—*Booklist*, STARRED Review, for *The Sussex Downs Murder*

"First-rate mystery and an engrossing view into a vanished world."

—*Booklist*, STARRED Review, for *Death of an Airman*

"A cunningly concocted locked-room mystery, a staple of Golden Age detective fiction."

—*Booklist*, STARRED Review, for *Murder of a Lady*

"The book is both utterly of its time and utterly ahead of it."
—*New York Times Book Review* for *The Notting Hill Mystery*

"As with the best of such compilations, readers of classic mysteries will relish discovering unfamiliar authors, along with old favorites such as Arthur Conan Doyle and G.K. Chesterton."
—*Publishers Weekly*, STARRED Review, for *Continental Crimes*

"In this imaginative anthology, Edwards—president of Britain's Detection Club—has gathered together overlooked criminous gems."

—*Washington Post* for *Crimson Snow*

"The degree of suspense Crofts achieves by showing the growing obsession and planning is worthy of Hitchcock. Another first-rate reissue from the British Library Crime Classics series."

—*Booklist*, STARRED Review, for *The 12.30 from Croydon*

"Not only is this a first-rate puzzler, but Crofts's outrage over the financial firm's betrayal of the public trust should resonate with today's readers."

—*Booklist*, STARRED Review, for *Mystery in the Channel*

"This reissue exemplifies the mission of the British Library Crime Classics series in making an outstanding and original mystery accessible to a modern audience."

—*Publishers Weekly*, STARRED Review, for *Excellent Intentions*

"A book to delight every puzzle-suspense enthusiast"

—*New York Times* for *The Colour of Murder*

"Edwards's outstanding third winter-themed anthology showcases 11 uniformly clever and entertaining stories, mostly from lesser known authors, providing further evidence of the editor's expertise…This entry in the British Library Crime Classics series will be a welcome holiday gift for fans of the golden age of detection."

—*Publishers Weekly*, STARRED Review, for *The Christmas Card Crime and Other Stories*

Poisoned Pen
PRESS

poisonedpenpress.com